Julie Shackman is a feel-good romance auth... journalist.

She lives in Scotland with her husband, two sons and their little Romanian rescue pup, Cooper.

julieshackman.co.uk

Also by Julie Shackman

THE HIGHLAND LODGE GETAWAY

JULIE SHACKMAN

One More Chapter
a division of HarperCollins*Publishers*
1 London Bridge Street
London SE1 9GF
www.harpercollins.co.uk
HarperCollins*Publishers*
Macken House, 39/40 Mayor Street Upper,
Dublin 1, D01 C9W8, Ireland

This paperback edition 2023
2
First published in Great Britain in ebook format
by HarperCollins*Publishers* 2023

A catalogue record of this book
is available from the British Library

ISBN: 978-0-00-859520-3

Printed and bound in the UK using 100% Renewable Electricity
by CPI Group (UK) Ltd

This book is dedicated to my Mum and grandparents – thank you for making every Christmas so magical.

Miss you all.

Chapter One

I offered a smile to the elegant, ice-cool blonde woman who had just entered the shop and was admiring our latest range of rose-gold tinsel and matching baubles.

I glanced down at my to-do list, which was making its way to the bottom of the pad. I still had a couple of suppliers to chase up. We hadn't received the order I had placed for illuminated holly wreaths, and the ceramic penguin and robin decorations had arrived smashed to bits in the bottom of the box.

All around me, fairy lights dazzled and there was the warm, festive scent of cinnamon emanating from our Christmas pot-pourri for sale.

I was just about to ring the ceramic decoration suppliers and ask for them to arrange delivery of ones that weren't like a Mensa jigsaw puzzle, when I realised there was a customer on the other side of the counter, waiting to be attended to.

'Excuse me? I love these tear-shaped baubles. You don't happen to have any in silver?'

I snapped my attention back to the woman who had entered Christmas Crackers just a few moments ago. 'I think we may have some through in the stock room. Would you like me to check for you?'

She scooped up an eclectic mix of the two-tone rose-gold and lilac baubles. 'If you wouldn't mind, that would be helpful. Thank you.'

I hurried towards the stockroom, located at the rear of the shop.

Christmas Crackers was located on Craig Brae high street, stationed between the local optician's and the card shop.

It was a sweet little place, with two huge, bevelled windows, covered in fake snow and tinsel, with a tree and a couple of illuminated Christmas cottage decorations.

The counter, a huge, old-fashioned mahogany affair on the right, greeted you as soon as you stepped inside the door and running down either side of the length of the shop was a number of matching wooden shelves and hooks, displaying everything from snow globes and festive table decorations to advent calendars and holly wreaths.

It used to be the local ironmongers until Mr and Mrs McIntosh decided to retire and sell the business just over three years ago to my boss, Vivian Sangster.

After completing my degree in interior design at the Glasgow School of Art, I worked for a couple of different department stores in the city for a few years. I ended up being able to indulge my love of Christmas by using my imagination and creating eye-catching window displays, which I loved doing but especially at my most favourite time of the year.

I glanced around the stockroom with a frisson of excitement. Only a matter of months now and Mrs Sangster would be retiring, heading off to the States and selling the business to me, as she had promised. I beamed from ear to ear.

I located the surplus baubles stock, marked up in sturdy silver boxes on the shelves in the stockroom and tapped back down the wooden floor of the shop, carrying several silver baubles. The wintry November sunshine shot through the shop window, making them sparkle even more. 'How are these for you, madam?'

She beamed, displaying, large, white teeth. 'Perfect. Thank you so much.'

'Which ones would you like?'

'Oh, I'll take all of them. I've got three trees to decorate.'

Three?! Wow!

I tried not to stare at her as I prepared her purchases. I wondered where she lived and how big her house was, if she was going to be decorating three Christmas trees. Perhaps she was a day-tripper or was visiting for a few days?

I didn't recognise her.

Perhaps this well-dressed, middle-aged woman was a new weekender? I smiled to myself. That would please Mr Clarkson, the caretaker down at the town hall. He was always grumbling, 'Aye, all these darn incomers pushing up the prices of the properties in the area,' and, 'parking their bloody great SUVs all over the place, like they've been abandoned.'

While I reached for some of our embossed Christmas Crackers red and green tissue paper to wrap her purchases in, the woman appreciated her surroundings. 'You have a beautiful shop. Are you the owner?'

I retrieved one of our large, glittery bags from under the counter and secured it with blue and green tartan ribbon.

'Thank you. No, it's not my business – well, not yet anyway. I'm the manager at the moment.'

I proceeded to explain to her about Mrs Sangster retiring and how I would be buying the business and taking over.

She nodded over at our white and gold wooden Nutcracker soldiers. 'Well, it's gorgeous. I could spend a fortune in here.'

'Oh, please do!' I joked, accepting her credit card.

While I processed her purchases, she pointed to the window and then the shelves, groaning with assorted festive gifts and decorations. 'Do you do all of this? The displays?'

'I do. It's a labour of love for me. I studied interior design.'

The woman laughed. 'Well, it's stunning.'

'Thank you. That's very kind of you to say so.'

She cocked her head to one side, making her blonde hair swing around her jawline. Her expression was open and intrigued as she studied mine. 'You must love Christmas then.'

'I'm obsessed,' I admitted, blushing. 'I always have been.' I indicated to everything that surrounded us, from the ornate, scented candles, infused with berry and vanilla, to the gingerbread tree decorations and the rainbow waterfall of tinsel, cascading down from the racks. 'Every day I come to work, it's like stepping into Christmas all over again. It's the most magical time of the year and I never tire of it.'

I let my attention fall on our miniature Christmas trees for sale, complete with dinky white lights, that I had lined up behind her. 'It seems like at Christmas, anything is possible.'

I was aware the woman was staring at me and I let out a self-conscious cough. 'Sorry! I'm prattling on. If you stay here any longer, I shall start boring you about Christmas traditions in Italy and Scandinavia.'

She grinned, hitched her shoulder bag up and clutched her

purchases. 'Not at all. It's so refreshing to hear someone so enthusiastic and in love with what they do.' She flashed me an intrigued look. 'So where have you worked before? And where do you get such innovative ideas from?'

'I used to work for Canterbury's, which was like a Scottish Harrods – I'm sure you will have heard of it.'

'Indeed, I have.' The woman smiled, apparently impressed. 'And did you create gorgeous displays like these for them too?'

'That's very kind. Thank you.' I blushed. 'I certainly tried. I used everything from tinsel animals to scented candles to create scenes which were like something out of a children's picture book.'

I lowered my voice, even though there were no other people in the shop. 'The owners, Barbara and Stratton Canterbury, were forward-thinking, approachable and open to any and all suggestions about how to make their store the biggest and brightest in Glasgow, so they gave me free rein.'

I smiled as I thought about my job and how much I had enjoyed it there. 'I loved working for them. But when Canterbury's began to lose money as people cut back on their luxury purchases, they had no option but to economise and that meant their generous staff quota had to be addressed. I was one of the members of staff who was let go, two years after I joined them.'

The blonde woman nodded. 'That must have been awful.'

'It was, but luckily Mrs Canterbury tipped me off about a new store across the other side of the city, Sanders, who were looking for someone with my skillset to turn their drab, average window displays into something magical.'

The woman listened with interest and seemed to be on the

verge of saying something else, but we were interrupted by Mrs Sangster sweeping in.

The woman thanked me again and then departed the shop with a wave of her gloved hand.

'Everything going well?' Mrs Sangster asked, resplendent in her long berry coat and white winter scarf. The glistening from the ruby fairy lights strung along the shelves behind her cast a soupy glow on top of her yellow-blonde hair. Vivian Sangster was a very well-preserved lady in her sixties, who had dabbled in fashion modelling for a bit during her younger years and enjoyed telling everyone.

'Business has been very steady.'

'Good.'

She hovered around, her attention alighting on the blue and silver fluffy robin redbreast I'd propped up by the cash register. We had received a job lot of them a few days ago and I was hoping that by positioning one there, they might start to sell.

The sound of Elton John stepping into Christmas began to play from Alexa.

'I've been having a think about when I buy the shop,' I enthused, coming out from behind the counter. 'There is a new magazine coming out next year, which will focus on Scottish women in rural communities. I'm going to drop them an email.'

Mrs Sangster's expression shifted. Her fingers tweaked the cute little bird's knitted winter hat. 'Lottie, I need to talk to you.'

I was on a roll and carried on. 'And I've already had a word with Mrs Crill and she said she would be happy to start

6

making edible Christmas cracker decorations which I can sell and we can share the profits—'

'Lottie!' Mrs Sangster's sharp voice made me start.

She dragged a hand over her blonde bouffant. 'This is very important. I should have spoken to you sooner. I'm so sorry.'

She clipped towards the shop door in her boots and spun the red and white painted sign hanging from it, to say *Closed*. 'Come through to the office.'

Oh God. Was this about those broken ornaments? No. It wasn't about Mum, was it? My mother worked behind the counter for a few hours each week, helping out, and loved it almost as much as I did. She had been doing such a great job too.

Mrs Sangster stalked ahead of me. I followed her through to the office.

An uneasy feeling was taking hold. What did she want to talk to me about?

Chapter Two

I couldn't process what she was saying.

No. This was a mistake. She wasn't making any sense.

Christmas Crackers was going to be mine next year. Everything had been agreed. It was only a matter of time. Vivian was going to retire and disappear into the Californian sunset with Ridley, and I was buying the business.

I shot forward in the office chair. 'Sorry. I don't follow. What about the lease?'

Vivian was struggling to speak. She repeated herself. 'The landlord has refused to renew it for Christmas Crackers.'

My mouth opened and closed several times. 'Why? But... but I was going to buy the business and take it over for five years, remember?' My brain felt addled – scrambled.

'I'm sorry, Lottie. They received a substantial offer for the lease from Roberto's, that chain of expensive Italian restaurants, and they have accepted it.'

I gripped the arms of the chair tighter. My knuckles

throbbed. This couldn't be happening. 'So, they've sold the lease to them?'

Vivian was struggling to look at me. 'Our lease expires on 31st December.' She looked like her heels were agony. 'I'm so sorry. I only just heard about it myself this morning, when the landlord rang me. I feel dreadful. We don't deserve this. You certainly don't.'

I jumped up from my office chair and prowled backwards and forwards in front of Mrs Sangster, like a traumatised zoo animal behind bars. This wasn't happening. I was hallucinating or something. Everything was planned out. It had all been agreed.

I wrapped my arms around myself. My fingertips were digging into my skin. Vivian watched me with a look of agony.

This was a bad dream.

Any moment, I was going to wake up in a panicked then relieved sweat.

I waited.

Nope. I wasn't asleep. This was real.

Vivian repeatedly smoothed down the woollen dress she was wearing, for something to do. She looked like she wished she was anywhere else, rather than telling me all this as she occupied her swivel chair on the other side of her desk.

I waited for her to burst out into tinkles of laughter and tell me this was all a wind-up. 'You're joking, aren't you?'

Mrs Sangster squirmed. 'Oh, how I wish I was, Lottie. I'm sorry. I'm so sorry. There's nothing we can do.'

I stared around our office with its heavy, rosewood desk, claret carpet and framed pictures of festive snow scenes. As of 31st December, Christmas Crackers would be no more. All my business plans and ideas, they were going up in smoke right in front of my eyes.

My chest was pumping with confusion. Where did this leave me? What did it mean? What about Mum and Orla? They both loved working here too. Mum enjoyed it as it got her out of the house after losing Dad.

'But I'm going to buy Christmas Crackers,' I struggled. I didn't care that I was repeating myself, like an annoying toy. That was the situation. That was what we had agreed. 'We talked about it so many times. You were retiring and I would buy the business.' I stared down at her, as though I didn't recognise her. 'This is all wrong. It's ridiculous.'

Vivian crossed and uncrossed her hands in her lap and struggled to make eye contact with me. 'I have been dreading telling you ever since they rang me earlier.' She let out an agonised sigh. 'I've been pacing up and down Craig Brae, trying to think of how on earth I was going to break this news to you. There's nothing we can do. Archibald and Strang have sold the lease to Ronaldo's. As of 6th January, they take over this place.'

I sounded like an incandescent Minnie Mouse now. 'They must know how much this shop means to us. We have worked so, so hard to make Christmas Crackers the success it is.'

'And I appreciate all your sterling work. You, your mum and Orla have been amazing.'

Burning anger shot through me.

Ronaldo's were a chain of expensive, successful Italian restaurants who had swept through the big cities and were now targeting tourist areas, in their quest for world domination. They were all glass roofs, rustic charm and quilted booths.

I slumped down into the chair opposite her.

Dear God. What was I supposed to do now? All my plans, ideas and energy had been pumped into this shop.

It only seemed like yesterday, but was in fact three years ago now, since Mum had tipped me off that Vivian Sangster, the Craig Brae force of nature and well-known local businesswoman, was starting a new venture.

Vivian had dabbled in everything from selling high-end handbags, purses, wallets and wheelie cases to shoes, jewellery and hats, with varying degrees of success. However, stories were rife that she was moving in a different business direction. My mum had told me that on one of her holidays to New York, Vivian had spotted a shop in the Big Apple, which she was certain she could replicate back in her Scottish hometown.

It transpired that she had come across a gorgeous little shop selling anything and everything festive and that it was open all year round.

In fact, it had become rather a celebrity in its own right and tourists would flock to see its bottle-glass windows, bursting with clockwork reindeer and glowing fairy lights, even in the soupy, cloying New York heatwaves.

I was becoming more and more disillusioned with Sanders and the lack of appreciation from my line manager. I had also spent the last six years studying, working and living in Glasgow and felt that returning to Craig Brae might be just what I needed.

So, I applied for the role of full-time retail assistant with Vivian at Christmas Crackers. I think my obsession with anything Christmas-related, together with my interior design degree, was a definite plus.

I was therefore delighted when Vivian told me I had got the

job the day after my interview, working alongside part-time Orla Cunningham, one of Mum's friends from her Zumba class.

I soon found myself making suggestions to Vivian about possible festive promotions we could run, as well as starting social media accounts for the shop and how to set out the shop interior displays for major impact.

I wanted the locals to forget that Christmas Crackers was once an ironmonger's and hoped they would view it in the same vein as the New York festive shop.

So, I started introducing things like Find the Christmas Pixie competitions for the local children, where they would have to bring their parents into the shop, to locate the naughty pixie who was concealed somewhere.

I also put up pictures in the windows of Christmas Crackers, of famous people, concealed behind Santa beards and shoppers had to guess who they were under the disguise.

I spent so much of my time trawling the internet, researching ideas and innovations that we might be able to adopt in the shop ourselves.

I enjoyed gathering together similar colour schemes of tinsel, lights and ornaments. Sometimes, the windows would be decked out in a rose-gold Christmas theme. At other times, I would opt for electric blue and silver or gold and green.

Vivian Sangster was very wary of social media, so I worked on pulling together ideas for what we could do to launch Christmas Crackers on Twitter, Facebook, Instagram and Tik-Tok.

When she saw my proposals for things like putting up pictures of an antique Christmas tree of the week, asking customers for their oldest Christmas tree decoration and competitions for the local children to design their very own bauble, she embraced them with relish.

In fact, Vivian thought my suggestions for her new business were so good, that after just twelve months of working there, she appointed me shop manager. She even gave Mum a part-time job helping out Orla, as we needed more hands-on deck.

Christmas Crackers was attracting people from all over Scotland and everything was going so well; it almost felt like a dream.

Cold, hard reality took hold of me again and wouldn't let go. My shocked mouth popped open. Three years of effort and all for nothing.

Vivian angled her powdered face to one side. I could see tears clustering in her pale eyes. She had suddenly become fascinated with her office carpet.

This was as agonising for her as it was for me.

I thought about all the decisions I'd made, in order to ensure I could afford to buy the business. I had been so careful with the money Dad left me in his will.

I cringed as I thought about my old second-hand car…

And now what? All that effort? It was for nothing? I flopped back in my chair, defeated.

My emotions skittered in all directions.

I threw my head back, as I thought about all the evenings and weekends I had spent on this, setting up social media accounts for the business; working behind the counter; dropping leaflets through doors; even dressing like a bloody reindeer and pounding the pavements in torrential rain!

Mrs Sangster's cool blue eyes were clamped shut, as if that might help make all this sorry mess go away.

If only it would.

It was as if my dreams had been ripped up in front of me.

I started through the open office door and across the shop floor, where the mahogany shelves groaned and shimmered with our festive ornaments. The lights, laced along the burgundy walls, slipped from electric blue to acid green in an almost effortless manner.

Vivian came hurrying after me, her pointed face brimming with concern.

'So that's it?' I managed. 'To be told I'm out of a job, just seven weeks before Christmas?'

'I'm so sorry,' croaked Vivian for what seemed like the twentieth time in the last five minutes. 'I really am.'

She bundled me into her arms. She smelled of lavender. We stayed that way for a few moments, clinging onto one another.

Dear God.

I was twenty-nine years old. What was I supposed to do now? My stomach felt like it was full of lead. I thought of Mum and Orla and how devastated they would both be at the realisation that Christmas Crackers would have to close.

I eased myself out of her arms. She looked like someone had just stomped on her toes. 'So, come December 31st, that's it?'

She winced and struggled to look at me. 'Yes. They have said they want to get cracking on renovating and redecorating come the start of January.'

I couldn't stem my disbelief. Closing down on Hogmanay. When everyone is supposed to be gearing up and looking forward to the future. I wanted to let out an incredulous bark of laughter.

I dragged a frustrated hand down my face.

It was already November. What were my prosects of

securing another job, with Christmas just around the corner? I had bills to pay. I had a mortgage. The money Dad had left me in his will had been generous, but it wouldn't last forever and I didn't want to end up frittering that away.

I reckoned the chances of me finding another suitable job right now would be zero, unless I could get a temporary, seasonal post?

Vivian gazed at me, tears glittering. 'I know it won't be much comfort, but I'll make sure you, your Mum and Orla receive an extra generous Christmas bonus.

'You've done wonderful work for me, Lottie, and Christmas Crackers would not have been able to achieve the sales and publicity it has without you.' Her words were appreciated, but I was struggling to pay attention.

I stared around myself at all the glossy, glittery ornaments and lights.

Everything was happening so fast. It was like my life was out of control all of a sudden and all I could do was stand there like an idiot and watch from the side lines.

Shakin' Stevens had started crooning 'Merry Christmas Everyone'. Not great timing.

Vivian moved on to talking about supplying me with a glowing reference. 'What with your interior design degree and the amazing work you have done here and in the department stores you worked in before… you should have no problems getting another job.'

I know she was trying to make me feel better, but the thought of being out of work and facing job hunting, made my stomach sink further. It wasn't as if I could stroll into a top job at Apple or as if Elon Musk would recruit me as his right-hand woman. Where were there interior design-related vacancies in Craig Brae? It was a small town an hour and a half away from Glasgow, so most of us knew each other. It was also a very popular tourist destination, thanks to its spectacular scenery, salmon ladder, the stunning vista of Loch Strathe and the treacherous but captivating mountain, Ben Linn. But as for an abundance of high-profile jobs, you could forget it.

I felt that if Christmas were an actual place, Craig Brae would be it, with its cosy community spirit and the glow from sitting-room windows winking out from the cottages.

I dragged my attention back and caught sight of a couple of intrigued tourists gazing through the shop window.

The woman, sporting a bobbly red hat, pointed at one of the illuminated thatched cottages drizzled in snow.

I dropped my voice. I didn't want to scare off a potential sale, especially when the shop was on borrowed time. We were known for our friendly and excellent customer service and I wasn't about to allow that to change.

Pictures of Mum and Orla flitted in front of me. There was still the horrible prospect of telling them. 'Don't say a word to Mum or Orla about any of this. I'll tell them.'

'No, I can do that.'

I shook my head so much, I almost cricked my neck. 'Thank you but no. It might be better coming from me.'

How could this be happening, after all the hard work we put in? The business was going to be mine.

After we had agreed on the sale, I had finally felt like my life was beginning to move on again. All the evenings I had slaved over a hot laptop, pulling ideas together and working on social media posts, studying catalogues for new stock, drafting adverts.

Mum and Orla had been so conscientious and loyal. They didn't deserve to be treated like this. None of us did.

I took a steadying breath. I had to try and keep it together for now, especially in front of the customers. Me banging about, bursting into tears or throwing things wouldn't help anyone.

I plastered on a smile for the lingering customers outside, keen to still do the job that I loved while I had the chance.

They started to make their way in through the shop door.

My heart plummeted. Next stop was studying situations vacant.

Chapter Three

I t was fitting that Halloween and Bonfire Night had just taken place, seeing as I'd been put through such a horrendous and shocking event, that had sent a rocket bursting through my life.

I had been bobbing along, happy in my work, bolstering the reputation of Christmas Crackers to take over the business. I had gained so much satisfaction from seeing customers eyes light up when they purchased something festive that captured their imagination or triggered a memory from a past Christmas.

I closed up Christmas Crackers as usual at six o'clock, switching off the lights and plunging the little shop into darkness.

Vivian had looked dreadful, so I insisted she head home. I told her I saw no point in both of us standing around in the shop, being miserable.

She had given me another fierce hug, which had threatened to make me burst into tears, and then vanished, citing that she had to speak to her estate agents about putting her house up for sale.

Now, I made my way along the cobbled main street of Craig Brae for the short walk towards Mum's cottage, to tell her what had happened. I was dreading it.

It had been several months after Dad had passed away suddenly that things had taken even more of a surreal turn, when divorced Vivian had invited me into her office and informed me that she had met and fallen head over heels in love with Ridley Moore, an American tourist and owner of his own chain of golf accessory shops, who had been on holiday and visiting the area.

She said that me losing my dad so suddenly and her having gone through a nasty divorce had made her consider her life and she had therefore decided she would retire and snatch happiness with both hands. She would be moving to Santa Barbara with Ridley.

At first, I had difficulty comprehending what she was getting at. I started burbling that Christmas Crackers was doing well and why on earth would she consider packing it all in at this moment in time? It was crazy!

That was when she had beamed at me from under her big blow-dried blonde do and told me that yes, she was going to sell the business next year, but would I like to buy it from her?

I remember sinking down in the chair opposite hers, unable to say anything sensible for a few minutes.

I could afford to buy the business. Tragically, that was only because of the death of my father, but he had been very money savvy and had left both Mum and me well provided for.

I remembered sitting there, my heart clattering against my chest.

The tantalising prospect of being my own boss and running this gorgeous shop meant that I took the challenge of buying it head-on and thanked Vivian so much, I ended up almost breaking her hand when I shook it.

Now, it was as if my whole future and all the plans I had made had been ripped away from me. This Christmas was going to be another tough one.

My ex-boyfriend Kyle Foster, a Craig Brae landscape gardener, hadn't understood or appreciated my love of the festive season. He was bemused by it when we first started dating three years ago. He became even more irritated when he moved into my flat and had to contend with my myriad decorations, including my singing Santa and Rudolph.

I received a discount from Christmas Crackers and made the most of it, much to Kyle's disdain.

He was tall and willowy and would more often than not bang his head on a dangling snowflake or not look where he was going and accidentally stab himself on a holly wreath.

He would throw his arms about, swear and insist that Christmas would be a much more enjoyable affair 'without the glitter and shit.'

Dad had referred to him as The Grinch.

Craig Brae was dipped in inky black night, its Victorian-style town centre thronged with old-fashioned lamps. The last thing I wanted Mum to do was worry but I knew that would be like telling a bird not to fly.

I arrived at Mum's, a detached cottage in a little cul-de-sac just off the main throng of the town.

A whirlpool of dread swirled in my stomach.

Her amber lamps cast smudges against the closed curtains.

My attention fell on the front garden that Dad had always

tended to. There were fresh breadcrumbs on the bird table. I could still see him there, breaking it up in his large hand and throwing it for the birds to hoover up. He always used to laugh when I said that it reminded me of Beast, feeding the birds breadcrumbs in *Beauty and the Beast*.

I huddled deeper into my belted coat and adjusted my sparkly beret. There was a stiff breeze coming down from the hills.

I raised one gloved hand and knocked on the glossy white door, with its stained-glass window. Well, this was it.

My heart ached at the bewildering array of emotions that crossed Mum's face as I told her about the shop.

Mum stared up at me in disbelief from her armchair. She gasped, her hands turning over in each other. Photographs of Dad surrounded her, his twinkly dark-blue eyes a mirror image of mine, as well as his thick conker-brown hair.

A golfing weekend with the boys, a family visit to Blackpool, sporting a hard hat while out on site during his construction career – they all merged together to tug at my heart.

I whipped my attention away from my late dad's photographs.

'But that's awful!' she gulped. 'I don't believe it. How could they do such a thing? But you were going to buy the business…' Her voice faded. 'And what about poor Orla and those kids of hers? Three teenagers now. What is she supposed to do?'

She shook her brunette head in disbelief.

'Vivian was intending on telling you and Orla, but she is in bits about it all too, Mum. I said I thought you might take the news a bit better coming from me.'

Mum let out a weary sigh. 'Thanks to your father, I'm not struggling or desperate to find another job straight away, but I really enjoy working there. It's the company and being busy, you know? But Orla...' Her voice erupted. 'And you, lovey! You were so looking forward to taking over.'

Her mouth flattened. 'Thank goodness your father isn't here. He would have been storming up to that landlord's office.' She pressed her lips together. 'Any time to receive news like this is awful, but just before Christmas? Don't these people have a conscience?'

'Mum, when it comes to money, the answer is no.'

Renewed worry swamped her delicate features. She sat and fiddled with her toffee-highlighted hair.

'I'm sorry about your job, Mum. Yours and Orla's.'

'Och, don't worry about us. We will be all right. I might be able to get a few more odd hours with Susie, just to get me out of the house. It's you I'm most bothered about.'

She stared across from her squashy wheat-coloured hessian armchair. 'So, end of December closing, you say?'

I nodded.

'I can't believe all this. You have worked so hard in that place.' Realisation dawned across her anxious features. 'But what does all this mean for you, sweetheart? What are you going to do?'

I forced my mouth into a smile. 'Oh, don't you worry about me, Mum. I'll be fine. I'm sure I'll get something else at some point.'

She raised her plucked, fair brows. 'Yes, but when? Where?

Craig Brae isn't exactly bursting at the seams with business opportunities.' Her expression fell further. 'You were so excited about buying Christmas Crackers.'

'I know. It isn't fair, is it?'

'No, it isn't. I don't know how those people will be able to sleep at night, after treating you and Vivian like this.'

She was pensive for a few moments. 'Surely, there are some vacancies around in the run-up to Christmas? At least it would be something to tide you over.' I could see her brain working away. She crinkled her nose. 'I could ask Susie if there's anything going for you at Eternal Flame? I know she's only just taken on a couple of new part-timers though, to help out with packaging and gift-wrapping in time for Christmas.'

Mum had started helping out one of her friends occasionally with her online scented candle making business. I thought it was more a diversion after losing my dad. 'If she does have anything for you, it would probably only be a few odd hours there and there, but at least it's better than nothing.'

I didn't want to appear ungrateful, so I said that would be great and thanked her. If I found I was struggling to get something else, it might prove to be a godsend to get something like that to keep me going for now. Now more than ever, I was grateful for the money Dad had left me in his will. I no longer needed it to put towards buying Christmas Crackers, I realised with mounting anger again, but I didn't want to start dipping into it to keep me going while job hunting.

At that rate, I would have none of it left in six months.

I watched Mum as she suddenly shot out one arm for her mobile beside her. Her eyes were hard. 'I want a word with that bloody landlord. It won't do any good, but it will make me feel a darn sight better. What's their number?'

'Mum, don't. They won't speak to you or will just feed you a bunch of excuses anyway.'

She rose from her armchair and pushed a hunk of hair back behind her ears. 'Have you told Orla yet?'

'No. I'm dreading it.'

Mum nodded her understanding. 'She's attending a crafts fair tonight and then meeting up with her cousin for a bite to eat. She's been looking forward to it for the last couple of weeks.'

'Well, in that case, I won't spoil her evening by going round to her house to tell her,' I decided. 'I will break the news to her face to face tomorrow at work.'

Mum agreed that sounded like a better idea.

She surveyed me, sympathy swimming in her eyes. 'Right, young lady. You need to take a break and forget about things for a bit.'

I rolled my eyes. That was easier said than done.

Mum encouraged me through to the kitchen.' I'll make us something to eat and we can have a good natter.'

I pulled a face and stood up. 'Sorry, Mum, but I'm not very hungry.'

She frowned at me. 'That's as may be, but you need to keep your strength up.' When I didn't answer, she gave me a nudge with her shoulder. 'We can have dinner and come up with an action plan for you.'

'Listen to you.' I managed to smile, even though my insides felt like mush. 'An action plan, eh?'

'You know what I mean. Another job won't come to you. You'll have to go out there and find it.'

The very thought of it made my stomach roll. The initial shock was beginning to give way to cold, frightening truth.

From going-to-be-a-business-owner to unemployed in a matter of hours.

No more cosy Christmas Crackers to go into every morning. No more being surrounded by festive frivolity every day of the year. What I had created washed away just like that.

I followed Mum into her kitchen, with its heavy farmhouse-style table and chairs and the blond wood cabinet fittings that Dad had been instrumental in erecting. I tried not to stare around the space. There were echoes of him everywhere.

I noticed Mum still kept his coffee mug with his name on it, sitting out by the kettle. 'Well, you need to be proactive. Get your CV out there.' She rummaged around in her freezer and produced two fat slices of haddock.

'I will do. I have no other choice, do I?'

She swung round to face me. 'I want you to promise me something, Lottie.' She took both of my hands in hers. 'Don't let me hold you back.'

'What? You don't. You never have.'

She squeezed my fingers between hers. 'There's every chance you'll have to move further afield for another job. Let's be honest. There isn't usually an abundance of vacancies in Craig Brae.'

I appreciated her soft smile and the mistiness in her green-flecked wide-set eyes. 'Mum, you never hold me back.' I gave both her hands a playful shake up and down. 'I don't want you to worry, ok? Everything will sort itself out.'

Her smile drooped again.

She took a breath and composed herself. 'I mean it though, sweetheart. If a good opportunity comes up away from Craig Brae, I don't want you to think twice. I want you to take it.'

'Mum…'

'Promise me.'

I let out a frustrated sigh and didn't say anything.

'Lottie Grant!'

'Ok. Ok. I promise.'

'Good.'

I reached for the cutlery drawer and began to set the kitchen table for two.

Mum wrapped the slices of fish in foil and drizzled them with lemon juice. She set her shoulders. 'Right. Enough maudlin talk. Let's make this Christmas a special one. Last year, well, I just wasn't in a good place.'

I nodded, my throat constricting. I dumped down the cutlery and bundled Mum into my arms. 'This will be our second Christmas without Dad, but we will make it one to remember for him.'

Her expression melted with memories. 'Yes. We will.' She gazed up at me, probably seeing the echo of my dad in my features. 'He was just like you. Christmas obsessed. He would have had our tree up in July, if he'd thought he could have got away with it.'

A watery smile appeared on my face, thinking of him rigging up the Christmas lights with a huge, excited grin; his cracker party hat on his head at a rakish angle; him pretending to be Father Christmas one year when I was little and almost tripping over next door's cat. He had been like a big, affectionate bear. 'We'll have a Christmas to remember, Mum. Whatever you want to do, we will do it.'

I fiddled with one of the forks I'd laid out. 'Do you want to get away from Craig Brae for Christmas? Have a change of scene?'

I suppressed a bolt of worry. Lord knows whether I would

have another job by then, but even if I didn't, if Mum wanted to get away from everything for a few days, I'd find the money to go with her from somewhere.

Mum frowned. 'What? You mean go somewhere else for Christmas?'

I almost laughed at her expression. 'Yes. A lot of people do it. We could go to a hotel for a few days if you like, or rent a cottage.'

I fetched two water glasses from a cupboard. 'It would be a change of scene for both of us over Christmas.'

Mum looked doubtful.

'If we booked a hotel somewhere with a spa, we could be pampered and get a massage and manicure.'

Mum faffed around at the sink. 'That's a lovely idea darling, but I really would rather stay at home for Christmas, if you don't mind. I wouldn't feel as close to your dad, if I was sitting in some hotel bar.' Her sorrowful eyes swept the kitchen. 'At least if I'm here at Christmas, I'll still feel like a part of him is with me.'

I was determined not to cry. I sunk my teeth into bottom lip. 'I understand. Whatever you want to do, we will do.'

No matter what, Mum and I would be here for one another. I knew that much.

The end of the week marched on to greet me.

Even though it was only the second week of November, Christmas was on the horizon. The supermarket shelves were brimming with selection boxes and glitter-strewn greetings cards.

Telling Orla about Christmas Crackers earlier in the week had been horrendous. As soon as I'd asked her to join me in the office, she had noticed Mum and me exchanging sorrowful glances.

Orla had tried to remain stoic about the whole thing, but Mum had overheard her crying in the stock room a short while later.

I so wanted to rip the heartless landlord's face off and I didn't care that those were NOT the sort of feelings you were supposed to be harbouring for a fellow human being at this time of year.

Local events were starting to appear in calendars and the local council had pinned up posters, advertising the *Craig Brae Grand Christmas Lights Switch-on* for two weeks' time. Excitement amongst the local school children was building at the news that this year, Santa's sleigh would be pulled by four real reindeer.

Christmas Crackers trade was brisk, and Vivian, Mum, Orla and I did what we could to remain cheerful. Having to act professionally and courteously in front of customers was zapping our energy but we knew we had no choice.

We hadn't informed our customers and the wider locals that Christmas Crackers was closing down and that was something we were dreading. I mulled over how and what to tell our loyal customers. This would have to be done much sooner than later. We couldn't keep delaying the inevitable.

So, in between the flurry of customers, keen to begin restocking our Christmas garlands and ornate door wreaths, I drew up a to-do list. The business would soon be no more and sitting here on our hands wouldn't achieve anything.

When one o'clock arrived, I closed the shop for a bit.

I had decided in the end to compile a general notice to put up in the shop window and on the door, and I would also upload it onto the Christmas Crackers social media accounts.

It would save us all from having to tell everyone directly.

I blew out a cloud of air. I suspected that the gossip grapevine wouldn't be long in sharing the horrible news.

Fury charged through me again. We were stuck in this awful, gut-wrenching situation.

Vivian was struggling to make many decisions after everything, so I instructed Mum and Orla to sell off what stock we could. I also suggested we put everything on discount. Buy one holly wreath, get one half price; two slivers of tinsel for three pounds. It was up to me to deal with things the best way I could.

For the remainder of that Friday afternoon, business was very brisk, which struck me as ironic, seeing as we would be closing down in a matter of weeks.

Once the end of the day swung around, I suggested to Mum and Orla that they head home and that I would close up. Vivian was up to her eyes with sorting out her house, prior to it going on the market, as well as trying to pack what she wanted to take with her when she emigrated to the States.

I retreated into the office. I was more than happy to deal with everything else. I suppose I wanted to spend as much time here as I could and make the most of it, before the shop disappeared.

I lowered the volume of the Christmas music still pumping from the speakers and was discomfited to realise it was annoying me. A sarcastic smile played on my lips. Good God. I almost sounded like my ex-boyfriend then.

Kyle would complain about not only the cost of the decorations (forgetting I received my treasured discount) but the 'mess' they made and the 'commercialisation of what is essentially an excuse for gluttony, excess and conglomerate exploitation.'

On more than one occasion, he would insist that Christmas Crackers had a limited shelf life and then proceed to laugh at his own, corny joke.

If he knew what was happening now, he would let out one of his dramatic sighs and say, 'I did warn you, Lotts.'

I made myself a mug of hot chocolate, which usually at this time of year would fire up my festive anticipation even more.

But these weren't normal times.

I sank into the chair behind the desk, the Christmas stock on the shop floor casting slivers of light.

After a frantic series of scorings out in my notebook and several frustrated mouthfuls of my hot chocolate, I managed to come up with the following:

IMPORTANT NOTICE – CHRISTMAS CRACKERS

For the past three years, we at Christmas Crackers have aimed to deliver the excitement of Christmas to our loyal customers all year round.

Unfortunately, due to matters out of our control, the business will have to close.

This is a very sad and difficult time, but I would like to extend our grateful thanks, appreciation and good wishes to you all, for your unwavering support. It has meant so very much.

Christmas Crackers will officially cease trading on 31st

December and Ronaldo's, the Italian restaurant chain, will be taking over the premises as of 6th January.

Have a wonderful Christmas and New Year and thank you once again for your loyalty. It will not be forgotten.

Vivian Sangster, Lottie Grant, Bernadette Grant and Orla Cunningham. X

Through a series of sudden, rasping sobs, I somehow managed to type up the notice on the office PC, before posting it on our Christmas Cracker Facebook, Instagram and Twitter accounts. I also made sure it appeared on our shop website.

I printed off two copies and just as I was leaving the shop for the evening, I attached a copy to the inside of the shop window and stuck the other on the inside of the shop door.

I then trudged home, bone-weary, to my flat at the other end of the town, feeling as though I'd been kicked by a bloody great horse.

I sat in front of my laptop that evening, nursing a huge glass of white wine and scanning job vacancies.

Mum had asked her friend about a few hours here and there for me at Eternal Flame, but Susie had apologised and said orders this year were down on previous Christmases, and she regretted she wasn't in a position to offer me anything. She was just about able to give Mum a few more hours as it was.

I had read her text with a degree of resignation and decided to check out any available opportunities.

It turned out there were a couple of part-time posts going in Craig Brae. One was behind the bar in the local pub, the

Hound and Hare, and the other was on reception in one of the hotels just a short distance away, but that was it.

I knew Mum had made me promise to look further afield but I couldn't. At least not for the moment. She had been slowly coming to terms with losing Dad, but the last thing I wanted to do was leave her at the moment. It just didn't seem right. Not yet.

A chill raced down my spine as I recalled that day eighteen months ago, when Mum rang me at the shop to tell me Dad was gone.

It had been a crisp beige and russet autumnal morning, with the sun kissing the roofs of the shops. I had just arrived at Christmas Crackers for the start of the day. We had received an early delivery of blown-glass reindeer and Christmas tree decorations and I was busy unpacking them, when the shop phone rang out.

I was surprised to hear it was Mum on the line. She always called me on my mobile. At first, I struggled to understand what she was saying. She was garbling words I couldn't make out. I asked her to slow down and she said something about ringing my mobile, but she didn't know if I would hear it over the morning buzz in the high street.

I started to ask her if she was all right and what was going on, but she broke down into a ragged series of gasps and sobs.

Dad had suffered a massive heart attack in bed. She had popped downstairs to make him a morning cuppa before he set off for work. He had been going on about the gorgeous new wildlife centre they were building.

Mum had only been in the kitchen a few minutes, she said. He had joked to her about her bringing him a full fry-up as well, as she had left the bedroom.

When she padded back upstairs in her slippers and dressing gown, she thought he had fallen back to sleep. Mum said she had laughed and told him to wake up.

He had only just turned sixty.

Mum and I blundered around in a dazed grieving fog. The local community rallied round. We had deliveries of flowers, hot meals left on the doorstep, offers of errands, and cards telling us what we already knew but that we appreciated and wanted to read anyway – that Tom Grant had been a gentle giant and that the mould had been well and truly broken when he was made.

His friends and colleagues in the construction industry were forever on the phone, checking to see how we were coping and offering their help.

Both of us were thankful to have Christmas Crackers to seek refuge in.

Visions of my late dad floated in front of my eyes, as my cursor hovered over the hotel reception vacancy on the job website. It wasn't ideal – it was less money of course – but the Heather Hill Hotel was very plush and it was only a fifteen-minute walk away from my flat. At least it would bring in some money and I would be nearby for Mum, until I could get my head around all of this and sort myself out.

I speed-read the job notice again, mentally ticking off the attributes they were looking for. I was presentable (most of the time) organised and was well versed in dealing with the public. I also knew the area well, should tourists interrogate me about places of interest, and I had a degree, even if it was in interior design and not hospitality or business.

I clicked on the link and took another gulp from my wine glass. If anybody from Archibald Strang Limited had been standing in front of me right now, I wouldn't have been responsible for my actions. How your life can change in such a short space of time.

No relationship and now I wouldn't be the owner of Christmas Crackers.

When we split, Kyle had announced that we were two very different people (boy, you could say that again) and that it would be best if we called it a day.

And to think that at one time, I had wondered if I might become Mrs Lottie Foster! Talk about dodging a bullet.

Strange thing was, six weeks after we split, I discovered he had been sleeping with Tula Lennox, a local part-time model and one of Santa's helpers in the Craig Brae Father Christmas Grotto.

He couldn't have been that averse to a bit of festive fun then.

When it all came out about their affair, Kyle and Tula packed up their rake and elf tights and took off to live together in Glasgow.

After that fiasco, my wounded pride and I decided to concentrate on building up the shop's profile and concluded that I didn't seem to have much of a future in terms of romance. I was far better off throwing myself into my career and putting all my energies into the love of my life that never let me down: Christmas.

I had a far better and more rewarding relationship with the festive season than I had with my love life.

But then again, now that I'd lost Christmas Crackers, that wasn't turning out so well either!

I glanced around at my cosy two-bedroom flat. It overlooked a section of the local park and beyond that, the view from the sitting room window provided a tantalising glimpse of treetops and the claret and dark-chocolate hillsides.

Well, I had to find another job.

My mind turned over all the hard work Mum, Dad and I had put into my flat. I couldn't lose my home because of a ridiculous sense of petulance and pride. I needed to maintain an income. I'd lived here in my flat for a couple of years now, ever since taking on the mantle of managing Christmas Crackers. Before I bought it, it had belonged to an elderly lady who was struggling to remain living independently, so her family took the difficult decision to move her into residential accommodation.

A swell of injustice promised to swamp me again, but I gave myself a stern mental shake. *Come on, Lottie. You've got a job application to compose.*

I straightened my back and decided to just get on with it.

'I'm so sorry Lottie,' burst out Mrs Crill the next morning, as she served me in the bakery, Sugar 'n' Spice, a few doors down from Christmas Crackers. 'I've just heard about the shop.'

I managed to smile. 'Thank you.'

She folded her arms against her floral apron from behind the cake-festooned glass counter. 'Terrible business. Some of these landlords have no morals.' She hesitated. 'I hope you don't think I'm gossiping…'

Ah, here it goes.

'But that pharmacy chap said there are rumours Vivian Sangster has met some handsome American and she's moving to California with him. Is that true?'

'Good old Mr Frew. Yes. All true.'

Mrs Crill gasped. 'Oh well. Good for her. That toerag of an ex-husband of hers treated her like a bloody workhorse.' She flashed me a sympathetic look. 'So, what happens now?'

I shrugged my shoulders under my padded winter jacket. 'We've just got to push on for the next few weeks, until the shop closes for good on 31st December.'

'And you?'

I flapped one gloved hand. 'I'll get myself sorted with something else. I applied for a local job last night.'

She offered a supportive smile from out of her creamy, freckled face. 'Here. This is on me. Put your money away, love.'

She bustled about, fetching me a takeaway latte, before scooping up one of the chocolate brownies from inside the polished glass cake cabinet.

'No, really, Mrs Crill.'

'Och, away with you. You enjoy.'

I blinked back a grateful tear. People were being so sweet and that was making the whole horrible situation even worse. 'Thank you.' I started to head towards the bakery door.

I would have to get used to this.

———

I followed my usual routine in the shop, moving from shelf to shelf, switching on the looping fairy lights, lighting a couple of festive scented candles – this morning, I chose cranberry and orange – before selecting more Christmas songs to play.

Nine o'clock was fast approaching, so I savoured what was left of my latte and took a couple of bites of the delicious chocolate brownie. I would save the rest of it to have with my lunch.

I looked out of the bottle-glass shop window. Fine droplets of rain were slithering over the cobbles, sending a gauzy sheen over everything. I hoped that wouldn't deter the locals or any hardy tourists from coming in to treat themselves to some Christmas decorations!

Mum and Orla were due in later, so it was just me manning the fort for now.

I hurried into the office, fired up the PC and rattled off some discount notices to attach to the shelves. The printer whirred into life.

I heard the dainty tinkle of the shop doorbell. 'Just coming!' I called, snatching up the printed pages. 'Good morning. How can I help you? Oh, hello again, madam.'

It was the willowy middle-aged blonde woman from earlier in the week. She was accompanied this time by a well-dressed man, who looked about the same age as her. He had well-cut salt and pepper hair and quizzical brows.

'Good morning,' she smiled. Then her face became serious. 'We were just reading your notice outside. Dear me. We're so sorry.'

'Thank you. Yes, it has all been rather a big shock.'

The air hung with unanswered questions. For something to do, I clapped my hands together and then wished I hadn't. I must have looked like a performing seal. 'The landlords wouldn't renew our lease.'

I thought I was being very circumspect about the whole thing. It was far more than the wretched lot of them deserved.

They nodded and murmured their sympathies and apologies.

'So how can I help you? Here to treat yourself to a couple more trinkets before you leave and head home?'

'Oh, we're not tourists,' clarified her companion beside her. 'We moved here a few months ago.'

'We've been very busy,' interjected the woman. She gave the man a charged look. 'With limited success.'

'You can say that again,' he agreed.

There was another pause.

'Sorry,' said the woman, refocusing. 'I was interested in buying one of your snow-covered ceramic cottages that are in the window.'

'Of course.' I led her over to the display. 'Have you seen one in particular that you like?'

Her gaze trailed over the cluster of roofs, surrounded by puffs of cotton wool I'd dotted around them. 'That one is gorgeous,' she said, pointing to the thatched one with a red door and sprigs of ivy attached to the roof. 'I'll take it.'

I carried it over to the counter and fetched a small cardboard box to pack it up in. As I padded it out with old newspaper and a couple of sheets of tissue paper, I became aware of the man examining me. 'You've done a brilliant job, promoting the Christmas Crackers brand.'

'Thank you.'

'You came up with some great promotional ideas when the business was starting out.' When he noticed me looking curious, he smiled. 'I used to work as a copywriter for *Business First* magazine. I remember us giving your shop a mention once or twice.'

I picked up the ceramic cottage, placed it in amongst the folds of paper inside the box and returned his smile. 'Oh, that's right. I recall us getting a mention. It has been a challenge, but

I've loved every minute of it.' I swallowed, fighting to maintain a professional veneer. 'It was a labour of love working here. I've always been obsessed with Christmas.'

The man pushed his tanned hands into the pockets of his long tweed coat. It was pricked with speckles of rain. 'So, when the shop closes down, what will you do?'

I concentrated on taping up the lid of the box. 'I'm sure I'll find something else. I've started looking, so…' I allowed my words to tail off. This was excruciating. How many times would I find myself having to endure these sorts of questions over the next few weeks?

The woman offered her credit card and I processed the payment.

I expected them to thank me and leave, but they continued to hover in front of the counter, appreciating the displays in the shop and then me. 'Was there something else?'

The man admired a quilted cloth Father Christmas and Rudolph behind him. 'I've done some research on you, Ms Grant.'

'Er, thank you?'

The man breezed towards some vintage-style lilac baubles dangling from one of the hooks. He plucked one from it and toyed with it in his fingers. 'Your marketing and PR strategies for Christmas Crackers pushed the business to another level. I thought your Secret Santa advertising campaign with those celebrities was very clever and I loved what you did with the Tinsel-itis competition for schools.'

I continued to shoot looks from the woman to the man and back again. 'That's very kind of you.'

Wow. They had done their homework on me. I didn't know whether to be flattered or a little terrified.

The gentleman studied me. 'I read on LinkedIn that you have a degree in interior design from Glasgow School of Art?'

'Yes. That's right.' I frowned. What was all this about?

The blonde woman must have sensed my slight apprehension. 'Ms Grant,' she said. 'Please let us explain.' She clutched her snowy cottage purchase in the tartan-ribboned gift bag. 'We have moved to Craig Brae because we want to launch a new business.'

Her dapper companion took over. 'That's right. But let's just say it hasn't been plain sailing.' He offered me an encouraging smile, that made his smoky eyes crinkle. 'We need someone with enthusiasm and creativity – someone who isn't afraid to use their imagination.'

I could feel my head snapping between the two of them in confusion. Why were they telling me this? 'Okaaaay…'

The blonde woman's long, wide mouth slid into a warm smile. 'How would you like to come and work for us?'

Chapter Four

I realised my mouth was forming a series of ridiculous shapes.

'Sorry?'

The man indicated to the woman. 'Please let us explain. This is my wife Stephanie and I'm Max. Max Styles.' He proffered his hand and I shook it, before she did the same.

My head was reeling, but I managed to say, 'Very nice to meet you.'

'Likewise.' He flicked me a look. 'This has no doubt caught you off-guard a bit.'

A bit?!

Stephanie Styles jumped in, her powder-blue eyes expectant. 'Rather than take up any more of your time trying to explain what we're doing, how about you come up to our place and we can show you our project?'

Max nodded. 'That's a great idea. We've moved into Rowan Moore House. Do you know it?'

Pictures of the gated, impressive house flooded my mind. It

had been lying empty for a while, since the previous owner, a retired politician, had passed away last year. It was located on the outskirts of Craig Brae and was situated in sprawling grounds that cradled woodland. So, they had bought that?

Max Styles plucked a business card from his coat pocket and handed it to me across the shop counter. I was still so stunned; I stared down at the card but wasn't processing what was printed on it.

'Would you be able to drop by at some point today?' he asked.

I opened and closed my mouth again like an idiot.

'There's no pressure,' insisted Stephanie Styles. 'How about you just come and take a look and see what you think?'

I had only just applied for that part-time hotel receptionist job. I wasn't swamped with offers. And whatever this job was that the Styleses were talking about, was also based locally. Thoughts of Mum and being around for her tripped through my mind.

I was still clutching Max Styles's business card. I gazed down at it. It was a navy-blue and gold affair; *Max Styles, Property Developer* ran across it, with his email, mobile and business numbers underneath.

'As you can see, I've changed careers,' he pointed out with a wry smile.

'In other words, my husband retired from copywriting and then got bored stupid,' added Stephanie with a grin.

I laughed and examined the business card again.

'And he roped me into his new vision too.'

'What did you do before?' I asked her.

'My parents owned their own chain of jewellery businesses. I was involved in that for a long time, but I always wanted to do something on my own, something more challenging. And believe me, this is it!'

My curiosity was piqued, not to mention that I was flattered by their interest and the research they had undertaken about me. What harm would it do? I wasn't committing to anything. I could just take a look at this mysterious project of theirs. And it wasn't as if I had another offer lined up already.

My heart rattled against my ribs. 'All right,' I found myself saying. 'Thank you. I'll come up and take a look.'

Stephanie Styles beamed with delight. 'Wonderful!'

'One of my work colleagues will be here soon and can take care of things on her own for a little while.'

Max nodded his approval. 'That suits us too. See you just after one o'clock then, Ms Grant.'

'Please. It's Lottie,' I called after them, but they were already disappearing out of the shop door, all flapping coats and expensive tailoring.

———

'So, what is this all about?' called Mum out of her passenger side car window.

I jumped in beside her.

'Why do you want a lift up to Rowan Moore House? What's going on, Lottie?'

I fastened my seat belt and we set off. 'Would you believe I've been offered a job?'

Mum was stunned. 'What, up there? Doing what, though? I don't understand. It's an empty house.'

'It was,' I explained. 'But apparently, this couple – the

Styleses – have bought it and they're starting some sort of business up there and they've asked me to go and take a look.'

'What sort of business?'

'I have no idea, Mum. That's why I'm going up there to see.'

She indicated past the roundabout and took us along past the dry-stone walls. 'Well, that sounds very promising, sweetheart. Dear me! You haven't wasted any time.'

The sun was trying to push its way through the clouds, now that the rain had faded away. It shimmered against the damp, bare tree branches. 'It does all sound rather mysterious,' said Mum, concentrating on the road.

I tugged down the passenger side mirror and pulled back my loose waves into a ponytail. 'I know. I keep wondering what it is they're planning.'

Mum's cat-like green eyes blinked as she took us past the shining mirror of Loch Strathe on the left-hand side. 'I didn't even know people had moved into Rowan Moore House, although I'd heard the odd rumour that the property had been screened off some months back.'

I finished tightening the elastic band around my high ponytail. 'Neither did I and I'm sure if the local gossips had known what was going on, they would have been telling everybody by now as well.'

She shot me a sideways glance. 'And this couple – the Styleses – they seem very nice?'

'They do. They were very enthusiastic and approachable. I said I would go up there just after one o' clock today and take a look. I haven't committed to anything.'

'Good job you haven't, not until you know what it is.'

'I know. I am intrigued though.'

Mum's little apple-green Polo glided past the spears of pine trees. There was a winding lane up and away on the right, with a black and white painted wrought-iron plaque, proclaiming *Rowan Moore House.*

'You've got me wondering now,' said Mum, slowing down to negotiate the bend. 'Well, whatever this job is, it would be very convenient for you…' She hesitated. 'But I meant what I said before, lovey. I don't want you taking a job, just because it's local and close to me.'

'Mum, the fact this position – whatever it is – happens to be just up the road, has nothing to do with it. Well, very little.' I offered her a smile.

Then I leant over and patted her arm. 'I'm just going to hear what they have to say and take a look at this project of theirs.'

Mum slowed her car as we reached another sharp bend. 'Ok. Oh, goodness me!'

The path up to the house fell away, to reveal Rowan Moore House, but not as I remembered it from years ago, during a secondary school trip. Back then, it had been owned by Sir Samuel Carter, a prominent politician, who was rather an eccentric.

He had been striding about the gardens, decked out in a red tartan kilt with his two springer spaniels at his side.

I recalled the house had also possessed splashes of tartan curtains and even Sir Samuel's two dogs were sporting the same material on their coats. Sir Samuel had spoken in a booming, confident voice about the history of his impressive home and that there were stories the ghost of a deceived seventeenth-century Highland warrior would roam the gardens at night, wailing about how treachery by one of his own soldiers had cost him his life.

Sir Samuel had then launched into an impersonation of said ghostly warrior, sending most of us into fits of giggles – and that included our teachers.

Back then, the turreted Edwardian house had been in dire need of a lick of paint and the gardens had been crying out for a spruce-up.

Now, Rowan Moore House was boasting sweeping tartan tie-back drapes at the many sash windows and two potted trees were standing to attention by the grand arched entrance. Glowing white lights were wrapped around each tree and the path leading up to the steps was also lit up by ornate carriage lamps.

Bursts of pink and lilac heather had been planted in front of the bank of manicured high hedges either side of the drive and at the rear of the house.

The property was all glowing grand pale-grey stone and was like an extravagant Christmas card.

'Isn't it beautiful?' breathed Mum, resting both her hands on top of her steering wheel to appreciate the house. 'It's donkey's years since I've been anywhere near this place but it never used to look anything like this.'

I managed to close my shocked mouth. 'It's gorgeous.' I glanced down at my watch. 'Crikey. I had better head in.'

'I'll wait for you,' insisted Mum, not managing to pull her eyes away from the stunning house. 'I'm dying to know what this Mr and Mrs Styles have been doing.'

'Thanks. Yes, you're not the only one.'

'I'll turn the car around and park a bit further down the lane.'

I pecked her on the cheek and clambered out, my stomach giving a series of excited flutters.

Mum threw her car into reverse and headed back down round the bend and out of sight to wait for me.

I drew up and gazed, enchanted, at Rowan Moore House. What was the business they were launching up here? Were they going to turn their home into a boutique hotel? Tourists would love it, what with its dramatic turrets, sweeping tartan drapes and sprawling gardens.

'Lottie. Hello!'

Stephanie Styles emerged out onto the steps of the house. Behind her, followed her husband.

I hoped I'd managed to disguise my trepidation with a friendly smile. I approached both of them and we all shook hands again and exchanged pleasantries.

'Thank you for coming,' said Max.

'Thank you for inviting me.' I nodded behind them. 'Your house is beautiful.'

Stephanie beamed. 'Thank you. We're slowly getting there with it.'

Max indicated over his shoulder. 'It has been a bit of a money pit, having to put things right. The window frames were on their last legs and the whole place needed re-wiring, but we had a rough idea what we were taking on.'

He pulled a rueful smile. 'Stephanie and I are therefore hoping we can recoup some of the money swallowed up by this place by making a go of our new business venture.'

He threw one hand out to the right, where there was a gravelled buttery path between the lawns and the hedges. 'Now, we know you don't have a great deal of time as you need to get back to the shop, so shall we show you what we've been working on?'

'Yes please.'

I had expected both of them to whirl around and lead me into their glowing, sumptuous home, but instead they began walking away from Rowan Moore House and guiding me along the gravelled path. That was odd. Where were we going?

We made our way through a kissing gate that took us through some crunchy, damp woodland. Thank goodness the rain had stopped!

I bundled myself deeper into my quilted jacket, glad that I was wearing my flat riding boots. Above us, the bare branches of the trees formed an intricate criss-cross roof. My hair bobbed about in its ponytail as we strode on.

We reached the other side of the woodland. I spun round to talk to them. 'All this land is yours?' I asked.

The air was earthy and laced with the scent of wet bark.

Stephanie nodded. 'It is. That's why we wanted to do something with it, and hopefully bring some money and extra tourism to Craig Brae too.'

Max agreed. 'That's why we decided to do this.'

'Do what?' My back was still turned away from what they were now gesturing at.

Max smiled and pointed over my shoulder. 'That.'

I turned.

My eyes widened. *Oh, my goodness.* This wasn't what I was expecting.

Chapter Five

Facing me were four gorgeous log cabins.

They were clustered together in a semi-circle, with more trees thrusting up behind them in the background. Each possessed their own porches and sweet chimney pots.

I immediately conjured up an image of them, dusted with snow and sporting festive wreaths on their doors.

'Is this your project?' I asked, whirling back round to look at Stephanie and Max.

'It is,' he said. 'We started building them several months ago, just before we moved into the house.'

Stephanie studied my stunned expression. 'So, what do you think?'

My face broke into an appreciative smile. 'They look lovely.'

Max arched one brow. 'From the outside they do. Wait until you see inside each of them. You might not be saying that then.'

Stephanie rolled her eyes and strode on, pulling a set of

keys from her jeans pocket. Max and I tapped up the steps of the first log cabin behind her.

I expected the interior to be all fringed woven rugs, an amber log fire spitting in a heavy ornate fireplace and stout candles casting shapes against framed paintings on the walls.

Instead, I was met by cheap plastic furniture and limp Christmas decorations hanging around the kitchen doorway. Bright orange cotton curtains were at each of the windows, clashing with a loud paisley rug on the floor.

Stephanie and Max eyed my bemused expression. 'Come and see the kitchen,' she encouraged, moving ahead.

That wasn't any better. The dark wood cabinets were smart, but more tacky festive decorations cluttered the windowsill. The kitchen floor consisted of amber laminate, that was almost as migraine-inducing as the curtains.

'They're supposed to be cosy, indulgent self-catering holiday accommodation,' muttered Max. 'Our plan was to have our first guests stay in them at Christmas and then accommodate more tourists for the rest of the year.' He pulled a face. 'They look more like they've been thrown together and then stirred with a stick.'

Stephanie encouraged me to look into the master bedroom. There was a silver skull sporting a Santa hat on one of the bedside tables and black and red bedding. I recoiled in horror. It was more like a sacrificial pit than a sumptuous bedroom.

'Come and see the rest of the cabins,' said Stephanie.

As I thought, the other three were very much in the same vein. The second was decked out in plum and berry, with weird Perspex furniture and a bedraggled Christmas tree made out of paper stationed in the corner of the sitting room.

The third and fourth cabins carried a checked theme and

reminded me of a Scottish biscuit tin. Again, they had Christmas decorations that looked like they had been stashed in someone's attic gathering dust for the past thirty years.

As we wandered from room to room, cabin to cabin, the Styleses explained that each one was fully self-contained, with an electric shower, bathroom, fully kitted out kitchen with wood-burning stove, as well as gas hob, oven and fridge.

'We've tried to be as environmentally friendly as we can,' said Stephanie. 'We insisted the builders use sustainable timber, as well as sheep's wool insulation and even sheep's wool duvets.'

'Even the water we supply to each cabin comes from our private spring,' added Max.

I followed Max and Stephanie out of the last cabin.

'So,' exclaimed Max. 'What did you think?'

My cheeks heated up. Oh God. I had to be honest. But what if I was too honest? I could end up talking myself out of prospective employment. I eyed him and then Stephanie. 'I think the environmental considerations you have undertaken are wonderful. It's a pity more businesses didn't think like you.'

'But?' asked Max with a hint of a wry smile, that made fine lines appear around his mouth.

'I'm sorry,' I faltered, flashing awkward glances at them both. 'I don't like them. In fact, I think they look awful – on the inside,' I quickly clarified. 'From the outside, they're gorgeous.'

'We agree with you,' sighed Stephanie. 'That's what we get for employing the granddaughter of one of Max's closest friends.'

Max flinched. 'I won't be doing that again.' He rubbed at

his tanned forehead. 'My friend assured me she was good. Very good. She's studying fashion in Edinburgh.'

Stephanie squinted under the washed-out November sky. 'As Max just explained, we wanted to launch the four cabins in time for Christmas and asked Millie to make them a reflection of the perfect woodland getaway dream.'

'Instead, they're a ruddy nightmare,' seethed Max, shoving his hands into his coat pockets. 'She's gone all quirky and that isn't what we asked for.' He gave me a hopeful smile. 'If you were in charge, Lottie, what would you do with them?'

'Do?'

'Yes. How would you improve them? Make them more appealing?'

I surveyed the four cabins under the moody Saturday afternoon sky. They carried so much potential, surrounded by the tangle of thick woods, with the tantalising glimpses of Loch Strathe facing them through the trees.

Pictures of them drizzled with snowflakes leapt into my head. I envisaged the porches each carrying a different colour of Christmas tree: white, silver, electric blue and rose gold.

There would be ivy wrapped around the porch bannisters and a sparkly, illuminated wreath on each door.

'Lottie?'

'Oh, sorry.' I blushed at Stephanie. I cleared my throat. 'Well, if I were to improve them for the festive season, I would start off by giving each of them an individual Christmas-related theme.'

'Go on,' said Max.

I described how I would have a pretty Christmas tree on each porch and wreaths on the door. Warming to my theme, I indicated to the lovely expanse of woodland they were set in.

'I'd have lit up reindeer situated around the cabins and string some lantern-style lights in the woods, leading up here.'

Stephanie's eyed glowed. 'That sounds so lovely.'

'And I would have someone playing the part of Father Christmas, serving toasted marshmallows and hot chocolate as the guests arrived.'

Max's lined mouth twitched with appreciation. 'And how would you go about marketing them?'

My head was buzzing with enthusiasm. 'Maybe as a Magical Escape or a Woodland Wonder. There could be a reindeer ride through the woods here for families and a present hunt. Each cabin would have its own name...' I realised I wasn't pausing for breath and pulled myself up. 'Sorry. Anything to do with Christmas and I get carried away.'

I noticed Stephanie and Max were bathing me in wide smiles. I glanced over at the cabins and back at them. 'You said you have taken on board environmental considerations, so you could easily continue to incorporate them into the lodges.'

Max and Stephanie exchanged intrigued smiles. 'In what way?'

I called on my degree learning and mentioned things like kindle cone fire-lighters, reusable paper decorations and even newspaper decorations for the tree. 'I've seen dinky little felt decorations and stained-glass baubles.' I carried on. 'You could also have wooden snowflakes and biodegradable glitter, which instead of plastic, uses forest wood pulp.'

They both appeared impressed.

'Did you say they would be available throughout the year to stay in too?'

'Absolutely. We're serious about making a success of this,' emphasised Max. He jerked his head back at the four vacant cabins. 'So once Christmas was over, what do you think you would do with them for the rest of the year?'

Blimey. They were really pushing me, to see how imaginative and forward-thinking I was. I took a nervous breath. 'Well, I would suggest simple tweaks to each interior, to reflect the season or the event. That would mean you wouldn't have to invest in more pricey interior makeovers.' I started to describe how red and pink hearts and decorations could be put up for Valentine guests. 'There could be glowing love heart lamps everywhere and a bottle of champagne and chocolates in each cabin.'

I carried on, drawing on more ideas and started to talk about Easter. Yellow, cream and white furnishings could be drafted in to reflect the springtime celebrations, together with vases of daffodils and fluffy toy chicks. 'There could be Easter egg hunts and find the Easter bunny and strings of yellow lights in the woods.' I realised I was wittering on and stopped.

'No, please continue,' urged Max. 'That sounds terrific.'

I felt my cheeks ping. For Mother's Day and Father's Day, I suggested laying on croissants and tea and coffee in the cabins for guests to enjoy. 'You might even be able to come to an agreement with the local beauty parlour for them to give a reduced voucher for a manicure or pedicure for the mums and perhaps a cheap round of golf or a reduced-price visit to one of the distilleries for the dads.'

Stephanie awarded Max a triumphant grin.

'Then at Halloween, it could be all pumpkin decorations, orange lights, ghost stories...'

My voice tailed off as I watched the two of them, gazing at me.

Stephanie wrapped her arms around the navy gilet she was

wearing. 'I knew it. I just knew it that first time I came into your shop, Lottie.'

'Knew what?' I blushed, feeling like an awkward teenager.

'That you are a very hard-working, creative and conscientious young woman,' jumped in Max. 'You've done such a brilliant job with Christmas Crackers.'

'Thank you. It's just a pity I couldn't have carried on with it as promised.'

Max's craggy, dashing features were sympathetic. 'That's dreadful and no way to conduct business.'

'Everybody's talking about it in Craig Brae,' qualified Stephanie, shaking her head in disbelief.

'I thought they might. Word soon gets around.'

Stephanie pointed to the empty cabins. 'Well, onto more positive matters. We'd love for you to come and work with us, Lottie. You would do such a fantastic job, turning this accommodation into something really special.'

I blinked, processing it all.

'We have a dedicated team of decorators, ready to overhaul them,' emphasised Max. 'Millie's vision, as you have seen, was the polar opposite to ours.'

Stephanie nodded her blonde shoulder-skimming hair. 'They are already all reserved for Christmas. We only have a matter of weeks and it's going to take some effort, but we know it's do-able.'

I blew out a cloud of apprehensive air. It sounded a wonderful opportunity.

Max let his hands rise and fall by his sides. 'You are a terrific businesswoman with a great eye for detail and lots of drive. Anyone can see that.'

I hadn't known what I had expected when I came up here, but I hadn't expected this, that was for sure.

Max reeled off a salary that was double what I was earning currently. 'You will be responsible for overhauling the cabins for each occasion; overseeing their revamps; making sure they are marketed and promoted; and coming up with social media enterprise. Essentially, you will be the lodges' project manager. You will also receive six weeks' holiday a year.'

My stomach performed an impressive series of forward rolls. 'Crikey,' was all I could manage. Could I do this? It was going to be one hell of a challenge.

Pictures of Christmas Crackers popped behind my eyes. 'But the shop,' I stuttered. 'It's closing down in a few weeks.'

'If you were to accept our offer,' suggested Stephanie, 'we really would need you to start as soon as possible. Is there anyone you could call on who could take over in the shop until it does close?'

'We wouldn't expect you to abandon the shop,' clarified Max. 'But of course, time is of the essence for us.'

My brain screeched in every direction. I couldn't just leave Christmas Crackers in the lurch. But then, I wouldn't have to. Mum and Orla were both very reliable and Vivian kept insisting she would be around for the time being, if we needed her.

My head snapped round, drinking in the empty log cabins and their obvious potential.

With lots of imagination, they could be transformed from the cheap and loud affairs they were at the moment, into warm and luxurious havens. But it would be such a change from what I was currently doing… 'It's a lot to take in,' I confessed. 'I don't know…'

'You don't have to give us an answer straight away,' said Max. 'Go away and take a day or two to think about it.'

I managed a shaky, excited smile. 'Thank you. I will.' I glanced down at my watch. 'I'm very sorry, but I really should be heading back to the shop now. I said to Orla I would be back before two.'

We made our way back through the woods, arriving out in front of the lemon glow of Rowan Moore House.

Mum's Polo was waiting for me. Instead of parking further down the access road, she was stationed not far from the house. She gave Stephanie and Max a smile and an awkward little wave.

After I'd got in the car, we trundled away, back towards Craig Brae.

'I thought they'd kidnapped you,' joked Mum, flashing me sidelong looks from the passenger side. 'I was about to ask inside the house if anyone had seen you.'

I smiled. 'Do they look like kidnappers, Mum?'

'No, but you tell me what kidnappers are supposed to look like.' She kept glancing across at me as she drove. 'So?' pushed Mum. 'Come on. Out with it, lass. What happened? What's the job?'

I laced and unlaced my gloved fingers in my lap. I still felt rather stunned by it all. 'It's not what I expected it to be.'

Mum waited and when I didn't say anything, she let out an impatient sigh. 'Och, stop teasing me, young lady, and just tell me!'

And so I did, regaling her about the log cabins in the

woods, their potential and the awful, gawdy interiors they had each been given. Then I went on to explain that Stephanie and Max wanted to recruit me in a project manager role, to turn their business into something successful, with a Christmas launch.

'Well,' gasped Mum when I'd finished, as she eased the car round the roundabout and back into Craig Brae. 'Goodness me!'

I glanced out of the passenger side window at the balls of sheep scattered in the fields. 'I don't know what to do,' I groaned. 'They've offered me double what I'm earning right now, but I'm not sure I could do it.'

'Whyever not?'

I fiddled with my gloves, before whipping them off and dumping them in my bag. My confidence was being pushed and pulled. 'I've never done anything like this before and on such a huge scale.'

'No, you haven't,' agreed Mum, taking me by surprise. 'But what you have done is promote and push a business that has become a nationally recognised brand. And you turned that shop into a gorgeous little haven. Your displays are admired and you know it!'

I pulled a face and laughed, despite my inner turmoil

'Plus, all those wonderful competitions you ran and the social media promotions you have done.' Mum's pink lips pursed. 'You came up with all those ideas on your own. I bet there are a lot of people out there in retail management who wouldn't have had the first inkling what to do.'

We eased up outside Christmas Crackers and Mum turned off the ignition. 'At the end of the day, lovey, it's your decision.'

I leant over and planted a kiss on her cheek. 'I will give their job offer serious thought. Thanks Mum.'

'Ok. You do that. Now, I'm just going to the bank and then I will be in to start my shift. Is that ok, boss?'

As I reached the shop door and waved through the window at Orla, I noticed a few eager locals bombing up the pavement, eager to get in, to stock up on their Christmas decorations.

I had a lot to think about.

Chapter Six

I felt emotionally wrung out, after a hectic Saturday afternoon.

A huge variety of decorations now on discount were snapped up and our regulars expressed their shock at Christmas Crackers closing down, having read the notices I'd put up or heard the news from other locals.

The Craig Brae gossip line was in full operational order, but that came as no surprise, since Stephanie and Max Styles, who had only been living in the area for five minutes, had heard all about our closure too.

Another hot topic of conversation was Vivian's whirlwind American romance with Ridley.

A wide variety of comments and observations were made, ranging from 'Jings! Fancy her running off with someone she's only known five minutes and at her age!' to 'Good luck to her. I don't suppose he has a twin brother?'

I tried to focus on the shop, but my mind travelled back to

Stephanie and Max and their log cabins. I couldn't take on something like that... could I?

It was such a huge responsibility and the Styleses would be investing so much in me. After splitting from Kyle, losing Dad and now the shop, I didn't know whether I felt capable of rising to such a demanding challenge.

As I wrapped up baubles, slid coils of tinsel into bags and enthused over our sets of Chinese lantern-style Christmas lights, thoughts turned over and over in my head. It would be such a rewarding job. Not to mention that I would still be working locally and therefore be around for Mum. Despite her protestations, I knew she appreciated me being there for her and, likewise, her for me.

But making a success of the lodges was going to take a monumental effort. My nerves jangled again like Christmas bells as I thought about it.

My phone pinged under the counter, signalling the arrival of a new email. I fetched it out and located my inbox.

It was from the local hotel, inviting me to interview for the post of part-time receptionist I had applied for.

I chewed my lip, frowned and clicked away from the message.

That night in bed, I lay lost in my thoughts and thrashing around.

After a few more disgruntled minutes, I threw back the covers, padded through to the kitchen and made myself a cup of relaxing camomile tea to take back to bed.

My alarm clock proclaimed it was 3.15am.

Oh, bloody hell!

I clambered back under the covers, cradling my mug and taking a few grateful sips. Through the gap in my hessian curtains, I could make out the spikey treetops, as though they had been dipped in ink and the silhouette of the surrounding hills, like slumbering giants.

The imposing hillsides that surrounded us in Craig Brae drew in keen walkers and coach holidays, not to mention the two distilleries positioned at either end of the town.

We experienced mild summers and cool winters and the visitors just kept coming back for more. I loved it and had missed the crisp zing of fresh air and the swathes of piercing pine trees while I had been away studying in Glasgow.

We were all about outdoor pursuits and glowing with the energy of fresh air in these parts. It had been known for the odd visitor to fall in love with Craig Brae and move here permanently, or at least buy a property to use as a weekend retreat.

Even in the stillness of the middle of the night like this, I could understand the appeal of my hometown and the magical spell it cast.

I took another mouthful of my tea. What would my dad say to me right now, if he were here? I could feel my eyelids drooping, as I set my tea down on my beside table.

'Lottie. Why are you hesitating?' asked Dad, tilting his brown floppy-haired head to one side.

'I'm not.'

'Yes, you are. You're procrastinating.' His dark-blue eyes shone. 'You know, you never give yourself enough credit.'

I brushed off his comment. 'That's not true.'

'It is. Look at what you've achieved with Christmas

Crackers. You turned that shop around and have kept things going. Vivian couldn't have done any of that without you and she's very open about that.'

I stared across at my father, noting the way one of his brows would always arch upwards when he was thinking about something. It made him look like he was surprised.

'You're just like me,' he grinned, displaying that familiar, slim gap between his two front teeth. 'Christmas crazy. That's why you have made such a success of things. That shop was a labour of love for you.'

I swallowed. 'But that's the thing, Dad. What about the shop?'

'What about it?'

His interested, kind face was every bit as caring as I remembered it.

'I can't just up and leave, especially not right now when we're closing down in a matter of weeks. If I did that, it would be like all the hard work I put in, was for nothing.' I blew out a mouthful of frustrated air. 'I know that sounds crazy, but I can't.'

'Oh, you'll think of something. You always do. What is it I always tell you?'

'That things have a habit of sorting themselves out in the end.'

I wanted him to stay. I wanted to reach out to him, be scooped into his capable, supportive arms for one of his bear hugs.

'Go for it, Lottie. Be proud. It's the things you haven't done that you regret, not the things you have.'

But I was beginning to lose him again. I shot out one hand

in the hope he would take mine, but it melted into the November night air. 'Dad? Dad! No! Don't go. Wait, please!'

I shot up in bed, almost knocking over the half-drunk mug of camomile on my bedside table. It took a few moments for my head to unscramble itself. My chest rose and fell in ragged breaths.

When I came that day to view the flat with Mum and Dad in tow, it had been clean, but a lot of the fixtures and fittings were tired and dated. Dark wood panelling ran along the length of the hallway and the walls had been painted a disturbing shade of green.

The bathroom was fitted out in white but the shower cubicle leaked and the kitchen was also begging for a makeover, with its flowery tiling and amber linoleum on the floor.

The spare bedroom was painted in cream and had a russet carpet, but my bedroom had wonky shelves and a loud, paisley patterned carpet which gave you a migraine whenever you looked at it.

As for the sitting room, that was all Venetian blinds, brass wall lamps and was painted a duck-egg blue.

Nevertheless, I could see the potential it had, as did my parents, so I bought it. We each rolled up our sleeves and set to work on dragging the whole place into the twenty-first century.

It took several months, but thanks to Mum and Dad's efforts and Dad calling on the expertise of some tradesmen colleagues of his, it had been transformed into a pastel-hued comfy home with a stone fireplace and scatter cushions that I could call my own.

• • •

I stared around my bedroom, with its mirrored wardrobes and cream and coffee bedding. It felt like my dad had been here, but then he'd slipped away again. Even in my flat, my late father's presence was imprinted everywhere – and I wouldn't have wanted it any other way.

Loss crushed my insides as I sank back under the covers again. I had conjured him up. I had willed him to be there and yet, his advice rang true as it always had.

It was like he had whispered to me while I was asleep. Dad always maintained that every problem had a solution.

After wriggling around under the covers, I sat up again and propped myself up against my pillows. It was almost nine o'clock in the morning.

I reached for my mobile by my bedside lamp and switched it on. Outside, I could hear the comforting, rusty peel of church bells.

Mum's number rang out several times before she picked it up. I didn't give her time to speak. 'I dreamt about Dad,' I blurted. 'It was like he was here, chatting to me.'

I heard Mum swallow down the line. 'I dreamt about him again last week. He was telling me off after I said I would only be ten minutes down the shops and I ended up being two hours.'

I laughed at the memory. 'And his car battery went flat waiting for you. He was always trotting that story out.'

'And it was exaggerated,' insisted Mum. I could almost hear her smile. 'I was not two hours... well, not quite.' She paused. 'So, what did Dad say to you?'

I pushed my bed head around. 'He said I should accept the Styles cabins job.' I rubbed at my creased face. 'I received an email yesterday, inviting me for an interview for the part-time hotel reception vacancy.'

Mum listened. 'Oh right. What's your heart telling you to do, lovey?'

I played with the edge of my crumpled duvet. I could see the woodland dusted with snow in my imagination and the glow of lamps from inside the log cabins, throwing a lemony warmth everywhere. There was the smell of pine needles. The cabins were furnished with sparkly cushions and woven rugs.

'But the shop, Mum,' I said, pulling myself back to the real world. 'If I did accept that job with the Styleses, they said they would like me to start straight away. Who would oversee the closure of the shop? I mean, I'd still be able to pop in and out, but I wouldn't be around like I am at the moment.'

'Well,' steeled Mum. 'I was having a think about all this last night and I don't see why Orla and I can't do it.'

I sat up straighter in bed. 'Really? You are sure?'

'Of course, I am, otherwise I wouldn't have suggested it.' Her voice took on a more assertive edge. 'We know how the shop works. You just give us a list of what needs doing and when – retail accounts to be closed, the electricity company to be notified, that sort of thing – and we can get on to it.'

'Are you sure?'

'Totally. It will give me something else to focus on for a bit and you know the personal issues Orla has had to deal with of late. I'm sure she will feel the same.'

Orla had got divorced a couple of months ago and, like Mum, was relieved to have Christmas Crackers to focus on to break up the monotony.

Optimism bloomed inside me. 'But what about Eternal

Flame? I mean, that would be great but you really should speak to Susie first, Mum.'

'Ah. I'm well ahead of you there. I rang her last night. I had a feeling this situation might come up. You looked so bewitched by those lodges when you got back in the car, I thought you would want to take the job with the Styleses.'

Mum then went on to explain that Susie had been fine about it. 'She said as long as I can do the odd shift mentoring the two new girls, then there's no problem.'

I turned over everything in my head. 'Blimey, Mum. You don't hang around, do you?'

'Well, it's best to just get on with things.'

Thoughts raced through my head, as though I were strapped to a roundabout and couldn't jump off.

'Will you please stop trying to take on responsibility for everything, Lottie? I know how capable and hard-working you are, but you aren't alone with this. There are people who are only too willing to help.' Her voice softened. 'Christmas is lovely but it can also be a very lonely time of the year when you've lost someone or you end up by yourself. I'll be happy to keep busy.'

'I know, Mum.' I tried to let everything settle in my head. It still seemed like such a monumental task and the Styleses livelihood was riding on the lodges being a success. 'Please pass on my grateful thanks to Susie for being so understanding, but...'

Mum interrupted me. 'I know you want this job with the Styleses, Lottie. But you're worried you won't do it justice. You have to believe in yourself more.' She sighed into my ear. 'I know how Christmas Crackers works. I've been behind that counter more than a few times with you, you know.' I could hear her smile down the line.

'You know I trust you, Mum.' My voice cracked. 'I'm just worried that I'll find this role is too big for me and I'll let the Styleses down. Managing a shop like Christmas Crackers is a completely different prospect to project managing four luxury cabins.' I let out a sigh. 'I just wish Dad were here.' All the emotion, the dream about my father, the fate of the shop... it was all pushing down on me.

'I wish he was still here too, sweetheart. But you know what? I think he still is. Your dream proved that.'

I bit back a sob.

'In your dream,' said Mum, 'what did Dad advise you to do?'

I waggled my feet under the bed covers and tried to compose myself. 'He told me to go for it. If I didn't, I would regret it.'

Now it was the turn of Mum's voice to splinter. 'He was always such a positive, optimistic man.'

More images of those sweet log cabins popped back into my head.

'So,' announced Mum down the phone. 'What's it to be then? What is your heart telling you do to?'

A surge of adrenalin took me by surprise. I clutched my phone tighter to my ear. Dad's words reverberated in my mind. *'Don't regret the things you have done. Regret the things you haven't done.'*

I imagined myself stationed behind the reception desk at the local hotel, handing out maps and tour guides to holiday-makers, receiving complaints from guests that their morning newspaper didn't arrive or that there was no soap in the shower. I could do that. Or I could accept the generous job offer from Stephanie and Max and turn my love of Christmas and my interior design degree into something that could be profitable, not only for them, but for Craig Brae.

They trusted me. They admired what I had achieved with Christmas Crackers. They were giving me free rein to start from scratch with the cabins and relaunch their business. And they had offered me double my salary. I shouldn't forget that.

A whirlwind of rising excitement blew through me, almost taking my breath away. I wasn't going to punish myself or procrastinate any longer by debating all of this. I had to believe in myself more. If I didn't take their job offer, I could end up regretting it. I banished any shred of lingering doubt. 'I'm going to ring Stephanie and Max now,' I announced to Mum, setting my shoulders. 'And tell them I accept.'

Chapter Seven

'That's wonderful news! I'm delighted,' enthused Max down the phone. 'Stephanie will be thrilled too. She's on the phone to Andrew and Dominic, who are our two construction supremos at the moment. They focus on structural changes and tasks like painting and making minor repairs.' I could hear his delight at me accepting the job. 'But I can assure you that you will be completely in charge of and overseeing the interior design and decoration of the cabins.'

I couldn't help but smile at his infectious enthusiasm. My stomach rippled with a combination of nerves and excitement. 'Well, thank you so much for the job offer. I'm really looking forward to it.'

'Well, we're looking forward to working with you.'

I straightened my pale-pink pyjama top and explained I'd spoken to my mother and she and Orla were going to take on the lion's share of duties in Christmas Crackers until its closure. I had also rung Vivian, who sounded almost as delighted as I did about my new role. I think underneath it all, the poor woman felt somehow guilty that she was going to be heading off to the States for a new life, while I wasn't going to have Christmas Crackers after all and was staring down unemployment. She, too, insisted I accept the 'wonderful' job offer and said that she would make sure she was around if needed by Mum and Orla.

I relayed this to Max. 'That's excellent,' he boomed down the line. 'But we meant what we said earlier, Lottie. If you need to dash off to attend to something important with the shop, just let us know. We don't want you to feel you are being pulled in two directions. We know how much Christmas Crackers means to you.'

'Thank you,' I breathed. 'That's much appreciated.'

I caught sight of my reflection in my wardrobe mirrors as I sat on the edge of my bed. Thank goodness this wasn't a Zoom call. My pyjamas were rumpled and my hair was exploding in a dark-brown mass down my back.

'So, Lottie, we were wondering if you would be able to attend a meeting at Rowan Moore House on Wednesday morning? It would give you a chance to meet everyone.'

'That should be fine. Can I just double check with Mum that it's ok with her and then I'll call you straight back?'

'Of course,' he agreed.

I heard tapping down the line, which I presumed was Max checking his computer. 'How does 10am sound? Let me know if that is all right with her.'

I ended the call to ring Mum and in a garbled rush explained that I had now accepted the job and would she be ok if I attended a meeting with the Styleses and the rest of the team up at Rowan Moore House at 10am on Wednesday morning.

She ushered me off the phone. 'Of course it is. I'm so excited and proud of you!'

Grinning like an idiot, I rang Max back. 'Sorry about that. I've just spoken with my mum and 10am on Wednesday morning is all good.'

'Excellent! Well, we look forward to seeing you then and hearing more about your wonderful ideas for the cabins.'

Then he was gone.

I clicked off my mobile and gawped at my apprehensive image in the mirrors. Today was Sunday. Right. I had three days to pull together more detailed ideas and get prepared for that meeting.

I didn't want to rock up looking unprofessional.

After jumping in the shower and washing my hair, I threw on my jeans and one of my Christmas jumpers, emblazoned with gold and silver sequinned Christmas trees. Ok, so it was still November, but it was never too early for a Christmas jumper in my opinion.

I hoped that the winking sequins might help me channel some extra inspiration.

I fetched myself two slices of toast smeared with butter and apricot jam, together with a steaming mug of tea and made myself comfortable at my kitchen table. I pulled my notebook and pen towards me, as crisp winter sunshine seeped through the window.

I would jot down more details about my ideas

At least I had the next couple of days in Christmas Crackers to help Mum and Orla out. With the festive season on the horizon and us keen to shift as much stock as we could before 31st December, any extra help would be welcome.

I took a pensive bite of my toast. It was going to be a very hectic time, but I could handle it, especially with Mum's support.

I tried to quash bubbling resentment inside me, as I thought again about the shop. I had come up with so many plans about what I was going to do, once I had bought it from Vivian next year.

I'd already had a chat with a local artist about producing special Craig Brae Christmas cards to sell, as well as running more promotional competitions and having personalised Christmas stockings for sale.

All the ideas and notions I had been excitedly coming up with… How could I have been so close to owning Christmas Crackers and then have it whisked away from underneath me, just like that?

My mind returned to that horrible conversation Vivian had with me in the office. Her croaky voice and tearful apologies. She had been every bit as distraught about the situation as I had been.

I glanced down at my fingers which were threatening to crush my pen.

Right. Sitting here seething about it all wasn't helping. I had to focus.

I imagined the four log cabins again. I had to hit the ground running with some great but affordable ideas to transform them in time for Christmas. What would I want in a cosy cabin like those? What would appeal to me?

I doodled random shapes on the empty white page staring back up at me. The cabins weren't just for Christmas, though. Stephanie and Max were intending on having them occupied throughout the year.

The proposals I had initially suggested to them bounded

about in my head. Potential colour schemes and themes rampaged. In that case, if I could make the revamped makeovers cost effective – use colours that could be adapted for other possible themes for the rest of the year – that could prove to be a significant saving. It sounded like Max and Stephanie had spent a great deal of money already on making the cabins environmentally friendly, not to mention all the gadgets and the private water source they had constructed.

That was a real selling point too, even if it had cost them a lot of money. Playing on the environmental aspects of the lodges would appeal to a very large section of the general public, with climate change at the forefront of so many people's thoughts.

While studying for my interior design degree, sustainability was always emphasised. Creating environmental awareness was stressed again and again, while reusing materials that might previously have been single-use was a definite advantage.

For my major project in my last year, I had decided to go with the biophilic interior trend, with rooms taking advantage of good natural light, colour schemes derived from nature and a very large quantity of house plants.

I tapped my pen against the notebook while I considered the cabins and their pine tree clustered surroundings, with the glimmer of Loch Strathe just a ten-minute walk away. Shades of blue in powder, electric and sky rippled in front of my eyes.

If I could harness the beauty of the natural surroundings and make use of the colour schemes to complement other events during the year…

What if one of the cabins had a winter wonderland theme? It could have cushions in navy and white, with a blue and silver Christmas tree on the porch. My enthusiasm and imagination were firing up and I made some notes. There could be snow-themed ornaments placed on the tree, like sparkly snowmen and snowflakes, together with blue fringed rugs and matching ornaments. That could be adapted with the introduction of yellow and white fittings for the spring and Easter reservations.

For the second cabin, I jotted down a possible Nutcracker theme, with pale-gold walls and champagne and white fittings. The cabin could be dotted with characters from *The Nutcracker*, such as the carved wooden soldiers we sold in the shop, and the tree on the porch for this one would be decked out with yellow and gold decorations such as teddy bears, trains and ballerinas.

Those colours would work with daffodils and Easter eggs come the spring.

I moved on to the third cabin. Pictures of a more traditional Christmas entered my head. What if this one could reflect that wonderful story *A Christmas Carol*? There would be rich cranberry curtains at the windows, ornate lamps and antique baubles dripping from a white Christmas tree by the door. More Victorian-style decorations, such as tiny porcelain dolls and tin soldiers, would dance from its branches. Again, such rich colours could be easily tweaked for the rest of the year, such as Halloween.

And for the fourth and final cabin, I decided to suggest to Stephanie and Max the theme of Christmas in nature. There would be woodland animal decorations and pine cones, with features of wood and flashes of red interior. There could be pretty red ribbons attached to the traditional Christmas tree on the porch. The walls would be neutral, with just a hint of beige, which shouldn't prove difficult to adapt for the year's other events.

I read over my notes again: *Winter Wonderland; The Nutcracker; A Christmas Carol;* and *Christmas in nature.* They were all unique in their own way, but each of them wouldn't require much to adapt them for Valentine's, Easter, summer, autumn, Halloween...

Whoa, Lottie! Just focus on Christmas for now!

Once I was satisfied with my initial ideas and had printed off a chart with my suggested paint colour scheme for each cabin, I decided I would take a look at ideas for social media posts for the business.

I might be wrong, but something told me that the Styleses might not have placed Twitter, Instagram, Tik-Tok and Facebook very high up on their list of priorities.

I rubbed at my weary eyes and stretched. Images of my dad shimmered in front of me. He was smiling from ear to ear in that big, clumsy way of his. 'See, petal? Your old dad was right. Things have got a habit of working themselves out in the end.'

I gave a watery smile. I would give this opportunity everything I had. I had to start believing in myself and my capabilities more. For him and for me.

The remainder of Sunday vanished and Monday morning swung around so fast, my head felt as if it were spinning.

As I made my way out of my flat and headed down towards the main street and Christmas Crackers, a handful of council workers were busy erecting the Craig Brae Christmas lights above the shop roofs, in advance of their grand switch-on, next Saturday.

Giant snowflakes, a beaming Santa and reindeer pulling a sleigh groaning with presents, were being jostled into position. I hoped the footfall and usual influx of families, keen for their little ones to meet Santa, would find their way into the shop.

Kate Bush was proclaiming that December would be magic again through the shop speakers.

Just at that moment, Mum bustled in, followed by Orla. 'The cavalry has arrived!' joked Mum, embracing me. 'I'll go and pop the kettle on and then we can get started,' she added, vanishing off.

Orla appreciated her surroundings. 'We've shifted a lot of stock already.' She forced a bit of a too-bright smile out from under her straight brown hair.

'Yes,' I sighed. 'I know I should be delighted, but what with the background to it all...' I shrugged. 'Customers have been making use of the closing down sale – buy one, get one free and the heavy discounts. They've been getting some real bargains.'

I gestured to her. 'Thank you so much to both of you for agreeing to step up. I really appreciate it. I hope Mum didn't twist your arm up your back.'

'More like a half-nelson,' joked Orla. 'No seriously, she didn't. I'm more than happy to help out.' She pushed her fringe out of her eyes. 'I was spending too much time digging out old photo albums of Martin and me.'

'Well, thank you again for agreeing to do extra hours. And don't worry. Vivian has insisted you both receive overtime. It's the least we can do.'

A few moments later, Mum returned with one of the trays

she'd located in the kitchen area, laden with three mugs of strong tea and a plate of white chocolate cookies. 'I just bought them from Mrs Crill's place.' She eyed us with a smile. 'Well, it'll soon be Christmas, so what the hell?! With everything that's been going on these past few weeks, I reckoned we deserve a treat.'

Mum cast her eyes around the shop. 'So, this is it then. Not too long to go now,' she said, gripping her mug. 'Goodness knows how this Ronaldo's bunch will get on setting up in here. Some Craig Brae folks can be funny. They like tradition and familiarity.'

Orla nodded in agreement. 'They're probably hoping they can make money from the weekenders and the second-homers.'

Mum pulled a funny expression. 'You'd better not let old man Frew hear you talking about "incomers". He'll have a coronary.'

I laughed and picked up my mobile from the top of the counter. I took the opportunity to check the notes I had made on my phone about making sure Christmas Crackers was closed down properly and all loose ends were tied up. 'We need to tell HMRC as soon as possible that we're stopping trading. We also need to make contact with our suppliers and close down our accounts with them. Then there are the utility companies, the telephone to be disconnected...'

Mum shot out one caring hand and rested it on my arm. 'Will you stop fretting, young lady?! Orla here and I can make a start on things like that.'

'And Bernie says Vivian is still around to answer any questions or help out?' piped up Orla over the rim of her tea.

'Yes, she is. She was emphatic about it. Said not to hesitate to contact her, even if she is knee-deep in estate agent quotes for her house.'

'Well then,' assured Mum. 'We can deal with it and if we hit any brick walls, we will speak to you or get Vivian involved, ok?'

'Ok. Thanks.'

Mum angled her head at me. 'You just concentrate on your new job and get those log cabins ship-shape for all these tourists.'

Orla cradled her mug in her ringed hands. 'They sound fantastic. They will be even better after Lottie has finished with them.' A naughty smile crept across her red lip-sticked mouth. 'I hear your new boss is a bit of a silver fox.'

'Orla!' said Mum. 'You're only just divorced.'

'I know, but when you're on a diet, you can still admire a Snickers bar.'

I burst out laughing. 'Thanks for that. Now every time I see Max, I'm going to imagine him as a chocolate bar. And anyway, he's married.'

'Story of my life,' grumbled Orla into her tea.

Monday morning evaporated, with the four of us occupied by a constant stream of customers.

'All the mini fibreoptic Christmas trees have now sold out,' stated Mum with satisfaction.

'And we've only got half a dozen of the ceramic candy cane tree ornaments left,' added Orla, surveying the hook where a host of them had been dangling.

The swell of eager locals and day-trippers, keen to bag

themselves a pre-Christmas bargain, trickled away and by lunchtime it was a good feeling to be able to pause and take a breath.

'Go and get some lunch, ladies,' I said. 'Make the most of a quiet spell while we get it.'

'Are you sure?' asked Mum.

'Absolutely.'

'But what about you?' asked Orla, shrugging on her camel coat. 'You need a break too.'

'I'll go out for some fresh air when both of you get back."

'Well, make sure you do,' instructed Mum. 'Can we bring you any lunch?'

I requested one of Mrs Crill's turkey and cranberry salad paninis and a latte from Sugar 'n' Spice.

'Won't be long,' trilled Mum, as the two of them headed out the shop door, all billowing coats and handbags.

When they had gone, I slumped against the nearest wall. The shelves were beginning to look patchy and empty.

I pulled my eyes away. I didn't want to dwell on Christmas Crackers closing down. It still didn't seem real.

I straightened my shoulders. I couldn't afford to brood about it now. *It is what it is*, I concluded. I had to focus on my new role with the Styleses. They had thrown me a lifeline when everything in my life had felt like it was crashing down.

I moved back behind the counter and located my notebook from my bag. I leafed through a few pages of my scribbles. It would be good to suggest something we could do at the local Christmas lights switch-on, on Saturday, to promote the cabins and get the word out there. All those excited families and loved-up couples filled with festive cheer! It would be a captive market.

I remembered the Styleses saying all four were already reserved for over the Christmas period, but if we could start securing bookings for Valentine's weekend and possibly towards Easter, that would really kick things off.

I toyed with my pen. If we could produce a few alluring, teasing fliers to hand out in the crowd, that might stir up some interest. If we could be proactive, we might even be able to secure a few reservations there and then or at least get some interest and enquiries going forward.

It would feel like we had hit the ground running then.

My pen skittered over the blank page. I would type up all these notes this evening after dinner and then I would feel more organised ahead of Wednesday morning's meeting. I also thought it would be an idea to try and come up with an umbrella brand name for all four cabins, something appealing and escapist.

I cringed at my frantic handwriting. Imagine how embarrassing that would be if I couldn't read my own notes in front of my new employees!

I would take a folder to that meeting with everything typed out and printed off.

Revamping and making over the cabins would be just the start. My brain had been addling itself, trying to come up with a wide assortment of marketing and promotional suggestions.

As well as the Easter egg hunt in the surrounding woodland that I had suggested, I also thought about hiring out little daffodil-yellow boats on the loch. And Halloween could see a fancy dress party, find the magic pumpkin and orange lanterns strung through the naked tree branches, against the backdrop of inky black sky.

We could even hire a children's entertainer or magician to

dress up as a wizard (nothing too frightening for the little ones) and have them recite stories and perform magic tricks and spells.

I laughed out loud at my rampaging enthusiasm. I had Christmas to concentrate on first! Still, the Styleses knew how obsessed I was about this time of year. It was important to let them see that I wasn't a one-trick pony and that I was capable of coming up with inventive suggestions for other important months of the year too.

I was chewing over other whacky ideas for the lodges, when something caught my eye out of the shop window.

A strange, unoccupied vehicle I'd never seen before had appeared and was parked up on the pavement. It was a bronze Land Cruiser Invincible and was glinting under the winter sun.

'Whose is that?' I muttered to myself. 'Bloody cheek parking there.'

I hovered by the window for a few moments, but there was no sign of the driver. It was causing difficulty for a few shoppers, who were attempting to negotiate their way around it.

A couple more local residents gave it disapproving looks as they edged past. A young mum with her little boy strapped into his buggy was negotiating her way past it now.

Another five minutes rolled by and it was still residing there, with no returning driver.

I marched back over to the counter and fetched one of the loud pink post-it notes from the shelf. I snatched up a pen and wrote:

Who is the clown who has parked their car here?!

Sorry, but you are blocking the pavement.
Christmas Crackers.

With the note in my hand, I breezed out of the shop and stuck it under one of the windscreen wipers.

I returned to my notebook and was about to jot down initial ideas about a name for the log cabin enterprise, when the shop doorbell rattled from side to side, as if indignant at being woken up.

Mellow winter sunshine spilt through as it swung open.

A tall, broad-chested figure, clad in an olive-green fleece and sporting a knitted black beanie hat, appeared out of the corner of my eye.

I didn't pay too much attention at first. I glanced up from my notes. His back was facing me. I saw him reach out and pick up one of the rose-gold hearts, inscribed with the words *Festive Love* from the nearest shelf.

He looked at it as though it were about to bite him and then thrust it back and muttered something. He did the same with one of the elf snow globes.

I stopped my note-taking.

He angled himself around, staring at the interior of Christmas Crackers, as though he'd come face to face with a three-headed gorgon.

I downed my pen. 'Can I help you?'

His challenging eyes were a shade of bitter chocolate. He had long, sooty lashes and a dark beard. He was very attractive.

His gaze lingered on me. 'I'm not sure. No. There must be some mistake.'

I refocused. 'Sorry?'

He rooted around inside his jeans pocket and produced a slip of paper and read from it. 'Can you tell me where I can find Lottie Grant?'

I blinked across at him from behind the counter. 'That's me.'

His dark arched brows fenced. 'You?'

'Yes.'

He turned around and drank in the shop. 'No. There must be some mistake. Max said you ran a successful business.'

At first I thought I hadn't heard him correctly. I could feel my indignation rising. Of all the bloody cheek! Hang on. Who was this man? I jutted out my chin at him. 'It is successful.' Or at least it was.

He folded his muscular arms. 'I thought Max said you ran a…' He squinted down at the piece of paper in his hand and muttered something about Max's illegible handwriting. 'Good grief. It looks like he wrote this in a hurry.' He drew the piece of paper closer. 'It says here you run a freestyle shop?' His voice was deep and rumbly.

I narrowed my eyes at him, confused. 'Freestyle? No, this is a Christmas shop.'

He stared around himself with growing horror. 'I can see that.' He offered a withering look to my singing Rudolph on the shelf behind him. 'I expected skateboards and sporting gear. At least that's what I thought it said here.'

'Can I see Max's note please?'

The bearded man frowned at me. After considering this request, he reluctantly handed me the note.

I examined Max's manic scrawl. 'Ah. It says festive, not freestyle. It's the way he's squashed the letters together.'

I handed the note back to him.

'Oh. Right.' He glowered at the rows of assorted stars, destined for the top of Craig Brae Christmas trees, which were spinning and dangling from a nearby shelf. 'It's like someone emptied half a ton of glitter in here.'

'Well, the clue is in the name,' I said through a forced smile. 'Christmas Crackers.'

His dark eyes swam over everything. 'I would never have guessed.'

I clenched my jaw, riled by his off-hand attitude. What was this rude man doing, carrying a note from Max? They must know each other. But what did he want? He hadn't introduced himself; he was too busy delivering frosty looks at the festive merchandise. 'Sorry. Who are you?'

Our chilly conversation was interrupted by my mobile jumping to attention under the counter. It was Stephanie Styles.

'Excuse me a second,' I said, reaching for my mobile. The cross bearded face didn't respond.

'So sorry to bother you, Lottie,' she breathed. 'Max meant to tell you earlier, but he's juggling so many things at the moment.'

'Tell me what, sorry?' I asked, aiming daggers at Beardy in the woolly hat. He had meandered over to where we stocked some felt festive mobile phone covers. While Stephanie chatted to me, he picked one up and proceeded to turn it upside down and around, arched his brows and then shoved it back into the box.

'One of our new employees was popping into the high street at lunchtime today and Max left him a note and suggested he drop in and introduce himself.' Stephanie let out a little tinkle of laughter. 'We thought it would be good for the newbie members of the team to meet one another. After all, you will be working together.'

A sudden jolt of apprehension made me widen my eyes at the man, who was now eyeing the holly wreaths with contempt. I turned my back to him. No. Not him. *Him?* 'A new employee?' I repeated.

'Yes. Max said he was in a real hurry and was dashing from one meeting to another when Blake was about to have a chat with him, so he left him a scribbled note about where to find you. Max couldn't remember if he gave him all the details about you and the shop.'

My feeling of trepidation ramped up. My attention shifted to Beardy again. I dropped my voice. 'This new employee,' I faltered. 'What's his name, did you say?'

'Blake. Blake Dempster.'

'Could you hang on a second please, Stephanie?'

'Sure.'

I lowered my phone and turned around. He must have heard the call and got the gist of it, because he had stopped glaring at the wreaths and was focusing his attention on me.

'Sorry. What's your name?' I asked him, anticipating what he was about to say, but hoping I might be wrong.

I mentally willed him to say anything – Bert Twaddle, Conrad Goggins, Sylvester Starburst…

The man flicked me a cool look. 'Blake Dempster.'

My stomach sank. Bugger. Of course, it was.

I raised the phone again to speak to Stephanie and ground out, 'We've just met.'

'Great! Well, that's one member of our team you've been introduced to now. Right, must dash. Sorry about all that. Bye!'

I lowered the phone and set it on the counter. 'You work for the Styleses too?'

'I've just started.'

'And what is it you are doing?'

'Providing walking and hiking activities for locals, tourists and their cabin guests. Or at least, I will do.'

I took in his beard and muscular build.

Well, he might have the physique of Henry Cavill, but the same couldn't be said of his personality. He was coming across as a right morose twat.

Blake Dempster leant against the frame of the shop doorway. His dark gaze was unwavering. 'I hear the Styleses want you to do up their cabins like something out of *The Nutcracker*.'

I shoved my hands into the pockets of my trousers. 'If you mean have they asked me to give them a festive makeover, then the answer is yes.'

He arched one thick brow. 'This I must see.'

I watched him turn and open the shop door. The bell went crazy. Then he drew up and turned around again to look at me. 'Waste of time and waste of money.' His black eyes flickered. 'I've worked in the mountaineering and hiking game for years. I know what I'm talking about. Guests won't want to feel like they're trapped in a department store on Christmas Eve. Perish the thought.'

Well. He didn't believe in honeying his words. 'I don't dispute for a second, Mr Dempster, that you know your own business inside out but the same applies to me. I studied interior design and within the space of a couple of years of me becoming manager here, the Christmas Crackers brand has become recognisable across the country.'

I forced my mouth into a cool smile. 'I know what customers want at Christmas. It's about nostalgia and feeling cosy. It's about being with family.'

Blake Dempster curled his lip and rolled his eyes. 'How every saccharine.'

I shrugged my shoulders. 'Maybe it is. Call it what you like. But whether it's saccharine or not, that's what people look for at this time of year and I don't intend to let them or Mr and Mrs Styles down.'

Without saying anything, he dug one hand into his jeans pocket and produced a bright-pink post-it note. He sauntered back over to the counter and stuck it down in front of me.

It took me a few seconds to realise it was the one I had slapped on the four-by-four occupying the pavement outside.

Below my message, was a reply

This is my car.
Good afternoon and best wishes,
Coco the Clown.

I jerked my head up, my annoyed eyes narrowing at him.

Blake Dempster's hard gaze flashed. 'Welcome to the team, Ms Grant, and good luck. Something tells me you are going to need it.'

Chapter Eight

Just great!

Just sodding great!

So, I had to work with Laughing Boy?! I let out a deflated sigh.

The dismissive way he'd spoken about Christmas Crackers and his superior attitude! What the hell was his problem? And what was all that passive-aggressive macho stuff about him knowing about hiking and mountaineering? Then he had the damned cheek to stand there and say I needed luck, because the cabin venture was doomed to fail?

I scowled down at the note and his sarcastic reply. So that figured. That big car belonged to him. Oh, he must have thought he was so witty, writing that response.

I folded my arms and remained standing behind the counter, seething. Saccharine?! The damned cheek of the man.

Mum and Orla reappeared, clutching my lunch and a latte.

Blake Dempster would not be involved with the cabins. He couldn't be, I kept reassuring myself. He would be there to encourage visitors to take up his hiking tours. He had said so himself. Well, he hadn't really said it. It had been more like a growl.

Pity he wouldn't take a tumble in a huge great cowpat! That would knock the supercilious smirk from his face – well, what you could see of it, through that privet hedge of a beard.

I thought about Max and Stephanie. Should I ask for a discreet word with them? Perhaps I could tell them about his negative attitude – something of an understatement – towards what I was aiming to achieve and they might have a word with him.

I stuck my tongue to the inside of my cheek as I debated it all. But on the other hand, if I did that, it could cause tension and complications even before we really got going with the cabins and how conducive would that be? Blake Dempster might even think I was telling tales after school and incapable of standing up for myself.

I didn't want them to think I was a troublemaker.

'All quiet?' asked Mum, handing me my lunch and then peeling off her coat.

'Yep.'

Mum eyed me. 'What's wrong?'

'Nothing.'

'Then why are you doing that thing with your tongue?'

I pulled my tongue out of my cheek. 'I wasn't.'

'She was,' explained Mum to a bemused Orla. 'Lottie has always done it ever since she was little. If something is troubling her, she stands and thinks about it with her tongue in her cheek.'

'Well, I'm not doing it now.'

'No awkward customers?' asked Orla.

'I wouldn't say that.' I thought about Blake Dempster pouring a bucket of freezing cold water over my cabin ideas. Fingers crossed, I never had to deal with the man again.

I didn't sleep very well on Tuesday night, ahead of my first day working for the Styleses.

After my shower and hair wash, I got dressed and put on my candy-pink pussy-bow blouse, a matching tailored jacket and slim-fitting black trousers.

I pushed my cereal around my bowl, managing only a few mouthfuls.

On the way out the door, I pulled on my glittery pink beret, scarf, gloves and my thick maroon belted coat, which I reserved for special occasions.

I jumped in my car, a cantankerous but rather sweet second-hand VW Golf in sky blue. That was another thing I had compromised on, in order to ensure I had the money to buy Christmas Crackers. I only used my car when I was forced to, to economise on petrol and whenever I had needed to fill the tank, I would put in the minimum amount.

I tried not to grind my teeth at the thought. *Move on, Lottie. Move on.*

I mentally ran through everything, checking I had all my notes about the cabins with me. I had placed them all in a buff folder and popped that inside my big fringed shoulder bag on the passenger seat.

I tugged off my beret and flicked a look at myself in the rear-view mirror. My dark-blue eyes popped out of my distracted face. I tried to smile at my reflection, but rather than looking confident, I appeared constipated.

I adjusted my ponytail and set off for Rowan Moore House. The hills were coloured in a kaleidoscope of purple and jade as the sharp winter sunshine played hide and seek with the scudding clouds.

As I drove along the winding country lanes, I hoped the weather on Saturday would be like this for the local Christmas lights switch-on. I reminded myself to mention this at the meeting with the Styleses and their other employees, although I knew I'd already taken a note to do so.

I was sure that everyone that was part of Stephanie and Max's team would be welcoming. Well, apart from Beardy McGrump-face. Still, there was a good chance he might not be attending this meeting anyway. He might be marching up some mountain right now, barking orders at the wildlife to stay out of his way. Maybe, with any luck, one of the stags would take a dislike to him like I had and give him one almighty jab up his arse with one of their antlers.

I reached Rowan Moore House and parked beside a couple of other vehicles, one of which looked like a trades van. It had the company name Care and Construct splashed across it in multi-coloured lettering.

No sooner had I got out of the vehicle and fetched my things, than Max came bounding down the steps to greet me.

'I'm sorry. I think I'm a bit early,' I apologised, clutching the folder to my chest.

'Not at all. Come on in Lottie.'

Max led me through a grand tiled hall that was studded with tall potted trees and boasting an ornate ceiling that looked like whipped cream.

He clicked open a heavy oak door on the right. The room had a thick chocolate-toned carpet with a long cream table and several high-backed chairs. Heavy, dark curtains framed two floor-to-ceiling windows at the end of the space.

Stephanie jumped up from her chair. 'Welcome, Lottie. Coffee? Tea?'

I didn't feel very thirsty, but smiled and said, 'Tea please.' Having a cup and saucer would give me something to do with my hands before the meeting started.

I set my folder down on the table and slipped my bag from my shoulder, removed my coat and draped them over the back of one of the chairs. A bundle of excited butterflies let rip in my stomach.

'We're just waiting for the other three to arrive,' said Max, reaching for a steel coffee pot in the middle of the table. 'Our construction guys are just taking an urgent call at the minute. But in the meantime, let me introduce you to someone else.'

Max glugged some tarry black coffee into his mug and took a welcome sip.

I turned, smiling. Then it died on my lips. Oh bugger. Not him again!

Blake Dempster strode over from the other side of the room. Gone was his woolly hat and the fleece. He was sporting a sharp navy three-piece suit, with a petrol-blue tie and white shirt. His black eyes flashed.

'We've already met.' I forced a tight smile.

Max pretended to slap himself on the forehead. 'Of course. Silly me! Steph told me the other day that Blake got my note and was going to pop in to Christmas Crackers to introduce himself.'

'Oh, he did that all right,' I grimaced.

Max carried on, oblivious to the stony atmosphere. 'I'm so sorry about that scribbled message, Blake. Steph said you told her you thought Lottie's shop was some sort of sports freestyle outlet?'

Blake Dempster ran a hand over his short, dark hair. 'Yes,' he replied, firing up one thick brow. 'It wasn't at all what I was expecting. It's certainly a unique experience going in there.'

I could feel my lips pulling themselves back into a ferocious snarl. I rearranged my expression. 'Yes, well, it's for discerning customers only.'

Blake Dempster's dark eyes hardened.

Max afforded us both odd looks and let out an awkward cough. 'Yes. Well. Blake has just opened up Rock Solid Ramblings, his new guided walking and hiking business in the town, but he has also very kindly agreed to provide his services to our cabin guests.' Max flashed us another glance each. 'So, I thought it might be a good idea for us all to get together, so we can update everyone on what's happening with the cabins. After all, we will all be working very closely as a team.'

Max tried to lighten the atmosphere further. 'After all, there is no "i" in team, is there!'

Oh shit! Dealing with hotel guests' complaints about their cooked breakfasts and finding out what had happened to missing newspapers suddenly seemed a rather more attractive prospect than it had done before. 'How wonderful,' I forced. 'I can't wait.'

Blake Dempster stared back levelly at me.

I was grateful when the meeting room door opened and in trooped three other people.

Stephanie introduced the two men as brothers Andrew and

Dominic Clark, owners of Care and Construct, who had built the lodges. They were both intense looking men in their late forties.

Behind them, was a pixie-faced young woman called Kim Wu. Her hair was white and cut into a Peter Pan style, which enhanced her fine features and high cheekbones. Stephanie explained Kim had just been recruited as their PA, after Max had enticed her away from a former publisher he had worked for.

Everyone took up their seats at the table and cups of coffee and tea were passed around. Blake Dempster ended up stationed on the opposite side of the table to where I was and a couple of chairs down. Thank goodness for that. At least I didn't have to look across at his glowering expression every time I lifted my eyes.

Kim sat herself down next to me, with Andrew and Dominic opposite, Blake beside them and Max and Stephanie at either end.

'So, the cabins,' announced Max with trepidation. 'As you all know by now, they are NOT how Stephanie and I envisaged them to look.'

Stephanie pulled a face. 'That's an understatement.' She glanced at each of us around the table. 'So that's why we have recruited Lottie here to work her magic on them.'

I could feel my cheeks zinging, as all interested eyes swivelled to me.

From further down the table, I could have sworn I heard Blake Dempster let out a grunt.

'I am delighted to confirm that all four of the cabins are now reserved for Christmas and so Lottie is going to transform them for us into a festive cornucopia!'

'No pressure then,' grinned Max from down the table. He took a mouthful of his black coffee. 'So, Lottie, it's over to you.'

This was my moment.

I swallowed.

I flipped open my buff folder lying in front of me and looked up. Blake Dempster had his arms folded and was reclining back in his chair studying me, as if to say, 'I can't wait to hear this!'

I snatched a mouthful of tea and set the cup down with a decisive clink against its saucer. Ok. This was it. I took a breath, ignoring the writhing nerves in my stomach. 'I'm obsessed with Christmas. I always have been. I suppose it helps when you work in a shop with the name Christmas Crackers!'

There were chuckles from everyone except Blake, who remained stony-faced.

I carried on. 'I wanted to come up with colours and themes for Christmas that could also be adapted for the rest of the year. So, I am going to run through my initial suggestions for revamping the cabins. I would be very interested to hear your views.'

I took another sip of my tea and then proceeded to explain the four individual themes I had come up with, describing my vision for everything from the glittery snowflake decorations to the sequinned, white cushions, the *Nutcracker* soldiers and woodland animals constructed from wood and pine cones.

I then went on to explain what I thought could be done with the interiors after Christmas was over, so that they could be adapted for everything from Valentine's weekend and Mother's Day, to spring, Easter, Father's Day, the summer months and then the arrival of autumn and Halloween.

'We can tweak each of the cabins,' I emphasised. 'I suppose it's all about being savvy with our colour schemes.'

I snatched the opportunity to look across at Andrew and Dominic Clark for their approval and much to my relief, they were nodding and making lots of notes.

I returned to my folder again and then laced my hands together on top of the table. 'Stephanie and Max, please correct me if I'm wrong, but I think you said to me you wanted something welcoming, cosy and magical and what better time to start as we mean to go on than Christmas?'

From Blake Dempster's direction, there came a small but audible groan.

He really was an abrasive cretin! What the hell was the matter with what I had just said?

I shot him a frosty look and continued. He was not going to distract me!

'I have been giving some thought to a brand name and I wondered about Magical Occasions Cabins?' I flipped my buff folder closed. 'I thought that encapsulates what we are trying to do here. We are all about giving customers a magical and memorable experience, no matter the occasion they wish to celebrate. I'm really looking forward to hearing all of your thoughts.' *Well, not your thoughts*, I concluded darkly at Blake. *You can piss off*.

I cleared my throat. 'I hope my love of Christmas and all things festive will go some way in helping to get this business off the ground. Thank you.'

There was a ripple of appreciative applause and positive murmurs.

'Excuse me?' Blake's voice rumbled down the table, cutting

through the clapping and making me start. 'May I say something?'

'Of course,' replied Max.

Blake straightened his tie. 'Look, all these fanciful suggestions sound all right in theory and I have nothing against Ms Grant. I am sure you are very enthusiastic and capable, but do guests really want to be trapped in something that reminds them of a cheap snow globe for a few days?'

Bloody hell! Could he be any more condescending? Any moment now, I expected him to pat me on the head and tell me I was a good girl.

Stephanie's brow furrowed. 'I think that's rather strong, Blake.'

'Is it?' His white teeth flashed through his dark beard. 'I'm an experienced hiker and walking guide…'

I rolled my eyes and folded my arms. *Oh, not this again.*

'I've stayed in a variety of accommodation. I can't see people like that wanting to be drowned in glitter and Rudolph.'

I could feel my back stiffening. Had his soul been sucked out of his body at some point? 'Our guests won't be drowning in anything,' I bit back, trying to keep my tone calm. 'Craig Brae becomes even more of a special, spectacular place to visit at Christmas, so why should the log cabins be any different?'

'We agree,' piped up Dominic Clark. 'The way the interiors are right now, they're very unappealing.'

Blake shook his dark head. 'I'm not disputing that their current features are a mess, but is there any real need for all this fairy lights and fir trees nonsense?'

Stephanie and Max, together with the assembled throng at

the table, swapped charged looks at one another. The atmosphere in the dining room prickled.

Good grief. What was his problem? Had he experienced some sort of joy bypass?

'Well, I think most people do want all that festive romance at this time of year,' interjected Kim.

Blake's top lip snarled through his beard. He muttered under his breath, 'You said it. Most people. Not all.'

'I take it you're not a fan of Christmas then, Mr Dempster?' I asked.

Blake's expression was stony. 'Not particularly.'

'Well, you might not be but a lot of people are,' exclaimed Andrew. 'If you ask me, Lottie's suggestions sound wonderful and they wouldn't cost an excessive amount to achieve either.'

'I think so too,' beamed Kim beside me. 'All that sparkle and festive decorations, it sounds beautiful.' She pinned me to my chair with wide, light eyes. 'I'd be more than happy to assist you in any way I can. I can help with furniture quotes, arranging deliveries, that kind of thing.'

'Thank you, Kim. I appreciate that.'

Blake's beard stiffened.

Stephanie jumped in with appreciation. 'Thank you, Kim. The offer of help is always welcome.' She added that she had already had a word with the lady who had been recruited to undertake the cabin cleaning and she was very enthusiastic about lending a helping hand too.

'Oh, that's wonderful. Thank you.' I switched all my attention back to Max and Stephanie. 'I was thinking that a small team of us could put in an appearance on Saturday at the Craig Brae Christmas lights switch-on. Perhaps hand out a few leaflets. I've drafted and printed off an example for you all to take a look at.' I reached into the folder again and pushed copies of the leaflets across the table to everyone. Blake stared down at it as though he had just been presented with an extortionate electricity bill.

The draft flier read:

> *Magic, festive, cosy cheer,*
> *Can be yours throughout the year,*
> *Book a luxury cabin stay,*
> *And watch your worries float away!*

Underneath the verse were Max and Stephanie's contact details, as well as mine.

'A poet as well?' chimed Blake from further up the table. 'Is there no end to your talents, Ms Grant?'

I ignored him and addressed Max and Stephanie again. 'If you're happy, I can print these off and include photos of the exterior of the cabins and a couple of shots of things like sequinned cushions and roaring log fires? Once the cabins are re-decorated, we can include proper photographs of the interiors, but at least images like that will give prospective guests an idea of what we're doing here.'

Max looked down the table at Stephanie and grinned his approval. 'This is great.'

I then moved on to describing a few more competition ideas I had. 'I thought we could have one where the local school children have to find Rudolph hidden somewhere around the cabins and another competition idea I had was to invite people to tell us who they would love to spend a weekend in a log cabin with and why—'

'Did you say this Christmas light thing is this Saturday?'

interrupted Blake, unable to conceal his horror. 'Are we all expected to attend it?'

'*This light thing*,' I remarked, 'is one of the highlights of the Craig Brae calendar.'

'That says more about this place than anything,' he muttered.

Andrew, Dominic and Kim exchanged awkward looks.

'Blake, we would appreciate it if we all could get involved in this venture,' said Stephanie. 'We want everyone to feel included.'

Blake glowered from under his brows at my leaflet, before pushing it back across the table. 'I'm not sure I'll be available at the weekend. I have ramblers booked in.'

How convenient. Something told me he was rambling himself.

Chapter Nine

B lake had just marched out of the door, when Stephanie gawped down the table at her husband. 'What on earth was all that about?' She pursed her lips.

Max toyed with his mobile phone. 'I agree, darling, that Blake can sometimes come across as a bit sullen…'

'Sullen?!' she repeated. 'Downright rude is more like it!'

'But he's a very experienced professional hiker. He comes highly recommended.' Max glanced down the table at me. 'I know he can seem a rather morose character, but he was instrumental in setting up that outdoor education centre for deprived children in Glasgow last year.'

I shuffled my papers in my file and glanced at Kim beside me. He might have achieved something deserving for deprived children, which was commendable, but as long as I didn't have to have many – or preferably any – dealings with Blake Dempster, that was fine by me.

I had planned to drive back to Christmas Crackers to check in with Mum and Orla that everything was ok.

But as I negotiated the tree-lined country roads, I decided against it.

They were both more than capable of dealing with the shop. Perhaps I could drop by just before closing time.

I decided instead to head back to my flat, make myself some lunch and then start pulling together the finalised fliers about the cabins to hand out at the Christmas lights switch-on this coming Saturday.

Once I changed out of my officious-looking work clothes into my jeans and a sparkly sweater, I made myself a chicken salad bagel and peppermint tea and set up my laptop on the kitchen table.

Bloody Blake Dempster, I thought to myself. He might not want to bring festive joy to people, but I did! What the hell was his problem with Christmas? Why so prickly about it?

Oh, stuff him! I wasn't going to dwell on him any longer. I had that leaflet to pull together.

As the cabins had not yet been revamped, I searched the internet for pretty, alluring images of sequinned cushions, cackling log fires, decorated Christmas trees and heart-shaped fairy lights.

I then arranged the images down either side of the verse I'd written and topped it all off with *Magical Occasions Cabins* in glittery red text.

Once my printer through in the spare bedroom was rattling out coloured copies, I finished eating my bagel, drank the dregs of my peppermint tea and then switched my attention to the social media accounts that Max and Stephanie had set up for the cabins.

Just as the meeting was drawing to a close, Kim had provided me with the necessary username and passwords to gain access to the Instagram, Facebook and Twitter accounts. 'Once you're in, you can set yourself up with access,' she'd whispered. 'I had a look at each account and they are rather bland.' She'd pulled a hesitant face. 'I don't think the Styleses are very tech savvy.'

I scrolled through each social media profile in turn. They all consisted of sparse information and bland photographs of the cabins from the outside. The shots were a bit blurry and had been taken on a day when it had tipped it down, so everything looked dank and forlorn. The images didn't fill you with the urge to rush up and visit, that's for sure.

There was nothing cosy, eye-catching or alluring about the social media content at all.

I chose instead to use the images that I'd pasted on the fliers, adding in a couple of extra ones of squashy, inviting sofas and crackling wood burners and used the text I'd inserted on Instagram for Facebook and Twitter so that I wasn't reinventing the wheel.

A log cabin isn't just for Christmas!
Soon, we will be unveiling our exciting revamped luxury log cabins, set amongst the rugged beauty of Craig Brae woodland.
Christmas, Easter, summer, autumn, Halloween… Enjoy the dramatic and breath-taking changing of the Scottish seasons with Magical Occasions Cabins.

Once I'd finished everything I wanted to do on social media for the time being, I rang Andrew and Dominic Clark and told them I would be emailing over a list of the colour schemes we had agreed on with the Styleses for each of the cabins, together with an itinerary of what new furnishings I was suggesting should go in each of them. I also said I would email them details of the Christmas decorations (mostly all end-of-line products) that I could obtain from Christmas Crackers, to decorate each of the cabins in time for the festive season. These consisted of woodland animals made out of Christmas pine cones, ceramic tree ornaments, spare tinsel and an eclectic mix of baubles and strings of fairy lights. That was one of the benefits of working in a Christmas shop!

By the time I'd done all that, my eyes and head felt like they were beginning to fry, but it was a very satisfying and rewarding sensation, nonetheless.

I scooped the printed leaflets out of my printer tray, before popping my phone in my bag. I was about to close up my laptop, when I found myself sinking down at the kitchen table again.

My fingers danced over the keys, as I typed 'Rock Solid Ramblings' into the search engine. I had sworn I wasn't going to do this, but my curiosity got the better of me.

An all-singing, all-dancing website appeared, complete with a rolling banner of colour photographs, featuring moody mountains and snow topped peaks.

There were also a couple of photographs of Blake atop mountains, wearing sturdy climbing gear and a helmet. He was all beard and flashy amber sunglasses.

Further down the page, there was a bio of him:

Blake Dempster's home is where nature and the mountains are.
From rugged peaks to sparkling ice, Blake, who is from Fife in

Scotland, learnt from an early age that the outdoors was his real family.

Now thirty-seven years old, Blake is a professional mountaineer, who since qualifying as a mountain leader and rock-climbing instructor ten years ago, has acquired the Mountaineering and Climbing Instructor Qualification (MCI) which is the highest qualification a climber can hold for summer mountaineering in the UK.

He belongs to the British Mountaineering Council (BMC) the Mountaineering Instructor Association (MIA) and the Association of Mountaineering Instructors (AMI).

Blake has conquered a variety of challenging, international peaks including K2, Kilimanjaro and Denali, but he says his most rewarding pastime is taking novice climbers to the likes of Cat Bells in the Lake District, when people who don't believe they can commit to or even attempt such a climb, reach the top and witness the beauty of the likes of Skiddaw and Derwentwater from the majestic peaks.

Blake writes for several mountaineering publications, has written two novels about his climbing experiences and has hosted his own TV show on Discovery Channel, Dempster's Nature Revealed, which drew wide critical acclaim amongst the mountaineering and rambling fraternity.

Now he has started a new chapter by unveiling his own exclusive hiking and rambling business in the picturesque Scottish Highland town of Craig Brae.

Rock Solid Ramblings provides a safe, informative and reassuring service for those who want to push themselves harder or for those who wish to enjoy a more relaxed ramble in gentler terrain.

Blake will accompany you on your chosen route or suggest an alternative he feels would be more suitable, based on your capability and previous climbing experience.

For further information and to discuss the climbing and rambling packages available, please compete the form below or telephone Blake on the following numbers...

I scanned the bio again.

That was odd.

Why was Blake not presenting his TV show now?

To come to somewhere quiet and out of the way like Craig Brae and set up your own business... It just seemed a rather strange choice of venue for someone whose career had appeared to be taking off on TV. Maybe he had upset someone in the television world and had decided to diversify. That wasn't hard to imagine!

From what I had seen of Blake Dempster's 'charm', him upsetting someone in television and therefore having to abandon his TV series was not an outlandish possibility.

I recalled again his opposition to my Christmas plans for the cabins and the way he sat during the meeting, looking churlish. Good grief. Working alongside Darth Vader would be preferable.

I scrolled again through some of the photographs on the Rock Solid Ramblings website and then clicked off it.

I relocated my search engine and typed in 'Blake Dempster'. The screen rippled, before producing links to his now defunct TV show. There were a few questions from irritated members of the public on an appreciation website about his show, asking why it had suddenly been removed from the schedules. Nobody seemed to know, until further down the comment feed, someone had remarked that Blake had decided to quit TV 'for personal reasons and his agent had refused to elaborate on the subject.

There were a few other pictures of his two published novels as well and the same images of him, all snow-encrusted beard and wraparound sunglasses, that he had on his website.

With regard to any personal information, it was scarce. In response to a couple of questions about his private life, his agent had responded with a terse, *'Blake is very protective of his privacy and does not give interviews.'*

My eyebrows arched as I exited the page and switched off my laptop.

I locked up the flat and jumped in the car to go and visit Mum and Orla at Christmas Crackers. We could place some of the leaflets on the counter and pop a couple in the shop window. I didn't want to get too ahead of myself as there was a terrifying amount still to do, but things looked like they might be starting to come together.

It was the Saturday of the grand Christmas light switch-on in the town.

Craig Brae high street was awash with pink-faced chattering children and their parents, the odd meandering tourist accosting the locals for directions and the warm aromas of roasted chestnuts, hot chocolate and mince pies wafting from not only Mrs Crill's bakery, but also a couple of decoration-strewn mobile snack vans.

Santa had already sailed statesman-like past Christmas Crackers, complete with four of his trotting reindeer and his sleigh. I recognised the twinkly, pale eyes of Mr Dalgleish behind his mass of white beard. He played Santa every year and was also the owner of the local garden centre.

Now, a choir of children from the local primary school which I had attended, all sporting loud Christmas jumpers and Santa hats, began belting out 'We Wish You a Merry Christmas,' across the other side of the cobbles.

The grand light switch-on was due to take place at five o'clock, about ninety minutes from now. This year, the local provost, Mr Reginald Jay, had been invited to do the honours, although Mum told me he'd been dropping hints since March that he would be more than happy to do it.

He was mingling amongst the buzzing crowd, no doubt pressing some flesh and trying to secure re-election next year.

Further down the pedestrianised town centre, a handful of brightly painted fairground rides swirled and danced, with squealing, laughing children aboard unicorns.

I stepped out of Christmas Crackers, clutching a handful of the fliers I'd created. The air was laced with chatter. It already felt as though Christmas had arrived in Craig Brae, even though it was still only the third week of November.

A little boy and his sister sauntered past, devouring toasted marshmallows.

The shop had been operating at a very brisk pace and today had seen a surge in customers. They came and went, armed with their purchases.

Just past the cluster of roundabouts and attractions, the shiny foil and cottonwool dome of Santa's grotto could be seen, rising phoenix-like over the paintbox lights of the fairground.

Stephanie, Max and Kim had arranged to meet me outside the shop at four o'clock and as soon as the velvety black descended and anticipation began to build at the prospect of the Christmas lights being switched on, the three of them arrived. They were all wrapped up against the biting cold, while the children surrounding us were hopping from foot to foot and squealing at everything.

Kim was wearing a black and silver pom-pom winter hat and matching scarf. Stephanie clapped her gloved hands together. She grinned at the glowing windows of Christmas Crackers and the stream of people ferrying in and out. 'Business looks good.'

'Oh, it is,' I assured her. 'The stock is flying off the shelves.'

Max tightened the tartan scarf knotted around his neck and gestured to the fliers I held in my hands. 'They look terrific, Lottie. You've done a great job with them. Right, let's make a start, shall we?'

The four of us turned around, appraising the sea of pink-tipped noses and winter coats.

We had just begun moving through the crowd, handing out the leaflets and chatting, when Andrew and Dominic Clark appeared in front of us. 'Need a hand?' asked Andrew.

He proceeded to introduce his wife Lisa, a petite blonde with friendly hazel eyes, and his two little girls, Lola and Anna. Their mouths were falling open at the colours and sounds.

Beside them was Dominic and a tall, attractive, brown-haired man in trendy spectacles. 'And this is my husband Sandy,' he beamed.

Handshakes and pleasantries were exchanged all round.

'We thought we could help too, before the big switch-on,' explained Dominic.

'Well, that's very kind of you,' said Max. 'The more, the merrier.'

'We're not going to miss the Christmas lights being turned

on, are we, Uncle Dom?' pleaded one of his little nieces from under her red fringe.

Dominic crouched down in front of her. 'Of course not, sweetheart. That's a promise.'

I handed out leaflets to all of them with grateful thanks, before we broke off into different directions.

The reactions from the locals and from the tourists alike were encouraging. A large number of them, over the sound of the school choir, asked for more information while others assured us they would check out Magical Occasions Cabins on social media.

I took a breather for a moment, savouring the scent of cinnamon in the air and the chips of stars breaking out across the black sky. It was great that all the team were so enthusiastic and willing to pitch in. Well, almost all of them.

Blake hadn't shown up. He was conspicuous by his absence.

That was no surprise. He seemed to view me and my suggestions as some sort of weird oddity that weren't deserving of his time or attention.

I could see Kim and Stephanie laughing with members of the public, as they answered questions and pointed through the dark towards the country lanes that slid away from the centre of Craig Brae and in the direction of Rowan Moore House.

As I watched them, a hopeful feeling grew inside of me. I was sure I could make the log cabin business work. I just had to give this everything I had.

A booming, self-important voice blasted out from the makeshift stage further down the street. 'Good evening, ladies, gentlemen and children. Welcome to the Craig Brae Christmas lights switch-on!'

Everyone turned in unison to see Brian Chiltern, one of the local Christmas Committee fundraisers, addressing the throng. There was enthusiastic applause.

'Each year, our light switch-on is an even bigger and brighter affair and this Christmas is no exception.'

More crackles of applause rose up over the intermittent wail of crying babies.

'I'd like to take this opportunity to thank those local businesses that have contributed so generously again this year, making this lights switch-on such a popular event.' Brian Chiltern scanned the crowd. 'In particular, we would like to express our deep gratitude to Blooming Lovely Garden Centre, Good Wood Furniture and to Christmas Crackers for their continued support.' He hesitated. 'And this seems like the perfect moment to wish Vivian Sangster and Lottie Grant all the best. We will miss Christmas Crackers. It has been a delightful feature of our main street and you have done our little town proud, Vivian and Lottie.'

My smile wobbled as people standing close to me clapped and expressed their sadness at the shop's closure.

Brian Chiltern waited a few moments for the applause to fade, before beckoning over the provost from the other side of the stage. I noticed Reginald Jay was shuffling from foot to foot like an excited toddler desperate for the bathroom. 'So, without further ado, I would like to invite our esteemed provost, Mr Reginald Jay, to officially switch on the Craig Brae Christmas lights.'

The provost marched up to the podium in his loud checked

suit, where a box had been set up. Jutting out of it was a red switch, tied with a green satin ribbon.

With an exaggerated flourish, Mr Jay raised his arm and yanked down the switch. The sky over Craig Brae was illuminated by rows of lights strung above all our heads. Giant snowflakes, Santa's sleigh, a glowing Rudolph and dazzling, multi-coloured stars glimmered down on all our upturned faces and onto the stippled roofs of our little town.

Gasps, shrieks and claps echoed around the streets.

I hugged my arms around myself, as pictures of my dad, mum and me leapt into my mind. The three of us would always attend the switch-on every year. Even if it rained, we would huddle together under an umbrella or in one of the other shop doorways, marvelling at the anticipation and the start of the festive frivolities.

I stepped back up onto the pavement again, weaving in and out between the crowd, until I had a clearer view of Christmas Crackers on the opposite side.

Mum and Orla had made the most of the temporary break in customers piling in and were standing out on the street, admiring the decorations. Mum's expression was wistful and forlorn. I could tell she wasn't seeing the lights, even though her eyes were turned up towards them. She was seeing my dad.

A brass band struck up by the stage and a rousing rendition of 'Rudolph the Red Nosed Reindeer' stirred up the exhausted children even more.

I only had a couple of cabin leaflets left, folded up in my coat pocket, so I wandered around, smiling at people and making polite conversation. I also suggested they take a look at the Magical Occasions Cabins website.

It was as the brass band began playing the haunting carol – and my favourite of them all – 'Silent Night', that I paused and drank in the echo of the heart-tugging melody.

Now that I had parted with the last few fliers, I pushed my gloved hands into the pockets of my long winter coat and glanced around. My attention drifted from shiny apple-cheeked children to parents attempting to calm their over-excited offspring and grandparents swathed in thick coats and scarfs.

Susie from Eternal Flame waved at me from across the moving heads of the crowd. 'I'm sorry I couldn't offer you any work,' she called, struggling with two wrapped-up toddlers. 'But your mum tells me you're all sorted. Congratulations.'

'No problem at all, Susie. Thank you.'

We both exchanged smiles and she vanished again. Then I caught sight of Vivian and a tall, tanned sandy-haired man, all wrapped up in their winter coats and hugging one another as they admired the decorations shining down on them. That must be Ridley.

They were chatting to another couple.

Vivian made eye contact with me, beamed and gave a cheery wave, which I returned.

I turned away.

Then I stopped. One face jumped out at me again from across the street.

It was him.

Blake Dempster.

He was standing on the pavement close to the barber shop on the other side of the road, his beanie hat tugged down over his dark hair. He was staring up at the illuminated decorations, as families and couples breezed up and down and around him.

The silver light from the snowflakes shone down on his upturned face.

He glanced around himself, as though sensing he was being watched. Then he stared right across the street. He had noticed me.

We appraised one another, like one of those Spaghetti Western stand-offs between two cowboys. Then he dropped his gaze, thrust his hands deeper into his puffer jacket pockets and melted away into the crowd.

Chapter Ten

The first week of December saw a flurry of activity as the revamp of the Rowan Moore House cabins was well under way.

Andrew and Dominic were ensuring that the colour schemes were put in place in the correct cabin and in the correct shades, while Kim continued to liaise with me and keep me informed of when the new furniture and fittings had been ordered and their schedule for arrival.

The local school children were busy rehearsing for their Christmas panto, *Rapunzel*, and Christmas trees were springing up in sitting room windows all across town. There was a general atmosphere of frantic excitement and harassment everywhere.

Front gardens boasted tangles of fairy lights draped in their trees and hedges and there was a sharp, fresh crispness to the air that teased snow might be on the way.

All stock in Christmas Crackers had to be gone by New Year's Eve and the keys were to be handed over that day too.

I still didn't like to dwell on it all, but at least customers were availing themselves of the bargains and three-for-two offers we had running.

Sadness about not having Christmas Crackers as my own business still festered, but at least I had the cabins to focus on.

Max and Stephanie had requested that I attend a short meeting with them, Kim, Andrew and Dominic on the Monday morning for an update on how things were progressing.

When I arrived at Rowan Moore House, I was relieved to see that Blake wasn't there.

'We're on schedule with the decorating,' confirmed Dominic. 'Our team should be finished all four cabins within the next few days. Then you can access them for the new furniture and fittings going in.'

I grinned at him. 'That's great!'

'Well, time is money,' Max smiled.

'And we have received half a dozen emails enquiring about reserving the cabins at Easter,' added Stephanie, her eyes sparkling with enthusiasm at me across the table. 'Plus, we have had two reservations for the Valentine's weekend. They all came from the fliers handed out at the Christmas lights switch-on.' She glanced at Max beside her. 'Things are looking much more positive than they were a few weeks ago and that's thanks to all of you for working so hard and pulling together.'

Andrew made a point of staring around the table. 'Well, not all of us. Where's that rock climber guy? Blake, is it?'

Stephanie shot a hot look at Max. 'He couldn't make it. We did ask him along, as he's supposed to be part of the team after all but he apologised and said he had a prior engagement.'

Yeah, right. I pursed my lips. No doubt he thought he was above all this sort of thing.

We moved on to discuss the furniture I had selected and suggested for each cabin, which had been approved by Max and Stephanie. We then moved on to scheduling delivery dates, and I provided everyone with a print-out. 'Kim has said she is more than happy to assist, if we find that there are any issues.'

Kim nodded at my elbow. She was wearing a shirt with pom-poms stitched on it and reminded me of a pretty Christmas elf. 'Fingers crossed, everything will be ok. I've checked and double checked with the furniture companies and all the suggested dates are still fine for delivery.'

Stephanie brushed her hand in the air in a sign of confident dismissal. 'I'm sure everything will be fine.'

We rounded off our update with a suggestion from me about the idea of launching a couple of competitions, to attract extra publicity and I also spoke about investing in local and regional newspaper and radio advertising. 'I'm sure the other local businesses would be more than happy to put up posters in their windows and give us a boost.' I also mentioned the local and regional radio stations, which I was going to approach for advertising quotes.

Minutes later, I was tugging on my coat, keen to go and take a look at the cabins to see for myself how things were progressing, when Max emerged out on the steps of Rowan Moore House behind me. There was a stiff breeze today and the steely sky burgeoned with the promise of rain. 'Everything going ok back at the shop?'

I raised my brows. 'I'm beginning to think I wasn't needed after all. Mum and Orla have been doing a sterling job. Vivian has been popping in and out too.'

Max smiled and nodded his salt and pepper head. 'It

sounds like everything is in order then. You, your mum, Orla and Vivian are all doing a wonderful job under very trying circumstances.'

I blushed. 'Thank you. Mum and Orla are doing amazingly, selling off as much stock as they can and winding everything down.' I took a breath. Even now when I heard myself say it, it still didn't seem real.

Max's clear eyes swam with sympathy. 'I know it's easy for me to say, but you will bounce back from all of this. And you really have hit the ground running with the cabins.'

'I'm enjoying it. Very much. It has also helped distract me from wanting to rip the head off our landlords.'

Max let out a bark of laughter. 'Steph and I are really keen on your competition ideas, especially the one you mentioned about asking local children to find Rudolph hidden somewhere around the cabins and the other, asking people who they would love to spend a weekend in a log cabin with and why… Oh excuse me a second.' His phone pinged, interrupting us.

He fished it out of his trouser pocket and pulled up his inbox. His warm smile slid away.

'Is everything all right?'

'Yes,' he forced, his eyes not reflecting what he was saying.

'Are you sure?'

A rush of frustrated sounding air came out of his chest. 'Actually, no.'

'What is it?'

His attention moved from me to his phone screen and then back again. I noticed that Max's cheeks were smudged with pink. 'This is all a bit awkward.'

'What?'

'Blake has just sent me an email.'

'About what?'

Max's cheeks deepened with colour. 'About the makeover of the cabins.'

I adjusted the strap of my shoulder bag and folded my arms across my chest. 'Oh, yes?' My trouble-detecting radar was going into overdrive.

Max blinked down at his mobile phone. 'Oh, just forget it,' he rushed. 'It's not important.'

It clearly was.

'Max, what's up? What has Blake said? Please tell me.'

He looked pained, as though someone had just kicked him hard in the shins. He didn't answer.

'Look, we all need to pull together as a team. You said so yourself. If we keep things from one another, it's not going to work.'

Max clicked his tongue and waggled his phone. He almost smiled. 'It's very annoying when someone points out something sensible that you've said.'

'Sorry.'

He smiled briefly, before handing over his phone for me to take a look. I scanned through the email.

Hi Max.

Apologies I was unable to attend the meeting this morning. I had a prior appointment.

I hope you don't think I'm being too presumptuous, but I have been thinking long and hard about the cabins and in my opinion, you should reflect again on going down the frivolous route favoured by some of the team.

I suggest you consider a Western frontier theme for all of them. This would be a much better option and keep continuity.

As you of course know, I have stayed in a wide variety of accommodation during my mountaineering and hiking tours and I have to say that introducing these sorts of glitzy, sentimental ideas are at odds with what I had envisaged the cabins to look like.

I stopped reading and jerked my head up to look at Max. Frivolous? Glitzy? Sentimental? Damned bloody cheek! He was trying to undermine me! How dare he do that! I was the one who had been tasked with the cabins, not him. How would he like it if I interfered with his sodding rock climbing and tried to advise him on climbing Ben Nevis? And to write all this down in an email, instead of trying to speak to me about it?

I opened and closed my mouth, struggling to form a coherent sentence.

'Of all the—'

I swallowed a ball of temper and forced myself to read the rest of the email.

I have a friend who can lay his hands on unique wooden furniture, reflecting that period. Instead of the themes Ms Grant has suggested, I believe we should go down the more rustic route, which would appeal to our clientele.

I have no doubt at all that Ms Grant's vision for the cabins would be appreciated and indeed suitable in another setting, but I feel it would be a mistake to introduce them for your venture.

I had to stop reading for a few moments. My eyes felt like they were scorching. That bloody man! Who the hell did he think he was?

I forced myself to read to the end.

I can provide you with costings of the Western frontier theme and have taken the liberty of attaching a few images of the type of thing I had in mind. I know that with a change in direction, the cabins would appeal to a wider mass market than the current themes Ms Grant is implementing.

I have no doubt that Ms Grant is very competent, but I feel this is the wrong direction to take.

Let me know what you and Stephanie think.

Best,

Blake.

I have taken the liberty? *Very competent*?! Yes, he sure as hell had taken the liberty!

Struggling not to let rip with a frantic stream of expletives, I clicked on each of the attachments Blake had included with his email. Images of cast-iron frying pans, copper-bottom pots, hurricane gas lamps and simple cotton tablecloths and curtains flashed before my eyes. There were no pastel painted walls in sight. No plump cushions or woven rugs. Instead, there were pictures of thick wooden panelling. Dear Lord. It all reminded me of props from a Clint Eastwood movie.

I thrust Max's mobile back at him.

'Don't worry,' insisted Max, catching my furious gaze. 'We won't be considering Blake's suggested route. We know what our vision for the business is and have done from the outset and we share that same vision with you.' He brandished his phone at me again. 'No doubt he thought he was being helpful. I will reply with a polite decline.'

Being helpful?! Being an interfering tosser, more like! I was the one with the interior design degree here!

I stood there, frothing with fury. What did he think he was

playing at? Going behind my back like that to Max? What was he hoping to achieve? No, that was a silly question. I already knew the answer to that one.

Blake had made it plain from the start that he thought my ideas for the cabins were a waste of time. He'd clearly been giving it a great deal of thought, going by the images of pots, pans and panels he had included. The sly, underhand cretin!

Max stared down at me. 'Lottie? Are you all right?'

'No,' I ground out. 'Not really.'

Max ran a frustrated hand over the top of his hair, as a robin fluttered in and out of a nearby hedgerow. 'I shouldn't have told you. I should have just replied to him and said thank you for the suggestions, but no.'

'No, I'm glad you did tell me, Max.' At least now I knew what I was up against.

Max examined me. 'Just forget all about this, Lottie. As I say, Blake must have thought he was helping in some way by making alternative suggestions, but he hasn't gone the right way about it.'

My mouth pinched. Blake Dempster being helpful was about as likely as pink rainwater. I pushed out a tight smile. I didn't want to come across as awkward and combative, even if Blake Dempster did. I was new to the job and I wanted to make a good impression. 'Yes. Something like that.'

Max shoved his phone back into his trouser pocket. 'Don't give it any more thought. He's been clumsy and thoughtless in the way he's done this, but I'm sure it was well-intentioned on his part.' He clapped his hands together in an embarrassed action. 'I'll give him a quick call and explain. I'll also tell him I don't approve of how he's handled this. He should have discussed it with you.'

'Thank you. I'd appreciate that.'

I didn't say to Max that I was also intending on having a discreet word with our bearded mountaineering professional. If he thought he could act like this, he was much mistaken. He might be able to conquer snow-capped peaks in a pair of flip-flops, but that didn't give him the right to treat people like they didn't matter.

Max brandished his mobile. 'Right, I'd better get on. You go up and take a look at the cabins before you leave. They really are coming on a treat.'

I waited until Max's tall, distinguished frame retreated into Rowan Moore House. Then my frozen smile collapsed. I had no intention of going to visit the log cabins. At least not at the moment. That could wait until another day. The more I thought about Blake Dempster and the whole situation, the more frustrated and resentful I was becoming.

Even if Blake had approached me first with his idea, I still would have been irritated but I wouldn't have felt so stupid. Why hadn't he mentioned all this to me? Did he think I was insignificant? Inconsequential?

I gritted my teeth under the milky, wintry sky. I couldn't let this go. It would be gnawing at me all day.

I made a decision. I would drive straight back to Craig Brae and have a chat with Mr Dempster. Right now.

Chapter Eleven

I switched off my car engine and sat there, staring out at the plush new glass and pine wood office of Rock-Solid Ramblings, which had once been our local community centre.

It was situated on the outskirts of Craig Brae and atop a small hill, with the shores of Loch Strathe resting like a ghostly mirror in the distance.

I snatched my bag from the passenger seat, locked my car and marched towards the three stone steps that led up to the double door entrance.

It had been a peeling white-painted affair in its former guise as the community centre, but was now almost unrecognisable.

I had no idea whether Blake would be here, but seeing as I'd walked straight in and the place wasn't locked up, I reckoned he must be lurking around somewhere.

Soft pan-pipe music wafted out.

There was a mannequin in the right corner of the entrance, dressed in an expensive-looking waterproof jacket and thermal hat, and a chrome stand next to it, set out with an assortment of snazzy-looking drinking bottles and T-shirts, emblazoned with the words *Rock Solid Ramblings*.

Blake Dempster didn't seem to do discreet.

I jutted out my chin and yanked open the double doors. My blood was boiling in my veins.

The music followed me into a space with a polished wooden floor and a reception desk on the right, which was also wooden but semi-circular.

On the mint-green painted walls hung dramatic black and white photographs of mountain ranges and moody hillsides. I noticed there were also other portrait-style shots on the opposite wall.

When I got closer, I realised they must be of Blake Dempster rock climbing and looking rather pleased with himself. They weren't close-up shots, rather more arty efforts with him photographed from a distance, gazing over ravines. Then there were a couple others of him, standing miles away from the camera and posing on some wild-looking crevice in tight T-shirt and canvas trousers.

What a bloody bighead!

I started as his voice rang out of what looked like a store room at the back of the place.

'Will be with you in a minute!'

Seconds later, one of the willowy yummy mummies emerged, clutching a pink waterproof jacket. 'Pity you didn't have my size,' she purred over her shoulder. 'Never mind. I'll have to come back next week when you have more stock in.'

She spotted me standing there and delivered a cool smile. She dispensed with the jacket onto the counter as she sashayed towards the double doors.

Heavy footsteps crossed the floor behind her. 'No problem at all,' grinned Blake at her, flashing his canines.

'Hi there. How can I help you?' His smile dissolved when he realised it was me. 'Oh.'

I glowered over at him, all chest and beard. 'Yes. Oh. Providing excellent customer service, I see?'

'Of course. Service with a smile.'

With a snarl, more like.

Blake assessed me. 'So how can I help you? Have you thought things through and decided you don't want to turn the cabins into a funfair after all?'

I shook my head, fighting to appear unruffled, when inside I was simmering. 'I saw your email to Max.'

Blake pushed both hands into his combat trouser pockets. 'Yes. And?'

A cross between an incredulous gasp and a laugh shot out of me. 'That's all you have to say? You try to undermine me and that's it?'

He cocked his dark head to one side. 'I didn't try to undermine you, Ms Grant.'

I picked up on the formality in his tone.

'Look, it isn't anything personal. I was merely pointing out to Max that I don't consider drowning our cabin guests in ornamental snowmen and the Easter bunny to be a recipe for success. In fact, far from it.'

'And you think making them feel like they're trapped in the middle of a Spaghetti Western is?'

Blake's penetrating dark eyes challenged mine. 'In case you hadn't noticed, I do have some experience of the rock climbing and rambling industry.'

'Have you? Good grief. You've never mentioned that

before. You really must stop hiding your light under a bushel, Mr Dempster.'

His mouth twisted into an irritated line.

'If you had just mentioned to me that you were going to send that email to Max or even spoken to me first, I would have appreciated it.'

Blake's thick brows flexed. 'Since when did you become the boss? Correct me if I'm wrong, but I was under the impression that Max and Stephanie Styles employed you, not the other way round.'

He really was an arrogant git. I folded my arms tighter. 'Max and Stephanie have put me in charge of the cabin refurbishments, as well you know.'

'Oh, believe me, we know.'

Now it was the turn of my brows to fence. 'And what do you mean by that?'

Blake surveyed me out of his blazing, dark eyes. 'Nobody else is getting a look-in with suggestions.'

I pulled a sarcastic face. 'Er. Yes. Because as YOU might not have noticed, that's MY job. Project management.'

There was a charged silence. 'So why do it then?' I pushed. 'Why make those alternative suggestions?' I sighed, frustrated. 'You heard what the Styleses said. We're all working as a team – or at least we should be.'

Blake listened, but didn't comment.

'In just a few weeks, it's Christmas and those cabins are going to look magical.'

Blake leant against the door frame of his store room. 'I am aware of that. You've just got to step into Craig Brae. It's like some drug-induced hallucination.' He pulled an appalled face.

'It's all hearts and romance and bloody tinsel sprouting everywhere. It's not normal.'

I blinked at him. 'Excuse me?'

Blake's dark eyes burned. 'Sentimental clap-trap, if you want my opinion.'

'Well, I didn't ask for your opinion.'

Undeterred, he continued with his dark rant. 'Good grief. Don't tell me it's as bad at Easter and Halloween round here.'

I glowered at him. 'Well, if it's so appalling around here, why move to the area?'

Blake's bearded jaw throbbed. 'Sorry?'

'Why move to Craig Brae if you think it's such a godawful place? It's not exactly a heaving metropolis.' I eyed him. 'I would have thought that for someone like you, a quiet town like Craig Brae would be too provincial.'

His muscles flexed under his tight jumper. 'I wanted a change of scenery, to escape the city life for something calmer...' His voice tailed off for a few seconds. 'And anyway, I don't have to stand here and explain myself to you, Ms Grant.'

Ouch. I definitely touched a nerve there. But it was a valid question. Why had he chosen to set up a business here?

I tutted at his hard expression. 'What is it with you?'

Blake stiffened and stood up straighter. Now it was his turn to fold his arms. 'What do you mean?'

'All the negative comments; the sarcastic asides; the eye rolling and the grunting when I make creative suggestions; not showing up to help us out at the lights switch-on...' A picture of him shimmered into my head, glowering up at the illuminations. 'What is your problem? Do you have something against fun and frivolity? Are you some kind of anti-happiness police inspector?'

Blake's mouth twisted into an expression of barely concealed fury. 'You know nothing about me, Ms Grant, so please don't make sweeping assumptions.'

'Likewise, Mr Dempster. It's a pity you felt you couldn't assist the rest of us with handing out the leaflets at the lights switch-on the other Saturday.'

Blake gave a dismissive shrug. 'I was busy.'

'All day?'

'Yes. Why?'

Now it was my turn to shrug. 'That's odd, because I did actually see you there.'

His black eyes challenged mine. 'I happened to unfortunately have to walk through the main street on Saturday afternoon very briefly, but I had a rambling tour booked in.'

'So that was you I saw, looking up at the Christmas lights. Or should I say, aiming thunderbolts at them from your eyeballs?'

Blair didn't answer my question.

'You looked right across the street at me.'

He ground his jaw. 'You must have been mistaken. I didn't hang around with all that going on.'

'You must have a twin brother then, because I saw you standing on the opposite side of the street.'

Blake dismissed what I was saying. 'Well, they say everyone has a doppelganger somewhere in the world, don't they?'

Bloody hell, I simmered to myself. One Blake Dempster was

hard enough to deal with, without the nightmare scenario of two,

He flicked the conversation back to emailing Max. 'Look, Ms Grant, if I have an idea that I think can benefit a business, I'm not just going to sit on it. And I happen to think that your apparent obsession with Christmas and all things Disney isn't going to benefit the cabins in the long run.'

I made a snorting sound. My anger was taking off. 'All things Disney? Well, I would rather have an obsession with Christmas than be a muscle-bound Ebeneezer Scrooge with a beard that looks like it could nest a flock of birds!'

Blake looked momentarily stunned. Then his gaze challenged mine. 'Muscle-bound?' His eyes, which had been hard and uncompromising, raked over me now. I felt my cheeks scorch and swallowed. Suddenly, I felt rather vulnerable under his relentless gaze. 'So, you have noticed then?'

My mouth dropped open at his sheer audacity. How confident was this man? How sure of himself was he? Pathetic! I gripped the strap of my bag tighter. 'Unfortunately, I can't choose who I work with, but what I can do is try my utmost to make Magical Occasions Cabins a success.'

I whirled away in my riding boots and then spun round again. 'You might like to know that Max is intending on calling you to tell you that your idea to turn the cabins into some wild west arena is a no. He is also going to suggest you don't send an email like that again. It's most unprofessional.'

I could feel Blake's gaze searing into me. 'All these airy-fairy ideas of yours won't work, Ms Grant. The hearts and flowers and happily-ever-afters. People will see it for what it really is. A sham.' His dark, penetrating gaze hardened. 'Don't say I didn't warn you.'

I drew up at the double doors on the way out. 'Do you know what? I almost feel sorry for you. You really don't have any Christmas spirit at all, do you?'

There was a chilly silence. A concoction of emotions raced across his features. Then without saying anything, he stalked back into his storeroom, granite-faced, and slammed the door shut behind him.

I left, got into my car and drove away.

Wow! I'd pricked a nerve there.

Blake's reaction when I asked him why he didn't like Christmas echoed around my head. And what was he going on about, when he mentioned happily-ever-after being a sham? He'd looked very irritated when I pointed out I had seen him at the local lights switch-on. God, he really was a piece of work.

I headed back towards the cabins. Now would be a good time to return there and have a look at how things were progressing. I had intended to do that earlier today, but I was so furious at Blake, I knew I had to confront him about it.

The way he had commented on me noticing his muscles as well! My face flooded with colour. What a bloody big-head! Dear me, he had a high opinion of himself.

I drove back through Craig Brae, still burning with anger as I played over our argument. His furious face when I accused him of not having a fun bone in his body. He looked like he'd been burned when I said that. What was going on with him? He was such a prize grump. Talk about being able to rub people up the wrong way!

I negotiated past the trees, stippled with the faintest chinks of sunlight slithering through the bank of clouds.

Well, I'd show Mr 'I've climbed Mount Everest with my hands tied behind my back' that I could make the cabins work! Sod thinking I wasn't up to it or that this role was too big for me. I was even more determined now.

The log cabin front doors were flung open and light sparkled against their windows when I arrived back.

The smell of paint mingled with the scent of pine needles and damp moss.

Three decorators had been allotted by Andrew and Dominic to each cabin, delivering coats with wide brushes and rollers, overlaid with the odd, happy whistle and the thrum of radios.

Licks of powder-blue and white, hot ambers and cranberry were already transforming the interiors into something warm and welcoming. Each cabin was beginning to show its own character and personality. I couldn't wait until the furnishings and decorations were in!

I exchanged pleasantries with each of the decorating teams as I moved from cabin to cabin.

Each cabin having its own name seemed even more of a good idea, now they were beginning to take shape and develop their own unique character. Hopefully, the "Name the Cabins" competition I had thought of would throw up some fantastic suggestions. The winner with the best and most original entry would win a free weekend stay for a family of four. What if we could persuade one or two of the local businesses to contribute towards a prize as well? I thought of Mrs Crill and the baking decadence she was famous for in Craig Brae. In the last few years, she had sold a number of Christmas hampers that she had made up herself. What if I could persuade her to part with one of those and contribute it as a gift in the competition? It would be a lovely little bit of extra publicity for her and the bakery.

I meandered up and down in front of the cabins, mulling it over. I was certain Stephanie and Max would think this competition suggestion would prove to be a popular one.

My thoughts insisted on returning to Blake and his comments, however.

Oh God. Had I made an awful mistake accepting this job after all? I mean, I was enjoying it so much. I was able to use my interior design skills and let my imagination and creativity run wild, but at what expense? At the expense of having to work with Craig Brae's Grumpy McGrumpface?

How could I do my job properly when he persisted in sticking that dark beard of his into everything? Trying to undermine me? Making sarcastic asides?

I stared across at the cabins, their doors open and the smell of freshly applied paint wafting out.

No. Sod it. If he thought he could intimidate me and prevent me from doing what I set out do, then Blake Dempster didn't know me at all.

Chapter Twelve

'You ok, Lottie? You look like someone's held you at gunpoint and stolen your lunch money.'

I twisted round to see John, one of the decorators, standing on the porch of the second cabin.

'I'm fine,' I forced. 'Just having to deal with cretins who think they're superior to everyone else.' I sighed. 'I don't know why I'm so surprised.'

John reached into a bucket down by his feet and plucked a smaller, clean paintbrush out of it. 'Don't sweat it. The more I get to know some folks, the more I love my dog.'

I laughed. 'I think you're onto something there.' I gestured to the cabins. 'You guys are doing such an amazing job. I really appreciate it.'

'No worries. Oh, here he comes. It's Scotland's answer to Bear Grylls. How's it going, Blake?'

Oh no. You have to be kidding me. What the hell was he doing up here? Didn't he have any more woolly hats and puffer jackets to sell? Or perhaps there was some dangerous precipice he could bugger off and climb?

I closed my eyes for a few seconds. Great. I did not need more of him right now. I rearranged my face into an expression which I hoped was one of professional indifference and spun around.

Blake was striding up. He'd changed clothes and was now wearing a pale-blue shirt, dark trousers and a navy tie. The shirt strained across his muscles. I jerked my attention away.

'Well, well. It's a real hive of activity around here,' he murmured, his dark eyes piercing me. 'Hello again.'

I managed a stiff nod. 'Hello.'

'So, what are you doing up here, Dempster? Come to see what real work looks like?'

'Don't kid yourself. I've got a 5am sunrise walk tomorrow with half a dozen wealthy Americans.'

'That's not work,' teased John. 'That's a hobby.'

I observed their banter and my anger flashed again. I jutted out my chin. 'Sorry to interrupt, but are you up here for a meeting? Or are you planning on sending any more of your two-page emails? Perhaps you've managed to dash another one off to Max on the way here?'

Blake turned to me and flexed one brow. 'I've got a catch-up with Max about the hiking services I'm going to be providing to the cabin guests.' He gave me a measured look and then turned to John. 'So, what do you think of all of this?'

'All what?'

Blake pointed to the cabins. 'These being turned into Scotland's version of Disney Land.'

Here we go again. *Stay calm, Lottie. Don't allow him to rile you. That's what he wants.*

I arranged my mouth into a frosty smile. 'It's called style, Mr Dempster. I'm not sure you're familiar with the concept.'

John struggled to hide a grin.

I paused and then gave John a megawatt smile. 'Do you like Christmas, John?'

John's close-cropped brown head was swinging between Blake and me like he was struggling to keep up. 'Yes, I do. In fact, I love it. Not so keen on New Year mind, but I've always enjoyed Christmas.'

I couldn't conceal a small smile of satisfaction. 'So do I. Most magical time of the year.'

'No such thing as Christmas magic. I'm more likely to bump into ET.'

'I would feel sorry for ET,' I muttered.

The woodland light sifted through Blake's dark layered hair. Under his generous beard, I could swear I saw his jaw tense. 'Each to their own. A load of commercial, overrated crap."

'Yes, I'm well aware of your thoughts about the festive season,' I smiled sweetly. 'But thanks for your input.'

Blake glowered and was on the brink of saying something else when his mobile rang out.

He tugged it out of his back trouser pocket and peered down at the screen. I noticed his eyes turning hard. He stared down at the flickering phone for a few more seconds.

'Are you going to answer that, mate, or communicate with the thing telepathically?' asked John.

Blake blinked at his phone and then back up at John and me, as if he had forgotten for a moment that we were both still standing there. He reluctantly raised it to his ear and strode a few feet away for some privacy.

John waited until Blake had turned away from us both and waggled his brows at me in a 'I wonder what's going on?' kind of way, before vanishing back inside the second cabin.

It was time I headed back to Craig Brae. I had now seen for myself how great the log cabins were looking already and the prospect of being in Blake Dempster's company any longer than I had to was about as appealing as a bout of flu.

I hitched my bag further up my shoulder and proceeded to leave the woodland and head back in the direction of my car.

I had taken several steps away, when Blake's agitated voice rang out behind me.

'Amy, don't give me that. Two years ago, you cleared me out, so enough of the bullshit!'

Blake's voice reverberated through the trees. Even though he was trying to keep his conversation private, his voice was becoming louder and more agitated. This Amy, whoever she was, was sending his emotions all over the place. He clamped his phone tighter to his ear and shot me a self-conscious look from over his broad shoulders. 'I'm not continuing this conversation. I'm at work. I've got a meeting in five minutes.'

Blake fell silent, listening to what the woman at the other end of the line had to say.

I moved off until he let out a burst of sarcastic laughter that made me draw up again. 'Are you joking? After what you did?'

I stopped and peered over my shoulder at him, back through the trees.

His expression had darkened. 'You are not getting another penny from me, is that understood? Don't you think you got more than your fair share?' He paused to listen again, before snapping back, 'Now trot off back to lover boy and leave me alone.'

My feet had ground to a halt on the crunchy twig-strewn mass.

What was all that about?

He lifted his phone and jabbed at the screen. He kept his broad back facing away from me for a few seconds.

What should I do? Should I pretend I hadn't heard any of that and just head back to my car? Or should I do the decent thing and go back and ask him if he was ok? He was an arrogant sod, but just because he behaved like he'd had a soul bypass, didn't mean I should. He must have known I'd heard at least some of the conversation.

He had sounded shocked and thrown by that phone call. Whoever this Amy was, she had rattled him.

I looked around myself, debating what to do. I hovered, caught between letting him get on with it and asking if everything was ok.

Before I could think about it any longer, I realised my feet were taking me back towards Blake.

He had turned around by this time and spotted me returning. He struggled to make eye contact with me.

I hopped from foot to foot. What should I say? Should I just be bold and ask him what that was all about? Who was Amy and why was he arguing with her? Or should I not refer to the call and just stand there like a prize lemon, like I was doing now?

It was almost a relief to see I wasn't the only one on the receiving end of frustrating messages today.

I took a couple more steps towards him and stopped. Blake adjusted his tie. He still wasn't looking at me.

I shuffled from foot to foot on the crunchy woodland floor. What should I do? Maybe I should have pretended I hadn't heard and just carried on walking? Oh well. It was too late now. I flashed him a look. 'Are you all right?'

His almost-black eyes narrowed, as though he wasn't sure whether he'd heard me correctly or not. He cleared his throat. 'Why shouldn't I be?'

'You look upset.'

Blake's unreadable gaze flickered over me. 'It's fine. It was nothing.' He pushed his phone into the inside pocket of his suit jacket.

'Are you sure? It didn't sound like nothing.'

'It's ok. I'm ok,' he ground out.

Clearly, the situation wasn't ok and neither was Blake, but his shutters were well and truly locked down and were not prepared to budge anytime soon.

'All right.'

He stood for a few moments longer, with the bare winter trees a tangle of dramatic criss-crossing branches behind him like spindly arms.

I couldn't stand here any longer. He wasn't saying anything.

'I'll be off then,' I said, turning away and starting to head back to my car.

I'd taken several strides when his voice surprised me. It rang out at my retreating back. 'Thank you.'

I turned around and blinked over at him. 'Sorry?'

He let out a cough. 'Thank you for asking if I'm ok.'

I stared at him for a few seconds. 'Oh. Er. Ok. No problem.'

We both stood, looking at one another, with just the woodland sounds like an orchestra surrounding us.

Then, like the flick of a switch, the traces of vulnerability I'd glimpsed in him just seconds ago evaporated. The intense, focused edge in his eyes was back.

Smoothing down his tie, Blake waited for a few moments to let me get ahead of him. Then he set off himself, back towards Rowan Moore House, for his meeting with Max.

Chapter Thirteen

L ife can often be like buses, can't it?

Nothing comes along for ages and then two pull up at once.

This is what happened with the furniture, fittings and decorations ordered for the cabins, which decided to arrive a couple of days earlier than we had expected.

As I'd hoped, Max and Stephanie had been very enthusiastic about my other suggestion of allowing the public to suggest names for each of the four Magical Occasions Cabins.

'Once we've got them finished, I thought we could post pictures of the interiors and exteriors online and ask people to come up with suitable names for each one,' I'd explained to them at our most recent catch-up at Rowan Moore House. 'The four most original suggestions that we like the best will win.'

The Styleses had nodded enthusiastically. 'That's a wonderful idea,' beamed Stephanie.

'Thank you. I thought the prize could be a gift voucher of

£200 towards the cost of a long weekend stay and a Christmas hamper supplied by Mrs Crill who owns the local bakery, Sugar 'n' Spice.' I added that I had already spoken to her and she was very keen on the idea. 'Is that agreeable to you both?'

Max and Stephanie said that they thought the hamper was also a great suggestion and so I explained I would post details of that competition once the cabins were completed on the Magical Occasions Cabins social media accounts.

It was a couple of days now since Blake's fraught phone conversation with the mysterious Amy.

I'd glimpsed him around Rowan Moore House, deep in conversation with Max and he had given me a nod of greeting.

Now I was darting between each of the cabins with Stephanie, as well as Ruth, the newly recruited cleaner of the cabins, having just received the arrival of cushions, lamps, chairs, sofas and bedding for each one.

The air was fresh and tinged with the promise of frost, as the helpful delivery men offered to manoeuvre the sofas and chairs into each cabin for us.

My heart lifted with excitement and a bout of trepidation, as I assisted Stephanie and Ruth with positioning the lamps, plumping and arranging the new cushions and flapping the new, fresh bedding.

We had been here since just after 5am this morning. The sleepy hot-orange sunrise had spilt across Loch Strathe and the tops of the trees, washing over everything and making it look as though it was catching fire.

Each cabin was now transforming in front of our eyes, into bright little havens of joy, with their own unique colour schemes and fittings.

The Winter Wonderland cabin was a sea of glittery snow

globes on the glossy shelves, powder-blue and cream bedding and a squashy dark-blue sofa and matching chairs.

The *Nutcracker* cabin was all soldiers and sugar plum fairies, decked out with gold and white, wooden soldier figures and matching Christmas flower arrangements thrusting out of frosted vases.

The bedding was crisp and white with gold detail and there were matching coloured star ornaments in the bedroom and sitting room, complete with the sheepskin fleeces adorning the backs of the sofas and beds in each cabin.

The next cabin, reflecting *A Christmas Carol*, invited in guests with its splashes of rich burgundy and Victorian-style decorations. There were long, dramatic velvet drapes at the windows and a couple of paisley printed rugs and an ornate candelabra on the dining area table.

The lamps were small and unique, topped with detailed fringed lampshades.

And the fourth cabin, reflecting a rustic woodland theme, boasted animal ornaments made out of wood and pinecones, a roaring log fire and fringed hessian rugs. The heavy stone fireplace carried a red and green string of ivy at the top of it, decorated with bright-red ribbons.

We worked from first thing that Wednesday morning, shuffling, adjusting, arranging and tweaking, before Kim appeared from the office based in Rowan Moore House to tell us the small Christmas trees and their decorations for each of the cabin porches were about to arrive.

Stephanie had greeted us outside the cabins with a couple of warm croissants and a flask of coffee for breakfast when we had first arrived, but it had seemed so long ago now. That was why I was so delighted to see Kim was carrying a tray laden with a pot of tea, mugs and a plate of warm scones. We were all running on adrenalin.

We threw ourselves at her like three relieved and famished shipwrecked passengers spotting a lifeboat.

'If you let me know what each of you would like for lunch, I'll pop down to the town and get you something.'

'You are a star, Kim,' I grinned, dusting my hands down the front of my old jeans and taking a welcome gulp of my tea.

Stephanie pressed two hands at the base of her spine. 'That would be great, Kim, if you don't mind. Thank you.'

After a bit of debate, Stephanie and I agreed that we both fancied one of Mrs Crill's turkey, cranberry and salad toasties and one of her spiced lattes, while Ruth requested a baked potato with coleslaw and salad. Definitely winter comfort food!

'I'll get those and bring them over around midday then,' said Kim. 'And none of you overdo it, please! If you need another pair of hands, please just let me know.'

And off she hurried in her patchwork, rainbow jacket back to the house.

We had just finished the tea and devoured the warm buttered scones between us when there was the sound of tyres through the woodland and the sharp slam of a vehicle door.

Three delivery men approached us, clutching four fake Christmas trees between them and boxes of decorations. The child in me zinged with excitement.

Stephanie and I proceeded to unwrap the four trees – electric blue, white, gold and silver – together with the boxes of decorations to accompany them, which gave a gentle rattle.

I had also remembered to bring with me two cardboard boxes of the end-of-line ornaments I had bought from

Christmas Crackers and which I thought would complement the new decorations.

Then there were the matching cabin door wreaths, which reflected the colours of the trees. The baubles that were studded into each one alongside the holly and tiny lights shone out.

Stephanie stood back, a look of joy riven in her handsome, elegant features. 'They are all going to look so pretty!' She thrust a finger in the air. 'I just had a thought. I've got a small blue and silver cuddly robin that we could put in the Winter Wonderland window. I think it would really compliment the blue in the tree.'

I looked up from where I was kneeling down on the porch, separating the branches of the newly arrived tree. 'That sounds lovely.'

Stephanie started to walk in the direction of the house. 'I'll go and get it then. I think it's in our Christmas box in the loft. Max should be around, so I'll ask him to give me a hand locating it. Won't be long.'

'Don't rush,' I said. 'I'm fine here.'

Ruth admired the door wreaths. 'Well, I can press on with putting these up then, and making sure all the tinsel has stayed put.'

'That would be great. Thank you.

While Ruth trooped off with the door wreaths, I finished draping and winding some strands of baby-blue and white tinsel in and around the tree branches of the Winter Wonderland lodge. Then I headed inside to locate the digital radio, which I'd spotted in the kitchen.

I clicked it on. The sound of 'All I Want for Christmas is You,' made my feet tap and move with the beat.

There was a strand of silver tinsel framing one of the sitting room windowsills, so I reached for it and tied it around my head. I began to dance and move, wiggling my bottom and flailing my arms, as Mariah belted out the lyrics.

I weaved this way and that, singing along and waggling my hips in time to the music. I put my arms above my head, sashaying backwards and forwards, and swung round with a flourish. With too much of a flourish, in fact.

I could feel myself lose my footing and stagger to the side. I shot out one arm to try and grab something to steady myself, but my hand flapped in mid-air.

That was until I felt a solid grip take hold of my arm and pull me upright. Surprise didn't register until I realised I had barrelled into a man's chest. It was solid and muscular. He smelled of citrus and the outdoors.

My heart stilled.

I dragged my horrified eyes upwards.

Blake was towering over me, with a look that could only be described as puzzled bemusement.

I could feel his arms still holding mine.

I jumped out of his grip, flustered and smoothing my hair.

Blake was dressed in his walking gear, his arms now folded and his mouth twitching. That was bad enough, but he wasn't alone.

Gawping over his shoulder at this spectacle of me in tinsel and jiving around, before I almost went over like an old tree in a gale, were three older ladies and a grinning gentleman, all swathed in hiking gear.

My cheeks burned.

My horrified hands flew to my neck. I was still wearing the tinsel. I yanked off the decoration and threw it over the back of the nearest new armchair, before reaching for the digital radio on the table and jabbing it off.

'Oh, please don't stop on our account,' insisted Blake. 'You carry on throwing some shapes – or whatever it was you were doing.'

Smug sod!

I didn't know what to do with my arms. I pushed them into the front pockets of my jeans before removing them, flailing them around and thrusting them into my back pockets. 'Why were you creeping up on me?' I blurted. I really wanted to give him a mouthful, but now wasn't the time. Not with members of the public spectating.

'I didn't creep, Ms Grant. I thought I would drop by at the end of our ramble to see how things were going with the cabins.' His eyed glittered. 'Good job I did too by the looks of things, otherwise your dance routine could have left you with a sprained ankle.'

I tried to swallow the ball of growing horror stuck in my throat. I was still struggling to look at him, let alone his accompanying audience. 'Well, as you can see, everything is coming along very well.'

My attention shifted to one of the ladies behind Blake. 'Mrs Stritch?' I asked, all at once recognising her open, inquiring face and cropped silver hair.

She blinked over at me. 'Lottie?' she beamed. 'Oh, my goodness! How are you?'

Oh great. Not only was I making an utter tit of myself in front of Blake, I also knew another member of my rapt audience.

'Mrs Stritch was my primary school head teacher,' I

explained to an intrigued Blake, keen to move matters on from my wiggling, jiggling bottom.

'Oh, I see.'

Marigold Stritch and her companions exclaimed and admired the cabin surroundings. 'If they all look like this one, you'll have guests queuing up for return visits,' said the smiling older man in an orange knitted hat.

'Let's hope so,' I smiled back at him.

I turned back to Mrs Stritch, trying not to make eye contact with Blake.

Oh, I was glad he was finding this whole situation so amusing. He was still fighting the urge to smile, which annoyed me.

His hot eyes flickered over me. I cleared my throat and clasped my hands behind my back like Prince Charles. 'So, is the school all set for Christmas?' I asked Mrs Stritch, keen to talk about something else, other than my dancing. She had been one of those teachers with a quiet, calm and reassuring smile. She was still heavily involved with the school, volunteering on occasion to help out with various events. She was every bit as much a part of the Craig Brae community as Loch Strathe was. 'I bet it is if you're involved. You were always so wonderful, organising things.'

'Och, away with you,' she beamed, delighted. Then her expression grew more serious. 'And in answer to your question, we were all set for Christmas,' she sighed, her smile fading. 'Unfortunately, Mr Shaw, our janitor, has broken his leg in a five-a-side match. It only happened last night. He always plays Santa for our younger children.'

'Oh no! So, what are you going to do?'

She raised her gloved hands. 'I don't know. The Christmas

party at school is tomorrow afternoon, so we have very little time to find a replacement Santa.' She frowned. 'Mr Shaw is a former body-builder. He's such a big, broad chap and so is his Santa outfit, of course.' She shot a troubled look at her walking compatriots.

Poor kids! It would ruin their Christmas party if Santa wasn't there. *Hang on… Former body-builder… broad build…*

An idea popped into my head. Of course! He would no doubt be furious, but it served him right for smirking at me just now and for trying to change the theme of the cabins to some wild west nonsense.

And anyway, he had chosen to move to Craig Brae and this was a close community. If he wanted to fit in and make a life for himself here then he would have to make an effort, and what better way than to help out at the local school Christmas party?

I could do something for my old school, while ensuring the kids weren't disappointed by their Christmas party – and of course, there was the delectable prospect of getting my own back on the smirking Blake.

He was glancing down at his chunky watch, oblivious to the plan hatching in my mind and the charged glances I was giving him.

'Right, ladies and gent,' he announced. 'Let's head back to Rowan Moore House now, where I'm told some coffee, tea and mince pies are waiting for us.'

I folded my arms and gave Blake a wide million-dollar smile.

He blinked at me, discomfited. 'What is it? Why are you grinning at me like that?'

'Like what?'

'Like Jack Nicholson in *The Shining*. It's very unnerving.'

I savoured his apprehension for a few more moments. 'Santa. You could do it.'

Blake's dark eyes grew with horror, as the realisation of what I was saying began to sink in. 'What? No. No. Sorry. No way.'

'But Mr Dempster, you would be perfect,' pleaded Mrs Stritch, her expression suddenly alive with hope. 'What a wonderful idea. You're a similar build to Mr Shaw: broad-shouldered, muscular…' My retired headteacher's eyes were twinkling with appreciation.

'Yes, and you've already got the Santa beard,' I chipped in. 'Pity it's the wrong colour, but hey, you can't have everything.'

Blake's cheeks were turning puce. He narrowed his eyes at me, his lips drawn back in a promise of a snarl. That made me smile even wider. Gotcha!

He turned to Mrs Stritch, floundering. 'I'm very sorry, but—'

'It would only be for an hour or so,' she carried on. 'You would be doing the school and the children such a huge favour.'

Panic shone out of his face. 'I think I have another ramble scheduled for then. Sorry about that.' He was fidgeting in his heavy walking boots.

'Oh, I'm sure you could rearrange it,' I said. 'If you explain how community-spirited you're being, I'm sure your rambling clients would understand.'

He snapped his head round to look at me. His white teeth were grinding through his beard.

I gave him a cheeky wink.

'Please Mr Dempster,' implored Mrs Stritch again. 'I can't

tell you what it would mean to us and the children. If we don't have a Santa for them tomorrow afternoon, it's going to ruin their school party.'

I angled my head to one side. I spotted a shred of silver tinsel still in my hair and snatched it out.

Blake appeared to be in mental agony and it wasn't helping that Mrs Stritch and the three other walkers and I were studying him like a museum piece. My eyebrows rose. 'It should only take up a small part of your day tomorrow, Blake.'

Blake's eyes bored into mine.

Perhaps doing something like this for the local school at Christmas would let him see what a warm and welcoming place Craig Brae was. It might also trigger a bit of Christmas spirit in him, although the daggers he was aiming at me right now made me think I was being a tad optimistic on that front.

Blake looked at me, Mrs Stritch and the expectant faces of his fellow walkers all crowded round him in horror. He let out a whimpering noise and closed his eyes for a few seconds, as though willing us all to vanish. 'Oh, for pity's sake!' he hissed under his breath. There was an agonising silence for a few seconds. 'All right! All right. I'll do it.'

Mrs Stritch clapped her hands together in delight. 'Oh, thank you. Thank you so much, Mr Dempster. You've saved Christmas for the little ones!'

Blake tried to smile, but he looked more like he was suffering with an ingrown toenail.

Mrs Stritch couldn't contain her delight. 'I'll email you the details when I return home, but if you could be at Craig Brae Primary School for one o'clock tomorrow afternoon please, that would be grand.'

Buzzing with relief, Mrs Stritch and her walking

companions began to file their way out of the cabin and tap back down the porch steps.

I beamed over at him.

'I won't forget this, Grant,' he ground out.

'I'm sure you won't. Still, I'm looking forward to seeing you do your yo-ho-ho act tomorrow.'

Blake looked stricken. 'What?'

I hooked my thumbs into the beltloops of my jeans. 'Oh, I'll make sure I'm there, don't you worry about that. I wouldn't miss this for the world.'

Chapter Fourteen

My old primary school was just as I remembered: a big, stately grey stone affair from the Victorian era, with sash windows and a large playground. The only new addition was an Astroturf football pitch.

As soon as I pressed the intercom, I was allowed entry and directed by a young teaching assistant to the school office.

A sharply dressed woman with curly hair smiled through the glass partition at me. It was all so different to when Mrs Edmond was the head school secretary. Her Dame Edna Everage-style glasses would glint at you with irritation if you dared to approach the hallowed ground that was the school office. It was most unnerving. She viewed all the kids as a damned nuisance.

I explained to the smiling woman that I was here to see Mrs Stritch and she told me to take the first right down the hallway to the main hall.

Paintings and drawings of everything from treehouses to volcanoes dotted the walls.

The playful tinkle of a piano sent the sound of 'Frosty the Snowman' across the hall to greet me, making me smile.

The polished wooden floor of the hall gleamed up at me. The air smelled of wax crayons and the remnants of school lunch.

A Christmas tree, popping with multi-coloured lights, sat in the far corner. Underneath it were several foil-wrapped boxes masquerading as presents.

Ahead of me and to the left were a number of occupied classrooms. Memories of my school Christmas parties trailed through my mind. The hall had been strung with paper chains and dangling spinning snowflakes, and we had played pass-the-parcel. I remembered Mum tonging my hair into ringlets especially for the occasion.

Mrs Stritch was chatting to a gangly, young male teacher. When she saw me, she smiled and excused herself. 'Lottie. How nice to see you again.'

'Likewise.' I glanced around myself, noting over her shoulder a classful of five-year-olds, chatting and giggling to each other, through a gap in the partially open classroom door. They reminded me of miniature princes and princesses, in their party outfits of smart shirts, waistcoats, glittery tops and velvet dresses. 'Is Blake here yet?'

'Oh yes. He arrived ten minutes ago and has gone to the gents' teacher's toilets to get ready.'

As if on cue, a blur of red and white emerged out of the corner of my eye.

Mrs Stritch reached behind her and tugged the classroom door closed, so that the children wouldn't be able to see anything.

Blake was clumping along in heavy, shiny black boots and

glowering out at me from under a long white wig and matching false beard.

Oh dear. Something told me he was still rather annoyed at me.

'You look terrific, Mr Dempster,' exclaimed Mrs Stritch. 'The real deal!'

Blake flapped his ankle-length cloak. 'It will only be for about half an hour, won't it? The wig and this cloak are rather hot.'

'Oh, I'm sure you'll be able to cope,' I beamed up at him. 'Playing Santa will be a walk in the park for someone who conquers three mountains before breakfast.'

Blake scowled out from under his white wig.

'An hour maximum,' clarified Mrs Stritch. 'Thank you so much for this.'

Blake scratched his real beard under his false one and attempted a pained smile. 'You're welcome.'

I was still grinning. 'You do look the part.'

Blake walked over to me and glowered from under his black brows.

'How are you coping with the double beard thing going on underneath there? It can't be very comfortable. Must be awful for you.'

Blake ground his teeth together. 'You wait, Grant. I will have my revenge.'

'Oh, you mustn't be tetchy,' I teased him. 'Santa is a sweet old gent. The children will love you.' I took an exaggerated step backwards and looked him up and down. 'Nobody would recognise you.'

'I bloody well hope not!'

'Oh, that reminds me,' gasped Mrs Stritch. 'Goodness!' She

hurried over to a passing teacher. 'With everything going on, I almost forgot. Could you bring me Mrs Shaw's Christmas elf outfit please, Cara?'

The young woman disappeared, returning moments later with an olive-green felt ensemble, complete with a pointy hat and bell attached to the end of it. Mrs Stritch took it from the other teacher and held it up towards me, as though she were trying to persuade me to buy it.

'Mrs Shaw always plays Santa's little helper at our Christmas parties, but she telephoned a short while ago to say she can't do it today. Her husband is in a lot of discomfort with his sciatica and she didn't want to leave him.'

What was going on? Why was she holding that ensemble up against me?

She fluttered the outfit, almost striking me in the face with it. 'The children are so observant. If any of the staff were to do it, they would recognise them straight away.' She fixed me with her clear, pale gaze. 'I'm so sorry to spring this on you, Lottie, but I don't suppose you would…?'

From behind me came a peal of deep laughter. Blake grinned through his flowing white beard. 'Yes, she would be more than happy to oblige. What is it you always say about being there to help out in the community, Lottie?'

Bugger! I shot him a hot look. The outfit was hideous. I stared with a feeling of dread at the fringed skirt and stripey red and white tights.

'Mrs Shaw is slim, but on the curvier side like you,' carried on Mrs Stritch, an imploring desperation creeping into her voice.

I managed a tight smile.

Blake was relishing this turn of events. 'Go on, Lottie. You don't want to disappoint all these children, do you?'

I swung around to look at him. His dark eyes danced with amusement from beneath his mane of white wig.

Well, I wasn't about to let Blake think he was getting one over me, or that I was dreading putting on this awful outfit.

I pushed my pinched mouth into an overly bright smile. 'Of course I'll do it, Mrs Stritch. Anything to help. No problem at all.'

'Wonderful. Thank you so much, dear.' She thrust the elf outfit at me and I threw it over one arm.

'The ladies' teachers' toilets are through the alcove.'

'On the left?' I asked, ignoring Blake, who was still grinning at my evident discomfort.

'On the left,' she confirmed with an appreciative smile. 'Well remembered.'

I made my way around the corner, clutching the garish elf outfit. At least I would be able to wear my snazzy knee-length riding boots with it.

'Oh, Lottie. Sorry. I meant to give you these.'

Scratch that.

I buried a tragic sigh, as Mrs Stritch hurried towards me with a pair of matching green slippers, tied with red laces.

'Lovely,' I murmured.

I was relieved to see that the ladies' toilets were empty, so I threw off my clothes, slid them into my bucket shoulder bag and pulled on the offending outfit.

I cringed at my reflection in the full-length mirror. My cheeks were hot and flaming, clashing with the screaming loudness of the green outfit and my ponytail was a mess.

I tugged on the stripey tights next. Dear God. If I had my

face painted green, I could have passed for Princess Fiona's sister.

I shook out my ponytail, letting my hair fall down my back and plonked the jangly hat on my head. The green and red slippers were a little too big for me, so I slipped my socks back on. Not perfect, but it would have to do.

I fiddled with my tunic and smoothed down the frilly white, Peter Pan-style collar. I looked more terrifying than festive. I would be giving the kids nightmares for the next month.

I raked about in my bag and reapplied my lipstick and a slick of mascara in the vain hope that might improve the overall look of the outfit. It didn't make that much of a dramatic improvement. To be honest, I think setting fire to the whole damned thing wouldn't have made much of a difference.

I lurched around the ladies' toilets, tugging at the tunic again and running one finger inside the scratchy white collar. I couldn't loiter in these toilets any longer. It would be Christmas at this rate by the time I plucked up enough courage to head back outside.

And I was not prepared to give Blake the satisfaction of thinking that I was trying to hide out here in the ladies' toilets, rather than face him.

I puffed out my chest and threw my bag back over my shoulder. 'Right. Let's do this,' I said, my voice echoing around the vacant cubicles. 'If I can make over four log cabins, I can bloody well go out there and humiliate myself for an hour, dressed like Kermit!'

I strode with what I hoped was a confident gait back around the corner and into the school hall again.

Blake was chatting to Mrs Stritch. On seeing her smile over at me, he turned. His dark eyes danced with amusement. He let out a gale of laughter. 'Well, well. Look at you, Ms Grant.'

My plan had been to ignore him, but Blake was intent on enjoying himself and exacting revenge. His white teeth flashed through his Santa beard.

I tried not to fidget on the spot.

'Nice legs,' he whispered, sauntering past in his red jacket and trousers. 'Even in those tights.'

My cheeks burned. Idiot!

Mrs Stritch guided us over to the opposite alcove on the other side of the hall, where pretty fairy lights and dangling streamers surrounded a high-backed chair, which was woven with gold tinsel. Beside that sat a large brown sack, bulging with wrapped presents for the school children.

'We're just going to play a couple of short party games and then start to bring the children through to you both in small groups,' whispered Mrs Stritch. 'We won't be long.'

Blake flicked out his wig and arranged himself on his 'throne'.

I stood to the left of him, grinding my teeth. Something told me he might be beginning to enjoy himself – at my expense.

'Having fun?' he twinkled, turning round to look up at me.

'Absolutely. It will be great. I love doing this sort of thing. Very rewarding.'

He appraised me from head to toe. 'I'm actually pleased now that you talked me into doing this.' His lips twitched through the trailing false beard. 'Are you always so persuasive?'

My cheeks now matched the ridiculous red stripes on my

tights. I clapped my hands together and ignored his comment. 'I can't wait to see the kids' faces.'

One of Blake's brows rose up to the hairline of his white wig. 'Yes, their faces are bound to be a study when they see you.'

I scowled at him from under my elf hat. A couple of moments later, the first of the children, guided through by a couple of teachers, appeared in Santa's grotto.

I stepped forward and ushered them in, with an enthusiastic smile and a 'Merry Christmas!'

Blake took one look at the expectant round little faces of the children. I heard him clear this throat. He angled himself round. There was a flicker of panic in his dark eyes.

The children gawped up at him and then at each other. There was a stony silence.

I expected Blake to say something, but it was like he had developed a bout of stage fright. He opened and closed his mouth.

Disappointment and confusion were creeping over the children's expressions. Even their teacher was beginning to shoot us desperate looks.

I had to do something, otherwise things could turn ugly.

I leant close to him and grinned over at the children in the hope of reassuring them that Santa was in fact all right. 'You've got this,' I reassured him in a whisper. 'You've climbed bloody great mountains in all sorts of weather. A classful of primary one children is nothing.'

Blake fidgeted, glancing at the expectant faces staring back at him. 'You think?' he hissed out of the corner of his false beard.

'I know.'

He shot me a look and managed a nod. Then he puffed out his chest. 'Ho-ho-ho!'

He did sound rather stilted with the first few children, but after a few more minutes, he began to relax and channel his Santa vibe.

Blake even surprised me by cracking a few corny jokes with the kids, which saw them erupt into giggles and groans.

'Not so bad, is it?' I muttered to him during a brief break.

'I wouldn't go that far,' he said, appraising my Kermit-green outfit again. 'Still, at least I didn't have to dress up like Shrek.'

I pulled a face at him. 'Any more sarcastic wise cracks and I'll set fire to your beard – both of them.'

I straightened up and grinned at a little girl with long, straight, glossy black hair who had appeared at the entrance to the grotto. Her big blue eyes scanned us both from beneath her thick fringe. She shuffled forward, encouraged by her teacher, who was trying to control a couple of buzzing little boys who were up next. The little girl was wearing a lemon-yellow party dress. She reminded me of a bright butterfly.

From through in the main hall, the sounds of dancing children and Little Mix drifted in.

'And what is your name, young lady?' rumbled Blake in his best Santa voice.

The little girl eyed him. 'Natalie.' She sidled up to Blake's elbow and gave me a shy little smile out of her freckled face.

'Hello, Natalie. Have you been a good girl this year?' asked Blake.

She thought long and hard. 'I think so.'

'I'm sure you have,' he assured her.

Natalie's attention fell on the sack by Blake's booted feet, the wrapped presents peeking out of the top of it. 'I know what I would like for Christmas, Santa.'

'Oh good. And what might that be?'

Natalie shot a glance over at her teacher, who was still preoccupied with the two little boys. She dropped her voice. 'I would like my mummy to come back home. Can you do that, Santa?'

An emotional gasp shot out of my throat, but I managed to turn it into a cough. Blake blinked at the little girl as she stood by his elbow.

While she waited for Blake to reply, Natalie wrapped her arms around herself and examined her sparkly party shoes.

Blake spun round in his chair to see my reaction to her request. I gave a sad, sympathetic shake of my head, forgetting that I had a bell at the end of my elf hat. It dinged.

Realising Natalie was waiting for him to say something, Blake swung his attention back to her. He puffed out his chest again. His voice was gentler now, but faltering. 'Where is your mummy at the moment, Natalie?'

The girl shrugged her slight shoulders. 'We don't know. Mummy told Daddy she was very tired and she needed a little holiday.'

My heart felt like it was going to wrench itself out of my chest. Bless her.

I glanced down at Blake. Under the white cloud of wig and false beard, his dark eyes were swimming with sympathy. He opened and closed his mouth a couple of times.

Miss Turner, Natalie's teacher, was listening from the grotto entrance, her expression an agonised one.

'So, can you bring my mummy home please, Santa?'

Blake shuffled forward in his throne. He looked pensive.

'Sweetheart, Santa can't make people do things. I wish I could. It's not the same as wishing for a bike or a doll's house.'

Natalie nodded, making her thick, straight fringe shake.

Blake shuffled round on this throne and shot me a cautious look, before turning all his attention back to Natalie. 'But I'm sure that once your mummy has her holiday, she will come straight home. And I bet she's been thinking about you and your daddy a lot.'

The girl's serious face eased into a small, pleased smile.

I leant forward and plucked a present, wrapped in lilac and silver paper, from inside Santa's sack and knelt down in front of her. 'Here you are. Merry Christmas.'

Miss Turner offered us both awkward but appreciative smiles and ushered Natalie back out of the grotto to join her classmates in the hall, who were bouncing around to 'Nellie the Elephant'.

'You were lovely with that little girl,' I admitted to Blake.

He twisted round, surprised, as he sat on Santa's grand throne. 'Well, don't sound so shocked. Anyone would think I was some sort of ogre.'

I flexed both my brows.

It was the turn of one of the rowdy blond boys next. He came bounding up to Blake, breaking the emotional hush. He informed him that his name was Caleb and proceeded to reel off a dizzying list of everything from a new football and goal posts to the latest mobile, that he wanted for Christmas.

At the end of the party, Blake and I gratefully gulped down a cup of strong coffee each, supplied by Mrs Stritch, together with generous slices of Christmas cake. We were both rather frazzled around the edges.

We had ended up having to contend with two girls arguing over the same gift, a boy who interrogated Blake/Santa about what he fed his reindeer and another little boy who insisted that underneath his wig and beard, Blake was in fact his Uncle Keith.

We were both relieved to call it a day and get changed!

I emerged out of the ladies' toilets, my hair still loose and hanging in light-brown waves past my shoulders. I was in my silky grey shirt and dark denim jeans again. The offending elf outfit was draped over one arm.

I rounded the corner and was back inside the school hall, with its splashes of children's paintings, decorations and winking Christmas tree.

Blake had changed out of his Santa outfit and was now dressed back in his civvies of a chunky cable-knit cream jumper and black jeans.

He was also engaged in an animated conversation with Miss Turner, the pretty blonde teacher. I noticed him rooting around inside his back pocket and handing her one of his business cards.

She flushed a fetching shade of pink. Was Blake asking her out? Was she asking him out?

I pretended to fish about in my shoulder bag and reach for my phone. Not that I was at all bothered or interested in what Blake did. It was none of my business. Brave woman if she was entertaining romantic thoughts about him. Good luck to her.

Blake strode back over to me and we made our way out of the school and towards our respective cars.

I didn't ask Blake about Miss Turner and he didn't offer

any explanation, as we got ready to drive off separately. He seemed preoccupied. He just muttered something about it being 'one hell of an afternoon' and then said bye and drove off.

I made my way back to the town, thinking of Natalie and wishing her and her father a lovely Christmas.

The next morning, I'd just finished breakfast and was about to hit social media to update the Magical Occasions Cabins accounts with photos I had taken of the made over cabins, when my mobile erupted with a number I didn't recognise.

'Hello?'

'Hi. Is that Lottie Grant?' asked a female voice.

'Yes. Who is this?'

'It's Sarah Turner. Miss Turner from school?'

The call threw me for a few seconds. 'Oh hi. Yes. Sorry. How are you?'

'I'm very good, thanks. I got your number from your mum at Christmas Crackers. I hope that's ok and I'm not troubling you at all.'

'Yes. No problem at all.' I fiddled with one of my pens on the kitchen table. 'So how can I help you?'

'I tried to call Blake but he isn't picking up.'

I glanced at my glowing laptop screen. 'Right.' I tried to ignore a stab of irritation. Miss Turner had tried to call Blake. He had given her his business card. It all pointed to a mutual attraction. No doubt she was calling me because she was keen to speak to him to arrange a date.

I refocused on what she was saying.

'First of all, I just wanted to thank you both again for yesterday. The children had a fantastic time.'

'Don't mention it. You're very welcome.'

'Well, what you both did was appreciated by everyone.' Then she said, 'The reason I'm ringing is because I wanted to ask you if you knew anything about a present left for little Natalie Scott this morning here at the school?'

I clicked on the cabins' Twitter account. 'A present? No, I don't know anything about that. What sort of present?'

'A very lovely and generous one,' replied Miss Turner. 'It's a Santa sleigh ride around Loch Strathe, followed by a slap-up lunch for Natalie and her dad in The Heather Grove.'

'The Heather Grove?' I repeated. 'Wow! That gorgeous new restaurant in town?'

'Yes. There was a gold envelope, topped with a red ribbon, handed in to the school office for Natalie this morning.'

'And who is it from?' I asked, intrigued.

'The tag on it just says, "From Santa" but I think we can work out who that is.'

Miss Turner allowed her words to hang.

I blinked, turning over what she meant. 'It was from Blake?'

'That's what I'm thinking. Mrs Cash, who's always in early, said we had a prompt delivery of stationery. When the delivery driver came in, he said a guy in a hoodie approached him, thrust an envelope at him and asked him to hand it in to the school office on his behalf. Then he disappeared.'

Was it Blake? It sounded like it. My mouth popped open, stunned. I processed this kind, caring gesture. Shocked didn't even begin to describe how I felt on hearing about this. Talk about left field. I realised I was almost stuttering. 'Are you sure about this? Did the delivery guy get a look at the hoodie-wearing man at all?'

'A very brief one. He said the chap was tall, muscular and looked like he had a beard. It must have been Blake. There's no other explanation.'

I sank back in my kitchen chair, thrown. My mind shot back to Blake's reaction when he heard Natalie's story and the way he had tried to reassure and comfort the little girl.

'You've got a good one there,' sighed Miss Turner, shattering my thoughts. 'I don't suppose he has a twin brother?'

'Sorry?'

'Blake,' she clarified.

I realised what she meant. I shot forward in my chair, flustered. 'Oh no. We're not... you know... I mean, we aren't... together. We're not a couple.'

'Oh, sorry,' she apologised. 'I just assumed...'

'Not a problem. No. We're just work colleagues.'

Miss Turner rounded off the call. 'Oh, I see.' Her voice lifted with relief. 'Well, sorry for bothering you. Thank you again to both of you for yesterday and if you see Blake, please pass on my grateful thanks to him for doing this. You should have seen Natalie's face when she opened that envelope!'

The call ended and I sat there in my kitchen for a few more moments, turning over everything in my head. So, Blake had arranged all that for Natalie and her dad? What a lovely and thoughtful thing to do. She seemed such a sweet little girl and her story must have really affected him.

I fiddled with my mouse, not paying attention to my laptop screen. I was still stunned. That wasn't the Blake Dempster I knew. Or at least, who I thought I knew. I felt off-kilter, all at once.

I finished loading up the new cabin photographs I'd taken and then gathered my things together to head up to Rowan Moore House to catch up with Max and Stephanie.

I also wanted to drop in on Kim to get details about the families and couples who had reserved the cabins over Christmas.

But my journey up there was preoccupied by Blake and what he had done for that little girl and her father. Maybe there was a heart buried underneath that surly exterior after all.

I was just pulling up in my car outside Rowan Moore House when I caught sight of Blake striding past. He was throwing a bulky backpack on.

I jumped out of my car and locked it. 'Blake? Hold on a second. Can I have a quick word please?'

He squinted over at me in the morning light.

I hurried towards him. 'Sarah Turner just called me. She tried to ring you.'

'Who?'

'Sarah Turner? Natalie's teacher from Craig Brae Primary School?'

Blake scratched his beard. 'Oh. Right. Yes.'

'Someone left a gorgeous Christmas present for that little girl and her father at the school office this morning.'

Blake continued to look down at me, his expression unreadable. 'Did they?'

'Yep. It's a reindeer sleigh ride around Loch Strathe and then lunch at a gorgeous new restaurant in town.'

Blake continued with his poker face. 'Ok. Sounds like a nice gift.'

'It was signed "from Santa".'

'That makes sense, I suppose,' he said, his expression impassive. 'It is coming up to Christmas, as you know, and as you take great delight in reminding us all.'

I angled my head to one side. 'Stop pretending. It was you, wasn't it? You arranged all that for Natalie.'

Blake broke eye contact with me and gazed off past my shoulder.

'What a wonderful thing to do.'

'I didn't say it was me.'

'You didn't have to.'

He gazed down at me with those penetrating, dark chocolate-brown eyes of his. Then he gathered himself. 'Yes, well, it's no biggie,' he insisted, adjusting his backpack.

'I disagree. I think it is. I've been thinking about her a lot too.' I paused. 'She got to you, didn't she? Natalie, I mean.'

The wind ruffled through his dark hair. I blinked up at him. He looked like he was on the brink of saying something, but then snatched it back. 'I felt a bit sorry for the kid, ok? That's it. It's almost Christmas, perish the thought. I just thought I would do something for her and her father. End of. Now, if you'll excuse me, I've got to get back to the office to arrange another tourist walk.'

Then he strode back to his car, threw his backpack on the back seat and shot off down the winding drive and away from Rowan Moore House.

Chapter Fifteen

It was only ten days now until Christmas and Craig Brae was buzzing.

Christmas Crackers looked like it had been ransacked during a daring raid. A lot of the shelves were bare, or emptying at a rapid rate. Mum and Orla were doing all they could to sell off as much of the stock as they could before the 31st.

I thought of how the shop had looked only a month or so ago: like a spangly, glittery craft box that had been upended. It was starting to look like a shell of its former self.

Vivian had informed us that her detached cottage had been sold to an affluent young couple from the London area, who were planning on using it as a holiday home, so she could get on with final arrangements for heading to the States with Ridley. 'At least that's one less thing to worry about,' she'd sighed during her afternoon visit. 'And now that I know the house sale is going through, please don't hesitate to let me know what else needs doing.'

I could only imagine how that news about yet more second homers would be received in the area!

Things were moving at pace elsewhere too. Representatives from Ronaldo's had dropped by Christmas Crackers to introduce themselves and to take a look around.

The man and woman, both in their thirties and well dressed, had been polite and professional, but it was clear they were intent on making their mark and had ambitious plans for transforming the shop into a rustic Italian restaurant to reflect their other city-based ones.

Once they had taken measurements and chatted to Mum, Orla and me, they departed.

I was left with an empty pang of sadness after their visit, but then acceptance took over.

Once they had set off, I made my way up to the cabins and Rowan Moore House to make sure Ruth was aware of which families were arriving on Christmas Eve and in which cabins our guests would be staying and for how long.

I hadn't seen much of Blake over the past week, since his surprising and heart-warming gift to Natalie and her dad. I'd caught glimpses of him a couple of times when he had come up to meet with Max and Stephanie. He had waved and smiled, asked how I was and then moved on. I suppose that was a big improvement on how we had been with each other before.

In the meantime, I'd managed to come up with some wording for the launch of the naming of the cabins competition and wanted to run it past Max and Stephanie:

Magical Occasions Cabins are just that – magical!

And that's why we want you to come up with an original and appealing name for each of our four wonderful, cosy cabins.

Take a look at the photos of our revamped cabins and then come up with a name that suits each one.

You might want to take inspiration from nature, book characters, countries or cities around the world. It's totally up to you. Just use your imagination!

Once you have your four suggestions, please email your entries to the following email address with your name, address, and a contact telephone number, no later than 3pm on Christmas Eve.

We will choose the four names we like the best and the winner will receive a three-night stay for a family of four in the cabin of their choice, together with a New Year Hamper, kindly donated by Mrs Crill of Sugar 'n' Spice bakery and Mr Hughes, owner of Pop the Cork, both local and respected businesses in Craig Brae.

These luxurious hampers contain everything from delicious lemon shortbread, two bottles of champagne and three delicious fresh loaves, to water crackers, Scottish salmon and a selection of cheeses.

So go and take a look at the photos of the cabins on the Magical Occasions Cabins, website and social media accounts, get your thinking caps on and come up with names we won't be able to resist.

Good luck!

Max and Stephanie approved the competition wording straight away, saying they thought it was a great idea and another perfect way to engage with the local community and get them involved.

'I'll get that typed up and posted up on the website and social media this afternoon,' I assured them. 'Thank you.'

Rowan Moore House was like the cover of a Christmas card.

Stephanie had two smaller Christmas trees, decked with simple gold lights, stationed at the entrance, together with strands of holly, studded with red ribbons, framing the archway of the door.

Inside the huge hallway, she had erected another larger tree. This one was draped in the rose-gold lights and decorations she had bought from Christmas Crackers.

I dropped by Kim's office to collect details about the guests arriving on Christmas Eve. Then I decided to take a wander up to the cabins before I headed back.

I still wasn't relishing saying a final goodbye to Christmas Crackers. In fact, the closer it came, the more I found myself dreading it, but not quite as much now as I had been. At least I had the cabins to focus on. They were definitely taking the sting out of the unhappy state of affairs. I was so grateful to Mum for all her extra help, as well as Orla and Vivian for throwing themselves into the deep end, and to Stephanie and Max for trusting in me and giving me this opportunity in the first place.

As I trampled over the dry twigs in my long boots, the sky, pushing through the ceiling of woodland, churned with low, heavy clouds and the wind chill was brisk and biting.

Snow on the way, perhaps? I crinkled my nose. There was a running joke in the family that I could 'smell snow'. I used to insist I could and Mum and Dad would tease me about it.

I reached the four cabins and stopped to appreciate the sparkling wreaths on each of the doors, the Christmas trees sat on their porches and through their windows I could see their individual interiors: pastel blues, golds, burgundy and apple greens.

Wooden soldiers winked out at me; encrusted star

ornaments and festive decorations shimmered through the glass.

I heaved a sigh of relief, mingled with apprehension. I could only hope our guests appreciated it!

I bundled myself deeper into my long belted coat. The wind from the east was cutting a chillier swathe through the trees.

I decided to start making my way back home so I could crack on with updating the website and socials with details about the cabin names competition, when something landed on top of my head.

My hand, toasty in gloves, reached up. I lowered my arm to see a couple of snowflakes sitting on my coat sleeve, before they vanished.

'Snow!' I gasped aloud, snapping my head to gaze up at the sky.

The bank of moody grey clouds of moments ago had given way to a swathe of snowflakes floating down, shrouding everything in a veil of white.

I shot out both hands now, marvelling at the diamond flakes. They were like white feathers, delicate and fluttery.

I threw my head back, closed my eyes for a few seconds and opened my mouth. The chilly flakes shimmied in, momentarily taking my breath away.

I let out a short laugh, as the snow continued to tickle my tongue. They tasted sparkly, like I imagined diamonds or stars would.

'What are you doing?'

I jumped at the voice and whirled round.

Blake was standing there watching me, looking confused.

'Enjoying the snow,' I gulped, the flakes tickling my lashes as I blinked across at him. 'What are you doing up here? Bumping into you seems to be becoming a bit of a habit.'

His face was impassive. 'Getting details of who is arriving on Christmas Eve and who has booked themselves on one of my festive rambles.' He arched a brow. 'Nice to see you're busy.'

I pulled a sarcastic face at him. 'Sometimes it's good to just savour the moment.' The snow continued to spin down, flakes clotting in my ponytail. 'You should try it sometime.'

'Try what?'

I flung my head back and stuck out my tongue. 'Having fun. It's catching.'

'What, like the flu?'

More flakes swayed down and landed on it, zinging and chilly. I straightened up. 'Try this. Go on. Catch snowflakes in your mouth. I used to do this with my dad when I was little.'

'So, he's Christmas obsessed too, is he? What is it about this town? It must be catching.'

My smile withered. I swallowed a lump in my throat. 'He was. We lost him suddenly eighteen months ago now.'

Blake's sarcastic expression collapsed. 'Shit. Oh God. I'm sorry.'

'It's ok. My mum and I are still trying to adjust to life without him and get on with things.'

'Lottie, I would never have—'

'I know. There's no need to apologise.'

There was an awkward silence, except for the crisp snow carpeting everything around us.

Blake flashed me a look, before jerking one thumb over his shoulder. It looked like he was busy trying to find the right words. 'I can't believe I'm about to say this and as much as it pains me to do so, those cabins are looking good.'

I performed an exaggerated blink. 'Good grief. Just give me a second to process this. Was that a compliment?'

Blake's black brows flexed under his woolly hat. His lips twitched. 'Don't get used to it. There won't be another one for three years.'

'Now that I can believe.'

He glanced down at his feet for a few seconds. Then he raised his eyes to mine. 'Look, Lottie, the truth is, I was hoping I'd find you here.'

'Oh?'

He flashed me a look from under his thrusting black lashes. There it was again: that slightly discomfited glint in his eyes. 'I should never have gone to Max like that, complaining about your plans for the cabins. I don't know what I was thinking.' He shook his head. 'That wasn't my finest hour.'

I allowed his apology to sink in while the snow spun around us. I didn't know what I was more taken aback by: the sudden snowfall, Blake's generosity to Natalie and her dad or Blake saying that he was sorry. I noticed a couple of flakes landing in his thick, dark beard.

My thoughts reeled. 'So why did you?' I asked.

'Why did I what?'

'Why did you email Max and say you didn't think my themed ideas were a good suggestion?'

Blake buried his hands deeper into his ski-jacket pockets. His dark eyes glowed. 'It wasn't aimed at you, nor was it me trying to upset you. I'm sorry that it did.'

'But that doesn't explain why you did it?'

He made a frustrated sigh. 'If I'm being honest, I've never really had a great relationship with that kind of thing.'

'What kind of thing?'

He rubbed the back of his neck as he considered my question. 'Celebrations, Christmas…'

'Right.' I wasn't sure exactly what he was hinting at but the very fact Blake was talking without his usual growl, was a big leap.

'So, you complained to Max about my ideas because you don't like Christmas?'

Blake flashed me a guilty look through the tumbling snowflakes. 'I mean, if I'm being honest, I thought everything you were suggesting to the Styleses was rather over the top.'

'Why, thank you so much!' I remarked. 'And there he is. Thank goodness for that. I wondered what you had done with the real Blake Dempster there for a moment.'

Blake's lips almost slid into a smile.

'So, you're not into Christmas?' I prompted again, my curiosity soaring.

Blake gave the briefest of nods. 'No. I'm not. In fact, that's an understatement.' He paused. 'All the lovey-dovey romantic sentiment of it… well… it just doesn't sit well with me.'

Wow. I turned over what he had just said.

I bit my lip and wondered if I should push it. Should I ask him why? What was it about this time of year he didn't like? I debated whether now would be a good time to broach the subject with him. Why on earth didn't he like the festive season? What had Christmas ever done to him?

I studied him, questions spinning through my head that I so wanted to ask him. There was a softer side to Blake. He had shown it by giving that gorgeous gift to Natalie and her dad.

Then there was that outdoor centre for deprived children he had helped set up, that Max had mentioned before. There were tantalising glimpses of another side to him underneath the bravado. Flashes of who he really was were there under the armour, but he seemed unwilling to acknowledge this other part of him even existed. But would he be prepared to share it with me now?

I opened my mouth to ask, but as though anticipating what I was about to do, Blake let out a defeated sigh and then strode up beside me.

I watched as he stood there for a few moments, deliberating what to do. Then he surprised me by swiping off his woolly hat, throwing his dark head back and allowing the flakes to caress his upturned face.

His dark, spikey lashes fluttered as he then poked out his tongue and savoured the falling flakes.

I found myself unable to pull my eyes away from his compelling profile: the long, regal nose, his hooded lids and his thick, dark hair, which was turning damp with the snow. My eyes shifted to his beard. What would he look like clean shaven? What was the rest of his face like underneath all that hair? I bet he was handsome, even more handsome without his beard…

Bloody hell! Where was all this coming from?! I didn't like him! The man was a sour-faced grump! My cheeks sizzled as Blake stopped ingesting the snow. *Stop staring at him, for goodness' sake! You'll freak him out.*

He turned to look at me. I stood, self-conscious and suddenly feeling clumsy in my own skin. Oh bugger. Had he realised what I was doing? Did he know what I had been thinking just now, that I had been imagining him without his beard? And why was I thinking about that anyway? What was wrong with me?

I cleared my throat. and blinked away more thoughts about beards. 'You know what I think?' I said after a prolonged pause, hoping the woodland air would take the stinging blush from my cheeks.

'Something tells me I'm about to find out.'

'I think you have more of the Christmas spirit in you than you care to admit.'

Blake pinned me to the spot with those black eyes of his. 'How dare you!'

I couldn't help it. My face broke into a grin.

'And what makes you say that?'

I put one hand out and let the flakes decorate my gloved fingers again. 'What you did for that little girl and her dad.'

Blake pulled a face. 'Oh, not that again.'

'I know! I know. You don't want me to go on about it and I won't. But not everyone would have even thought of doing such a caring and generous thing.'

Blake shrugged his broad shoulders under his black ski jacket. 'I happen to know the guy who manages that restaurant. It's not a big deal.'

Flecks of snow dusted his woolly hat as his fingers tightened around it.

'You don't like accepting compliments, do you?'

Blake eyed me levelly. 'It depends on what the compliment is and who's giving it.' His lips curved upwards with amusement.' If you were to tell me you found me madly attractive and that my eyes reminded you of melted chocolate, I'd take it.'

I let out a bark of self-conscious laughter. 'I bet you would. As if that's going to happen!'

His mouth tilted into a gorgeous lopsided smile.

I realised I was doing it again – staring at him – and forced my attention away to the deepening snow around us. Why was I suddenly acting all weird?

'So, stuffed shirt,' I teased, hoping I sounded normal.

'Stuffed shirt?' echoed Blake, cocking one brow.

'Copy me.'

'Why? What are you going to do now?'

Distracting myself from more thoughts about what Blake might look like without his beard, I dumped my bag down beside me, lay down flat in the snow and began to flap my arms up and down. Making snow angels never got boring. 'Care to join me?' I asked.

Blake stared down at me lying there. His eyes shone with what looked like a mix of amusement and disbelief. 'I hope I don't see anyone I know. My reputation will end up in tatters.'

'Oh, stop grumbling and get down here.' As soon as the words left my mouth, I knew I had to clarify it. 'I mean, come and lie beside me.' Shit! That sounded like a come-on as well. I wanted to scoop up some snow and slap it onto my heated cheeks. 'I mean, come and be a snow angel.'

Blake glanced around himself.

'What? Are you chicken?'

He gave me a withering look.

'Oh, don't tell me the big, brave mountaineer is frightened of snow angels?'

Blake posed like Superman, which made me yelp with laughter. 'Certainly not.' He gazed down at me. 'Well, if it stops you from assassinating my character.'

Now it was my turn to offer him a smile.

Blake dumped his rucksack on the ground and came and lay down beside me, raising his arms up and down as the snow continued to wrap us both in its crisp whiteness.

'See? This time of year isn't so bad after all, is it?' I asked him, as the wet, chilly snow seeped against our coats while we lay there side by side.

'Don't push your luck,' frowned Blake with fake annoyance. 'I still think I'd much rather have root canal treatment than have anything to do with Christmas, but…' His voice tailed off and he rolled his eyes. He gave several more flaps of his muscular arms in the snow, which made me laugh.

He narrowed his eyes at me. 'What? Why are you laughing at me?'

'You look more like a buzzard trying to take off than an angel.'

Blake pushed himself up onto one elbow to look at me lying there beside him. He drank in my face. 'Maybe that's because I'm no angel.'

My heart took off in my chest. I swallowed and pushed myself upright. I suddenly felt all self-conscious and hot. I couldn't look at him.

After a few moments' hesitation, I raised my eyes to his.

He was watching me. Then he made a big show of looking at his watch. 'Ok. Well. Right. I'd better be off. I've got a pile of paperwork to do.'

He unzipped his ski jacket to give it a dust off from the snow and straightened his fisherman's jumper. I was sure I caught a glimpse of what looked like a black Marvel T-shirt underneath. I squinted at what was on his T-shirt. 'Is that Spider-Man?'

'It certainly is. The best superhero out there.' He raised his barley-coloured knitted jumper to reveal a picture of Spider-Man crouching down, with one wrist extended out in his usual pose.

I tried not to be side tracked by the teasing glimpse of his taught stomach and smattering of dark hair. I hoped my voice hadn't transformed into a ridiculous squeak. 'What makes you say that?'

Blake looked at me, incredulous. 'Really? You even have to ask that question?' He lowered his jumper again and crossed his arms as he sat there. 'He has a dry sense of humour and he isn't invincible. He has to work hard to beat the bad guy.'

'Like you have to work hard to conquer all those mountains you climb?'

His expression softened. 'I guess so.' He examined me. 'So, who's your favourite superhero then?'

'Deadpool.'

'Oh, interesting choice. Why's that then?'

'Because he's funny, fiercely loyal – oh, and he loves Mexican food.'

Blake remained sitting beside me for a few more moments, in no hurry to move. Our eyes shone across at one another, with just the glow of the empty cabins and the woodland for company. Finally, he scrambled to his feet. 'Though I would love to sit and talk to you about superheroes all day, I suppose I'd better go. No rest for the wicked.'

Oh, help me, Lord. There was that sexy twinkle again.

'Catch up with you soon, Christmas fairy.'

Blake dusted the snow from his jeans, hoisted his backpack over his shoulders and gave me a mock salute as he strode away through a flurry of snow.

I watched him leave, a weight of sudden disappointment taking me by surprise. I hadn't wanted him to go. Not yet.

Ok, so that had been unexpected.

Blake's comments about Christmas bounced around in my head. Why did he dislike it so much? He was as deep as Loch Strathe.

I thought again of just a few moments ago, when his lids were fluttering and the snowflakes were fringing his lashes and beard; when he grinned and his face lit up; the feathery creases at his eyes. There was his apology too, about complaining to Max about my ideas for the cabins. It was such a pity he seemed to have such a downer on this time of year. I realised I wanted him to confide in me about it. Very much. There was so much he wasn't telling me. But why?

I tried to ignore the way my heart was still fizzing in my chest at the proximity of him just now and sprang to my feet. Like I needed to get involved with anyone after my disastrous relationship with Kyle! Christmas fever. That's what it was I was feeling.

The snow was spiralling over the cabins, lacing them with icing sugar, but it wasn't spinning from the sky quite as fast as it had been.

I bit my lip. My insides were jumping.

I was beginning to think there was a lot more tenderness to Blake than he cared to admit. It just seemed such a shame that he was carrying this pessimistic view of this time of year. If only he would let me show him how magical Christmas could be.

Chapter Sixteen

Craig Brae reminded me of a delectable cake the next morning, sandwiched between layers of snow, like frosted icing.

I stood for a few minutes by my sitting room window, marvelling at the Christmas trees glistening in the houses and in the distance, the roofs and pavements of the main street smudged with amber street lamps, before they were switched off until the evening.

My thoughts harped back to my conversation yesterday with Blake up at the cabins.

I couldn't believe my eyes when he joined me in the snow and lay beside me, all broad chest and long legs, making snow angels; the way he had thrown his head back to swallow the flakes.

I tried not to dwell on his long lashes fluttering and his muscular body inches away from me. It was as though the breath had been stolen from me.

Nope. Not going there.

I had to keep all this in perspective. We were colleagues. Yes, I found him very physically attractive. I was certain most other women would too. You would be crazy not to. But I had to think logically about it all. I'd had enough of Christmas pessimists to last me a lifetime, thanks to Kyle.

My track record of putting my faith in people was a poor one.

I wasn't prepared to put myself in the firing line to be hurt again.

I'd done a lot of thinking last night. I had come to the conclusion that it had been the romance of the cabins, the snow, the festive decorations, a handsome man... Yes, the combination of all of that had made me feel a bit... well... odd. It wasn't anything else. Definitely not. I also had my new job with the Styleses to focus on and I was determined to make that a success.

But the fact that Blake disliked Christmas so much still gnawed at me. Could it be anything to do with that woman he had been having that tense phone conversation with in the woods? Amy, was it? Or perhaps he was like Kyle; some people just didn't enjoy this time of year and that was that. But there was something about his attitude towards this time of year and his demeanour towards anything remotely festive, that made me think there could be more to it than just a simple grump about Christmas.

I reached for my mug of tea and took a considered sip. I had to drop by the local newspaper office, the *Craig Brae Chronicle*, to hand in the advert that Max, Stephanie and I had composed to publicise the cabins. It was terrific that all four cabins were occupied over Christmas and New Year, but we had to secure many more reservations after that, going well into next year. It would be a case of building our brand, word of mouth and getting our name out there.

We couldn't afford to have the cabins sitting empty for the next six months. We had secured some bookings going into spring and the summer months, but I wanted to try and look ahead as much as we could. I was already brainstorming more ideas about what we could do around Halloween. I allowed myself a small, optimistic smile. *Lottie Grant, you are making headway.*

My thoughts moved on from the cabins and back to Christmas. The newspaper office was just a five-minute walk from Rock Solid Ramblings. I could drop by and see Blake after placing the advert. And if I happened to take some mince pies, a yule log, maybe some decorations and an advent calendar with me, what harm would it do? Just as work colleagues, of course. Ok, he might send me packing, but then again, he might secretly appreciate it. Maybe he just needed someone to give him a gentle nudge and let him see how wonderful this time of year could be? Then he might begin to change his mind and open up a bit more.

I downed the rest of my tea and hurried to the shower, before throwing on my black fitted trousers and cream jumper, with my pale-pink shirt underneath. I was well aware of how bitter Craig Brae winters could be and the wind chill was often biting at this time of year. Layers were the solution.

I decided not to take the car. The roads were slushy and I'd witnessed a couple of vehicles perform impressive spins already that morning from my sitting room window. It would be much safer to walk and I could drop in to the supermarket for my Christmas purchases for Blake on the way.

I deposited the advert into the newspaper office to appear

in this week's edition and then popped into the corner shop on the way to see Blake.

Just like in every other business in the town, the Craig Brae Cabin was no different. It was a newsagents, but was like a Tardis inside, crammed with not only newspapers and magazines, but greetings cards, a selection of food and confectionary.

Tinsel dangled everywhere, fairy lights flashed around the edge of the shop window and the shelves at the rear of the shop were bursting with everything festive from Christmas puddings to gingerbread men.

I perused the assortment of mince pies before deciding on a pack of six crumble-topped ones, filled with salted caramel. I also plopped a gorgeous, thick chocolate yule log, topped with a sweet little snowman and a sprig of holly, into my basket.

From the couple of advent calendars remaining on the shelves, I opted for a Cadbury's one, smothered in glitter and depicting Santa and Rudolph negotiating a snowy roof.

Then it was time to take a look at the corner shop decorations that were for sale. I had toyed with the idea of getting them from Christmas Crackers, but most of the nicer items had gone and I reminded myself how important it was to support other local businesses anyway.

Like the advent calendars, most of the decorations had already been snapped up, but there were several strands of postbox-red and bottle-green tinsel left, so I scooped them into my basket, together with four strands of matching red and green Christmas lights.

Mr McBain, the owner of the Craig Brae Cabin, had three miniature Christmas trees remaining on the counter for sale, dusted with fake snow and their pots tied with a fancy red ribbon.

'I'll take one of these as well, Mr McBain.' I smiled, appreciating Jethro Tull's 'Ring Out, Solstice Bells' drizzling out of the shop radio.

Mr McBain glinted from behind his half-moon spectacles. 'Dear me lass, I would have thought you would have been well prepared by now..'

'I am,' I confided, pulling my purse from my shoulder bag. 'These are for a friend.'

I heard myself saying the words and a strange pang hit me in the chest. It sounded odd. It felt odd too.

I recalled his apology from yesterday and the way his eyes reminded me of swirling dark chocolate…

I gave my head a severe mental shake and forced myself to concentrate on fetching my credit card from my purse.

I paid for my purchases and set off down the main street, with the council Christmas decorations glowing above my head and down onto the snow-clotted road and pavements.

The happy twinkle from shop displays threw out lively amber pools from their doorsteps and people bustled past, clutching gifts they had just bought.

My boots trampled through the snow, taking me towards the gritted set of steps and Blake's office.

I steeled myself and glanced down at my bulging shopping bag. Ok. Had I thought this through? No. Not really. Had this been such a great idea after all? Was I going to come across as some interfering, parochial busybody?

Oh God. I hadn't thought this through at all. Still, I'd been and bought all this now. I didn't want it to go to waste.

My gloved hand dug deeper into the shopping bag. I was

hoping Blake would accept them in the spirit with which they were intended.

As I began ascending the steps towards Rock Solid Ramblings' wood and glass entrance, a poster, tied to a nearby lamp post, was advertising the Craig Brae Christmas Market this coming Saturday. Goodness! I had been so preoccupied with Christmas Crackers and the cabins, I had forgotten all about it.

I made a mental note to drop by the market. That could be another great opportunity to hand out more fliers about the cabins. It was a mainstay in the Craig Brae festive calendar. Anyone who was anyone in the retail business in the surrounding area made sure they got involved.

As well as the local shops, local artists in jewellery, ceramics, soaps, condiments and scented candles usually pitched up a stall too.

A melancholy thought took hold. Christmas Crackers wouldn't be there at the market this year. Nor any year after that.

It had been a wonderful day for the shop.

I dismissed the lingering notion of making a voodoo doll in the guise of unscrupulous landlords and sticking nine hundred pins it. *Christmas thoughts, Lottie! This is supposed to be the time of year for forgiveness and kindness.*

My stomach stunned me by performing a sudden and impressive forward roll as I opened the swing doors and headed in to see Blake.

I ignored it. I was probably hungry.

As I suspected, Blake's business possessed not a trace of Christmas. Everything was the same as the first time I barrelled in here to exchange words with him about his complaint to Max. My cheeks stung at the memory.

I glanced around. Not a strand of tinsel, a bauble nor a shred of holly to be seen. It was still all dramatic photographs of soaring mountain peaks and racks of hiking clothing and equipment.

He was on the phone when I entered. He swung round, mouthed 'Hi' and indicted he would be finishing his call in a few moments.

My hand gripped the carrier bag handle that bit tighter.

He finished his phone call and leant against the reception desk. 'Sorry about that. Is this a social call or do you wish to book my services? For a ramble, I mean,' he added, deadpan.

I hoped I wasn't pinking up again. 'It's a social call.' I raised the bag and waggled it in front of him.

'What's in there?'

'Take a look.'

Blake accepted the bag and investigated its contents. He looked back up at me, his face impassive, but the dark eyes glittered. 'Are you trying to tell me something?'

I gestured around at the wall-mounted TV running relentless climbing adverts and his couple of mannequins decked out in the latest snow gear. 'I hope you don't think I'm being too forward, but I thought you might like to make this place a bit more festive.'

Blake plucked out a strand of the red tinsel. Then he investigated the other contents of the bag. He looked back up at me, taken aback. 'You got all this for me? For this place?'

My cheeks stung. Realisation gripped me. What the hell had been going through my head when I was performing Supermarket Sweep and stuffing all those festive goodies into my basket? I must have experienced some temporary leave of my senses. Blake had made it plain that he had no time for Christmas and yet here I was, clutching all this paraphernalia and offering to turn his business space into a glitterball. What had I been thinking? What was I hoping to achieve by bringing him these festive goodies? Just because I was Christmas obsessed, I wanted everybody else to be too – especially him.

It didn't sit right with me, that someone like him, who was so thoughtful and caring underneath the bluster, should have such a vehement dislike of this time of year.

I stared at the carrier bag and what was inside it. Oh shit. Was I was coming across as the local curtain twitcher, sticking her nose in where it wasn't wanted?

That was the very last thing I wanted Blake to think.

I should run out the door and rewind.

I took an embarrassed step backwards. 'I shouldn't have done this,' I blurted. 'I don't know what I was thinking.' I extended one hand for the carrier bag. 'I'm so sorry. I should have respected your decision and not come barrelling in here with enough mince pies and chocolate yule log to feed the whole of Hampden Stadium.'

Blake continued to look at me.

'I don't know what came over me. I'm not usually like this, all impulsive and wading in there.'

He arched one brow. 'Aren't you?'

'Ok. That's not true. I am. But I shouldn't be. Or at least I shouldn't be in this situation.'

I gestured for him to return the bulging contents of the carrier bag.

Blake eyed me. 'What are you doing?'

'Mum can use them.'

Blake flicked me a look from under his fencing brows. He peered into the bag again and then back at me. 'No, it's ok,' he said after several seconds. 'Now that I've clocked all this lot, I'm hungry, so good luck trying to take them back.'

'You're just saying that.'

'No, I'm not. I'm surprised you haven't heard my stomach rumbling from over there.'

I smiled.

The silence crackled between us.

He waggled the full carrier bag. 'This is very kind of you, even though I might spontaneously combust at the sight of tinsel.' He paused. 'Please let me pay you for all of this.'

'Not at all,' I replied, flapping my gloved hand around.

Blake rolled his eyes. 'Has anyone ever told you that as well as being impulsive, you also have rather a stubborn streak?'

'Yes. Once or twice. But I think that's very hypocritical coming from you.'

'I can't argue with that.' He studied me with a quiet look of bemusement. 'Well, thank you again.'

'You're welcome.' I gestured to the bag again, feeling even more self-conscious. 'Well, I'll leave you to it.'

Blake took a step closer to me. 'And where do you think you're going? You are not depositing all this stuff on me and then taking off.'

My mouth dropped open and I closed it shut. All this had seemed like such a wonderful and fun idea earlier, scooping anything remotely Christmassy into my basket, but now...

Blake pointed to the carrier bag in his hand. 'You can help me put up the tinsel and the lights. The mince pies and the Yule log can be a reward for us to enjoy after all our hard work.'

'Are you sure?' I gave him a tentative look.

'Do you mean am I sure about converting my respectable business into a tinsel-filled hell? No. I'm not. But seeing as you're here and we have all this lot, it would be a shame to waste it.'

Blake lifted out the miniature Christmas tree next and didn't say anything. He placed it on top of his semi-circular reception desk. 'You don't happen to have brought that elf outfit too, by any chance?'

'No, I bloody well haven't,' I laughed.

Blake examined the little tree and dived back inside the carrier bag for the yule log. A slow flicker of a smile enveloped his mouth. 'Shame. That hat with the bell is rather sexy. Oh well, you can't have everything.' He jerked his dark head. 'Come on then, Ms Grant. Tell you what, let's have a cuppa first and some of these goodies and then you can help me transform this place into a fairground attraction? No point working on an empty stomach.'

I tucked into a generous slice of the yule log, while Blake devoured one of the crumbly mince pies, washed down with a mug of builder's tea each.

I eyed him over the rim of my mug as we sat beside one another behind his reception desk. My imagination started to create tentative images again of what he might look like clean-shaven... I bet he would look gorgeous without his beard, but with a smattering of stubble...

I jerked my thoughts away. *For heaven's sake Grant, what is the matter with you?! Not this again!* What did it matter if Blake had a beard or not?

'So, when did you develop this fascination for Christmas? Have you always loved it?'

Blake's voice interrupted me and made be blink into my mug. I set it down beside me. 'It was my dad's fault. He was one of those people who would litter our front lawn with blow-up Santas, lit-up reindeer... You name it, Dad would buy it.' I gave a fond smile. 'I don't know who used to get more excited over Christmas, him or me.' I laced and unlaced my fingers together. 'My paternal grandparents were very religious and anti-Christmas frivolities, so when I came along, he told me that gave him the perfect excuse to behave like Chevy Chase in *National Lampoon's Christmas Vacation*.'

Blake sat forward, listening.

'My father told me on more than one occasion that when he was growing up, Christmas was a much more staid, low-key affair. Any presents his parents did give him, he wasn't allowed to open until after the Queen's speech at three o'clock.' I shifted in my chair, smiling at the warm memories of my dad. 'He always used to tell me that there was never any Christmas music permitted from the likes of Slade or Mud. It was strictly traditional Christmas carols.'

Blake studied me as I talked. 'I think that after the non-event Christmases he had with my grandparents, he was determined that if he ever had kids of his own, he would go full-on Christmas lights, garish decorations, party hats... "The whole nine yards," as he put it.'

I could feel my smile slipping. 'So, every Christmas was something special. It might sound corny, but it was exciting just seeing my dad laying out a glass of whisky, a mince pie and a carrot for Santa and Rudolph.'

I gathered myself together and carried on, trying to ignore

the growing lump in my throat. 'When I was little, the three of us would snuggle up on the sofa and watch the original *Scrooge* on Christmas Eve. You know, the black and white version with Alasdair Sim.' I could feel my smile returning at the memory. 'Then Mum and Dad would hang a pillowcase on my bedroom door.'

I picked up my mug again and took another sip of my tea. 'One year, my parents got hold of some fake snow, dusted it over the front doorstep and then my dad stuck his pair of wellies on and trampled about in it, to make it look like Santa had been. I wasn't supposed to see, but I crept downstairs and hid.'

Blake smiled. 'After all that, I can understand why this time of year means so much to you, Lottie.'

I realised with a jolt that he had called me by my first name, rather than *Ms Grant* like he usually did. It sounded lovely, rolling around his deep voice. I checked myself and continued talking, in the hope that my thoughts would get back onto an even keel, rather than dwelling on Blake's sexy rumble. 'Oh, that's definitely where I got my obsession from. Growing up, I started reading about Christmas traditions of old and what other countries do.'

Warming to one of my favourite subjects, I started telling Blake about other countries and their festive customs. 'In Australia, they hold a Carols by Candlelight event every Christmas Eve in a local park. People of all ages come together to sing along to carols performed by an orchestra or singer and hold candles.' I took another sip of tea. 'A goose feather Christmas tree, dyed green and decorated with small ornaments, was the first artificial German and later Victorian,

Christmas tree. They also used turkey, swan and ostrich feathers.'

I drained my tea but still clasped the mug. I realised I had been blethering on like a toddler who had just learnt to talk. 'Sorry. I can't stop going on about Christmas, once I get started.'

Blake shook his head. 'No need to apologise. I never thought I would say this, but listening to you talk about Christmas traditions with such enthusiasm and knowledge, well, it's really interesting.'

'Thank you. I think.'

We both smiled. I clasped tighter on to my empty tea mug. 'And how about you?'

Blake blinked at me. 'What about me?'

I wondered whether I might be treading on delicate ground here, but he had asked me about my love of Christmas and I had been pouring my heart out about my dad. I decided to go for it and venture onto more personal territory. 'What were your Christmases like as a kid?'

Blake's expression, which had been soft and open only a moment ago, tightened.

'Did you have any festive family rituals that you did?'

'No,' he ground out, downing the rest of his mug of tea and signalling that this particular line of questioning was off-limits. 'We didn't go in for that sort of thing.'

Whatever the reason was, he didn't want to talk about it. I shook my head. 'Look, I'm sorry. I didn't mean to upset you.'

Blake kept his eyes trained ahead of him. 'There's no need to apologise. You didn't upset me.' His expression had hardened. He was just saying that to be polite.

'I shouldn't have asked. You don't have to...'

He shook his head. 'No, it's ok.' He sat for a few moments longer, lost in thought. Then he stood up. 'Come on. Let's get this show on the road. I don't want the local kids throwing snowballs at my car and calling me Scrooge if I don't have a scrap of tinsel visible anywhere.'

I let out a laugh.

Blake put on a comic frown. 'It's nice to see the idea of me being persecuted by the local school kids is amusing you.'

'I'm just surprised they haven't done it already.'

We fetched the carrier bag and pulled out the tinsel and the lights. I began draping swathes of the tinsel around the frames of the dramatic scenery pictures and photographs on Blake's walls.

Once they were in place, we secured a strand of the red and green lights around the entrance doors, so clients would be greeted by them as they came in. There were still a few strands of the tinsel remaining, so we tied them around the branches of Blake's little tree and topped it off with some of the lights.

Then we stepped back to admire our handiwork. It wasn't Santa's Grotto, but it was much more festive and a darned sight cheerier than it had been.

'Now, I hope once I've gone, you're not going to accidentally on purpose set fire to this little lot?'

'Stop putting ideas in my head.' Blake shot me a sideways glance. 'Thank you, Lottie.'

I tried to sound blasé about it. 'You're welcome. Now, that wasn't so painful, was it?'

Blake's lips moulded into a ghost of smile. 'If you say so.'

There was an odd, charged silence. I found myself beginning to swing my arms backwards and forwards like an out-of-control propeller. Why the hell was I doing that?!

I clamped my arms back down by my sides. 'Right. I'd better be off then. I've got a radio advert to arrange now about the cabins with Craig Brae FM.'

Blake nodded. 'Sure. Thanks again for all of this.'

I tugged on my coat and slung my bag over my shoulder.

'Lottie.'

I jerked my head up.

'You probably know about it anyway. In fact, no doubt it will have been marked up in your diary for months.' Now it was Blake's turn to look somewhat uncomfortable. 'Against my better judgement, I've reserved a stand at the Christmas market on Saturday. I thought it might be a good opportunity to meet more of the locals. Then they might be less inclined to chase me with their pitchforks.'

'They only chase incomers on a Tuesday. Saturdays are the pitchfork bearers' day off, so you should be ok.'

Blake grinned, his even white teeth flashing through his beard. 'That's good to know.'

'No, seriously,' I continued, trying not to dwell on how captivating his smile was when it made an appearance. 'That's a great idea. I just hope you don't burst into flames when you hear Christmas songs or happen to smell a cranberry-scented candle.'

'It wouldn't be the first time.'

He stuffed his hands into the pockets of his dark jeans. The tight navy V-neck sweater he was wearing emphasised the sinewy muscles in his arms. I forced myself to concentrate on one of the mannequins over his shoulder.

'I take it you'll be going to the market on Saturday?' he said.

'Yes, I always do. Definitely this year, what with the cabins being launched.'

Blake nodded. 'Of course.'

He flashed me a quick look. 'So maybe I'll see you there then, on Saturday morning?'

I fiddled with my scarf, as the red and green Christmas lights flickered around us. I smiled, my cheeks flushing hot-pink for the ninetieth time. 'Maybe you will.'

Chapter Seventeen

The next few days were a cacophony of placing adverts for the cabins in regional and national newspapers and magazines and dropping by Christmas Crackers to give Mum and Orla a helping hand.

Mum had rung me to say they were swamped with customers, keen to snap up the chance of a last-minute bargain before we closed for good on New Year's Eve and was there any chance, I could ask the Styleses if I could escape from cabin business for a couple of hours? She said they could do with an extra pair of hands to help with some paperwork, re-stock the emptying shelves with more of our most popular decorations and close supplier accounts.

Max and Stephanie were very understanding about it. As the cabins were all finished and furnished, they insisted I help Mum and Orla and that it wasn't an issue, but I made them promise they would call me if they needed me.

When I arrived, Christmas Crackers was becoming a husk

of its former self. So many of the shelves were bare, except for the odd, forlorn ornament waiting to be sold.

I decided to make a start on fetching more of the cardboard boxes containing extra supplies of our most popular styles of decorations, to replenish the shelves.

The three of us stared around ourselves. 'All the advent calendars and blow-up garden decorations have gone,' Orla told me with a hint of sadness. 'Soon, all that will be left will be mismatched baubles and odds and sods.'

'I sold the last of the "Snowman family" cuddly toys this morning and because of the three-for-two offers on the star-trimmed tinsel we've been running, it's all vanished as well,' said Mum. 'I'm hoping to get rid of the last of the illuminated door wreaths and chocolate reindeer tree decorations in the next few days.'

I forced a smile. 'Thank you so much to both of you for being so supportive and understanding during all of this. I know it's been rather chaotic, what with me now working up at the lodges, so I really do appreciate it.'

I slipped one comforting arm around her slim shoulders and she nestled closer to me.

Orla wrapped her arms around herself and peered down at the contents of a nearby box. She fired up her plucked brows. 'Oh, Vivian and that dishy man of hers dropped in earlier. Have you heard the latest? The couple who bought her house are planning on installing a hot tub and a sauna in the back garden.'

'No!' gasped Mum.

'It's true. They've already contacted the council about it.' Orla tried to conceal a smile. 'Mr Frew is going around telling everyone that they'll be having sex al fresco and swinging all over the place if we aren't careful!'

Mum and I exchanged looks and started to laugh.

'Swinging from what?' I snorted.

'Exactly.'

Once our laughter subsided, I gave Mum and Orla a hug each. 'We're going to go out for a slap-up Christmas lunch when things have calmed down a bit. If Vivian is still in Craig Brae, I'll invite her too.'

I was pleased to have a chorus of enthusiastic responses to my suggestion.

'And don't forget there will be a bonus in your pay packets at the end of the month as well,' I confirmed. 'It should make things a little easier for a bit.'

I turned to Orla. 'And how is the job hunting going?'

She rolled her light-green eyes. 'Not well at the moment, but it's almost Christmas. At this time of year it's to be expected, but I'm sure I'll get something. Once the New Year comes, I'll have more luck.' She forced out a smile.

'Well, if you like, I'll keep my eyes and ears open up at the lodges and let you know if anything comes up?'

Orla nodded. 'I'd appreciate it, Lottie. Thanks.'

Mum beamed up at me with pride. 'You would have done such a sterling job as the owner of Christmas Crackers, sweetheart.'

I gave a shrug and started to make my way towards the store room to collect more baubles and tinsel to set out on the shelves. 'I would have loved that, but nothing stays the same.' Pictures of the snow-capped, illuminated lodges filled my head and a squiggle of excitement took over my stomach. For the first time, the gnawing despondency of not getting Christmas

Crackers wasn't at the forefront of my thoughts. 'Anyway, onwards and upwards.'

The Craig Brae Christmas Market was well underway.

There had been a fresh flurry of snow earlier that Saturday morning and all the stalls and canopies were laced with it.

The businesses that had rented a stall were set out down the length of the main street, which was temporarily closed to traffic to accommodate it.

Canvas flapped and rippled in the brisk December wind. There was the enthusiastic sound of Christmas songs blasting out of a few of the stalls. The council decorations shimmered down onto the market.

Everything from handmade Christmas cards and crafted soaps in a variety of delicious festive scents, such as pine and berry, to Christmas-inspired jams, marmalades and chutney, hand-painted puzzles and jigsaws, vied for people's attention. Susie, who made and sold her scented candles, had a stall there too.

I clutched more fliers I'd printed off, extolling how wonderful the cabins were and proceeded to smile and chat with the locals and visitors, in the hope of persuading them to take a leaflet and book the cabins next year.

My feet crunched on the snow. There was the tantalising, cosy aroma of roasted chestnuts and hot chocolate and the warm and spicy scent of mulled wine emanating from a couple of mobile kiosks.

I spotted Blake and my hand shot up to fluff up my loose hair under my sparkly pink beret. *Leave your hair alone*, I moaned inwardly. Then my stomach did that weird, wriggly thing again. I felt irritated with myself and tried to ignore it.

I meandered over to a stall selling picture frames and snow globes. I picked up one of the globes containing a sweet little cottage surrounded by swirling snow.

Blake's stall was the next but one down. He was chatting to a young couple with a shaggy champagne-coloured dog and hadn't spotted me.

He was wearing a black woollen hat and a long checked coat with the collar turned up. A thick grey and white scarf was knotted around his neck. He looked casual, but very attractive. Stylish even.

I found myself screwing up my eyes and trying to visualise him without his beard again. This was turning into a popular pastime of mine. Perhaps the authorities should turn it into an Olympic sport? If they did, I would be a gold medallist for sure. What was Blake's jawline like? Did he have a cleft in his chin, like Henry Cavill?

Ok. I was thinking about this way too much. I needed to get out more or start a range of new hobbies.

I dismissed any more thoughts about Blake minus his beard and waited until the couple and their dog wandered off.

I gave my coat an ineffectual tug and set my shoulders as I approached his stall.

Blake turned. His dark eyes crinkled at the corners. 'Hey.'

'Hi.'

I indicated to his stall layout as Christmas market visitors drifted up and down. There were leaflets about his hiking and rambling tours fanned out over the stand table, as well as several of the trendy drinking bottles Blake sold. There were also some of the protein bars and energy drinks he stocked. He had even brought one of his torso mannequins with him and he'd stuck a Santa hat on it.

The mannequin was sporting a pricey waterproof winter jacket for sale.

But like Rock Solid Ramblings HQ, before I rushed in with my festive goodies, there was not a Christmas decoration to be seen on his stall, apart from the lone Santa hat plonked on the mannequin's head. 'I see you've gone crazy with your stall decorations.'

Blake arched one black brow. 'We can't all be Kelly Hoppen. Or Lottie Grant.'

I grinned and glanced around. 'How's it going?'

Blake blushed under his beard and rubbed at the back of his neck. 'If truth be told, not very well. I've been here half an hour and, in that time, I've had one elderly gent come up to me to ask me the time and that couple you just saw... well, I recognised him from the hiking community.' Blake snatched up a couple of his leaflets about Rock Solid Ramblings and waggled them. 'So no, it isn't going great so far.'

My eyes flickered over Blake's stall. The other stalls surrounding us were creaking under festive lights and swirls of tinsel. 'You know what I'm about to say, don't you?'

Blake's eyes followed mine. 'Jock's Santa hat isn't enough?'

'Jock?'

'My mannequin.'

'No, I'm afraid Jock's hat isn't enough.' I pointed to the competition, glistening and flashing against the snow. 'I don't mean to be rude, but in comparison your set-up looks more like a dentist's waiting room.'

'Oh cheers.'

I gestured around. 'Look, Blake, I know you aren't a big fan of Christmas – you've said it often enough.'

Blake pulled a sarcastic face. 'I think it must be about ten minutes since I mentioned that.'

'But you aren't doing your business any favours, surrounded by all this festive competition.'

Blake watched me start to march away. 'Where are you going?'

I spun round. 'To Christmas Crackers. I'll be back in a few minutes.'

Mum and Orla were bustling up and down inside the shop when I entered. 'Just going into the storeroom to see what's left, Mum.'

She nodded over the bobbing heads of customers. 'Help yourself, sweetheart, although there won't be much to choose from.'

I whipped off my gloves and raked through a couple of the half-opened boxes.

There were a few strands of the green tinsel remaining and some of the pine animal ornaments. That would do. It wouldn't transform Blake's market stall into a Disney palace, but it would give it a bit more colour. Anything would be an improvement!

I hurried back through the market, carrying the box of decorations I'd pulled together. Blake was leaning against his stall, looking dejected. My heart sank for him. Now wasn't the time to ask him why he had no time for Christmas, although it was still niggling at me. It would be too intrusive in the middle of a festive market. And anyway, he was too preoccupied, trying to promote Rock Solid Ramblings.

I decided I might try and gently broach the subject another

time. I had wondered again whether it was just a casual irritation with this time of year, like some other people had, but his vehement dislike of it and refusing to elaborate… well, it just made me think that there must be more to it than that.

'Turn that frown upside down,' I called over to him.

Blake strode up and relieved me of the box. His eyes sparkled. 'Do you know, I think I detest that saying more than Christmas?'

'Well, that's a start,' I joked. 'I'll have you belting out "It's the most wonderful time of the year" and wearing Rudolph antlers in no time.'

Blake gave me a withering look. 'Lottie, you would have to sedate me first.' He indicated to the box and insisted he relieve me of it. It was now cradled in his sinewy arms. *Lucky box.* I blinked hard and threw that thought to the far corner of my mind.

'What have you got inside here?' he asked.

'Take a look.'

'Oh, don't tell me you've been doing your smash and grab of advent calendars and decorations again? I loved those mince pies, but if I eat any more of them, I'll be rolling down mountains, not climbing them.'

'I promise I haven't brought any more mince pies,' I laughed.

Blake opened the flaps of the cardboard box. 'Have you been raiding your own business?'

'It won't be our own business for much longer. Just a couple of weeks now.'

Blake's dark eyes glittered with sympathy. 'I'm sorry.'

'Oh, don't be. It is what it is.'

He gave me a considered look. 'Are you starting to come to terms with the closure of Christmas Crackers?'

I gazed over at him and thought about what I had been able to achieve in such a short space of time with the lodges. 'Do you know what? I think I finally am.'

I pointed to the box of decorations I had brought from the shop. 'Come on then. Take a look. We need to get cracking.'

I watched him set the box of decorations down on the stall table. He delved a hand inside and pulled out a sweet little Robin, made out of pinecones and a length of green tinsel.

'I'm sorry but we're really starting to run low on stock, so I just had to grab what I could.'

Blake shook his head. 'No need to apologise.' He stared at me. There was a charged silence. 'You seem to be making a habit of helping me out.'

My cheeks reddened. 'That's what we do around here,' I babbled. 'Community spirit and all that. Anyone who needs a hand, we all try to be there for one another.'

Our eyes stayed locked for a few more seconds.

'Anyway,' I announced, 'I thought the pinecone animals and the green tinsel tied in well with the outdoorsy aspect of what you do.'

'It does,' agreed Blake. 'Thanks.' He admired the little cone robin, before setting it down and fishing about inside the box again. This time he produced a couple of wooden foxes positioned back-to-back, each clutching a Christmas gift for one another.

I watched his long fingers trace over the pinecone and wood, caressing it. I found myself swallowing a bloody great lump in my throat.

Lottie Grant, for goodness' sake, get a grip of yourself!

What do you know about him? asked a small voice in my head. *What has he told you about himself?*

It was true. All I knew about his background was what I'd read on his website and that concentrated on his mountaineering career.

Like it said on the internet, Blake was protective of his private life. Guarded even. Any time I thought I might be finding out a little about him, he would haul the shutters down.

We busied ourselves setting out the ornaments across the stall, before wrapping and winding the poles of the stall in the green tinsel and sitting the little battery-operated string of white fairy lights along the edge of the stall table and across the canvas canopy.

It looked so much prettier and eye catching.

We waited.

The improvements to Blake's stall attracted more attention, but he was still lacking any concrete expressions of interest, let alone bookings. Of course, he had the reservations from the cabin occupants up at Rowan Moore House over Christmas, but I knew he couldn't rely on those to sustain him forever. Like the cabins, Blake needed a steady influx of clients, otherwise his business would be over before it even got started.

There was far too much surrounding competition from extravagant handbags and fresh baking. The market visitors were too occupied with the other stalls to take any notice of Blake's efforts.

I turned over one of Blake's glossy leaflets in my hands. He had put a lot of work into it. It featured stunning colour photographs of Loch Strathe, the woodland that surrounded us and the swell of the hillsides. I pointed at the leaflet in my hand. 'I love going for walks but at this time of year... well, there's something so calming and recharging about a walk – even a short one – on Christmas Day and Boxing Day. Gets you out of the house...'

I studied the pictures again that Blake had included on his leaflet, of the breath-taking mountain ranges, smudged with purple light from a sleepy sunrise.

A possible marketing angle pushed its way to the forefront of my mind. Might it garner some interest? It could do. We couldn't stand about here like this, watching locals, visitors and tourists sally past, ignoring us. It was worth a shot, anyway. Anything was. And putting forward a suggestion like this to the stressed, busy public in the runup to Christmas might encourage them to book a relaxing ramble with Blake. It would be something to look forward to; one thing less to worry about – a pre-planned outing that you could brag to your relatives and friends that you had the foresight to arrange, in between all the Christmas shopping, food-buying, present-wrapping and general silliness of the season.

I whirled round, my excitement growing. I could do this. I had taken on the lodges, so this would be a breeze. I hoped it would work. Would it work? 'Blake, can you pass me Jock's Santa hat please?'

'He'll get cold.'

I rolled my eyes. 'I'm sure he'll cope for a little while.'

Blake handed it to me. I snatched off my beret and plonked it at a jaunty angle on Jock's bald dome, before tugging the Santa hat onto my own head. 'There. Better?'

Blake folded his muscular arms. A small smile played on

his lips. 'Just when I think you can't surprise me anymore, you go and do something else.'

We stared at one another. He seemed self-conscious all of a sudden and straightened his shoulders. 'So, Ms Grant, what's the plan?'

I gave the Santa hat a final adjustment on top of my head. 'The plan is to offer the public something that they don't have to worry about themselves. They've got enough on their plates at this time of year, without worrying about how to keep demanding relatives and visiting friends happy and occupied.'

Blake frowned. 'But what?'

My lips moulded into a hopeful little smile. 'You'll see.' I took a couple of steps. 'I just hope this angle works.'

I moved a bit further away from the stall and set my shoulders. The smell of chestnuts and the sound of ringing Christmas songs was everywhere.

I gathered myself. I could end up looking like a class tit if this didn't work, but we had to do something.

I cleared my throat and raised my voice in the middle of the buzzing market. 'Book a beautiful festive walk with Rock Solid Ramblings,' I shouted out into the frosty air. My breath coiled out like a ghost. Emboldened, I carried on. 'Now is the time! Treat your visiting friends and relatives this Christmas to a wonderful guided walk, enjoying the best Craig Brae has to offer.'

A couple of passing market visitors paused to listen to me. I offered them a bright smile. I didn't dare turn around to look at Blake. I was worried he would put me off my stride or look appalled.

'Book now to avoid disappointment and take advantage of a ten percent early bird discount!' I paced backwards and forwards in front of Blake's stall. 'Come on, ladies and gentlemen. Book a walk with Rock Solid Ramblings. Keep your relatives and friends busy and happy when they come to visit.' I raised my voice higher. 'Walk off those Christmas calories and prevent those tense family arguments over Brexit!'

I paused and risked a look back at Blake. He was gawping at me with a look of disbelief. Then his mouth twitched. 'Ten percent?' he mouthed.

'You have to speculate to accumulate,' I hissed back.

His lips broke into a shadow of a smile. 'True.'

I picked up a couple of the leaflets and repeated my sales pitch again.

A middle-aged couple, their arms linked, came wandering over from where the woman had been admiring the handbags.

'My mother-in-law is able to walk only short distances,' said the man to me, his eyes glinting behind a pair of polished spectacles. 'I don't suppose you would be able to accommodate us on a gentler walk at all?'

'Good morning, sir,' said Blake, striding over. 'We would certainly be able to do that. What I can do is take you, your wife and your mother-in-law on one of the more sedate woodland walks here in Craig Brae.' Blake warmed to his theme. 'It's a lovely walk, set out by the Woodland Trust, which incorporates views of Ben Linn, but it's all proper paths and has disabled access.' He went on to describe that the walk he was talking about also possessed an abundance of wildlife and some glorious heather.

He dropped his voice. 'I also know where there are a couple of roe deer and a family of foxes. We may not see them, but we might be lucky.' Blake smiled at the couple.

'I've been walking with a couple of other groups and they caught fleeting glimpses of two of the juvenile fox cubs last week.'

I stared at him as he talked. He really could be very charming when he put his mind to it.

The fine-featured lady smiled hopefully up at her husband from underneath her cream knitted hat. 'Mum would love something like this. It sounds like a great idea and you know how much she loves watching all her nature programmes.'

I turned to Blake, who surprised me with a wink.

My stomach performed an excited little squiggle. I jerked my attention back to the interested couple and focused on them.

'Thank you,' Blake mouthed to me, after the couple asked if they could make the ramble reservation with him now. He offered me a full-blown grin. It lit up his eyes and made them crinkle like tissue paper at the corners. My breath caught in my throat.

I could see how white and even his teeth were and he had nice, full lips...

Oh, bloody hell! I was off again! I had to get a grip of myself.

This had to stop. These increasingly frequent, random thoughts about Blake had to stop. I had to keep things friendly but professional. We had started off on very, very shaky ground, but at least now our relationship had defrosted. All I needed right now, after starting a new job, was getting involved with a work colleague and making a monumental car crash of everything.

Nope. No way. I would not allow that to happen. I was enjoying working with the Styleses and they seemed very impressed with how I had been getting the cabins knocked into shape.

I couldn't afford to throw it all away... even if it was for someone with eyes like melting Cadbury's chocolate...

I reached into my bag, which I had stashed under Blake's stall. I had to do something. I realised I had been staring at him for much longer than I should have and was ignoring this very pleasant couple.

I pinned on a professional smile and banished more thoughts of Blake's smile. 'I don't suppose while you're here, I could also interest you in taking a leaflet about the new luxury cabins which are now available to reserve after Christmas?'

Once the couple completed their booking with Blake, they wished us both a Merry Christmas and meandered off to browse the other stalls.

'Well, Ms Grant,' said Blake. 'That was very impressive, especially when you managed to crowbar in a mention about the cabins as well.'

I let out a bark of laughter. 'You can't blame a girl for trying.'

And so we carried on in a similar vein for the remainder of the day, taking turns to entice, pitch and call over passing shoppers, pushing the 'Treat your family and friends to a festive ramble and take a look at the new cabins' aspect.

Blake managed to snare several more ramble reservations during the remainder of the morning, including two from a couple of the other stallholders who had happened to overhear us.

Then he took it upon himself to go and get us both some lunch. Ten minutes later he returned carrying two warm croissants filled with chicken, parmesan and salad, two caramel lattes and two apple and cinnamon muffins from Mrs Crill's bakery. 'Food for the workers.'

I savoured the succulent taste of the crumbly golden croissant and rewarded myself with a grateful mouthful of the hot, sweet latte.

Blake eyed me over the rim of his latte cup. 'Good?'

'Mm,' I sighed. 'More than good.'

Once we had devoured our lunch, we threw ourselves with abandon into the rest of the afternoon.

We double dipped, working in unison to ply Blake's hiking services and extoll the virtues of Magical Occasions Cabins at the same time.

Children danced and skipped in the snow, wearing moustaches of hot chocolate and chattering away to their parents. Couples, clutching onto one another in the bitter cold, appreciated the lights and shared boxes of roasted chestnuts, while grandparents argued about what gifts their families would like.

From where Blake's stall was positioned in the market, I could look down the run of shops and see Christmas Crackers, with its glowing windows.

A steady stream of customers had been going in and out, reappearing with the remnants of the bargain decorations.

I had done all I could. Now I had to focus on Magical Occasions Cabins.

Following another spell of Blake and me taking turns to beckon potential customers over, we managed to secure three more walking bookings for Blake after New Year and towards the end of January and two of the ladies who were selling the handmade Christmas cards reserved two of the cabins for the end of February for themselves and their husbands, to celebrate a milestone birthday.

The afternoon vanished and before we knew it the other market stallholders were packing up, the fairy lights on their stalls were dimming and disappearing and the snow was spiralling down from the darkening sky again.

The sound of Kirsty MacColl and The Pogues seeped away into the night, as our fellow stallholders wished us a good evening and crunched away to their vehicles.

I helped Blake clear away his leaflets, the drinking bottles, Jock the mannequin and remove the decorations, before packing them all up in the spacious boot of Blake's silver four-by-four.

The street lamps of Craig Brae cast a soupy, comforting glow down onto the snow-encrusted pavements.

'Fancy a drink before we call it a night?' asked Blake, removing his bobbly hat to smooth down his dark layers. 'I think we deserve one.'

I pointed to his car.

'Don't worry. I won't be drinking and driving. I can come back in the morning to collect it.'

I snuggled deep into my coat.

What are you doing, Lottie? You should be making a polite excuse, before heading home.

I struggled to comprehend that this was the same guy who I detested up until the other week.

I opened my mouth to give an excuse. I should head straight home. Run a bath. Lose myself in some of my mandarin bubble bath. Keep my distance. My head was too slow, though. Before I could think about it any longer, my heart galloped ahead in the race to speak. 'I'd like that. Thanks.'

We headed to the local pub just around the snowy corner. I insisted on buying the first round, seeing as Blake had bought me lunch.

He opted for a pint of Craig Brae's own ale, Amber Mountain, which I recommended. 'My dad loved it. He said it reminded him of the heather and local streams around here. He even used to say it tasted like them, but in a good way.'

'Are you working for the local brewery as well? You have one hell of a sales pitch when you get going. I'll try it.'

I chose a glass of white wine and we took our drinks over to a wooden table and bench situated in the corner, close to the gothic-style fireplace that was spitting and snarling over some giant logs.

A Christmas tree blinked nearby and there were lantern-style lights swinging along the edge of the bar.

We recognised a couple of the other market stallholders, who were supping pints and relaxing by the bar as they perched on stools. They nodded and smiled back at us.

'You were great today,' said Blake across the table. He clawed off his hat and plonked it down beside him. His raven-black hair was sitting up in clumps on top of his head. He reached up one hand and smoothed it down. Even with hat hair, he was still handsome.

We slipped off our coats. The log fire continued to blaze fiery orange and someone had just chosen a Christmas song from the jukebox. Greg Lake's 'I Believe in Father Christmas' started to play.

'You were great too,' I insisted. 'Once you got into your stride, there was no stopping you! You could have sold igloos to Eskimos!'

He took a grateful mouthful of his pint and savoured it for

a moment. 'Oh wow! I understand why your dad liked this. It's gorgeous.'

I relished the crisp, tangy taste of my wine. 'Thank goodness for that. I would have felt awful if I'd recommended it and then you hadn't liked it.'

I flashed Blake a quick look over the top of my wine glass. 'So, what's your opinion about Christmas now? Still detest it as much?'

Blake's lips morphed into a small smile. 'I'm still not a huge fan, but that Christmas Market wasn't quite as painful as I thought it might be.'

I hitched my brows up. 'Well, not a ringing endorsement, but it's something.'

Blake took another sip of his beer and set it down on the mat in front of him. 'You definitely made today much better than it would have been.'

My heart galloped a little faster at his words and I took another mouthful of wine, for something to do.

Right. Ok. Was Blake flirting with me? Talk about being out of practice with all this stuff! God, I was so rubbish at all of this.

If he was, I knew it was risky. Things could get messy.

And yet, sitting opposite him like this, in the cosy, amber warmth of the pub, gazing across into those intense, dark eyes of his, with his furling lashes and arching, black brows…

Oh God. Who was I kidding?

I didn't want to leave even though the sensible part of my brain was ordering me to finish my drink and go home. I wanted to just stay here like this. Talking to him. Sharing banter. Joking backwards and forwards. One of us trying to get the verbal upper hand on the other. It was flirtatious. It was fun and I realised, my stomach fizzing, that I didn't want the evening to stop.

'Thank you,' I grinned back at him. 'I'm glad I made the experience not quite as painful as it might have been. You are now viewing Christmas as not quite as horrifying a proposition as dental treatment, so it's a step in the right direction.'

Blake's expression was deadpan from under his beard. 'Now, let's not get too carried away.'

I watched his fingers drum up and down the side of his beer glass. 'So, have you always lived here?' he asked me.

'Yep. Born and bred in Craig Brae and I love it.' I leant a little forward on the velvet-cushioned bench. 'My parents are both from here too.' I stole a glance around at some of the locals, lost in conversation and laughter with each other and nursing their drinks. 'It's not just the wildlife and the stunning scenery around here, although that's a huge part of it. It's the feeling of community that I also love.'

My cheeks glowed with enthusiasm. 'I've lost count how many times tourists have said to me that it must be a privilege to come from here.' I reached for my wine glass.

'And you said your degree is in interior design?'

'Yes. I studied at Glasgow School of Art. Then I worked for four years at a couple of department stores in the city.' I told Blake about loving both jobs, especially at Canterbury's department store, but that in time, the gloss wore off while working at Sanders. 'My line manager was resentful over me taking the job, rather than his girlfriend getting appointed. I was coming up with all these fun, colourful ideas for displays and not getting the recognition I felt I deserved. Then, Mum happened to tell me about Vivian Sangster opening up her own Christmas-themed shop back here in Craig Brae and that she was looking for staff.' I gave a shrug. 'So, I came home that weekend, rang her up and she gave me an interview.' I took a gulp of my wine. 'She took me on as a retail assistant, while also taking Mum on part-time.' I smiled at the memory, which in some ways seemed so long ago now. 'She liked my suggestions for Christmas Crackers – display ideas, competition suggestions, that kind of thing – and after about a year, she appointed me shop manager.' I hitched one brow up. 'And the rest is history.'

Blake listened. 'You've achieved a lot.'

'Thanks. Well, I like to think so. My parents always taught me to never give up.' Over in the corner, there was a burst of laughter from a couple of the ruddy-faced market stallholders. 'So, what about you? What's your story?'

There was silence from across the table. His broad shoulders stiffened. 'Oh, there isn't much to tell. I don't have a story.'

'Everybody has a story.'

'Not me.'

I blinked across at him, surprised by his sudden sharp defensiveness. He was shutting down again.

I tried to keep my voice light. 'I just mean, where are you from? What's your background?'

Blake's dark-brown eyes took on a guarded flicker. Had I said something wrong? It was like the flirtatious guy I had been chatting to just a minute ago had walked out and been replaced by his reserved identical twin when I wasn't looking.

He fiddled with the stem of his pint glass. 'I lived in Edinburgh before moving here,' he answered. 'I wanted a change from the city. Somewhere quieter.' He flashed me an unfathomable glance. 'I've been living here in Craig Brae for a few months now. I bought one of the new flats over by Craig Brae Park.'

I wondered if he would elaborate or mention his background, but he switched his attention to out of the pub window. 'I checked out the forecast and they aren't predicting any more snow tonight. I hope not, as I've got an early hike scheduled with a honeymooning couple first thing in the morning.'

It was clear he didn't want to discuss himself. A pop of disappointment exploded in my chest, but I hoped I managed to disguise it. 'Oh, where are you hiking?'

'Ben Linn.'

A sliver of worry shot up my back. 'That mountain can be really tricky at the best of times, but in conditions like this, it can be dangerous.'

Blake gave me a long look. 'If I didn't know any better, I'd think you were worried about me.'

I pulled a funny face. 'I'm not worried about you, Mr Dempster. I'm more concerned about your clients.'

'Gee. Thanks.'

I let out a sigh. 'No. Seriously. Blake, that mountain has caught out a few experienced climbers over the years.' I awarded him a charged expression. 'I know you've climbed Everest but Benn Linn... well, she can be a right tricky madam.'

Blake shook his dark head. 'Please don't worry. I know what I'm doing and both Caitlyn and Dylan are experienced climbers too.'

I must have looked puzzled.

'They're the honeymoon couple I'm taking on the hike.'

'Oh. Right.'

Blake's white smile flashed through his beard at me. 'And we aren't tackling the whole of Ben Linn anyway. Just part of the north face. They have a flight booked to London for five o'clock tomorrow afternoon.' He indicated to his now empty beer glass. 'Can I get you one for the road?'

'Go on then. Same again for me, thank you.'

My eyes followed his broad back retreating to the bar. His muscles slid and tensed under his jumper.

Blake Dempster was deep, like a complicated puzzle you couldn't solve, no matter how hard you tried. You might begin to think you stood a chance of getting to know him, but then he would shut you down or say something or do something and you would be thrown off-kilter.

Once we'd enjoyed our second round of drinks, Blake insisted on walking me home to my flat.

We left the hustle, warmth and hum of the pub and stepped out into street. Craig Brae was like a scene from a festive calendar, covered in a lacy white blanket of snow, with the inky black sky and Christmas lights bursting their colours in the background.

He opened his mouth to say something, but his mobile in his coat pocket buzzed.

'Excuse me one second.' He reached in and pulled it out. He frowned down at the screen.

'Is everything ok?'

He slipped it back into his pocket. 'Yes. All good, thanks. It was a text from Sarah Turner.'

I blinked across at him as we strode along together.

'Miss Turner. The school teacher?'

A jab of something took me by surprise. 'Oh. Right. Of course.' I was struggling to look nonplussed. 'She's very pretty.'

'I suppose so. She's texted me a couple of times, but I'm not interested.'

I huddled further into my coat as the spray of stars winked and blinked above our heads. A frisson of happiness crackled inside me, and it took me by surprise. I tried to ignore the relief coursing through me. 'I see. Can I ask why?'

Blake's pace slowed. I could see the white spirally tendrils of his breath in the dark. 'She's not my type.'

We both drew up together at the same time. *Don't ask who his type is*, screamed an invisible voice in my head. Play it safe. You don't need awkwardness or distractions right now.

I wanted to continue the conversation so much; the words felt as though they were burning the tip of my tongue.

'Well, this is me,' I exclaimed, pointing to the communal flat door with its entry system.

I reset my thoughts and tugged at my gloves. Pictures of Ben Linn, packed with treacherous ice and mottled with freezing winds, rampaged through my head. Blake had only been living here for a short while. He hadn't grown up in the shadow of that striking but dangerous mountain. I had.

'Blake, you're going to roll your eyes again at me, but I'm going to say it anyway. I'm concerned about you doing that climb tomorrow. Why don't you postpone it? Just for a day or two until some of this snow melts?'

Blake read my face. 'Please will you stop worrying, Lottie.'

I chewed my lip.

'Look, tell you what, if the weather gets any worse tonight, I promise I will cancel it.'

'Promise?'

He twinkled down at me. 'Scout's honour.'

I angled my head at him. 'You weren't in the Scouts, were you?'

Blake pretended to be offended by my accusation for a few seconds. 'Yes. All right. You rumbled me. I got thrown out for being a disruptive influence.'

'Now, that doesn't surprise me.'

We both lingered for a few more moments, our breath mingling together into smoky white spirals.

Blake's attention travelled to my lips. My breath felt like it was trapped at the base of my throat. Then he reached up to his woolly hat and clamped it further down over his ears. He made no move to go. 'You sleep well. No doubt I'll catch up with you tomorrow up at Rowan Moore House, once that hike is done.'

'What time are you setting off?'

'Seven o'clock tomorrow morning,' he replied. 'The sun disappears much quicker at this time of year up there and the light fades faster.'

There was a prolonged silence again, where we just stared, studying the details of each other's faces. My imagination took off again, wondering what his lips tasted of; how they would feel, grazing against mine; what his skin would feel like. I tried to throw those images to the back of my mind. *Oh, for goodness' sake!* It wasn't working.

'Thank you again for all your help today, Lottie. You were amazing.'

My cheeks shone and not just with the biting effects of the cold. 'You're going to give me a big head.'

'What, even bigger than normal?'

I playfully smacked him on the arm and we exchanged silly, lopsided smiles at one another. Was he going to kiss me? *No! No! You don't want that to happen. Don't I? No. Too many complications.*

I fished my flat key from my bag and jabbed in the entry code. 'Well, I guess you'd better head home before you freeze on the spot.'

Blake nodded and jerked up the collar of his long coat. 'Thank you for your help today.'

'My pleasure.'

I typed in the code and the main door whooshed open. I stepped inside and turned. Blake held up one hand.

'You will be careful tomorrow?' I called. My concern raced out of my mouth and towards him in the bitter December night.

His white teeth shone back at me in the dark. 'Promise.'

Then he melted away under the street lights.

I woke up the next morning with Blake nudging at my thoughts.

I lay there, spreadeagled under my duvet. It was a good thing we hadn't kissed, I assured myself. Totally the most sensible outcome. Keep things on professional, friendly terms. Fine to have a flirt and lots of verbal banter. No problem with letting the old imagination fire up once in a while. There would be no harm done, by doing that.

But anything else was too risky. Yep. It was good nothing had happened.

I threw my legs out of the bed and sat there for a moment. So, if it was for the best in the long run, why did I keep imagining what Blake's lips tasted like?

———

After showering and getting ready for work, I snatched some tea and toast and gathered together my bag and phone. I had already decided to drop by Christmas Crackers before heading to Rowan Moore House and the cabins.

The sky was a deep milky white.

As I drove to the shops, my eyes strayed to the mountain range and to the imposing, sharp peak of Ben Linn.

Blake and his honeymooning couple had set off two hours ago on their trek. They would no doubt be traversing the north face of the mountain by now.

Oh, he would be fine. He was a very experienced climber and was no idiot. He knew what he was doing.

Nonetheless, I found myself peering again through my car windscreen at the sky and willing the weather to stay calm.

Mum was busy serving a couple of customers, while Orla was on the phone, discussing the return of some faulty fairy lights to the manufacturers.

'Hi Mum. How's it going?'

'Pretty hectic, lovey.'

I dumped my bag down behind the counter and slid off my coat.

'Right then. Let me lend a hand.'

I couldn't remember the last time my mother had looked so relieved.

It was good I was able to distract myself from thinking about Blake, by both helping Mum and Orla to serve customers at Christmas Crackers and then attending a planning meeting with Max and Stephanie when I arrived at Rowan Moore House later that morning.

First on the agenda, was an update on the naming competition for the cabins.

I had checked the inbox for entries and was delighted by the number we had received so far: almost five hundred and we still had a few days to go until the closing date of Christmas Eve.

I referred to my notes, which I'd taken ahead of the meeting so I could give Max and Stephanie a potted update. 'We have received name suggestions based on everything from species of trees to flowers, breeds of birds and someone even suggested naming the cabins after four famous Scottish architects.'

I jabbed my pen at my notebook page. 'And the entries have been submitted from far and wide too.' It wasn't just Craig Brae locals who had been entering the competition. We had received entries from as far away as Wick, so word had been getting around.

Max considered this. 'That's what we want. Excellent!'

Stephanie beamed across the dining room table at me.

'It is wonderful and so gratifying that we have received so many entries already,' enthused Max. He asked me to keep an eye on how the entries progressed over the next few days and then moved onto the next agenda topic of what activities we could put on during the spring and summer months for the future cabin guests.

'I was going to suggest we could organise an Easter egg hunt in the woods, name the Easter bunny, perhaps organise a plastic duck race on the shore of Loch Strathe?'

The Styleses met my suggestions with enthusiasm.

'I also wanted to come back to you both soon with some ideas I've been trying to pull together for Mother's Day and Father's Day? I know we've just received a couple of cabin bookings for Mother's Day in March, so I thought possibly making it a bit more of an event could make it a bigger draw.'

Stephanie nodded along. 'I think doing something a bit special for those weekends would be a great marketing ploy.'

The next topic to be discussed was looking at the potential cost of placing a few adverts on social media. 'I thought this might be a good way of reaching out to a more varied demographic.'

I referred again to the scrawls in my notebook. 'I will look into the costings for placing these ads.'

'Yes, please do that, Lottie. We would be interested to know how much the quotes are and then we can take it from there,' said Stephanie, making a few notes herself.

I jotted down a note on my to-do list to action that.

Max glanced down at his watch. 'Right, ladies. How about we stop for some lunch? I'll ask Kim if she wouldn't mind popping down to the village to get us some sandwiches.'

He gestured to his print-out of the agenda lying on the polished table in front of him. 'Once we've had something to eat, we can have a quick discussion about ideas for the cabin brochure and then call it a day.'

'I'm so sorry, Lottie, for you keeping you this long,'

whispered Stephanie, when Max vanished next door into Kim's office to speak to her. 'Max got called away by his accountant and it delayed things a bit.'

'There's no need to apologise,' I assured her. 'It's good to be able to discuss all this and get things moving.'

Kim vanished in her little lilac Ibiza to Craig Brae and returned twenty minutes later, bearing delicious hazelnut lattes and a selection of fresh sandwiches, oozing with everything from turkey, stuffing and cranberry to egg and cress and prawn salad.

I stared out at Rowan Moore House's lawns, slumbering under a quilt of thick, sparkling snow as I finished eating my sandwiches and clutched my hazelnut latte. Max and Stephanie were seated opposite me, enjoying theirs.

'It never ceases to amaze us how beautiful the scenery around Craig Brae is,' sighed Stephanie.

I nodded and smiled, as Blake drifted into my mind again. Yes, it was stunning, but it could also be treacherous in the wrong conditions. I hoped he and his climbing clients were safe and well. I glanced down at my watch and took a thoughtful sip of my latte. He should be back by now, or certainly very soon.

We resumed our meeting, mulling over possible ideas for a glossy colour cabin brochure. I had just started suggesting offering a discount for NHS employees when there was a knock on the dining room door.

Max boomed. 'Come in.'

Kim appeared in the doorway, looking self-conscious. 'Sorry to interrupt,' she said, hopping from foot to foot in her suede ankle boots and short tartan skirt.

'Don't worry,' said Max, sitting back in his chair. 'It's good to have a bit of a breather. What's up, Kim?'

She laced and unlaced her fingers in front of her. 'I don't suppose any of you have heard from Blake at all?'

I shot up straighter in my chair. 'What is it? What's wrong? Aren't he and his climbers back yet?'

Stephanie glanced across the table at me, a knowing look passing across her handsome face.

'I've just received a call from the Craig Brae Book Club. They go on a scheduled ramble with Blake every Monday afternoon at one clock.' Kim glanced at me. 'One of the group members has been ringing both Blake's office number at Rock Solid Ramblings and also his mobile, but he isn't answering either phone.' She paused. 'They were growing concerned, so they thought they would ring here, to see if Blake had returned from his earlier hike or was on the way back.'

An uneasy feeling clawed at me. 'And he hasn't returned yet from Ben Linn?'

Kim shook her white-blonde pixie cut. 'No. I've tried ringing him myself, but my calls are just going straight to voicemail on both numbers.'

Her concern was evident. 'Blake and his two clients haven't been seen since they set off for Ben Linn first thing this morning.'

Chapter Eighteen

I jumped to my feet.

'We need to speak to Craig Brae Mountain Rescue. They could be in danger.'

I whirled round to look out of the dining room window.

Oh bugger. It was snowing again.

In any other circumstance, the sight of fresh snowflakes, falling like feathers to the ground, would send me into an excited delirium, but not today. 'They weren't even going to do the full climb,' I rushed, my anxious thoughts jostling in my mind. 'Blake told me the couple were due to catch a flight to London at five o'clock today, so they agreed to hike some of the north face only.'

Oh God. More snow was spinning down from a gunmetal grey sky. What would conditions be like up on Ben Linn right now? Where were they? Was one of them injured? Were they lost in a blizzard? *No, come on, Lottie.* Blake was a seasoned climber. He had conquered other climbs which made Benn Linn look like a molehill.

Kim was about to say something when her office phone let out a series of insistent rings. We all swapped charged glances.

She excused herself and rushed to answer it and returned again a couple of minutes later. 'That was one of the receptionists at the Heather Hill Hotel. The couple with Blake are staying there.' She paused. 'They confirmed they haven't returned to check out.'

A sick feeling swished around in my stomach.

Max was next to leap to his feet, followed by Stephanie. 'We should give the local mountain rescue a call and take it from there.'

The three of us abandoned the dining toom table, strewn with lunch debris and scribbled meeting notes.

As I bundled out of the door, Stephanie reached out and lightly touched me on the arm. Her light eyes were understanding. 'Don't worry, Lottie. Blake will be fine. The three of them will be.'

I opened and closed my mouth, not sure what to say. In the end, all I could do was force a watery smile.

Max, Stephanie and I crowded into Kim's little office. It was all Japanese plants like peace lilies and miniature bonsai and pretty stationery on her desk.

Kim pulled up the Craig Brae Mountain Rescue website on her computer.

'The rescue team leader is Malcolm Shields,' I explained, pictures of Blake and his two companions flitting about in front of my eyes. 'He owns the local pet shop, Paws for Thought. He was a good friend of my dad.'

'Ok. Thanks.' Kim snatched up her desk phone and dialled the emergency number on the website.

It seemed like the phone was ringing out for an agonising

length of time. In reality, it wasn't, but my impatience made it feel like we were waiting for someone to answer for ten minutes.

My heart lurched with relief when I heard Malcolm's soothing voice answer his phone.

Kim gave him an explanation about Blake and the honeymoon couple not returning from their early morning hike up Ben Linn.

'Is that *the* Blake Dempster?' I heard Malcolm ask in surprise. 'That young man has bagged more Munros than I've had hot meals.'

Kim confirmed that yes, it was.

'He's a very seasoned climber. If anyone knows what they're doing, it's him. Nevertheless, the conditions up there are getting worse. What can you tell us about what time they set off? Who was Blake Dempster with? Where did they leave from?'

Kim gave me a flustered glance. I gestured for the phone, asking her if I could have a quick word with Malcolm. 'Malcolm? Hi. It's Lottie Grant here.'

Malcolm paused. I could hear his smile break out down the line. 'Ah. Tom's girl. How are you and your mother bearing up?'

I flashed a look at the expectant faces of Max, Stephanie and Kim surrounding me. 'We're not too bad thanks. Just keeping busy. Malcolm, we're really concerned about Blake and the couple he's with. The fact that they haven't returned yet is very worrying, especially as they weren't going to attempt the whole of the north face.'

I gathered myself, realising my voice was beginning to waver. 'It's a honeymoon couple that are with him. Blake told me they were experienced climbers too, but they're staying at the Heather Hill Hotel and the receptionist said they haven't returned to check out.'

I gripped Kim's office phone tighter in my hand. 'They were due to catch a flight from Glasgow to London at five o' clock today.'

Malcolm processed it all. 'Right. Leave it with me. I'll get onto the other team members now and coordinate the search party.'

I swallowed a ball of apprehension, tinged with temporary relief. At least we were trying to do something. 'Thank you. Thank you so much.'

'No problem, pet. I'll keep you informed of what's going on.'

And with that, there was a deafening click as he hung up.

I insisted on making us all tea.

Every so often, my attention strayed out of Rowan Moore House to the snow, fresh layers of it settling along the driveway and thick hedgerows.

I couldn't stop thinking about the treacherous conditions. My imagination was swamping me, suffocating me.

When my mobile let out its familiar ring, I scrambled across the dining room table to answer it.

It wasn't Blake, nor Malcolm with news. My heart deflated. It was Mum.

'Darling, is it true? We just had Jocelyn Crill in the shop here and she said she heard from one of her friends who's in the local book club that that handsome young man you work with has gone missing up Ben Linn with a couple of tourists?'

Hearing what had happened fall from my mother's lips made the situation even more concerning.

'Yes, that's right. We've contacted Malcolm at mountain rescue.' I forced myself to try and sound a bit brighter. 'I'm sure they're all fine and have just been held up on their way back down by the weather.'

'Yes, that's what it'll be,' agreed Mum. She paused. 'Please try not to worry, sweetheart. Your young man will be ok.'

'Oh, he isn't my young man,' I rushed. 'It's nothing like that at all. We're just work colleagues. You know, acquaintances.'

I watched the flakes tumbling from the milky sky.

'You like him though, don't you?'

I found myself pacing up and down in front of the dining room window, with its floor-length claret patterned drapes and the huge, stunning Christmas tree standing guard in the main hall. 'Blake is a friend,' I blustered. 'I know we didn't hit it off at all at the beginning, but…'

But what? What had happened between us? I thought about last night, when Blake had looked like he was on the verge of kissing me. I had wanted him to. So, so much. In fact, I couldn't remember the last time I had wanted something so badly. But if he had kissed me, what would that mean for our relationship working together? And did I really know him or even have a sense of who he was? I knew I didn't.

It was like he was worried about sharing part of himself, in case it made him vulnerable. Like Superman with kryptonite.

But even so… Although I knew so little about him, I'd found myself wanting to kiss him so much, it hurt… Jesus! It was like my common sense had evaporated! All the protestations and my insistence that I felt nothing for him.

Mum's voice hauled me back from where I was. 'Hmmm,' she muttered into my ear.

I sighed in defeat. It was no use. My mother could tell when I was being evasive even more than I could. I was aware that Max, Stephanie and Kim were within earshot, so I took my phone out into the hall and wandered close to the Christmas tree. 'Yes. Ok. I admit I have grown to like him a lot, but Blake is a dark horse, Mum, and the fact we work together… well, it's far from an ideal situation.'

She listened. 'Do you know what I think?'

'Go on.'

'When he arrives back safely – and he will – why don't you tell him how you feel?'

I closed my eyes in horror at the prospect. I couldn't do that. I wouldn't. Was there anything that I could tell Blake anyway? 'But Mum, didn't you hear what I just said? I've had enough of being hurt. After what happened with Kyle, well, I don't need all that pain and hassle again.' Putting my heart out there, just for it to be stomped all over… The prospect made the breath in my throat tighten. 'Imagine if I did open up to Blake? Imagine if it all went wrong?'

'But what if this Blake isn't another Kyle? Imagine if it all went right?' She sighed. 'We both know how fragile life can be.'

I thought of my dad and his sticking-up conker-brown hair and wide gap-toothed grin.

Once Mum had hung up, after making me promise to keep her informed of any news before she went, I tried to focus on updating the cabin website with a list of some of the wonderful names that had been suggested so far for the cabins. It was no good. I couldn't concentrate.

Max and Stephanie milled around, trying to look relaxed and not succeeding, while Kim typed up some correspondence for the Styleses, keeping one eye on her phone.

I was sitting staring at my laptop screen when Kim entered the dining room and cocked her platinum head to one side. 'How are you doing?'

'Not bad. I'm updating the cabin website…'

She offered a caring smile. 'I'm not talking about work. I'm talking about Blake.'

I flashed her an embarrassed look and pulled my hands away from the keyboard. 'Oh, bloody hell. Not you as well.' I slumped backwards in the dining room chair. 'And I was congratulating myself about how discreet I had been.'

'What do you mean?' She clicked the dining room door closed behind her and took up a chair opposite me. 'Has someone else guessed too? That you have feelings for Blake, I mean?'

'My mum rang me after hearing about Blake and the couple not returning yet from their hike.' I allowed my hands to splay on the gleaming wood dining room table.

'Ah.' Kim played with her huge emerald dress ring. 'So, she noticed it too?' She shook her head. 'It's obvious to the world and his dog that you and Blake are attracted to one another.'

I rubbed my face. 'You can't keep anything quiet in Craig Brae.'

'Nope. Well, not from me anyway. I have a sixth sense about these things.' She gave me a small smile. 'You two both need your heads banging together.'

My phone let out a ping to signal I had received a text

message. I snatched it up, willing it to be from Blake, telling me that he and his two companions were frozen, exhausted but otherwise all right. It wasn't. It was from Mum.

Just been told by Mrs Crill that the rescue team members, led by Malcolm, met at their rendezvous point of Loch Strathe over an hour ago and were on their way to conduct their search.
Thought you would want to know.
Love you and remember what I said.
Carpe Diem and all that!
Mum XXX

I raised my eyes from my phone screen and relayed the message to Kim.

'See?' she twinkled out of her sky-blue eyes. 'It's not just me telling you that. Your mum is a very wise woman.'

I was about to reply when a flicker of movement out of the dining room window caught my eye. There were still swirls of snow being caught by the breeze, but I was able to make out three weary figures making their way through it.

As they approached Rowan Moore House, I realised the three individuals were dressed in waterproof trousers, climbing boots and insulated jackets. Rucksacks bobbed up and down on their backs.

Behind them followed several people dressed in the same way.

I rose from my chair and gestured out of the window. Kim followed my hand. My heart jumped. Was it them? Was it Blake and the young couple? I was scared to get too optimistic.

But as they grew nearer, I could make out Blake's silhouette through the snow.

Relief whirled through me. 'Thank goodness for that,' I blurted. 'It's them. They're back with the rescue team.'

I raced out of the dining room, almost colliding with Max in the hallway. 'It's Blake. They're all ok!'

And I bolted down the steps of Rowan Moore House without thinking to throw my coat on.

Chapter Nineteen

'We found them sheltering halfway up Ben Linn,' explained Malcolm from under his waterproof hood. He batted snowflakes out of his grey, crinkly eyes. 'In Looter's Cave.'

Malcolm gave his head a shake, making his hood crackle. 'We told them we would take them to get checked out at the hospital, but all three of them refused, the stubborn buggers.' Malcolm jerked his head back, indicating to a young blond man. 'Luckily, young Campbell here is a locum GP, so he checked them over instead.' He narrowed his eyes at Blake and his two companions. 'They're cold and knackered, but fine apart from that.'

My head snapped from Malcolm to Blake and then to the embracing couple, Caitlyn and Dylan. My emotions were tearing through me like a hurricane.

I noticed there were smudges of weariness under Blake's dark eyes.

'It was too bad up there to start making our way back, so

we stayed in the cave, hoping that the snow would start to ease off,' said Blake. He surveyed me with concern from under his woolly hat. 'You're not wearing a coat, Lottie.'

I was too preoccupied to process what Blake was saying. My thoughts were scrambling around, drinking in the sight of him and the relief that he and his companions were safe and well.

My imagination had placed Blake down a rock face, incapacitated with a broken leg or blundering around, weak and confused in a snowstorm.

His words jolted me back. I glanced down at my polo neck and fitted trousers. I had been so anxious to see him and the other figures trudging back through the snow that pulling on my coat hadn't even occurred to me.

I wrapped my arms protectively around myself.

But now that Blake had mentioned it, I felt shaken and vulnerable, surrounded by the rescue team, who were trussed up for the worst that Craig Brae could throw at them.

I started to rub at my arms, but before I realised what he was doing, Blake had dumped his rucksack on the snowy ground in front of him, unzipped it and pulled out a red fleece.

He slid it like a cape around me and proceeded to drape it around my trembling shoulders. His gloved fingers skimmed against my skin. I swallowed.

He gazed down at me through the whirling flurries of snow. 'Put this on. You must be freezing.'

I tugged the fleece on, grateful for another layer. 'Thank you. But I'm not the one who was trapped in a mountain cave.' My mouth trembled and chattered. I stared up at him. 'We were worried sick.'

'Oh, there was no need to be.'

My mouth fell open. 'What? You take off in horrible weather up a dangerous mountain, are late returning and then you brush it off, just like that? I've been... I mean, *we've* been so concerned. Stephanie, Max, Kim and me.'

Blake studied me. 'It wasn't as bad as it seemed.'

'Oh, stop being so bloody macho about it!' I erupted, my worry and relief clashing. My feelings were in knots, tightening up my chest.

In frustration, I punched him on the arm.

All the assembled mountain rescue, Kim and the Styleses pretended to be engaged in conversation.

Blake almost laughed. 'Ow! What was that for?!'

'For being a dick! And stop laughing!'

'I'm not laughing, Lottie.'

'Yes, you are. I can see you are through that wild animal you've got stuck to your chin.'

'Wild animal?' echoed Blake, breaking into a wider smile.

'And stop repeating what I say.'

I bit my bottom lip and struggled to look up at him. Relief reared up inside me. God, I hated feeling like this. If he hadn't been channelling his inner Bear Grylls and gone walkabout up Ben Linn this morning, I wouldn't have been standing here in a fleece three sizes too big for me, like a raging Oompa-Loompa.

I huddled deeper into his red fleece with Rowan Moore House glittering behind us. 'The next time you decide to go all testosterone and take on the elements, I won't worry. How about that?'

Blake examined me. 'So you admit you were worried about me?'

I struggled to look at him. 'No.'

'I'm not used to someone worrying about me.'

I blinked up at him as he loomed lover me. His words tugged at my heart. Oh bugger. Why did he have to say things like that?

Blake's lips looked cold but inviting through his snowy beard. 'So you called the rescue guys out?'

I raised my chin up at him, still oblivious to the intrigued faces of the honeymooning couple, the rescue team and Max, Stephanie and Kim surrounding us.

'Yes. You're really late back. There was no sign of you and the hotel where Caitlyn and Dylan are staying rang here to say they hadn't been seen either for hours and they were growing concerned.'

The voice of Caitlyn made me start. I had been so preoccupied by Blake arriving back safe that the faces of the spectators around us had melted away.

Caitlyn's electric-blue waterproof rustled as she moved. 'That turned out to be the least of our worries. We owe a lot to this man here.' She pointed at Blake and managed a grateful smile.

'Goodness me, you must all be so exhausted and frozen,' exclaimed Stephanie, eyeing Blake and me. She gave me a small, knowing smile as she huddled closer to Max on the steps of their house. 'Come on in and get warmed and have something to drink and eat. All of you.'

One of the recue team members, a thin, wiry man, was insisting they should return to Craig Brae, but Stephanie was having none of it. The man accepted defeat.

'We're all fine. Relieved. Nothing a good night's sleep won't cure,' said Dylan to a concerned Stephanie, as he squeezed his wife's hand.

They filed past us, together with the rescue team, who were

talking about what a stunning house Rowan Moore House was. They were a sea of brightly coloured jostling waterproof jackets and trudging boots.

Blake and I lingered by the entrance steps, with its glossy holly decorations and scarlet ribbons.

The snow was slowing and the air was punctuated by a crisp sharpness.

Blake's eyes danced from under his hood. A couple of locks of damp, dark hair tumbled forward onto his brow. It made him even more irresistible. 'You do realise I have done this climbing lark once or twice before?'

I folded my arms. 'Nooo. Really? I don't recall you ever mentioning that before.'

Blake smiled and pulled a face. 'So, how worried were you about me on a scale of one to ten?'

I glanced up at him. He towered over me, all broad-shouldered and beardy. 'Now you're just trying to milk it, Dempster. Of course, I wasn't worried. I was actually sitting here all the time, giving myself a manicure and watching daytime TV.'

'Yeah, right.'

Oh God. He was doing that lip-gazing thing again. My stomach rippled. Part of me wanted him to stop staring at my mouth like that; the other part of me wished he would do something about it. What would it be like to have his lips greedily kissing mine?

There was an electrified silence. His mouth slid into a charming, lopsided smile. 'You've got snowflakes in your hair.'

My breath froze as he tugged off one glove and brushed a couple of flakes from out of my tangled, damp locks. His fingers glanced across my cheek and a brief gulp escaped from the base of my throat.

It was no good. I could protest all I wanted. I could try and compare him to Kyle, with his intense dislike of Christmas, but the truth was, he was a world away from my ex-boyfriend.

The shock of what I wanted ripped through me. I couldn't go on like this, fighting my feelings, insisting I was in control and that Blake was an acquaintance who meant nothing to me. I was fighting a battle I knew I couldn't win. I had to admit defeat. I wanted Blake to kiss me. I wanted to taste his lips; feel them moving against mine. Images of him pressing himself against me, raced before my eyes. I'd never experienced a burning desire like this before and although it was addictive, it was also frightening. My heart rocketed against my ribcage.

I didn't want to drag my eyes away from his handsome face. 'I was so worried,' I choked, unable to bite it back any longer. I had to tell him. My emotions were going to brim over otherwise. They were twisted up inside of me and I had to release them. 'I kept thinking about you up there and wondering if you were injured or worse…'

Blake's fingers stayed wrapped around one of the strands of my hair, his gaze grazing my features. I didn't want him to stop touching me.

I knew what all this meant. I knew the complications it could create, how I would be putting myself in a vulnerable position again, at the mercy of my feelings, but right now, with the snow drizzling around us and Blake stroking my face, I didn't care. I realised I was more than prepared to take a risk and deal with the consequences.

I lifted his un-gloved hand and rested it against my cheek.

'Oh Lottie,' he growled, moving even closer to me.

I savoured the sensation of his warm skin against mine. I could make out the glistening tips of his blue-black lashes. 'What's happening here?' I managed, searching his face. 'Up until a few weeks ago, we struggled to be in the same room together.' I was unable to control the wobble in my voice. 'Then things started to change. Until you went missing, I promised myself I would keep my distance. It would all get too messy. But then when I thought you might be in trouble up that mountain, I thought I would go crazy.'

'I can't say I enjoyed it much either,' joked Blake.

I arched one brow.

His eyes softened even further as he looked down at me. 'When the three of us were sheltering in that cave and the snow was piling up, all I kept thinking about was you, Lottie.'

My heart zoomed in my chest. 'Really?'

'Really.' A whole array of emotions swept across Blake's face. 'My feelings for you have crept up on me. They've caught me off-guard and I don't know what to do half the time.'

He took one long finger and traced it down the side of my face as we remained by the steps of Rowan Moore House, surrounded by what was like our own Christmas card scene.

I nestled my cheek further against his hand. 'Even though I don't know you, I feel the same.'

Blake blinked down at me. 'What do you mean?'

I lowered his hands from my face and squeezed them both in mine, entwining my fingers with his. 'You don't talk to me.'

'Yes, I do. I'm talking to you now.'

'Not in the same way I talk to you.'

Blake lowered his gaze to his hiking boots.

'I feel like you have these secrets stored up inside of you that you're afraid to let out. You keep me at arm's length.'

This could be the moment for us. I silently implored Blake to say something, to confide in me, but he remained quiet.

'Why won't you let me in?'

Blake looked agonised.

I squeezed his fingers tighter. 'Please, Blake. Why do you insist on shutting me out?'

I ran my fingers around and between his, savouring the grooves and his pronounced knuckles. 'All I know about you is the briefest details.' I gave both his hands a gentle, cajoling shake in mine.

Blake shifted in his boots. 'What do you want to know?'

'Anything. Everything.' I let out a short laugh. 'What were you like at school? Who was your first crush?'

His generous mouth glided into a shadow of a smile.

His reaction emboldened me and I decided to carry on. 'What's your favourite flavour of ice cream? What were you like as a kid?'

I blinked with shock as, all at once, Blake disengaged his hands from mine. It was as if he had just been struck with a poisoned arrow.

He took a couple of steps away from me.

My heart deflated. 'Blake? What is it? What's wrong?'

Something unreadable reared up in his eyes.

The wind whipped up the snow on the hedgerows around us.

'I... I can't do this, Lottie.'

It was like someone had punched me in the chest. 'Can't do what?'

Blake struggled to meet my gaze. A robin hopped in and around the trees, shaking the snow and sending it tumbling to the ground. 'This.' He shoved his hands into his jacket pockets. 'I've never been any good at this sort of thing.'

'This sort of thing?' I repeated, embarrassed, stunned tears clustering at the backs of my eyes.

Blake whipped down his hood, tugged off his hat and dragged a frustrated hand through his thick, dark hair. 'Relationships. Opening up. Whatever you want to call it.' His mouth was grim.

I hugged myself, still adorned in his red fleece. I was a stupid, naïve woman! Why hadn't I just kept a lid on my emotions? I should have locked them away and tried to forget they were there.

I had insisted I wouldn't allow myself to be swept away with my feelings for Blake and that I could control everything. I must have been so foolish. What did I think? That if I ignored my growing feelings for Blake, they would evaporate and I could just carry on as normal? Now look what had happened. What had been my mantra? Oh yes. I would not get involved with someone else, risking my feelings being tossed aside again. It could end up a complicated, emotional mess. *Well Lottie, guess what?!*

Now it was my turn to take a couple of faltering steps backwards, the snow slipping and crunching under my boots.

'Lottie.'

I shook my head so hard, I was in danger of dislodging my head from my shoulders. My loose, damp hair flapped against my cheeks. 'No. Don't. It's fine.'

Blake's eyes fluttered closed for a few seconds. He rubbed at his damp beard. 'You don't understand. It's complicated. It's not you.'

I held up both hands, almost laughing out loud. 'Please do

not insult my intelligence with that old chestnut. At least do me that courtesy.'

I rubbed at my jacket sleeves and realised I was still wearing Blake's fleece.

I wanted to remove it. I didn't want to feel like I was close to him at all. Let's face it, I wasn't. I wriggled out of the fleece, desperate to take it off and thrust it towards him. 'Thanks for this. I'm fine now.'

For something to do, I pulled at the hem of my polo neck. The chilled air began to gnaw at my skin again.

I summoned as much of my resolve as I could. This was for the best. Of course, it was. My pride was hurt. That was as far as it went, I reassured myself. 'You're quite right,' I announced through a wobbly smile. 'Best not to complicate things.'

Then I turned and clattered up the steps of Rowan Moore House.

I should never have opened myself up to Blake. Why did I think things would be different this time?

Stephanie's Christmas tree blurred through my mist of tears, its dangling, elegant teardrop baubles that she bought from Christmas Crackers taunting me from the hall entrance.

Chapter Twenty

Christmas week came screeching up to greet us, as did all the excitement, trepidation and frantic buying that came with it.

I purposefully kept myself occupied.

It had been a couple of days since Blake and I talked in the garden at Rowan Moore House and had our heart-to-heart. Well, heart-to-heart wasn't the correct choice of words.

On reflection, it had been me spilling my feelings out and him looking uncomfortable, bringing down the shutters and telling me he didn't want a relationship.

My eyes clamped shut with embarrassment every time my head returned to it. My heart stung but I knew I had to move on, brush it off and be professional.

Oh, why hadn't I just listened to my head in the first place?

I was grateful in one way that the final trading period for Christmas Crackers was drawing ever closer. There would be odds and ends to tie up, as well as Magical Occasions Cabins to keep me busy.

The cabins were all ready and sitting waiting in preparation for the arrival of our Christmas guests.

I had dropped in to Christmas Crackers earlier that morning to see Mum and Orla. Without telling them, I had arranged for two bouquets of stunning Christmas flowers to be delivered to each of them, as well as one for Vivian, by way of a personal thank you. They were an assortment of sweet roses, gold leaf, fragrant freesia and pistache, and both Mum and Orla were very grateful and rather tearful!

Most of the stock had been sold now and only a handful of miniature Christmas trees and random decorations remained. The walls were all empty, as was the office.

Mum eyed me from behind the counter, while Orla bustled through to the back sink to place the delivered bouquets in water. I had phoned her after Blake and I talked and explained to her what had happened.

'How are you today, darling?'

I pinned on a smile. 'I'm good, thanks, Mum. I'm looking forward to taking a break and spending Christmas with you.'

She faffed around with some sheets of tissue paper on the shelf under the counter. 'Have you seen much of Blake?'

My smile wavered. 'No, and that suits me fine.'

She tilted her shoulder-length highlights to one side.

'It's like I told you, Mum. I read the situation all wrong. Anyway, it's for the best.'

I leant over the counter and plonked a big kiss on her cheek. 'See you later.'

I drove along the frosty lanes up to Rowan Moore House. The snow from a couple of days ago was vanishing, making the scenery look rather forlorn and bare.

I was adamant I was going to stay out of Blake's way.

I negotiated the bends in the road, fringed with naked trees. How had I got this so wrong? From when we had first met and clashed, we had taken exception to one another and been resentful of each other's capabilities. Blake had been abrupt and cynical about my plans and hopes for the cabins. Then over time, we had moved on to where we began extending an uneasy truce towards one another.

Then there had been the friendlier chats, followed by frequent teasing smiles; intense looks; gazing down at my lips; flirting with me.

Then when we had been on the brink of taking things a step further, he had pulled back. Whether he was terrified of commitment or was a player, I wasn't sure. Was it anything to do with that woman called Amy, who he had been having that charged conversation with, that day by the cabins?

I blinked and blanked out more images of him. Whatever his reasons for reacting like that, better to walk away now than risk any more hurt.

Kim had one ear clamped to her office phone when I entered.

She indicated for me to sit down, rolled her eyes and mouthed, 'Won't be long.'

When she finished, she gave me an apologetic smile. 'Sorry about that. Max and Stephanie's accountant wanted to arrange a meeting with them for a catch-up, but trying to get them all together in the same room on the same date and at the same time is a nightmare!' She offered a small smile. 'And how are you?'

'I'm fine.'

'Are you sure?'

'Of course. Why do you ask?'

Kim's look was pensive. 'You're avoiding Blake, Lottie. Has something happened between the two of you?'

I couldn't resist a brief, wry attempt at a smile. 'No. Nothing happened.'

She arched her plucked brows at me.

I sighed. Good grief. I wasn't going to get away with being evasive that easily. 'I made a fool of myself.'

'How?'

I shook my head, my cheeks heating up. 'Let's just say I read far too much into the situation. So...' My voice vanished. I didn't want to talk about Blake.

Kim's kind smile made my eyes sting. 'Well, I'm here if you want to offload, ok?'

'Thanks.'

Kim gestured to some notes she had scribbled down on her notebook. 'So, let's not chat about moody mountain climbers and talk instead about the odd phone call I had about twenty minutes ago.'

I sat up a little straighter, my attention snapping away from Kim's cute Christmas tree on her desk. 'That sounds intriguing. What was that?'

Kim's satsuma-orange pinafore dress was almost as bright as the lights draped around her PC screen, but she carried the whole ensemble, complete with long black boots, with her usual aplomb. 'Well, you know that the four cabins are going to be occupied from the 24th of December?'

'Yes.'

Kim arched her brows in a dramatic fashion. 'Well, a gentleman rang a short while ago asking if he and his partner could reserve our Winter Wonderland cabin for tomorrow for one night.' She paused. 'He was literally begging. At first I didn't think anything of it. I presumed they might be travelling through Craig Brae and on to somewhere else.' Kim gave a shrug. 'Anyway, I started to explain that the cabins aren't officially opening till Christmas Eve, but he wouldn't take no for an answer. He wasn't rude or anything, just sounded desperate.'

I frowned at her. 'Ok. So, what happened?'

'He asked if there was any chance at all they could stay that one night and to tell you the truth, I felt a bit sorry for him. He said he wouldn't have bothered us if it hadn't meant a lot to him.'

Intrigued, I asked Kim to carry on.

'So, I spoke to Max and Stephanie and they said it would be all right, just for the one evening.'

I nodded. 'Ruth will still have time to change the bedding and get the cabin ship-shape again for our Christmas guests who have reserved it.'

'Exactly. No harm done. He also insisted on paying upfront.'

I narrowed my eyes, confused. 'Right. Ok. Sorry, Kim, but I'm getting a bit lost. You said you thought this was a bit odd?' At that moment, I was struggling to understand what was strange about any of it.

Now it was Kim's turn to nod her peroxide elfin hair. 'Yes. I mean no, not the paying of the rental upfront. It was all the questions he started asking afterwards.'

'Like what?'

Kim held me to the chair with her wide doll-like pale-blue eyes. 'As soon as I had confirmed the booking, he began reeling off a whole list of questions about Blake; what time does he start work; what time does he tend to finish; does Blake work with us full-time; how long has Blake worked here; does he live locally…'

I pulled a confused expression. 'Why all the interest in Blake?'

'Exactly. When I asked him why he was so interested in him, he mumbled something about being keen on hiking, but he didn't sound convincing.'

I turned this over in my mind.

I screwed up my eyes in thought. Who on earth could be so interested in Blake? And if so, why? 'Kim, what's the name this booking has been made under?'

Kim pulled up the electronic reservations screen on her PC. 'It's been made under the name of Jason Driscoll.'

That name didn't mean anything to me.

I shuffled further forward in my chair. 'And did you say he reserved the cabin for two?'

'Yep.'

'And you took the name of the other guest too?'

'Of course.' Kim squinted at the bright screen. 'The other man's name is Rob Tait.' She hesitated. 'Do you know either of them?'

'No. I don't recognise either name.'

I sat back in my chair. What was with all the questions this Jason Driscoll had been asking Kim about Blake? What relevance was it whether he lived locally and how long he had worked here? Why would a guest, keen to get away to the cabins for a short break, be so interested in things like that? The more I thought about it, the odder it seemed.

'Lottie. Lottie? Are you ok? Lottie?'

I blinked over at Kim, as though I'd just emerged from hibernation into the bright sun. I pushed out a smile. 'This Jason Driscoll, he'll just be some nosey bugger. Probably after a hefty discount, trying to give you the impression that he knows Blake or has met him before.'

Kim frowned. She didn't look convinced, but didn't argue.

I gathered up my bag. I would ring Blake now and give him a heads-up. Might it be something to do with his past? Although, I had to acknowledge I didn't know anything about his background.

Perhaps my imagination was playing tricks on me, but something was telling me that there was more to this reservation and phone call than an innocent set of questions.

Chapter Twenty-One

I hurried out of Rowan Moore House.

The winter sun was spilling through the tangled knots of trees in the garden.

I unlocked my car door and sank into the driver seat. I dumped my bag on the passenger side and retrieved my mobile.

I would ring Blake now.

My stomach squirmed while I pulled up my list of contacts and dialled his mobile number first. I knew I had to get what I was about to say straight in my own head. I couldn't just unleash, 'Hi there. How are you? Oh, by the way, someone has rocked up to the cabins and been asking lots of questions about you.'

I need not have worried. While my head was racing, forming what I was going to say, Blake's voicemail kicked in.

I listened to his deep Scottish rumble, inviting me to leave a message, but I hung up. I didn't want to sound deranged, rabbiting on like I was relaying the plot of a Martin Scorsese movie. It would be much better to actually speak to him.

I would try Rock Solid Ramblings next. I rang the number but had no success there either.

His business phone reverted to another voicemail recording:

'Hi. You are through to Blake Dempster at Rock Solid Ramblings. I'm sorry I can't take your call right now. No doubt I'm out with hiking clients at the moment. Please leave your name and number and I will call you back as soon as I can. Thanks.'

I jabbed at my phone and hung up.

I would drop by Christmas Crackers now and see Mum. Perhaps by the time I'd spoken to her, Blake would be back.

I fired up the engine, threw my car into reverse and headed back towards Craig Brae.

'That sounds odd,' murmured Mum.

She stopped dusting the shop shelves, her open, enquiring face frowning.

'Why was this person asking all these questions about Blake? Surely, if they wanted general information, they could have accessed the lodges' website. Or they could easily have looked up Blake's business.'

I nodded. 'That's what I was thinking.' I hesitated, mulling it over. 'You don't reckon this man is a journalist, do you, Mum?'

Mum dashed the duster on top of the shiny wooden

counter. Wizard and 'I Wish it Could be Christmas Every Day' serenaded us in the background. 'But why would a journalist be up here so close to Christmas?'

Orla emerged from the store cupboard, waggling a reel of Sellotape. 'One of the magazines I read often has a Where Are They Now? feature. They find celebrities and report on what they're doing with their lives after stepping out of the limelight.'

I considered this. Well, that was possible. Blake had written a couple of books and presented his own successful TV series.

Mum thought about what Orla had just said and began nodding. 'And don't forget about the local gossips we have living here. All it takes is one phone call to a newspaper to tip them off.'

'No doubt they would get paid for their tip-off as well,' added Orla.

A pang of concern punched at me. I could see someone like Casper Frew, the local pharmacist, taking great delight in ringing up one of the tabloids to tell them about Blake having moved here.

Mum folded the duster over and over. 'When it comes to money, you can't say what some people will do.'

I frowned. It did all seem to add up. The sudden booking, the stream of questions about Blake Good grief. If this man was a journalist and he was intending on writing an article about Blake coming to Craig Brae, Blake would feel deceived and exposed – just like anyone else would.

Then another worrying thought took hold. What if there *was* an article about him coming here? He might decide to leave… to move on.

My stomach lurched.

Mum rivered her hand through her caramel highlights, sending her hair flying back from her face. 'So, when is this man arriving at the cabins?'

I blinked and dragged my attention back to what she was saying. 'Tomorrow.'

Mum returned to fiddling with the bright-yellow duster. 'Well, please make sure you don't put yourself in any vulnerable situations with this character, just to be on the safe side.'

My jaw hardened as I thought about it all. If this man was a reporter, I had to try and get hold of Blake and warn him. Forewarned was forearmed. The wellbeing of the people I cared about was paramount.

Pictures of Blake's dancing dark eyes shimmered in front of me. Unrequited love was horrific. Had I been just some sort of passing diversion to him? A bit of flirtatious fun when he felt bored?

I gave myself a mental talking-to. I would just have to confront the heart-wrenching fact that Blake didn't feel the same way about me.

A leaden feeling settled in my stomach.

What if my suspicions were correct though, about this stranger asking so many questions about him?

I managed to rearrange my mouth into something approaching a reassuring smile at my mum. Despite feeling like an utter tit over Blake, I knew I couldn't just stand by and let some journalist tear up the life he was trying to build here in Craig Brae – even if it was a life that didn't include me.

If my dad were here, he would expect me to do the decent thing. The prospect of what could happen – Blake being embarrassed in the papers and his life here put under scrutiny – was making me feel ill. Whatever secrets he had in his life, they were his own business and though it was frustrating and painful that he hadn't confided in me about them, they sure as hell didn't belong splashed across the pages of a newspaper.

'Anyway,' carried on Mum, flapping her duster. 'It would take someone with not a lot of common sense to come to a small town like Craig Brae and start throwing their weight around. Can you imagine Mr Ferns?!'

I laughed at the thought of our bullish postmaster. 'He would be in his element.'

'Exactly!'

Mum planted her hands on her hips. 'Right. Seeing as there's a quiet spell at the minute, I'm putting the kettle on.'

'Sounds good to me.'

I shrugged off my coat and proceeded to tidy up the shelf under the counter, while Orla vanished to finish parcelling up a stock of garish Christmas candy canes that lit up and shouted, 'Season's Greetings!' in a nasally tone.

I had no idea why Vivian had ordered a job lot of them in the first place. The sales rep had been a bit of charmer, mind you. We were lucky if we had sold three.

It was as I finished throwing away some old post-it pads and a couple of broken pencils, that I glanced out of the shop window.

A handsome, older man was standing a few feet away, his long herringbone coat collar turned up. I didn't think too much of it and assumed he was waiting for someone. It was when I turned and glanced out of the window again a few moments later that I realised he was still loitering there, staring into the shop – and at me.

I took in his black trilby tipped down to shadow a lot of his face and the fleeting glimpse of his proud features.

After glancing down towards the office where Mum was bustling around with the kettle, I darted out from behind the counter and moved towards the window to get a closer look.

We both looked at one another and then, upon realising I'd spotted him watching me, the man dropped his head deeper into the collar of his coat, placed one hand on top of his hat and took off down the street.

I followed, clattering out of the shop door.

The bell above the door went wild. 'Lottie. Lottie? Are you all right? What is it?' called Mum after me, but I was too preoccupied.

I bounded out onto the pavement and peered down the street in both directions. The bodies of other shoppers weaved in and out, but there was no sign of the man who had been watching me.

I turned and went back into Christmas Crackers.

'Why did you dash out like that? Are you all right?'

Mum was lingering in the office doorway, clutching the teapot. I didn't want to worry her and anyway, it was most likely just a day-tripper being nosey, rather than an investigative journalist. Also, if I mentioned I was concerned someone might have been watching me or the shop, she would fret about it.

I plastered on a casual smile. 'Oh, I thought I saw Kim walking past and I was going to say hi.'

'And did you?'

'Did I what?'

'Did you see Kim? Was it her?'

'No, just someone who looked a bit like her.'

Mum gave me an odd look. 'Right.' She observed me for a few more moments, before returning into the office to make us a brew.

I didn't sleep at all well that night.

I kept replaying Kim's comments about this Jason Driscoll character asking her myriad questions about Blake, and then my thoughts harped back to the man in the black trilby outside Christmas Crackers.

Oh, this is ridiculous, I attempted to convince myself. My imagination was all fired up and going into overdrive! The questions this Jason Driscoll was asking could be nothing. Maybe he was a journalist, but his visit was an innocent one? Maybe he was going to write a review of the cabins?

As for the man hovering outside the shop, he might have just been checking out the opposition. Everyone knew that Ronaldo's had bought the lease. Perhaps he was from a rival hospitality chain?

As I lay there, I made constant efforts to stem my concern about this Jason Driscoll.

At this time of year, I was usually buzzing like a five-year-old at the prospect of Christmas but there was too much uncertainty and distraction swirling around inside me at the moment, what with the shop closure, my new job and Blake.

I prized open the glittery window of 22nd December on my advent calendar when I got up that morning, which was propped up in the kitchen, and plucked out the mini chocolate Santa. I had made another attempt last night to reach Blake, but his voicemails on his mobile and at Rock Solid Ramblings were still kicking in, rather than him answering.

Thankfully I knew he was all right, as Mum had mentioned last night that she had spotted him through the window of Christmas Crackers at closing time, wandering past clutching a pint of milk and a loaf of bread. She said he had paused for a moment, stared through our window and then moved on.

I got ready for work, mulling over what to do if Jason Driscoll was a reporter with a hidden agenda.

I had asked Kim to text me when he and his partner arrived to check in but it took me by surprise when her message popped up on my phone as I was throwing on my work clothes.

They were arriving earlier than originally planned. Why?

I replied as much to Kim.

Mr Driscoll rang last night as I was finishing up in the office, to ask if he and his partner could gain access to their cabin a few hours earlier. I chatted with Stephanie and she said that would be no problem, seeing as they had paid for their reservation upfront.

Then Kim fired off another text to me:

I know you're probably nervous about them being our first guests in the cabins, but don't worry. You've done a sterling job and they look amazing! Are you sure you're ok?

I gulped down my orange juice as I read her texts. I set down the empty glass and rattled off a response:

Just a bit jittery about everything, ahead of Christmas guests arriving. Want it all to go ok!

I hoped that explanation would answer Kim's curiosity. It seemed to do the trick, judging by her following reply:

Please don't worry [smiling emoji] It will all be fab. You'll see! X

I took a distracted bite of my buttered toast and a mouthful of my cold tea.

Guilt churned away inside me about not telling Kim about my concern. If I was wrong about Jason Driscoll and he wasn't a reporter here about Blake, I would look a right idiot, blaming some innocent man for something he wasn't involved with. If I was right, it would be best not to get her or the Styleses involved. At least not for the time being. The last thing I or they would want with their fledgling business, would be bad publicity.

———

I had just pulled up in my car in front of Rowan Moore House, when Kim emerged out of the elaborately decorated entrance.

Today, she was decked out in a glittery red Christmas jumper covered in huge snowflakes and a pair of slim-fitting tartan trousers. She bounded over to my driver side door. 'Blimey, it's chilly today.'

She waited until I had retrieved my coat and bag from the passenger side seat. 'Sorry to drop this on you as soon as you arrive, but I wondered if you could drop by the Winter Wonderland cabin where Mr Driscoll is staying?'

I found my hand clutching my coat tighter over my arm. I frowned. 'Why?'

Kim folded her arms over her sparkly jumper. Her pixie face broke into a smile. 'It seems that your interior overhaul has worked its magic already.'

'Sorry?'

'Mr Driscoll rang down to the office. He and his partner are very taken with their cabin and wanted to speak to you about reserving it for an extended period at Easter.'

I stared at Kim. 'But they only just arrived.'

Kim gave an easy shrug. 'It's made a big impression on them. Mr Driscoll was raving about the quality of the furnishings and the colour scheme.'

'And they asked to speak to me specifically about it?'

'Yes.'

I could feel my heart quicken against my ribs. Was this an innocent request? Perhaps it was a legitimate case of them wishing to make an extended booking. But asking for me, arriving early, raving about the cabin when they had literally just arrived... It all seemed a bit too convenient.

I dived into my bag and pulled out my mobile. 'I'll head over to the cabin now. If I'm not back in fifteen minutes, I want you to ring me, ok?'

Kim squinted at me under the grey, frosty sky. 'Er. Ok. Sure.'

I started to march down the path, away from Kim and the towering presence of Rowan Moore House. To anybody else spotting me striding along right now in my long burgundy winter coat and boots, I showed none of the apprehension that was clutching at my insides. *Give them the benefit of the doubt, Lottie*, murmured a calming voice in one corner of my mind.

But in the other dark recesses of my head, nagging doubts were taking over. This didn't feel right at all. It felt contrived, too neat and perfect. Something wasn't adding up.

I crunched over the woodland carpet of old twigs and discarded furled-up leaves, laced with crisp frost.

I remembered I had a personal alarm stashed at the bottom of my bag, should I need it. If they started to get pushy or insistent, I could give it a bloody great blast and hopefully deafen them for a bit.

Mum had insisted I buy one when I lived in town. *Oh bugger!* I hoped the batteries hadn't gone flat!

The pinpricks of the carriage lights outside each of the cabin doorways played hide and seek through the trees as I approached.

The Winter Wonderland cabin was the first of the four, its electric-blue and white tree on the porch throwing out twinkling sparkles. Inside, I could make out two tall figures wandering backwards and forwards.

It looked cosy and inviting, standing outside in the bone-tingling middle of December.

I stopped and sucked in a long breath of air. I recalled having a can of hairspray rolling around inside my bag, as well as my personal alarm. That might disable someone, if I sprayed a cloud of that in their face. Either that, or I could style their hair for them.

I performed an inward eyeroll. I was allowing my imagination to become hysterical. These two men turning up like this might not have anything at all to do with gossip-laden newspapers.

I tightened the belt around my coat and gripped my phone in my other hand. Well, I wouldn't know for sure, hovering here.

Chapter Twenty-Two

My fingers were wrapped, claw-like, around my phone, as I tapped up the porch steps of the Winter Wonderland cabin.

I raised my hand to the door and it lingered there, as though it wasn't mine. I took a breath and gave a sharp knock.

A few seconds passed before a tall, regal-looking man with greying collar-length hair and hawkish features appeared at the door. He gave me a slight smile. 'Ms Grant. I'm Jason Driscoll. Do please come in.'

My attention swept him from head to toe. I had to admit, he wasn't what I was expecting. I had imagined someone uber confident and brash, not the suave figure in front of me. Still, appearances could be deceptive.

I shook my head. I hoped I was coming across far more confident than I was feeling. My insides were like water. 'Thank you but I've got rather a lot on today,' I answered with a crisp smile. 'Kim tells me you're interested in taking an extended rental on this cabin during Easter. Is that right?'

From behind Jason Driscoll appeared a second man. He was a shade shorter, with dark-blond hair swept to one side and a pair of piercing green eyes. He was attractive in a public-school boy kind of way and looked a number of years younger than his partner.

He studied me from over Jason Driscoll's shoulder and gave him a gentle nudge, as if to ask what was going on.

If Driscoll was a journalist, was his companion a photographer?

Driscoll shot a brief glance back. 'This is Ms Grant, Rob. Ms Grant, this is my partner, Rob. I asked her to come over and speak to us about renting this cabin for an extended time at Easter.'

Rob's brow furrowed. 'Sorry?'

'You know,' prompted Driscoll, widening his eyes in a theatrical fashion. 'What we talked about after we arrived here.'

I caught sight of a confused-looking Rob.

After a few seconds, Rob corrected himself. 'Oh yes. Of course. Sorry. Don't think I'm quite with it yet after the journey here.'

I clutched my bag tighter to my side and narrowed my eyes at them. The trees echoed to the sounds of birds flitting and fizzing behind me.

The frost glittered through the woodland, like the remnants of a sparkly ballgown. 'If you can give me your email address, Mr Driscoll, I can send you further details and a costing for how much it would be to have an extended spring rental.'

My attention fell on the blue and white painted hallway table just visible through the open door. There was one of our new brochures lying on it, which contained all the information and prices. So why get me to come over here, when they were in possession of the details anyway?

I was right. This was some sort of ruse. They had got me to come to the cabin on a pretext.

I whipped my attention back to the two men and forced a tight smile.

Jason Driscoll searched my face. 'I really would prefer it if you could come in for a few moments, Ms Grant.'

As he continued to appraise me, an odd sensation took over. Wait. He seemed familiar. Hadn't I seen him somewhere before?

I tried not to peer at his long, proud nose and the sharpness to his chin. Hang on. I did recognise him. But where from?

Louder alarm bells started clanging at full volume inside my head. Then he dropped his chin as he looked at me and an image of the man outside Christmas Crackers from yesterday zipped through my mind. The glimpse of greying hair, the angle to his face and his sharp profile underneath his trilby; it was him. He was the same man who had been watching me through the shop window.

Why had he been watching me like that at the shop and why had he reserved one of the cabins? What was he doing here in Craig Brae?

I took a step backwards, my suspicion on full alert now. I had to try and stay focused and calm. If he was a reporter and here in the area for an ulterior motive connected to Blake, I would be far better not letting him know I recognised him from yesterday. He might try to trick me into saying or doing something that might betray Blake and that was the last thing I wanted.

My mobile phone was in my bag. I could lay my hands on

it quickly if I needed to. I squared my shoulders. 'I'm sorry, Mr Driscoll, but as I have already explained, I do have a great deal of work on today and with Christmas just a few days away, I'm sure you can appreciate how busy we are.'

A short, sharp, surprised breath shot out of the base of my throat when Jason Driscoll stepped out of the cabin doorway and started to make a move towards me.

'Ms Grant, I do need to speak with you.' His unwavering amber gaze raked me from head to toe.

'Jason,' muttered Rob from behind him. He followed up the rear and shot out one hand, placing it on his partner's shoulder. 'I don't think you should. Not here. Not like this.'

Was he trying to calm Driscoll down? To make him see that he was being unreasonable, or taking a risk? If he was, it didn't work. My mind pinged back to when Driscoll was watching me through the shop window. He had been alone. The blond man had not been with him then.

Driscoll shook off Rob's hand. 'Ms Grant, I didn't come all this way for nothing.'

I struggled to marshal my resolve. His tone was becoming more insistent. Growing fear rattled my chest. What did he want?

I found myself lurching backwards with another couple of clumsy steps. 'Mr Driscoll, what's going on?'

He and the other man watched me and said nothing.

I glanced around myself. The stillness was almost suffocating. At any other time, I would have relished it. 'You got me here under a false pretence, didn't you, Mr Driscoll?'

Jason Driscoll pushed both of his hands into the pockets of his dark jeans and flicked me a guilty look that confirmed I was right.

My heart drummed louder in my ears. I felt as if I were trapped under water and struggling for help. Pity the other three cabins weren't occupied already. Out here, it was secluded at the moment. At least I still had a couple of bars of reception on my mobile and Kim was under strict instructions to call me, if I hadn't reappeared in fifteen minutes.

I edged backwards again from Driscoll. Bloody Archibald Strang Ltd! If the landlords hadn't cheated me out of Christmas Crackers, I wouldn't be stuck in the middle of quiet woodland with two suspicious characters!

'We need to talk, Ms Grant.'

I grabbed at my bag, swinging it around in front of me like a shield and located my mobile. I brandished it at them. 'I've got nothing to say to you.'

I pointed to my phone. 'This thing is switched on, you know. I told Kim, my work colleague, to call me if I didn't return in fifteen minutes.'

Jason Driscoll's attention flew from me to my glowing phone.

'I know why you're both here,' I blurted, before I could think about what I was saying. *Shit!* Maybe that wasn't the best thing to say. Perhaps I should have pleaded ignorance. Now that I had revealed that, they might think they could persuade me to start talking about Blake.

Rob's boyish expression reddened behind Driscoll. 'You do?'

I folded my arms. 'Of course, I do! I'm not stupid!'

Adrenalin was racing through me; it was like all my building irritation and apprehension of the last couple of days was unleashing itself. 'I saw you yesterday, Mr Driscoll. You were hanging about outside the shop, watching me. When you saw me looking at you, you took off.'

Jason Driscoll shot me a look from under his brows. 'I spotted your details up on the cabin website. Then I contacted the local mountain rescue team here, hoping they could give me more information about Blake and he confirmed that the two of you worked together.'

Malcolm. It must have been him that this man spoke to.

Rob snapped his head to look at Jason Driscoll. 'What were you doing?'

When Jason didn't answer, Rob let out a sigh of resignation. 'Don't tell me you were lurking around the main street, hoping to see him.'

Him? They had to be talking about Blake.

My attention swivelled from one to the other. 'I won't let you intimate me, Mr Driscoll, or whatever your name is.'

I took another few steps backwards, hoping I wouldn't stumble and fall over. I puffed out my chest and hoped I appeared more self-assured than I felt right now. 'If you're here to dig up dirt, then you're asking the wrong person.' I gripped my phone even tighter. 'What is it about journalists like you? Why do you feel you have to trash people, when all they're doing is trying to make a different life for themselves elsewhere?'

Jason Driscoll's silvery brows knitted together like two warring caterpillars. 'Sorry?'

I carried on, making sure I had moved even further away from the bottom of the porch steps. 'Why don't you just pack up your things and crawl back to wherever you came from? The people of Craig Brae won't tell you anything. We are a tight-knit, loyal community here. Just because one bad apple snitched, doesn't mean the rest of us will.'

Jason Driscoll looked bemused. He and the other man exchanged frowns.

Fired up, I carried on. 'Yes, it is very likely someone from the local community here tipped you off, but people like that around here are very much in the minority.'

I folded my arms. 'So I suggest that you and your reporter buddy here, or whoever he is, leave. You are wasting your time.'

Driscoll blinked at me from the porch. He turned to look at Rob who gave a perplexed shrug. Driscoll turned back to me. 'Sorry. I don't understand. Reporters?'

I pursed my lips. 'Oh, please don't insult my intelligence! Blake is the reason you're here, sniffing around and asking dozens of questions, isn't he?'

Driscoll nodded his head. 'Yes. All right. I admit that we are here because of Blake.'

'I knew it!' I snapped. 'So, what sort of article are you intending on writing about him, eh? Why can't you people just give folks some peace?'

Rob looked perplexed. 'Why would we be writing an article?'

'Because you're journalists?'

Jason shook his head. 'I don't know where you got that information from, Ms Grant, but I can assure you that neither of us are reporters.'

'That's right,' added Rob. 'We don't know what you're talking about.'

Confusion stole over me. I digested what Jason Driscoll said. Were they bluffing? It didn't look or sound like they were.

My eyes flitted from him to Rob. 'Don't give me that! You're lying.'

'It's true,' insisted the young blond man. 'Neither of us is a journalist. You have our word.'

I gawped at both of them. What the hell was all this about then? 'So what were you doing outside Christmas Crackers yesterday, Mr Driscoll? Why were you staring in the window and hanging around?'

Rob frowned at his partner. 'Honestly, Jason, that wasn't one of your better ideas. I told you not to go there.'

Jason Driscoll blew out a puff of frustrated air. It swayed and disappeared into the woodland chill. 'Well, what was I supposed to do? We're only staying here the one night and I got desperate.' Jason shuffled from foot to foot. 'We were visiting Rob's elderly uncle at a residential home yesterday in Perth and booked in to a hotel there.' He shot his partner a guilty glance. 'I pretended to Rob that I needed to do some last-minute Christmas shopping, but I came to Craig Brae instead.'

What on earth was going on here? What were they talking about? Were they bluffing? Were they lying, just to get me into the cabin? 'What do you mean? What are you talking about? Why all the questions you asked Kim about Blake?'

'Blake,' murmured Jason Driscoll, an odd expression traveling across his features. 'Blake Dempster.'

'What about him?' I prickled. 'You admitted Blake is the reason you're both here.'

Jason looked agonised. He chewed his bottom lip. 'Yes.'

'But not for the reasons you think,' insisted Rob over his partner's shoulder.

'Then why are you so interested in Blake?' I asked. 'You're talking in riddles.' I rubbed my forehead.

'It's delicate,' explained Jason, with desperation in his voice. 'But yes, this is all about Blake.'

'Jason, take it steady,' warned Rob. 'This isn't perhaps the best way to go about all of this.'

'Go about what?' I pushed.

'Lottie! Lottie? Are you ok?'

I whirled around to see Blake striding towards me. His glowering dark-brown eyes flashed up at the two men on the porch of the Winter Wonderland cabin.

'Blake? What are you doing here?'

He came and towered over me. 'I dropped by Rowan Moore House and bumped into Kim. She was concerned about you and told me where you were.' Blake paused and studied me from under his black brows. 'She wasn't the only one.' He turned his attention back to Jason Driscoll and Rob. 'What's going on here? Everything ok?'

l managed a confused smile and a nod. Everything was ok. At least in a sense it was. I was still so bewildered though about what was going on. I'd read the situation all wrong. Or had I?

Driscoll and his partner were maintaining that they weren't journalists, but had admitted Blake was the reason for their visit. So why were they here? My head was fuzzy and churning.

I looked back up at Jason Driscoll and saw that he had paled when he saw Blake approaching and that he couldn't drag his eyes away from him.

I flicked a look up at Blake to see if he had noticed too, but he appeared oblivious.

'Did they do anything to you?' whispered Blake, gazing down into my eyes. 'Did they threaten you?' The wind ruffled up his dark hair, as he turned to glower up at the two men standing there.

'No, I'm fine. Thank you.'

'When Kim told me you'd come over here to one of the cabins to see two guys on your own and that you had seemed a bit spooked by it all, I insisted I check you were ok.' Blake rubbed at his beard. 'I would have come over here with you.'

Memories of Blake shutting me down after our heart-to-heart, of him backing off and refusing to confide in me, rocketed back through my head.

My smile wobbled and faded. 'I told you. I'm fine, thank you. There was no need for you to come riding up here on your white steed to rescue me.'

Blake's mouth hardened through his dark beard. 'Oh, I'm sorry I was worried about you.'

'Blake.' Jason Driscoll's voice sounded odd.

We stopped our frustrated exchanges and snapped our heads round to look back at him.

He took a few more steps towards us.

'Jason, don't you think you ought to think this through a bit longer? Is it really the best time and place to do this?' Rob was moving from foot to foot in his winter boots.

Jason didn't seem to hear his concerned partner. He just continued to stare past me at Blake, who eyed him back with suspicion. Blake's confused gaze swept over the man. 'Can I help you?'

Jason hesitated. 'I didn't mean for it all to happen like this. I'm sorry.'

Blake stared him down. 'Who are you? What is all this?'

Rob let out a long, low and frustrated breath from the cabin porch.

Jason hauled a hand through his thatch of silver hair that was furling up around his collar. 'Blake...' He faltered, his chest rising and falling under his chunky-knit cream jumper. 'I had all these plans about how I was going to talk to you when I saw you again – how I would tell you and explain everything.'

Blake looked at the older man as though he had taken leave of his senses. 'Look, I don't mean to be rude but I haven't a clue what you're talking about.'

From the cabin porch, Rob leant against the doorway with a look of awkwardness shooting across his features. 'I'm not surprised,' he muttered.

Blake gave him an odd look and turned back to Jason Driscoll. 'Tell me what?'

Jason gazed heavenwards for a few seconds at the churning ghost-grey sky through the ceiling of woodland. 'Look, Blake,' he faltered. 'I didn't want to tell you like this.' He regarded him out of conflicted amber eyes. 'I'm... I'm your dad.'

Chapter Twenty-Three

Blake stiffened beside me. 'Is this some sort of joke?'

Jason Driscoll shook his head. 'I'm so sorry, Blake. Like I said, I didn't plan on telling you like this.'

I looked up at Blake, my head swimming with concern for him. His dad?

Blake let out a strained bark of laughter. 'I don't believe you. I don't know why you're here or what you think you're doing.' He gestured to Rob. 'And who is he? My great-grandfather?'

Rob's boyish expression flooded with colour. He introduced himself and added, 'I'm your dad's husband.'

Blake stared at them both. 'So you're both in on this crap? Ok. Whatever floats your boat, I guess.'

'We aren't in on anything,' replied Jason. 'Rob is my partner. He didn't want me to tell you this way, to show up again like this, but I had to see you, son…'

Blake stood beside me, bristling. 'Don't call me that.' He gave a disbelieving shake of his dark head. 'I know my dad came out years ago, when I was a kid, but that doesn't mean you're my father. It doesn't mean anything.'

There was an icy silence, almost as chilly as the woodland air. Blake's attention swivelled from Jason Driscoll to Rob and back again.

'Look, what do you want? Have you found out I used to be on TV and thought you might have a crack at a bit of blackmail? Or have you fallen on hard times and thought you could go to the papers with your lies?' Blake gave a mocking sneer. 'Whatever your plans are, threatening me isn't going to work, but I suggest you leave Lottie out of it.'

Jason hovered on the cabin porch, his face stricken. 'I'm not here to blackmail or threaten you or anyone else.' He flopped his head back and gazed for a few seconds up at the churning winter sky. 'You've got this all wrong, Blake. I am who I say I am. I'm your dad.'

Blake's challenging sneer was wavering. 'So, if you're my father, prove it then. What's your name?

'Jason Driscoll,' completed Jason with finality. 'My name is really Jason Driscoll.'

Blake pushed a shocked hand through his dark hair.

I reached out and squeezed his arm. 'Are you ok? What's going on?'

But Blake flashed me a confused look. It was as if he didn't hear me. 'You still haven't proved it though. Well done. You know my AWOL father's name. Anybody could have found that out with a bit of detective work.'

Jason reached one hand into the pocket of his denims and produced his driver's licence. He offered it to Blake.

Blake stared at it for a few moments. The man was who he said he was: Jason Driscoll.

'And I have this too,' murmured Jason. He reached inside his wallet in the other pocket and pulled out a curling, faded colour photograph. He handed it to Blake.

Blake examined it. It showed a much younger Jason Driscoll with longer, darker hair, cuddling an adorable little grinning boy in a paddling pool in a sunny garden somewhere.

Blake swallowed and turned over the photograph. Scrawled in loopy pencil on the back was written:

Daddy and Blake, aged four, July 1989.

Blake's eyes looked like they were alight. He thrust the photograph and the driving licence back at his father. 'Well, well, well. Just in time for Christmas dinner. Was that the plan? I wondered when you might crawl out of the woodwork.'

Jason flinched. 'Please, Blake. I need to talk to you.'

'Well, this might surprise you, but I am going to politely decline. You are thirty-odd years too late.' His lip curled at his father. 'So why now? Why show up here, just before Christmas? Is this some sort of twisted joke?'

I blinked up at Blake, almost giving myself a crick in the neck in the process. So, it was true? This man was Blake's father? *Oh God.* And I had pegged him as a snooping journalist.

I studied Jason Driscoll's proud, long nose and his expressive brows and then turned to look at Blake. They were very similar.

Jason bowed his head for a moment. 'I had a car accident a few months back. I could have been killed. I know it shouldn't have taken something like that to make me think about my life, but it did.' Jason shifted from foot to foot. 'I realised the mistakes I'd made and wanted to put them right. I know I was never there for you growing up, son...'

'I never was your son. You relinquished all of that when you sodded off and left Mum and me.' He gave his father a scornful look. 'You told her on that Christmas Eve that you were leaving and that you didn't want to be a father.'

Jason's amber eyes popped with shock. 'What? No, Blake. It wasn't like that. Is that what your mother told you? Because it isn't true.'

Blake's muscles tensed. 'Don't you dare say anything about Mum. She isn't here to defend herself.'

A pained sigh escaped out of Jason. 'I know that and I'm so sorry you lost her. But what she told you, Blake... That isn't what happened.'

Blake looked like he wanted to stride across there and punch his dad.

'I don't know why she told you something like that. Please believe me. You deserve to know the truth.'

Blake fired his father a look. 'I wouldn't believe a bloody word that comes out of your mouth. Anyone capable of doing what you did to a young woman and a small child – abandoning them at Christmas...'

Then he turned to look at me. The hurt was alight in his eyes. 'Yes. That's right, Lottie. My father walked out on my mother and me on Christmas Eve. No awards for Dad of the Year. What do you think of that?'

My heart contracted for him. I wanted to throw my arms around him and tell him everything would be all right. 'Oh God, Blake,' I murmured. 'I'm so sorry.'

His Adam's apple bobbed up and down. 'I was five years old and spent that Christmas with my mother sobbing her heart out because of him.' His lips promised a brief, almost wry smile. 'Mum and I never celebrated another Christmas after he left. It was tarnished for both of us.' He struggled to conceal the pain. 'Now you might understand why I don't have a lot of fond memories of Christmas.'

Shock and empathy followed by an emerging understanding filtered through me. The festive season held too many horrible, painful memories for him. They were Christmases he'd never had. Ones that held no happiness for him. They were ones he wanted to forget.

'I never received a Christmas card from you, let alone a birthday card,' he spat at his father. Blake's black eyes fired up. 'Not even a short letter, asking how I was or how I was doing at school. But of course, you would already know that, as you didn't give a shit.'

'Whoa. Hang on a second.' Jason's face drained of all colour. 'Say that again.'

'What part? There are so many gems to choose from.' Blake's brows were thunderous. 'The bit about you turning Mum into a bitter, unhappy woman who never smiled again? The part about you never keeping in contact with me? Or the fact you never bothered to buy your own son a birthday or Christmas present?'

Blake glanced down at me; his handsome face riven with resentment. 'She never got over my dad walking out on us. She died five years ago.'

My chest heaved for him. 'I'm so sorry, Blake.'

Blake snapped his furious gaze from me to his dad's partner, as Rob spoke, breaking through my thoughts.

'Blake, your dad did send you birthday and Christmas

presents, as well as cards and letters, but Saffron kept returning them unopened, so in the end he stopped.'

Blake let out a dismissive snort, which made his breath coil in the chilly woodland air. 'And how the hell would you know? Oh yes, because he told you?' His gaze zoomed up and down Rob. 'Do you always believe what he tells you?' Blake scowled. 'A piece of advice: I wouldn't believe a word that comes out of his mouth.' Blake threw Rob a dismissive glower. 'You weren't around then, so you have no idea.'

'It's true,' croaked Jason, glancing back at Rob in a plea for support. 'If I had known about your mum and how tough she was finding it being on her own and bringing you up, I would have been there for her. I had no idea she was struggling...'

Blake folded his muscular arms. 'Oh, don't tell me. You would have come charging back to rescue your little boy.'

'Yes. I would have.'

Blake rolled his eyes up to the woodland sky. They were hard and unwavering. 'Yeah. Sure, you would.' He angled his dark head to one side. 'So where did you think I was? In Narnia? At Hogwarts?'

Jason rushed down the porch steps towards Blake, but he held up one protesting hand. 'Don't.'

Jason bit back evident disappointment. He did as he was told and stayed, rigid to the spot. 'You have to believe me.'

'I don't have to believe a word you say.'

Jason flicked his eyes heavenwards again. 'No, you're right. You don't have to believe anything I say. But I'm telling you the truth, Blake. Like Rob just told you, I did try to keep in touch with you, but every time I sent you anything, your mum would return it unopened.'

This was all so surreal. It must have been even worse for

Blake.

We were surrounded by frosty, festive woodland, with only a few days to go until Christmas and this painful scenario was playing out, dredging up pain, resentment and memories from years ago.

Jason wrung his hands together. 'When we first split up, your mother refused to tell me where you had moved to. She said I had relinquished all rights to contact with you when I left, but that was the last thing I wanted.' He swallowed. 'I tried to reason with her, but she wouldn't tell me anything. In the end, I had no option but to recruit a private investigator.'

Blake's mouth flatlined.

The agony and turmoil reared up in Jason's distinguished features. 'I didn't care what I had to do or how much it cost, I had to find you.' He attempted to steady his voice. 'Even your gran had no idea where you were either. Not until I found out through the investigator. She was as distraught as I was.'

Blake's eyes hardened. 'I don't believe you. That's lies. Mum told me when I was older that Gran was embarrassed about the whole situation and refused to have anything to do with any of us.'

Jason looked pained. 'That isn't true. Your gran was very understanding about it all. She was desperate to see you too, but your mum kept you away from her as well. It was like she was hurting so much over what I did, she just lashed out at everyone.'

Blake listened, his eyes flashing.

'I didn't want to cause all this heartache. That was the last thing I wanted. But if I had stayed married to your mum, we would have ended up destroying one another and I was determined you wouldn't get caught in the middle of it.'

Jason shot a look back at Rob and carried on. 'After about a month, the private investigator managed to track you down to an address in Stirling. I remember it was coming up to the Easter bank holiday weekend.'

Jason took a long, low breath. 'I arrived on the doorstep of Saffron's new address, armed with a giant Cadbury's Easter egg and a big, fluffy bunny for you.' His voice cracked. 'You should have seen her face when she saw me standing there. She wouldn't hear me out. After about ten minutes on the step, trying to reason with her, she said she would take the Easter egg and the bunny and give it to you.'

Blake shook his head in a dismissive manner. 'Never received them. I never got anything from you.'

A look of sad resignation stole over Jason's features. 'I thought as much.' His expression morphed into a pleading one. 'Blake, you have to believe me. I kept trying to reach out to you. I mailed letters, birthday cards, presents… but your mother returned them all.'

Jason took a gulp of woodland air. 'She point-blank refused to let me see you too. Then, when you were a little bit older, she insisted you didn't want anything to do with me.'

Blake stiffened beside me. 'That's not true. I never said that. She never told me you came to the house or that you tried to send me anything. Not once.' He ran a troubled hand through his dark hair. 'Mum told me you had gone to work in London and that you had cut all ties with both of us.'

Jason closed his eyes for a few seconds. 'She should never have lied to you like that. I can understand why she was so bitter and angry at me, but she shouldn't have involved you.'

He clasped and unclasped his hands as he spoke again. 'I

contacted your grandmother. We both agreed that we wanted to give you financial support growing up.'

Jason turned to me and took a breath. "I did think about pursuing Blake's mother through the courts for access, but I knew how unstable and hurt she was and I didn't know what she might do."

He gave a helpless shrug. 'Saffron worked as a childminder. She enjoyed her job, but it didn't pay a generous salary, so Blake's grandmother started a post office account for him and I opened up another account in your gran's name and with her knowledge to help with Blake's upbringing.' Jason's features were tortured. 'Even though we were no longer together, there was no way I was shirking my responsibilities as your father.'

Blake's brows rocketed to his hairline. 'No... That can't be right. Mum said all that money was from my grandmother. She said you never contributed financially for me at all.' Blake swallowed. 'She said Gran had a huge windfall from my great-aunt Janet's will and that she wanted to ensure I was ok.' Blake shot the three of us confused stares. 'Mum said she had moved that money from my gran into another account for me and that I could access it when I turned sixteen.'

Jason shook his head. 'No. That isn't what happened. That monthly amount wasn't a windfall from your gran. It was from me. For you.' Jason took a breath, trying to reconcile everything. 'I had the account closed, once I knew you were financially independent.'

Blake shot me a troubled look as I stood at his side.

'Yes, your grandmother did receive a payout from Janet's will, but it wasn't a huge amount,' explained Jason. 'She paid a thousand pounds into the post office account for you, but the monthly allowance was from me. It always was.'

Jason's appealing amber eyes softened. 'I was so proud of you. I still am. When I saw how well your career was going, with your TV series and your books, I realised even more what I had missed out on.' Jason hauled an agitated hand down his face. 'But that wasn't my choice, Blake. You have to believe me.' Jason wrung his hands. 'Do you think I wanted all of this?'

Blake glowered but didn't say anything.

'When I realised I was gay, I knew I had to tell Saffron. It just wouldn't have been fair on her, on me or on you to carry on limping along in that marriage like we were.'

Jason lowered his head and studied his walking boots for a few seconds. He gathered himself. 'I knew I couldn't carry on living the way I was. I loved her, but I realised I wasn't in love with her.' He rubbed at his refined face, as though willing all the pain and mess away. 'I should never have married Saffron. You can imagine what a shock it was for her, when I told her. I felt wretched.'

'Yes, but not enough to try and stay around for me,' butted in Blake.

'That's where you're wrong,' implored Jason, his low timber sounding increasingly desperate. 'I said to your mother that I wanted to be around for you. I turned up at that address in Stirling repeatedly, but she refused to let me see you. It's the truth.' Jason wrung his hands. 'I wanted to help her raise you. I still wanted to be a part of your life.'

Blake made a dismissive growl.

Jason's hurt flared. 'Do you honestly think I would have preferred to have deposited cash in some account for years, rather than spend time with my own son and watch him grow up?'

Blake's hurt and confusion was evident. 'That's crap. You told her you were gay and then you upped and left. You abandoned her. You abandoned me.'

'No! That isn't true. Saffron might have told you that, but that wasn't how it was.'

Blake's mouth twisted with fury and resentment through his beard. 'You told her that you had to get away, that you weren't cut out to be a father.'

'I never once said that, Blake. I did tell her I wasn't cut out to be her husband, but I never said I thought I wasn't up to the job of being a father to you.' His voice was pleading. 'I wanted that to continue more than anything. I still wanted to be your dad. I don't know what your mother was thinking.'

Blake's eyes were harsh. 'Really? I think I can guess. She was thinking that she had failed you and that the man she loved had left her and their son when we needed you. She was in love with you.'

Jason paced up and down a few feet away from us, as the twigs and frost crunched under his boots. 'I said I wanted to be a father to you. Ok, not living under the same roof, but be around to watch your grow up and support you both, not just financially but emotionally.'

Blake flicked him a long, pain riddled look. 'So why didn't you then?'

Jason closed his eyes for a few seconds. 'Don't make me do this, Blake.'

'Do what?'

There was another harsh silence, squeezing the air out of everything. 'Betray the memory of your mother.'

Rage charged headlong across Blake's face. 'You're lying. All of this is a shitful of lies.' He gestured to Rob, standing like a blond fashion model on the cabin porch steps. 'How dare you rock up after all these years with your pretty boy and try to tell me you tried? It took a car accident – a near-death experience – to make you think about me? That says it all. You couldn't wait to get away and live the life you should have lived.' Blake struggled to bite back the croak in his voice. 'And then you blame my dead mother for keeping you away from me?'

He threw his hands into the air.

'If I had known all that money hadn't come from gran but from you...' Blake let out a dry laugh. 'God, I must be so stupid. I did wonder how my grandmother was able to keep depositing money like that.'

Blake dragged a confused, tired hand down his face. 'I don't know what's the truth and what isn't.'

I snatched up one of Blake's hands in mine.

Blake didn't seem to notice. His voice was quieter. 'If I'd known that the money had come from you, I wouldn't have spent it. I wouldn't have wanted it in the first place.'

'I can understand that,' admitted Jason. 'But I wanted to try and ensure you were provided for.' He raked a troubled hand through his silvery hair. 'When your mum and I parted, I insisted that I financially support both of you. I wanted to look out for her too.'

Jason gave his head the briefest shake, as though even now, all these years later, he couldn't reconcile it all. 'Despite not earning much from her childminding job, she refused to accept any assistance from me at all for herself.'

I clasped Blake's hand tighter beside me. I could feel the

mixed-up tension rattling through him. It sounded like Saffron had been hell-bent on cutting all ties with Jason, even though she must have known it would be such a struggle for both her and Blake.

Jason puffed out his cheeks in frustration, as the cabin he and Rob were staying in twinkled invitingly behind him. 'I can understand why she refused help from me. She was hurting so, so much. She wanted me gone from her life and not to have the reminder of it. But to make you suffer like that too.' He gave his head a weary shake. 'Your mother must have wondered where all that money came from. She must have known your gran wasn't financially independent like that; she must have suspected the other money was from me.'

Blake took a few faltering steps away. 'I don't need to hear all this. You changed Mum from a happy smiling young woman into someone who didn't want to get up in the morning.' Blake's mouth twisted. 'She ended up in an early grave. You abandoned us both.'

His mouth sneered.

'It's not my fault you almost died in a car accident and then found your conscience. You should have thought about me long before now. If you had, my memories as a kid could have been happy ones!'

Blake's words about his childhood tore at my insides. They spun across to his father in a whirl of fury. 'When you walked out on us, you took any hope of a happy childhood I might have had with you.'

He fired a chilling stare at his dad and then at Rob. 'You can't tell me anything different.'

And with that, the three of us watched Blake stride off and disappear into the woods.

Chapter Twenty-Four

I didn't know whether Blake would listen to me, but I had to at least try. I pulled my coat tighter around myself, as the December breeze rattled through the bare trees. The last thing I wanted was him to be on his own, conflicted and emotional. 'I'll go and try to find him.'

A grateful expression reared up in Jason. 'We'll come with you.' He started to dash back up the porch steps of the Winter Wonderland cabin. 'We're only staying here in Craig Brae in the cabin for a night and then we head home to Brighton tomorrow for Christmas. I need to talk to him now.'

Rob shot out one arm. 'No, I don't think you should, Jason. At least not yet.' He offered his distraught partner a soft smile. 'Let him get it all straight in his head first that you're here.' He nodded at me. 'Lottie might be able to get through to him better than we ever could.'

'I don't know about that,' I blustered.

Jason studied me. He suddenly looked a little older and less sure of himself. 'No, you're right, Rob. I will speak to him, but not right now. Lottie, have you got your mobile with you?'

'Yes.'

'Then please let me give you my number.'

Jason reeled it off and I jabbed it into my phone.

Desperation rung out in his voice. 'Please let me know as soon as you find him.'

I offered them both my best reassuring smile. 'I will. I promise. And please try not to worry.' I pressed my lips together. 'Look, I can't promise Blake will even listen to me, but I will try to talk to him.'

Jason nodded. 'Thank you. That's all I can hope for right now.'

Where had Blake got to?

I trampled through the woodland, calling his name.

It must have been an awful shock for him, discovering his father was standing in front of him after so many years. It would throw anyone.

How wrong could I have been about the whole situation? And I had thought Jason Driscoll was some newspaper reporter, intent on revealing all about Blake and what had happened to him after his TV series was pulled. I had been right that all the questions Jason Driscoll had been asking were suspicious but it hadn't been for the reasons I had thought. That was why he had been hanging around outside the shop too, in the hope of seeing Blake there with me.

My cheeks flipped with colour as I thought again about how wrong I had been about everything. All I had wanted to do was protect Blake and make sure he wasn't hurt. That hadn't changed.

I called out 'Blake!' again as I pressed on, my boots scrunching across the woodland carpet of twigs and dead leaves. No wonder he'd taken off like that. He probably just wanted to put as much distance as he could between himself and Jason right now.

No doubt Blake wanted to get away and think things over, rake through his own thoughts and get everything clarified in his own mind. Everything Saffron had told him and led him to believe had been shot down in flames by his father. He had grown up thinking his dad couldn't care less about him and nothing could be further from the truth.

I hated the thought of him sitting somewhere on his own right now with what Jason had told him screeching around in his head. He must be struggling to comprehend everything and sort fact from fiction. Jason wasn't perfect, but Blake didn't know the whole story and he deserved to. He needed to. He shouldn't spend the rest of his life carrying around all these untruths.

I tightened the belt of my coat. I knew he wasn't interested in anything other than friendship. Blake had made that plain. But even though my hurt and disappointment still festered over him and what had happened between us – or more precisely, what *hadn't* happened – I wanted to be there for him. Even if he just wanted to sound off about his parents and how frustrated and let-down he felt. I would be more than happy to listen.

I reached the other side of the woods. I could just make out the stippled roofs of the log cabins. They seemed so far away now.

I whirled around on the spot, taking everything in from each direction. Where the hell was he?

A dark thought clung to me. Bloody hell. Blake wouldn't try to go climbing up some fierce hill, would he? The temptation to claw out his frustration and anger by taking himself off up Ben Linn again lurked at the edges of my mind. No. Surely, he wouldn't be so stupid and pig-headed as to do something foolish like that?

I conjured up images of him marching away from Jason and Rob without even so much as a backward glance. Goodness knows what he was thinking about everything right now. He might not be thinking straight. I so wanted him to know that he could talk to me and that he wasn't alone.

No wonder I had labelled Blake complicated. He had experienced an unsettled life growing up.

And no wonder he didn't like Christmas. What had happened on Christmas Eve all those years ago, would linger on in anyone's memory, especially when his mother refused to celebrate the festive season from then on.

I paused for a moment, my breath sliding out of my mouth into the frosty air and spiralling into smoky coils. The waggling, stripped tree branches and the odd bird darting in front of me was almost hypnotic.

Learning what I had about Blake's parents splitting up and him being told by his late mother that his father had in effect cancelled Christmas for them by leaving, let me see even more clearly now why he relished surrounding himself in nature. The mountains and the hillsides never let you down. They were constant and always there, ready to be appreciated.

But the idea of him taking himself off up another mountain right now filled me with horror. His head wouldn't be in the best place. He would be distracted and angry, his head jostling with thoughts that he couldn't reckon with.

My head brimmed with rising worry. I had to find him. My desperation was growing. 'Blake? It's Lottie,' I called out, before feeling foolish. Who else could it be? 'Please, Blake. Where are you? I'm worried about you.'

There was no reply.

I let out a panicky gulp of air.

I drew up again and tried to rationalise. So where might he have gone? Something told me Blake would not have returned to Craig Brae. At least not straight away. The town was a hive of activity with last-minute Christmas shoppers. He wouldn't want to be surrounded by festive jolliness. That would be his idea of hell.

Much more likely then that he would choose to go somewhere quiet and seek solace. If I were him, I would want to take myself off somewhere I could sort everything out. But where? The woods up here rambled on for a few miles. He could be sitting anywhere in amongst the trees.

The niggling worry that Blake might have ventured up somewhere like Ben Linn again in a fit of pique threatened to take hold. He had no proper equipment with him though, let alone his usual mountaineering clothing.

My stomach twisted.

No. I had to stop thinking like that. He wouldn't be so stupid. Unless he had dropped by Rowan Moore House to collect his things and then get ready?

I pulled my phone out of my pocket and rang Kim's mobile, wandering up and down and tilting my head this way and that till I secured a reasonable signal. I didn't think it would be likely that Blake would go to Rowan Moore, but I was getting desperate.

After a few seconds, she answered. I didn't give the poor woman the chance to say anything. 'Kim, it's Lottie. Have you seen Blake at all?'

'Only when he came by to see Max and I told him I was worried about you going to the Winter Wonderland cabin on your own.' She hesitated. 'Lottie, are you all right? You don't sound too good.'

I fell quiet. My head was swimming with worry about Blake. 'If he does show up, Kim, can you let me know straight away please?'

'Yes, of course I will. Is everything ok?'

My brain scratched around. I didn't want to say anything about what had happened. It didn't seem right. It was Blake's affair. 'Yes,' I faltered. 'It's fine.'

I ended the call and shoved my phone back into my pocket. My concern for Blake was gnawing harder at my insides. Every minute that ticked past, my imagination had him up some dangerous mountain, not thinking straight and putting himself in potential danger. If he wasn't concentrating and took a stumble, fell or got himself into a tricky situation...

'Blake,' I yelled even louder this time. 'Are you ok?'

Still no response.

I thrashed my way through the trees and came out the other side where the loch shone like a huge oval mirror.

I bit my lip and stared down the rolling hill and across the sleepy country road, towards the water. The hills were shifting and changing colour, swishing from moody grey hues to carrying a tinge of gold under the sun, fighting to break through the clouds. The snow was dusted across the peaks of them, glittering like shards of diamonds. Blake had better not have taken off up there. If he had, I would be having a right bloody go at him when I saw him.

I screwed up my eyes and scanned the loch. The light twisted and shifted. Wait. Was that a figure down by the shore? I lifted up one gloved hand and squinted downwards.

A tall, broad silhouette was standing on the shingled shore with his back to me. Was that him? It must be.

I picked up speed and raced down the hill, leaving behind the cabins, the bare, silhouetted trees and the aftermath of Jason and Blake's discussion.

Oh, thank goodness! It was him. As I drew closer, I recognised his dark hair and broad shoulders. Blake was lost in his own world, studying the flickering waters of Loch Strathe as they swished and murmured.

I called his name. 'Blake!' and bumped down the last of the slope, ran across the deserted road and squeezed myself between the crumbling dry-stone wall to reach him.

He spun round and stared at me. 'Careful, Lottie. You could break a leg, charging down there like that.'

Despite his attempt at light-hearted chat, my heart ached for him. His eyes were preoccupied.

He turned back to face the loch, which was throwing up haunting reflections of Ben Linn and the surrounding vista of heather-cluttered hills.

'Are you all right?' I asked, taking in his enviable lashes.

He scratched his beard as he considered my question.

As soon as the words were out of my mouth, I regretted it. 'Sorry, that was a dumb thing to ask you.'

'No, it wasn't. I mean, there's not a lot you can say, is

there?' Blake stood, gazing out at the view, before sinking down on a huge rock jutting out of the shoreline.

I observed him for a few moments. 'Budge up please,' I said, lowering myself down beside him.

His lips moulded into the briefest smile, before it vanished again.

I was aware of his strong, muscular thigh almost touching mine and I swallowed. God, I hated seeing him like this. He was gazing out again at the stunning view, but not processing it.

'Your father turning up like that must have been such a huge shock.'

Oh, for pity's sake! I was doing it again! Stating the bloody obvious.

Blake pushed both his hands into the pockets of his bright-blue puffer jacket. 'You could say that.' He scrunched up his eyes and considered what he was going to say next. 'I always thought he would show up again at some point. Great though, that it took a near-death experience.' He then let out a hollow laugh. 'You know, reeling off a series of excuses, telling me what a huge cock-up he had made.' He grunted. 'Made sure he wasn't about for all the hard stuff though, like when I had chickenpox, parents' evenings, snotty colds and school shows…' His voice vanished.

I fidgeted beside him. Blake was still clinging on to what Saffron had told him. Maybe he didn't want to believe that his father had wanted to be around for him. Perhaps it was easier in some ways not to think that his mother had prevented them from being a proper father and son. He didn't know the whole story. How could he? Saffron had only told him what she had wanted him to know. She had selected parts of the story to punish Jason.

I opened and closed my mouth. I had to say something. How could I sit here, in such close proximity to Blake and watch him put himself through the turmoil of his parents splitting up again?

Jason wanted me to try to speak to Blake on his behalf, but even if he hadn't, how could I remain quiet and watch this wonderful man think so badly of his dad? It seemed like Blake was clinging on to the memories he always had from all those years ago. In his eyes, his dad had abandoned him to the mercy of his troubled mother.

I lifted one hand and placed it on Blake's sleeve. He looked down at my fingers resting there. 'Blake, there's something I should tell you.'

He gazed down at my hand. 'Do you know it was the father of one of my friends who got me so obsessed by all of this?' He threw out one hand at Loch Strathe. 'It was when I got a bit older and we were living in Stirling.'

He appreciated the rise and fall of the water. 'It was thanks to me getting to know another lad who had moved into our street, who was just slightly older than me.' Blake gave a brief smile at the memory. 'He was keen on the outdoors too. His dad was one of those fresh-air fiends, who was really into rambling and nature. One day he took us both out on this walk.'

Blake's deep brown eyes melted at the memory.

'It wasn't a particularly amazing walk he took us on. We just went up some nearby fells and through a nature reserve, but something about the greenery and the smell of the damp moss captured my imagination.'

He shrugged his shoulders. 'That was it. I knew I belonged. I fell in love there and then with the countryside and the hills and I never looked back.'

Blake's mouth curled up with disdain. 'I remember feeling this punch of envy in my stomach as I watched my friend exchanging jokes and banter with his dad. It should have been my own father showing me these things, not someone else's.'

My back stiffened and I pushed myself more upright beside him. 'Blake, you don't know everything that happened between your mum and dad.' I cleared my throat. 'I don't mean to sound rude, but you only knew one side of the story.'

Blake angled himself round to look at me. 'Sorry?'

'You should hear him out.' I appealed to him. 'He never forgot you. You were always with him. You still are.'

Blake's brows grew stormy. 'Well, he's certainly made a good impression on you.'

'Blake, he just wants the opportunity to explain his side of things. Nobody is asking you or expecting you to forgive him.'

'He buggered off and never gave me another thought.'

I shook my head. 'That's not true. Please speak to him. Things aren't as cut and dried as you think.'

I shrank back on the rock as Blake's eyes burned into mine. 'Jesus. You've known him for all of five minutes and he's managed to charm you already.'

'He hasn't. You just can't see how upset and troubled he is. He's carrying around so much guilt, Blake.'

'And so he bloody should. I had my childhood stolen from me because of him.'

My insides tumbled around, as though they were on a spin cycle. 'You need to talk to your dad. Just hear him out.'

Blake's mouth flatlined. He jumped up from the rock we

were sitting on and prowled up and down in front of me, like a caged animal. 'I don't know if I can. I don't even know if I want to.'

'You know, you can press reset, Blake. It's not too late.' I pushed myself upright and moved towards him. 'It's almost Christmas. I know you don't agree with me, but it's a special time of year. Maybe this is the ideal opportunity.'

Blake switched his attention from me to the slapping water of the loch. The waves on the shore, sounded like they were whispering to each other. 'Christmas and I have never had a great relationship. I've told you that before.'

He gave his head a sad shake.

'I remember her lying there on the sofa on so many Christmases. She would be staring at the TV, not watching it.' Blake raked a hand through his hair. 'She would dissolve into tears at the festive adverts on the telly. Then she would get angry and resentful.'

Blake stared out again at the loch as he told me she would rant about Jason, telling him that they didn't need him and that they were better off without him. 'I think she thought if she told herself that often enough, she would start believing it.'

He steadied the rising resentment in his voice. 'You know what you're like when you're a kid. All the other houses would have Christmas trees and decorations, blow-up Santas on their lawns, and yet we would be sitting there in semi-darkness, without so much as a string of tinsel.'

Blake's hot gaze blazed down at me. 'He did that to her. He did it to me too. My so-called father.'

I gazed up at his handsome profile. 'I know your mum never celebrated it after she and your dad parted and that must have been so awful…'

Blake turned to me. 'It isn't just my mum who ruined Christmas for me after she and Dad split.'

I frowned. 'What is it? What are you talking about?'

'Oh, Christmas and I have previous form.' A sweep of emotions crossed his face. 'I was married,' he answered after a charged pause. 'Happily – or so I thought.'

I blinked up at him. surprised. Wait. Blake's comments about his pessimism over romance reared up in my head from before. That must have been what he was referring to, but didn't want to divulge. 'You were married? What happened?'

Blake gave me a fleeting, wry smile. 'Christmas chose to kick me up the arse once again.'

'What do you mean?'

He stared at me levelly. 'My wife had an affair with one of my best friends. I discovered them together three days before Christmas.'

Chapter Twenty-Five

B lake took a breath before he spoke. 'It was three years ago today, when I lived in Edinburgh.

'I had been Christmas shopping and bought a lot of things I thought Amy would like. I remember staggering through the door with everything from her favourite Chanel perfume, to a vanilla and coconut scented Jo Malone candle and a Kate Spade handbag in baby pink that she had been dropping endless hints about.'

My chest throbbed for him. 'Lucky girl. Go on.'

'Our last two Christmases as a married couple hadn't been what either of us had planned. I had been away on location the last two Christmases, recording my two specials for Netflix about spectacular walks in Canada and the States.' Blake paused for a moment. 'Amy was a successful hairdresser and make-up artist who I had met while filming a mountaineering documentary at the BBC. Because I had been away filming, she had spent both previous Christmases with her parents.'

Blake gave a small smile as he continued to talk. 'I had it all planned out: warm croissants and Bucks Fizz in bed on Christmas morning, before present-opening, a lazy Christmas lunch and then a romantic walk in Holyrood Park. I was determined it was going to be a Christmas to remember. And it was – for all the wrong reasons.'

Blake shot me a look before he carried on talking. 'I heard a clatter and noise coming from the bedroom and I was surprised as she had told me she would be late home that day, as she was working on a new Glasgow-based TV office drama and it was going to be a lengthy shift for her on set.'

He frowned as he continued. 'So I made us a snowball each and took the drinks down the hall to the bedroom, opened the door and she was in bed with one of my climbing buddies, Tyron Lang.'

I let out a shocked gasp. 'Bloody hell! I'm so sorry, Blake. She must have been crazy to do that to you.'

Blake offered me a small smile as the loch shimmered and sloshed ahead of us.

'What did she say?'

'They both apologised and said they didn't mean for it to happen. She tried to say it was Tyron who instigated it, and that what she had done wasn't really her.'

Blake pulled a face. 'Turned out they had been having an affair behind my back for a few months, but she attempted to also blame me, saying she felt neglected and that I was always away filming.' Blake paused as he remembered. 'Funny thing is, I kept insisting she join me on the trips, but she kept saying she was too busy with work.' He let out a snort. 'As it turns out, she was very busy – bedding Tyron over being with her husband.'

Blake bent down, picked up a random stone and skimmed

it across the mirrored surface of Loch Strathe. 'I called him Edinburgh's answer to Mr Potato Head and that really irritated her, because she knew it was true. The rock we're sitting on has a higher IQ.'

His dark, brooding face was stormy. 'Then she had the cheek to say she wouldn't have anything more to do with him and that she knew she had been stupid.'

'And were you tempted to give her another chance?'

Blake shook his head and watched the milky clouds scud overhead. 'No. Especially when she started going on about our posh flat and the standard of living we had and that we shouldn't throw it all away over someone like Tyron. That was all she cared about, not me.'

Blake stared at me as he sat there, all long legs, dark hair and beard. 'I told her she hadn't been the stupid one. That had been me. All along.'

Blake squinted across at the loch.

The water sloshed onto the stones and shingle, almost licking the tops of his chunky walking boots. 'So that's why I'm not keen on Christmas,' he explained. 'I suppose I associate it with some not very happy times in my life.' He shrugged. 'I much prefer climbing a Munro. There's less chance of hassle up there. You climb up, you get down.'

'You make it sound so easy!' I smiled. 'Although I guess it depends on the way you look at it.' I was struggling to comprehend why Amy could even contemplate cheating on Blake. He was so intelligent, handsome, brave… I pulled myself together. 'I mean, you could find yourself stranded.'

Blake's brows bunched together. 'Not if you're an excellent and expert climber.'

I pulled a comical face. 'Like you, you mean?'

'Possibly.'

We stood up in companiable silence, letting the steel-grey sky splinter with more marmalade sun. The wintery kaleidoscope of shades smudged over Ben Linn.

'So, what happened?' I asked in a gentle voice. 'After you discovered about Amy.'

'A messy, protracted divorce. Because I refused to try again with our marriage, she became spiteful.' He kicked at the shoreline. 'My mum had passed away two years previously and a couple of the newspapers were trying to make a big thing of my marriage breaking down.' He sighed. 'That was when I decided to leave Edinburgh and try to start over somewhere else. What was it you said? Reset?'

He offered me a wry smile that made my heart throb in empathy for him. 'My agent wasn't too happy about my decision to "go off grid" as he put it, but I felt I needed to. I had no choice.'

I nodded. 'I don't blame you. Sometimes, you have to put yourself first.'

'You do.'

I flicked him a look. 'Was that why you decided to quit TV? Because of your marriage breaking down?'

Blake rubbed at his beard and turned away from me to study the hills again. 'Yes. I didn't want to be in the middle of some media storm.'

The thought of him daring to blame himself for Amy's behaviour, just because of his sudden media success, was ridiculous. I risked a look up at him. 'I heard you on the phone that day when she called you up by the cabins.'

'I'm sure you did. It would have been hard not to.'

I took a moment to appreciate the scenery laid out in front of us, like a moody watercolour. 'What did she want?'

'Amy wanted what she always wants: more money. Turns out Tyron isn't making enough of it for her liking. She's a user. It took me a while to realise it. I think deep down I knew she was like that all along, but I thought she might change – or at least I hoped she would.'

Blake scuffed his boots against the shingle. 'I think the success I was having with my books and the TV series made her worse, not better.'

My heart lurched for him. 'What Amy did is no reflection on you. You didn't deserve it. It was her decision to cheat on you. It's obvious how much you love her.'

'Loved,' he clarified.

I paused, considering what he had just said. 'And can I ask you what happened to Amy?'

'She ended up marrying Tyron. Last I heard, he had qualified as a personal trainer and they had emigrated to Portugal. Amy has opened up her own beauty parlour out there with the proceeds she got from our divorce.' Blake shot me a look. 'But it obviously isn't enough, seeing as she was trying to squeeze more cash out of me by telling me that Tyron isn't getting the number of wealthy clients he thought he would.' Blake gave his dark head a shake. 'It never was enough money for her.'

I turned over in my mind what he was telling me. 'Well, more fool her for treating you like that.'

I realised the vitriol towards the woman was heavy in my voice. Blake studied me.

'And as for your dad turning up the way he did...' I pressed my lips together, couching in my head what was the best way to broach this delicate subject. 'I totally understand why you felt that you needed a new start after going through all that.'

Blake looked lost as he studied the patchy sun dipping and weaving behind the clouds. 'That money in my account, all the money I thought was from my grandmother… That helped me get started on my mountaineering training.'

'Did it?'

'Oh yeah. I was able to undertake my instructor's training in Wales and France. Like most things, these sorts of courses are not cheap.' Blake kicked at a random stone on the shore. 'I learnt everything from the technical aspects of rock climbing and mountaineering, to improvised rescue, teaching, mountain environments, navigation, group adventure activities. It really was the whole nine yards.' Blake stopped and almost smiled. 'Sorry. I'm going on a bit. I sound like you talking about Christmas.'

'Thanks for that.'

'You know what I mean.'

I eyed him. 'Blake, for what it's worth, you ought to know you aren't stupid at all. Far from it.' I let my hands rise and fall by my sides. 'From where I'm standing, you were the innocent party in all this. You were caught up in some sort of tangled, resentful game. I'm sure your mum didn't mean for it to get as out of control as it did or that you would suffer because of it.'

Blake flexed his dark brows at me, not appearing convinced.

'It sounds like her pride and her hurt got in the way.'

Silence fell between us. The slosh of the loch in front of us was almost hypnotic. 'Would you promise me one thing please?'

Even though it was evident he was still thrown by his father, he attempted a jokey lift of one brow. 'It depends what it is.'

'You're not going to like it.'

I bundled myself into the warmth of my coat against the stirring breeze waltzing across the water.

'Go on, Grant, out with it. The suspense is killing me.' He tried to keep an indifferent look to his face. 'If it's dressing up as bloody Santa again or becoming one half of a pantomime reindeer, the answer is no.'

I laughed and gathered my resolve. 'No, it isn't that, although don't put ideas in my head.' I hesitated. 'Please hear your dad out. You don't have to throw your arms around him or buy him a pint, although if you did I think he would be overjoyed.'

Blake scowled and whipped his attention back to the loch.

'Please. Just hear what he has to say before he leaves tomorrow to head home. He and Rob live in Brighton, so it's not as if you're likely to keep bumping into them.'

Blake kept his mesmerising eyes trained on the opposite shoreline. There was no noise, except for a random car negotiating the country lane behind us and the odd bird letting out an indignant cry.

'I don't know, Lottie. It won't change anything, will it?'

'No, it won't change what happened, but it might help you to understand the whole situation a bit better.'

Blake sighed.

I squinted up at him. 'My dad always used to say that it's the things you don't do that you regret, not the things you do.'

'And you think I might end up regretting not talking to him?'

'In the long run, yes, I think you would.'

Blake didn't appear convinced. He stooped down and picked up another pebble. He turned the flat, shiny marbled stone over in his hand, before pulling back one strong arm and launching it into a skim across the silver surface of the water.

The pebble twisted and danced over the top of the loch, bounding and leaping for what seemed like forever, before it finally lost momentum and vanished with a delicate 'plop!' into the depths.

'Oh, that was impressive!' I said, trying to lighten the heavy mood for a few moments. 'Please don't ask me to do that.'

Blake gave me an attractive, if fleeting, lopsided smile.

'How do you feel at the moment?' I asked him. 'About everything you just heard?'

'Angry, resentful, mixed-up and so, so confused.'

'There you are then,' I said simply. 'I think you've just answered your own question.'

Blake bent down to fetch another pebble. 'What do you mean?'

'You just said you feel mixed-up and confused, as anyone would be. And you will keep feeling like that, as long as you have all these questions swirling around inside your head.'

I stuffed my hands further into my coat pockets. 'At the moment, you don't know what to think or what you believe and the only way you stand any chance of coming to terms with what happened between your parents and why is to speak to your dad.'

Images of my own father lodged themselves in my mind and refused to budge. 'I would give anything for even five more minutes with my dad. When people go, they take that window of precious time with them and you can never get it back.' I bit back the crack in my voice. 'There are so many things I wish I could tell him.'

'I'm sorry.'

'Oh, don't be. I had him as my father for twenty-eight years and I wouldn't give up a single moment of those memories for anything.'

'You're lucky.' Blake shot me a wry look. 'Since when did you become so wise on affairs of the heart?'

I gazed at him, my heart twisting in on itself. 'Believe me, I'm not.' *Especially not where you're concerned.*

'Well, you sound like you are, Lottie.'

'So,' I announced, hoping I sounded breezy. 'What's it to be then, Mr Dempster? Do you ignore what your heart is telling you and carry on being the stubborn sod that I know you are? Or do you go and listen to what Jason has to say for himself?'

Blake fiddled with the pebble he'd just picked up by his feet. He toyed with it between his fingers and then lobbed this one across the loch too.

Just like the last one, it spun its way across the surface of the shiny water, before vanishing.

'Now you're just showing off.'

Blake waggled one eyebrow.

I folded my arms and tilted my head to one side in a questioning gesture.

Blake turned to me. He let out a world-weary sigh. 'Will you stop nagging me if I do?'

'Yes. Ok. Well, probably.'

There were more rhythmical swishes coming from the Loch Strathe water.

'I suppose that's the best I can ask for under the circumstances and knowing you as I do, Ms Grant.'

I blushed up at him. 'Is that a yes?'

Blake performed an eventual nodded. 'All right. I will speak to him. But don't expect me to come rushing back to tell you we're playing a round of golf together next week.'

'Of course not.' I beamed with relief. 'Jason will be delighted. Thank you.' I tightened my coat around myself. 'I'll leave you both to it then.'

I started off up the shingle, my boots smashing and crashing against the buttery stones. No wonder Blake had no time for the festive season. Bad enough that his Mum had banned it, but then to be deceived and treated that way by his then wife in the run-up to Christmas. That would colour anyone's view – even a Christmas fanatic like me.

I paused by the edge of the quiet country road and pulled up Jason's number. He answered almost straight away. 'Don't worry. Blake is fine. He's down by the shore at the loch.'

Jason let out a relieved rush of air. 'Thank goodness for that. Is he all right?'

'Yes. A bit preoccupied, as you can imagine, but he's ok.'

'Thank you, Lottie.'

'No problem.'

Jason hesitated. 'Have you told him that I would like to speak to him?'

'Yes, I have, and he said he will, but let him come to you.' I turned my attention back to Blake, who was watching me from the edge of the water. 'I've told him you're heading home tomorrow, so he knows that if he does want to talk to you, it has to be before then.'

'I'll wait for him to come to the cabin.' I could hear the rush of relief in Jason's voice. 'Thank you so much.'

I hung up, stuffed my mobile back in my pocket and performed a quick salute to Blake, before starting to cross the road and head back to my car, parked up at Rowan Moore House.

'Lottie. Wait.'

I turned around, brushing some loose hair away from my face. Blake was striding over the hillock of grass and rushes towards me. 'Don't go.'

'Are you all right?'

He considered my question. 'No. I mean, yes. Well, I think so.'

I offered him a kind smile. 'You need some time on your own to get everything straight in your head.'

I began to move off again, when he reached out one hand and caught my wrist. My eyes shot from Blake's fingers searing into my skin to his softening expression. I had never seen him look like that before.

He glanced down at my wrist, his fingers furled around it. 'I've spent enough time on my own, brooding.'

My breathing raced. I tried to steady it and failed. What was he trying to say? I gazed into his intent, dark eyes. 'What do you mean?'

Blake took a step even closer to me. I could make out traces of hazel in his eyes and the sexy tilt of his lips.

'I had it all planned out – or at least I thought I did. Get away from Edinburgh and the ghosts of Amy and my mother. I thought I would start again here in Craig Brae. Somewhere quiet and new.' He gestured around at the stunning vista. 'I'd researched a few places and the fact that I'd never been up here climbing before and its scenery and the tranquillity – well, the idea of it seduced me.'

The way Blake pronounced the word 'seduced' sent a frisson of excitement tripping up my spine.

I had a stiff, silent word with myself to get a grip.

Blake let out a sigh and scratched his dark beard. 'Everything in my life seemed to be finally falling into place. I was starting my own business and was beginning to think I could settle here and find some peace and equilibrium until…'

'Until what?'

His mouth twitched at the corners. 'Until the Styleses decided to employ Craig Brae's answer to the Christmas fairy.'

I blinked up at him as he towered over me. 'Me, you mean.'

'Well, I'm not talking about Mrs Crill, although I'm sure she's a very nice woman.'

There was a loaded silence. My chest gave a tiny fizz. 'What are you trying to say, Blake?'

'You were so dynamic and enthusiastic about the cabins, especially giving them their Christmas makeover.' Blake rolled his eyes and flashed me that grin of his, which made my legs melt. 'You were also a real champion of the area, what with helping out your local school and roping me in to becoming Santa.'

He let out a resigned sigh. 'I was determined to do my best to put a spanner in the works about your plans. The last thing I wanted was to be surrounded by or get dragged into anything remotely festive. I was trying to put all those painful memories behind me.'

My eyes searched his. Was Blake saying what I think he was? 'And then what happened? What changed?'

The breath stilled in my throat as Blake raised one hand and traced it down the side of my face. 'I told myself over and over that I felt nothing for you. You were just a pain-in-the-arse colleague, with a Christmas obsession.'

'Gee thanks!'

'But it didn't work. I thought you were so lovely that first day I came into Christmas Crackers, but the more I saw of you and the more I got to know you... When you were dancing around in the woods, eating snowflakes; all the help and support you gave me at the Christmas market; your enthusiasm in helping me put up decorations at Rock Solid Ramblings; the passionate way you stood up to me and faced me down about the cabins at the meetings, not to mention how worried you were when I was missing up Ben Linn...'

'I was worried sick,' I murmured.

Blake's mouth inched closer to mine. 'Yes. I know you were. You gave me a right rollocking.' There was that cheeky grin again. 'You punched me so hard on the arm, I thought you might have broken something.'

'What a big, tough, macho man like you?'

'It was rather sexy, actually.'

I swallowed, hypnotised.

'I had no idea how kind and genuine you are. You're like this gorgeous Christmas pixie.'

'I don't know whether to be pleased or offended.'

Blake rolled his eyes. 'Please don't interrupt me while I'm being all romantic. I'm trying to concentrate here.'

He brushed away a loose hair from my cheek. 'It has taken this knuckle head of mine a bit of time to realise that I'm falling for you.'

A rush of breath escaped from my chest. My eyes greedily took in every part of him, even his thick black beard. I thought my heart was going to explode.

His gaze lingered on my lips. Oh God. I wanted to taste him so much, it was almost painful.

'When I first arrived here, I was still hurting and so resentful. Remember that reply I left about Coco the clown when you told me off for parking on the pavement?'

I giggled at the memory. 'How could I forget that? It was rather clever actually, what you wrote, but you were rather up yourself.'

'Thanks for that.'

'Well, you were. But not anymore. You've changed.'

His eyes were teasing. 'So have you.'

'How?'

'You've grown,' he answered after a considered pause.

I grinned back up at him, the realisation of my increased self-belief burning even brighter in my chest than before.

'You've got more confident and have realised you can do anything. I don't think you know how dynamic and capable you are.' He gave me a sexy wink. 'See? That's what starting to fall for a good man can do for you.'

I pulled a dismissive, jokey face. 'If you tell me where this good man is, I'll try to track him down.'

'Oh, very funny.' Blake held me tighter, his arms wrapped around me. 'Now, I might be wrong but I think this is the bit where you're supposed to tell me that you have feelings for me too?'

My mouth broke into a silly grin. 'Of course, I have. Oh, you have no idea.'

Now it was Blake who was grinning like an idiot. 'Well, that's a relief, otherwise I would have been standing here, feeling like a right prat.'

We tilted our heads together so that our foreheads were

touching. It was like we were together properly now, in our own little world, where all the issues, problems and miscommunications couldn't touch us.

Blake smiled down at me. We were oblivious to the biting cold that was whipping up off the loch. 'You kept that shop going and supported your mum through such a difficult and stressful time, as well as starting work on the cabins. I don't think you have any idea what a wonderful woman you are.'

Now it was my turn to reach up one hand to his face. I brushed a stray lock of thick, dark hair from his brow that was flapping in the breeze. 'Well, I could say the same about you.'

'What do you mean?'

'You talk about me having had a time of it, but look at what you've been through and yet you kept going. You took a chance on making a new start elsewhere, you carved out a successful TV career for yourself and you've undertaken some great charity work.' I blushed up at him. 'You also started your own business.'

'Yes, well, after what happened with Amy, my head was all over the place. I didn't know what I wanted.' He hesitated, scanning my face, before resting his attention on my lips. 'But I do now. More than anything.'

I struggled to contain the bubbles of happiness exploding inside of me. I never thought we would be together. My hopes of meaning something more to Blake had died that day when he had told me that he couldn't be anything more to me than a friend. What was it he had said then? That he wasn't any good at relationships and they never seemed to work out.

Well, that was all about to change. We were strong together. We could see a future together. Nothing else mattered.

I couldn't, however, resist flashing Blake a jokey, pensive

look. 'The only fly in the ointment between us is that you don't like Christmas.'

Blake playfully rubbed at his dark beard. 'That is true. But I have a feeling we can work on that.' He arched one brow, as the loch whispered behind us.

'Can we?' I teased.

'Oh yes.'

Blake lowered his mouth to mine. We kissed over and over, our mouths claiming one another and deepening with intensity as we both let out uninhibited moans. The water continued to swish and sway behind us.

We moulded our bodies against one another, lost in the feel and sensation of each other, oblivious to everything else.

After a dizzying, delicious amount of time, we eased ourselves apart.

'I hope you don't suffer from beard rash after that,' joked Blake. 'I apologise in advance.'

I gave him a wink. 'It was worth it, although I'm very curious to know what you look like underneath that.'

'Oh, are you now?'

We clung to one another, the shimmering icy-cold water lit up by intermittent bursts of sunshine.

'Have I ever told you how wonderful you are, Lottie Grant?'

'No. Never. Not once. But I think you should start.'

Blake kissed me and grinned against my lips. Then a pensive angle to his features appeared. 'Do you mind if I slip away and speak to Jason back at the cabins? After all, you said he and Rob are heading home tomorrow.'

I beamed up at him, delighted. 'Of course, I don't. You go back over there right now.'

I ran my hands up and down the sleeves of Blake's bright-blue winter jacket. 'Just go and hear what he has to say and take it from there. It's a start.'

'I will.'

I watched his retreating back start to disappear but then he stopped and fired me that smile of his, which sent my heart spinning into orbit. 'Something tells me this Christmas is going to be something special for both of us.'

Chapter Twenty-Six

C hristmas Eve had always been my favourite day over the festive period. It was because of all the excitement and anticipation; the thrill of what was to come.

And this year was no different. In fact, I had a feeling it was going to be even lovelier than usual.

There was still pain about my dad once again not being around to share in the festivities with us, but this had been tempered by Blake, who assisted me, Max, Stephanie and Kim in preparing for the arrival of our Christmas cabin guests. Ruth pitched in too, which was a relief.

Thanks to us all getting involved, their stay with us got off to a gorgeous, Christmassy start.

There had been a light fall of snow and the woodland looked like it had been dipped in icing sugar, as two families and two couples, one younger pairing and one older, arrived and we introduced them to each other before settling them in each of their allocated cabins.

I had arranged for Mrs Crill to provide us with some of her

delicious cinnamon and hazelnut mince pies and Christmas cake from Sugar 'n' Spice together with some of Max's mulled wine from his secret stash, and the guests said how delighted they were by the warm Christmas welcome they had received.

The Christmas trees stationed on each of the cabin's porches twinkled like stars and the illuminated lights strung from the nearby bare trees gave the whole area a magical Santa's Grotto-type feel.

Max had been concerned that the lit-up almost six feet high pair of gold reindeer that Stephanie and I had spotted on the internet might be a little bit too much, but they enthralled the children of both visiting families, so everyone was happy.

I breathed a huge sigh of relief as we all wished our guests a merry Christmas and began to walk back to Rowan Moore House.

Max and Stephanie had tried to persuade me, Kim and Blake to stay on a little longer for some champagne to celebrate, but Kim politely declined. 'I'm catching a flight this afternoon down to Southampton to visit my parents but thank you anyway.'

'And I have something to do,' added Blake from behind me. 'But Merry Christmas and thank you again to both of you for all your support this year.'

I frowned at Blake as he started to make his exit. He didn't divulge where he was headed. 'See you back at yours in an hour or so,' he beamed, giving me a quick kiss as we stepped out of Rowan Moore House. 'I won't be long.'

I gave him a quizzical look. 'And where are you off to?'

Blake gave me a wink. 'Never you mind. See you in a bit.'

'Ok.'

I jumped into my car and headed towards Mum's. What

was he up to? Last-minute Christmas shopping? What a different Christmas it was going to be this year.

Rowan Moore disappeared in my rear-view mirror, like a vanishing Christmas card, as I trundled back past Loch Strathe and down the network of country lanes.

I arrived back in Craig Brae to see that some of the local shops had already closed their doors for Christmas, while beside the town clock a Salvation Army choir were belting out carols, their brass instruments glinting in the watery sun.

Last-minute shoppers jostled past each other with apologetic smiles, everything from rolls of wrapping paper and Christmassy napkins poking out from their bags.

I slowed down as I drove past Christmas Crackers. It was all closed now until after Christmas, when it would open for a few more days until the 31st. The council Christmas lights shimmered against the darkened windows.

Oh well. I supposed nothing ever stays the same and we all have to move on in the end.

Mum was busy wrapping up Christmas presents when I let myself in and called through to the sitting room. 'Only me!'

She thrust a half-wrapped gift behind her back, out of my line of sight. 'No peeking, young lady.'

'As if!'

The old black and white version of *Scrooge* with Alasdair Sim, which the three of us always used to snuggle up on the sofa and watch on Christmas Eve, was on the TV.

'Are you sure you and your young man want me round at yours tomorrow?' she asked. 'I mean, you've both been working flat out. I don't mind making Christmas dinner for us.'

I shook my head. 'And you've been busy too, getting all the loose ends tied up with the shop. No, Mum. Blake and I insist.'

Mum twinkled. 'All right. Thank you. That will be lovely.' She hesitated. 'So how are things going with you two?'

'Good. No. Great. It's like there's another side to Blake I never knew existed. If you'd asked me a couple of months ago if I thought we would be where we are now, I would have laughed.'

Mum played with a sparkly Christmas tag. 'Just goes to show you never know where life can take you.'

She flicked me an apprehensive smile. 'Are you sure I'm not going to be playing gooseberry tomorrow, Lottie?'

'Don't be daft, Mum. Of course not. It will be lovely.'

I instructed her to be ready to be collected for 11am, so she wouldn't have to drive and could indulge in a dry sherry or two.

'Ugh. Dry sherry!' she groaned. 'Perish the thought.'

Almost in unison, our attention moved to one of Dad's photos that Mum had dotted around the sitting room and along the top of her heavy stone fireplace.

'He would have been sitting on that sofa right now, mouthing along to the end of *Scrooge* and wearing one of his Christmas jumpers,' I pointed out through a sad smile.

Mum nodded. 'I was thinking just the same thing.'

She changed the subject, her light eyes melancholy. 'How did things go yesterday with Blake and his dad?'

'They had a good long chat. Blake said they've agreed to meet up again in the New Year. He said it was all a bit strained at first, as you might expect, but Rob went for a walk to make himself scarce and after a bit, Blake and Jason just heard each other out.'

I watched the flickering black and white credits at the end of the film scrolling up on Mum's TV. 'It's going to take some time for them both to get to know one another again, but at least things are moving in the right direction.'

'Good. I'm glad.'

I returned to my flat at the other end of Craig Brae.

I had expected Blake to be back by now, but there was so sign of him or his car.

I let myself back in to my flat and drifted around, switching on my Christmas lights laced around a couple of the sitting room walls and on my tree in the corner.

I'd already wrapped and stashed Blake's Christmas present in the bottom of my wardrobe. I 'd bought him a pen knife, made from Ben Linn stone, which I was sure he would love and appreciate.

Unbeknownst to Blake, I had accidentally come across the gift he had bought me for Christmas, when I was looking for a lost earring in the back of his car. He had stashed it under the blanket on the back seat, not realising I might have to venture there.

It was the most beautiful rose-gold bracelet, from which dangled three little Christmas trees. I'd spotted it in the local jeweller's window the other day. He must have noticed me admiring it.

Swallowing back happy tears, I tugged the tartan blanket back over the gift to conceal it and didn't reveal what I had seen. I didn't want to spoil the surprise.

I'd just clicked on my digital radio in the kitchen, which

was pumping out Maria Carey's 'All I Want for Christmas Is You', when I heard a knock on the front door.

Through the frosted pane of glass, I could make out Blake's tall, dark frame standing there. Where had he got to?

I started to tug the handle and opened the door. 'Well, hello you! Where have you been?! I hope the shops weren't too hectic for you...'

My voice died. I gasped.

It was Blake. But he was minus his beard.

I couldn't stop staring at him. His mouth cranked up endearingly at one corner. 'So? What do you think? Come on then. Out with it! Am I a new man?'

I took in his strong, angled jaw and the irresistible dimple popping like crazy in his right cheek, which I hadn't even known existed. He looked even more handsome. My stomach cartwheeled. 'I hope not! I like the man you are.' I drank in the smooth, clear planes and contours of his face. 'But I must say that you look... you look terrific. And at least five years younger.'

'Only five? Bloody hell! I was hoping for at least ten.'

He planted a kiss on my shocked and delighted lips. Then he enveloped me in his arms.

He never failed to surprise me. 'So, is that where you got to? You went back to your flat to shave?'

'Yep!'

His arms tightened around me. I felt warm and safe.

'What made you decide to get rid of your beard?'

Blake gazed down at me, all clear-skinned and fresh-faced. 'A new start. I've put my old life and disappointments behind me. After all that happened with Amy, I grew a beard and lost myself a bit. I think I retreated behind it.'

He rubbed at his strong, clean-shaven chin. 'It probably will feel a bit weird to begin with.' He kept his face straight. 'Maybe you could grow one instead, so I don't suffer from withdrawal symptoms.'

I punched him in the shoulder.

'Argh! That hurt!'

'Good. It was meant to.'

Blake looked thoughtful. 'You know, this might sound stupid, but getting rid of it is a bit symbolic, I suppose.'

I raised my head and gave his delicious chin a playful tweak. It was smooth and soft. 'It doesn't sound stupid at all.' My eyes widened in surprise. 'You've had your beard for three years?'

'Yes. When Amy and I first broke up, I wasn't in a great place.' He gestured to his freshly shaven chin.

A smile then broke out on his face. 'Time to let it go though, as the famous song goes.' Blake lowered his mouth closer to mine. 'Now I don't feel I have to hide from anything or anyone. That's thanks to you.'

Blake continued to gaze down at me. 'I realise that not everyone is like my mum or my ex-wife.'

He couldn't hide a playful smile. 'But the most important thing is that I won't feel guilty now about kissing you and giving you beard rash.'

'That's a good point. See? There's a plus side to everything.'

Blake's arms tightened around my waist.

I brushed my mouth against his and grinned. 'At least I can see your gorgeous face now and you no longer look like the fourth member of ZZ Top.'

Blake play frowned. 'ZZ Top? I think that's a bit of an exaggeration.'

'Yes, You're right.' I remained straight-faced. 'Not ZZ Top. More like Animal from the Muppets.'

He kept his face straight. 'So, when are you going to shave off your beard?'

'Would you like another punch on the arm?'

'Not particularly. Ok. I've had enough of the hilarious banter.'

With one swing of his muscular arm, Blake scooped me up and effortlessly threw me over one shoulder.

I started to laugh and squeal as he held me there and began to stride down the hallway. 'What are you doing? Put me down! Blake. Stop it. Where are you taking me?'

'To the bedroom. Any objections, Ms Grant?' he asked with a growl, as he bumped me along.

'No,' I sighed, my stomach performing that familiar delighted swoop. 'None at all, Mr Dempster.'

Epilogue

TWELVE MONTHS LATER, CHRISTMAS EVE

The last twelve months proved to be a hectic, exciting but rewarding time.

Magical Occasions Cabins, following the entries submitted for the cabin naming competition, were ultimately named after four successful Scottish architects and engineers: Adair, Playfair, Mackintosh and Telford.

There had been so many original entries, but in the end, Max and Stephanie opted for the suggestions put forward by a local ten-year-old girl who was studying Scottish architecture for a class project. She and her family were delighted to win a long weekend stay for four in one of the cabins of their choosing, plus of course the delicious hamper.

I continued with the tweaking and refurbishing of the cabins to fit in with Valentine's, Easter, Mother's Day, Father's Day and Halloween.

Yellow and white furnishings incorporated for the easter weekend, complete with Easter egg hunts in the woodland, little fluffy chicks and an easter bunny visit.

The other weekends during the year, such as Halloween, with pumpkins, orange lights strung in the woods and spooky stories, went down a storm too.

Max and Stephanie continue to be delighted with how things are going and Kim and I work well as a team.

Blake's Rock-Solid Ramblings business is going from strength to strength. Word has spread about Blake's former life as a TV presenter (more about that in a minute) and his rambling and mountaineering reservations have shot up, not to mention his reputation for providing Magical Occasions Cabins with a great hiking and rambling service for their guests.

Blake reached out to his agent and, after some thought, he is planning to return to TV to do some presenting again. He said he didn't want to give it up – not really – but after what happened between him and Amy, his confidence took a major hit and he needed to escape the spotlight for a while.

Now he thinks he could see himself venturing in front of the camera again to present more shows about hiking, rambling and the best nature walks in the UK, starting with Craig Brae.

I'm thrilled for him!

As for Christmas Crackers, Ronaldo's turned it into a rather fetching, rustic-looking premises at the beginning of the year, complete with high wooden beams, wall lamps and high-backed quilted chairs and tables.

Strange thing is, Mum dropped in with Orla for a coffee not long after it opened and she ended up being offered a job there. She works part-time serving drinks behind the bar and enjoys it. She still does the odd piece of scented candle packaging and selling for Susie, but working in the café has brought Mum something else.

Despite her protestations, she has become friendly with the manager, Mark. Things are in their early stages, but she and Mark, a divorcee, seem to get on really well and are good for one another. I know Dad would not want her to be alone.

Orla got herself another job too. She started work in the spring with us up at Rowan Moore House, as a part-time assistant to Kim. She's doing sterling work and it means that Kim has a bit of extra support with the increase in admin and bookings!

And as for Blake and I... well, we aren't together at the moment...

It's Christmas Eve, you see, and it's supposed to be bad luck for the bride and groom to see one another the night before they get married!

I'm busy getting ready at Mum's house and will hopefully spend the rest of my life with a man who showed me that it's never too late to turn your life around and that we are all stronger than we think we are, no matter what life may throw at us.

I stare back at my reflection in my old bedroom mirror. My hair is loose, spiralling down my back in brown curls and I've just slid into my winter wedding dress. It is a satin A-line design, with a sheer long-sleeved top, decorated with beads.

I'm going to slip on my tuille bishop-sleeved robe on over the top of it. After all, it is Christmas Eve and Craig Brae is chilly out there!

I finish putting in my pearl earrings and reach for my bouquet. It will be no surprise for you to learn that it too is festive-themed, comprising of deep-red velvet roses that remind me of burgundy wine. I chose gold pinecones and gold-tipped eucalyptus to accompany them, together with iced foliage and holly, studded with frosted berries.

I gaze around my old bedroom with its simple white furniture, lemon bedding and my dressing table with its oval gold-rimmed mirror.

Outside, the late morning sky is teasing the town with a possible delivery of snow.

'Lottie! The car is here!' calls Mum up the stairs, a trembly, excited echo in her voice.

She looks wonderful in her mother-of-the-bride outfit of a silver shawl maxi-dress, with embroidered matching coat and silk fascinator. 'Ok. Won't be a second.'

I take in a long, low breath, trying to steady my thrilled but nervous emotions. Mum and Mark; Jason and Rob; Stephanie, Max and Kim; Ruth; Orla and her three teenage daughters, Rose, Violet and Poppy; Mrs Crill and the girls from Sugar 'n' Spice, Vivian and Ridley (they insisted on returning to Craig Brae from their home in California for our nuptials – she said she wouldn't have missed it for anything) plus many of our loyal customers from Christmas Crackers; they would all be there at the ceremony. Everybody I cared about. Well, almost everyone.

As I'm reaching for my white-sleeved robe, which is hanging on the back of my bedroom door, I turn around.

My father is standing there, giving me that crooked grin of his.

'Well, Dad, how do I look?'

'You look like a princess, sweetheart. And a Christmas Eve wedding too!'

'I thought you'd like that.' I gestured out of the closed

bedroom door. 'Mum's giving me away and has written a speech. Mark has helped her with it. He's a good guy. You'd like him.'

'I'm sure I would. I'd hate the thought of your mother being unhappy and alone.'

I shoot him a smile. 'He's not you though, Dad.'

'Well, let's face it. Who is?!'

We both start to laugh.

'And this young man you're about to marry... well, I hope he knows how lucky he is.'

I roll my eyes. 'I think he does. I'm lucky too, Dad. Blake has been through a lot and yet he has such a kind heart.'

My father nods. 'You two are going to be ok.'

Another shout up the stairs from Mum telling me to get a shift on makes Dad shake his head. 'Bernie hasn't changed, has she? Still trying to organise everyone and loving every minute of it.'

Then his happy smile begins to melt. 'You had better go. We don't want the groom thinking you've stood him up.'

'Now that would never happen!'

I glance down at my winter bouquet through a gathering mist of tears. The rich ivory, peach and cranberry shades of the roses and dahlias melt against one another. 'No disrespect to Mum, but I wish you were giving me away, Dad.'

His mouth wobbles. 'I would give anything to be there for you; to walk you down that church aisle.'

I struggle to speak. 'I know you would, Dad.'

I finger the flowers of my bouquet.

'I wish you could be there.'

My dad takes a few steps closer to me. There is still that clump of hair on his head that insists on going in a different direction to the rest of it. 'You don't have to wish, Lottie. I'm always here. And I will be in that church congregation, watching you.'

I sniffle and turn to snatch a tissue from the box on my dressing table.

When I look back, my dad has gone.

I dab at my eyes, removing a smear of black mascara that has appeared under each of them.

'Lottie Grant!' bellows Mum. 'We need to go! Now! Thank goodness we don't have far to travel.'

I stand for a moment, gripping my bouquet and willing for it to snow. 'That would make everything perfect, Dad.'

And just as I tug open my bedroom door, a movement outside the window catches my eye. A few snowflakes begin to rock their way down like delicate kisses from the milky white sky.

Christmas really is the most magical time of the year.

Acknowledgments

My ever grateful thanks to my wonderful editor Jennie Rothwell, Dushi Horti, Lydia Mason, and to all the fabulous team at One More Chapter and HarperCollins.

Any author would be lucky to have such a wonderful group of talented people in their corner!

Eternal gratitude also to my amazing agent, Selwa Anthony, and also to Linda Anthony.

Love always to 'my boys'.

And a huge thank you to everyone who reads my books – this one is dedicated to all of you, with love and thanks.

Hope the magic of Christmas is with you always.

Read on for an extract from *The Bookshop by the Loch*

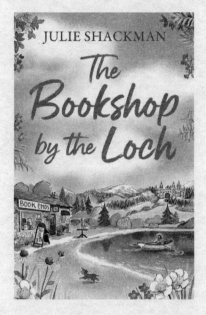

Available to pre-order in eBook and paperback now

The Bookshop by the Loch: Extract

Chapter One

Just ten minutes to go.

Ten minutes and there would be the announcement that me, Lexie Dunbar, was to become the new senior commissioning editor for romance and popular fiction, here at Literati Publishing.

My heart skittered against my ribs.

New, tailored navy suit. Tick.

Lilac, pussy bow blouse. Tick.

I had even had my long, straight, toffee coloured hair blow-dried and tonged into a cloud of tumbling curls first thing this morning, thanks to the magical capabilities of my amazing hairdresser, Fabia. Tick.

I drummed my fingers against the edge of my maple office desk, before remembering I had treated myself to a professional manicure yesterday. I drew my shiny, cranberry nails to an abrupt halt.

Around me, my colleagues were sliding knowing looks and encouraging smiles in my direction. The clock trudged closer to 11 o' clock.

This was agonizing!

I had worked here at Literati Publishing in Glasgow now for five years as a junior editor and boy, had I paid my dues!

Ridiculous hours; taking minimal holiday entitlement; working through my lunch break or devouring a sandwich whilst up to my elbows checking edits; chasing up manuscripts; taking work home evenings and weekends; massaging the rampant author egos of the likes of Dame Alicia Kilroy and Sir Stephen Todd; tackling an inbox which bred emails every ten minutes.

But despite the incessant pressure, working in publishing had been all I had ever wanted to do, since I was little and able to hold a book.

I grew up in Bracken Way, a small, Highland tourist town with a crumbling castle ruin and a beautiful loch, but moved through to Glasgow at eighteen to study English Literature at Glasgow University for four years and have lived here ever since.

Once I obtained my degree, I worked for the Scottish Civil Service for three years on one of their in-house newspapers, before hearing about the job of junior editor at Literati.

I knew I had to apply.

I ended up working under the auspices of senior commissioning editor Tabitha McGregor and learnt so much from her. When she retired recently, I knew her stilettos would be considerable ones to fill, but I knew it was what I wanted and had been working towards.

I turned my attention back to the office clock on the far wall.

Five minutes to go until our Executive Publisher, Grant Mullen, materialised to make the announcement about Tabitha's successor.

I shot out of my chair and paced backwards and forwards across the champagne carpet in my pearly heels. Well, when I say paced, it was more of a hobble. My toes were screeching out in protest but no other shoes matched my suit as well as they did.

Outside the panoramic office windows, Glasgow was a sea of stippled roofs, towering spires and winking glass in the Monday morning April light. The sun was pushing through the clouds.

Our offices were modern with floor to ceiling glass windows, situated in the trendy Byres Road area of the city. Surrounded by media types, students and struggling actors, Literati overlooked the emerald spread of the Botanic Gardens and their meringue shaped glasshouses.

I returned to my desk and sat down again for what seemed like the twentieth time in the last couple of minutes.

I smoothed down my skirt. My light grey eyes shone back out at me, wide and expectant, from my laptop screen.

"How are you feeling?" hissed a familiar voice as she hurried past.

It was Rhiannon, my best friend and head of marketing here at Literati.

"Like I'm about to throw up."

Rhiannon flashed me a white grin. She was all peroxide blonde bob, had just hit the age of thirty – the same as me – but seemed to possess far more attitude. "You're going to be a brilliant successor to Tabitha. Everybody knows it. Oh, stand by your beds, folks."

From the left, the doors swished open and Grant Mullen strode in, like an older, Scottish version of Pedro Pascal.

At once, chairs were squeaked back and bodies rose upwards, gravitating towards him.

Oh God. This was it. This was the moment.

With my legs resembling a new born foal's, I managed to make my way across the office floor and joined the others in a semi-circle. Rhiannon glided up beside me and gave my arm a supportive squeeze.

"Good morning, everyone. I trust you all had a weekend full of fun and debauchery?"

There were ripples of polite laughter.

"I take it that's a yes then?"

There was a chorus of more sycophantic chortles.

"Right, down to buisness. You will be aware of Tabitha's recent retirement. This has of course left us with the senior commissioning editor vacancy for romance and popular fiction to fill."

I was aware that dozens of sets of eyes were drifting my way. Grant glanced over. He gave me a knowing look. My stomach rippled with apprehension.

"Finding someone who has the same drive, flair, experience and creativity as Tabitha has meant, as far as me and the board are concerned, that there was only one candidate for the job."

Rhiannon gave me a nudge and I grinned at her, rolling my eyes.

"And so, it gives me the greatest pleasure to introduce you to our new senior commissioning editor. Please step forward, Anya."

A confused, ringing sound went off in my ears.

What? Anya? Who?

I felt like I was trapped underwater. There were sounds around me, but they were distorted. My colleagues were muttering and Rhiannon made a weird, gasping noise. Then she ground out a string of expletives.

An impeccably dressed ice blonde, who looked to be in her forties, emerged out of nowhere.

Heads turned to me for my reaction.

My stunned eyes swept over the woman. Her bleached wavy hair sat perfectly on her shoulders. Recognition punched me in the stomach. Shit. Anya. It was Anya Mills, from the top New York publishing house, Panache Publishing.

I was struggling to swallow. Was this some sort of twisted joke?

Grant began talking again, but my brain couldn't process what he was saying.

"Team, I'm sure this lady with her impressive publishing credentials needs no formal introduction, but for those of you who might have been living underground for the past few years, I'd like you to give Anya Mills, our new senior commissioning editor, a very warm welcome."

I have no idea how, but I managed to force out a few, awkward handclaps, before stumbling in the direction of the ladies' toilets, with Rhiannon in hot pursuit.

And there I huddled in one of the cubicles, a crying and snotty mess against Rhiannon's cerise blouse.

Chapter Two

I scuffed my dark leather ankle boots on the train platform and pushed my fringe out of my eyes.

Lugging my florally wheelie case behind me, I squinted around, until I saw Mum waving so hard at me from across the station car park, it was like she was performing semaphore. Her shoulder length, dark hair was being buffeted around her face.

My stomach sunk to the ground. I knew that once I confessed everything to Mum, she would be sprinting up to my old bedroom to turn it into a spa sanctuary for me, with soft towels and scented candles.

I had intended on telling her and my grandfather last week when I rang them to alert them that the prodigal daughter was returning home for three months, but the words lodged in my throat.

Instead, I'd mumbled something about the extended leave I'd decided to take to lick my wounds, as just being a "use it or lose it situation."

Oh God. Where was my life headed? That was the million-dollar question. What was I going to do with myself for the next twelve weeks? Did I really want to return to Literati? Did I want to stay here Bracken Way permanently? Would that feel like I was going backwards, instead of moving on?

What now? Was I even thinking straight? According to Rhiannon, I had lost leave of my senses, when I'd whooshed up in the lift to HR after Anya Mill's appointment last week, to announce that I had accrued a ridiculous amount of leave entitlement and I would be taking it with immediate effect.

When they appeared reluctant, I pointed out I could take

the money instead, to which they relented after working out the considerable sum involved and agreed yes, taking my accrued total leave of three months was the more sensible option.

I think because I also looked like a terrifying, tear-stained poodle, helped my case.

Grant had summoned me up to his ostentatious office after the announcement, to tell me that while my skills and abilities were much appreciated, the board had decided that Anya Mills' name carried more weight, which meant, "We would be in a better position to take on the other publishing power houses."

More swirling thoughts took over. The way I felt right now – cheated and foolish – I couldn't envisage myself returning to work there. But I loved the publishing world so much. Could I really turn my back on it?

I did have some savings put by, thanks to the money my late grandmother had left me in her will eighteen months ago, plus what I would make from temporarily renting out my flat in Glasgow for the three months I was back here in Bracken Way. The combination of both of those, would keep me going if I did decide to hand in my notice, but it wouldn't last forever.

I tried to give my head a mental shake. Right now, I was struggling to decide between peppermint tea or camomile, let alone what I wanted to do about my job.

I set my shoulders, plastered on a smile and started to stride over to where Mum was, but she had already abandoned her zesty yellow Hyundai and was bearing down on me, arms flung open.

She enveloped me and planted a huge kiss on my cheek. The wind carried wafts of her Estee Lauder perfume towards me, warm and flowery. "Three months," she breathed. "I've got my baby girl home for three months."

Guilt tugged at my insides. I fought to make my voice sound jovial. "You'll want to see the back of me after a fortnight."

"That long?" she teased. "Come on. Let's get you home and you can tell us all your exciting news."

Right. Enough. I would tell her and my grandfather the truth, once lunch was out of the way. I couldn't carry on, bottling up my frustration like this.

Mum held up the fob to the car and it let out a series of bleeps.

While I dumped my wheelie case in the boot, I realised that it only seemed like five minutes ago, that I was in the midst of the hustle of Glasgow and now, I was being blasted by hypothermic winds. And this was April, for Christ's sake! Bracken Way was a romantic, rugged part of Highland Scotland though, carrying echoes of the Vikings, so I guess the bracing weather was to be expected.

I buried my hands deeper into the pockets of my denim jacket, wishing I'd thrown on my thick, pink fleece instead and clambered into the passenger side.

Mum began talking about Grandpa complaining about his new reading glasses. I hoped I was murmuring and nodding in the right places. I was struggling to focus. My thoughts were jumping everywhere.

She indicated out of the train station car park and took us in the direction of the main street, moving the conversation on to the bad snow that had hit the area last month. I could see visitors meandering up and down the hill towards Bracken Castle.

Clusters of chattering American tourists were entering the castle courtyard in an array of multi-coloured waterproofs and clutching maps.

Chilly, Scottish dappled sunshine rippled down through the exposed towers.

To the right, was the gift shop, selling everything from Bracken Castle embossed bookmarks to postcards and clotted cream fudge. To the left, was the entrance kiosk and office. I recalled coming up here on school trips to hear about the history of the castle, with its links to hidden treasure, smuggled ladies of nobility fleeing from arranged marriages and the rumoured ghost of a knight searching for his lost love.

I gazed out of the car window, drinking in the achy, buttery stone work, with its narrow, grinning passages and elaborate crenelations. Busty balustrades erupted at every turn, depicting frilly flowers and rearing horses.

If you ventured through the gift shop and out of the exit on the other side, you were greeted by a hillside of sloping green grass, which overlooked the shimmering loch.

My heart sank. It was as if my life was contained in a snow globe and someone had snatched it up, given it a prolonged shake and then handed it back to me and said, "Right then. How are you going to deal with this?"

Perhaps I should have ignored that voice in my head at sixteen, telling me to indulge my dream of becoming a publishing editor. Maybe if I had chosen another career, I wouldn't feel so much of a withered, rejected husk right now at the age of thirty. Literati had chewed me up and spat me out.

It had been the love of our local bookshop, Book Ends, which had triggered my book obsession from an early age.

From the moment I had stepped in there with my late grandmother Pattie, the world of books and publishing had cast its spell on me and there had been nothing I could do about it.

I stared up at the castle, as Mum eased us up to the traffic lights. This place was the voice of the long-gone characters who had drifted in and around these walls; who had drunk up the sunshine in the sprawling lawns and hatched and plotted in its chambers hundreds of years ago.

I bit back a swell of disbelief as I played over in my head again, Grant's burring voice as he introduced Anya Mills and her perfectly pressed checked suit.

"Are you alright, sweetheart?"

Mum's voice made me sit up straighter.

"You're very quiet."

I huddled deeper into my denim jacket. "I'm fine." Out came another brittle smile. "Just a bit tired."

She weaved her way along the street. "You work too hard at that place."

Yeah. And look where my hard work has got me.

I shot a surreptitious glance back towards the bustling gift shop and then to the kiosk, where Nigel Carter, the dashing, elderly stalwart of the castle, was holding court with a group of visitors. Nigel, suited and booted and with his dark silvery hair combed, was pointing a gnarly finger towards the grounds.

I thought again about me returning home. My grandfather lived with my mother. I was looking forward to seeing him again too. They'd act like a moral boosting tag team, and right now I really needed it.

No sooner had I got through the front door and deposited my case and jacket in the hall, than my grandfather embraced me. He beamed at me from under his white moustache. He smelled of tobacco and fabric softener. "I don't know how many people your mother is expecting for lunch."

I popped my head around the sitting room door to see the dining table at the far end of the room laid out with her best crockery, on a starched white table cloth.

"I've made your favourite," she grinned at me, her eyes shining. "My chicken pasta bake."

"And then sticky toffee pudding and custard for pudding," added Grandpa.

I stared at the set table and at the familiarity of my old family home. I couldn't hold it back any longer. My emotions swamped me. My face crumpled.

Both of them shot forward, concerned.

"Lexie. What is it? What's wrong?" asked Mum, shooting worried looks at my grandfather.

I gave my head a shake, as they guided me into the sitting room and my grandfather encouraged me to sit down.

His sympathetic, papery hands seized mine. "Come on lass. You can tell us."

"How could they do it, Grandpa?" I gulped into his shoulder, not making any sense to either of them. "I've given them everything. I've worked so hard. I've sacrificed so much."

They exchanged puzzled looks.

And out it came; the kick in the teeth about the job I'd been led to believe was mine and which I'd worked so hard to earn; the appointment of someone who they believed held more gravitas than me.

My grandfather surveyed me out of his intelligent eyes. His long, considered face was framed with bristly brows and a thick sweep of white hair.

My mum's sitting room, with its well-worn sofa and armchairs and chestnut-coloured cushions, gave me a shred of familiarity and comfort.

My father had walked out on us when I was seven years old to pursue a career in journalism. Working on the local paper, The Bracken Way Observer, hadn't been high profile enough. Niall Dunbar had far more lofty ambitions than that, wanting to cover international stories and being awarded the Pulitzer Prize for intrepid journalism.

My parents got divorced a few years later.

I blinked several times, refocusing on my grandpa and my mother.

"This is just a blip. A bump in the road," he assured me.

"Yes. Well. It's a sodding big bump."

Grandpa pressed his lips together. "Things will sort themselves out in the end. They always do. You'll see."

Gerald Dunbar was still a dapper man, even at eighty years of age and had long possessed a penchant for snazzy waistcoats, which had endured from his twenties. Today, he was sporting a jade green Paisley style over cream shirt and dark trousers.

He had been a real father figure in my life.

He had been born and raised in Bracken Way like me and had worked for a local boat building company for years, until his reluctant retirement fifteen years ago. He was also an eternal optimist.

I moved my tear-stained attention to Mum, who looked like she wanted to commit murder. She perched beside me on the sofa and reached her hand over to rest it on mine. "I can't believe the way you have been treated. All the hours and weekends you've given that company! I hope they have a good think about what they've done and offer you another post." She sniffed. "So, this American woman was given the senior role instead of you?"

I dashed my face with the back of my hand. "Yes."

"And that's why you've taken this extended leave?"

I nodded and dabbed at my eyes with a clean hankie Grandpa had just handed me.

Mum's expression stiffened even more. "Still, with your experience and your ability, if you feel scunnered by the way they have treated you – I know I do - you should have no problem getting a position with another publisher."

My heart hammered in my ears. Saying the words out loud, sounded alien; like it was someone else speaking. "Right now, Mum, I don't know if I ever want to go back to publishing, let alone Literati, but I love what I do so much. That's why this has come as such a kick in the teeth."

She raised her brows in surprise. "But... but I don't understand? That is all you have ever wanted to do, sweetheart."

"I know Mum, but I had my heart set on that position. I'd been led to believe it was mine." I rubbed at my face. "I put my life on hold for Literati. I gave so much of myself to them and this is how they've repaid me. I don't know that I'm prepared to do that again."

She frowned. Then a sudden helplessness took over her features. "I just want you to be happy, love."

I leaned over and squeezed her hand.. "I know you do, Mum. I'm not sure what else I would do instead, though. If I did decide not to go back to Literati, I suppose I could offer freelance editorial services. That would bring in some extra income."

Mum mulled this over. "Well, you would need to think about your finances. What about your flat in Glasgow? What would you do about that?"

As I continued to sit there, thoughts tumbled through my head. God. There would be so many decisions to make. "I'm renting it out for the three months I'm here, to bring in some extra income and I still have Grandma's inheritance put aside."

Grandpa digested this for a few seconds and then gave me a confident nod. "Well, you know your own mind. In the meantime, don't make any decisions on anything. You'll know soon enough what you want to do.."

I bent forward and took gently clasped his weathered hands in mine, so grateful for his optimism. "I wish I had your confidence."

He gave a small smile. "You need time, lass. You don't know where you are right now or what you want. But you will."

Grandpa moved to speak again, but Mum got there first. "But what will you do, if you do decide you aren't going back?"

Maisie Dunbar could make worrying an Olympic sport. "Try not to fret, Mum. I'll just have to think about my options."

"Well, like I said, no making any decisions on your future right now," advised my grandfather, giving Mum a charged look. "You're still very upset."

I nodded, fixing a smile as grandpa suggested that Mum put the kettle on.

She surveyed us both, sighed and vanished into the kitchen.

Once she was out of earshot, he lowered his voice to a whisper. "Once your mother has a cuppa and a biscuit, she will be calmer and not quite as likely to want to go and rip the head off that boss of yours."

""It's going to take more than a cup of tea and a chocolate digestive to stop her worrying."

Grandpa nodded his head. "Och, like I said. A bump in the road, little dove. A bump in the road."

My heart constricted at hearing him call me what he had always called me since I was small, after we discovered an injured dove near the loch and fearing for its safety, we brought it home and nursed it back to health. I stood up, went over to him and planted an affectionate kiss on his cheek.

Then I made my way through to the kitchen.

Mum was clattering around with the jar of tea bags. In the sitting room, my grandfather had switched on the TV for the lunchtime news. He had cranked up the volume, which made Mum pull a disapproving face. "I'm surprised they can't hear that television set in Dundee."

She opened the bread bin next and stashed a new pumpkin and sesame seeded loaf inside. "Lunch will be ready in a little while."

"Thanks, Mum." I tried to gather my resolve. "Promise me you won't worry. I know what you're like. I just need some time."

Mum swung round to face me. "Why didn't you tell us last week, Lexie? You phoned but never said a word about the real reason for all this time off."

"I thought it might be easier telling you and grandpa face to face. I'm fine."

She picked up the kettle and moved to fill it from the tap. "You're not fine…"

"Maise! Lexie! Get through here!" Grandpa's voice erupted from the sitting room.

Mum and I exchanged worried glances as she dumped the kettle by the sink and we both took off together back towards the sitting room.

"Dad. Are you alright? What is it? What's wrong?"

My grandfather's expression was tense.

I crouched down in front of him, still seated in his favourite armchair. "Are you ok, grandpa? Aren't you feeling well?"

"No lass, I'm fine," he managed after a pause, his attention focused over my shoulder at the burble coming from the TV. "Or at least I was until I saw that."

I gazed up at Mum from my crouched position, but she was also now staring at the television with a strange expression on her face. "Mum?"

I got up from the carpet and turned to look at the TV, "Please tell me all six of our lottery numbers have come up."

It took a few seconds for my eyes to register what I was looking at – or should I say, *who* I was looking at – in glorious colour. The craggy smile, pointed chin and sun weathered complexion.

I blinked for several seconds. No. It couldn't be. It couldn't be him.

ONE MORE CHAPTER

YOUR NUMBER ONE STOP
FOR PAGETURNING BOOKS

The author and One More Chapter would like to thank everyone who contributed to the publication of this story...

Analytics
Emma Harvey
Maria Osa

Audio
Fionnuala Barrett
Ciara Briggs

Contracts
Georgina Hoffman
Florence Shepherd

Design
Lucy Bennett
Fiona Greenway
Holly Macdonald
Liane Payne
Dean Russell

Digital Sales
Laura Daley
Michael Davies
Georgina Ugen

Editorial
Arsalan Isa
Charlotte Ledger
Lydia Mason
Laura McCallen
Jennie Rothwell
Kimberley Young

International Sales
Bethan Moore

Marketing & Publicity
Chloe Cummings
Emma Petfield

Operations
Melissa Okusanya
Hannah Stamp

Production
Emily Chan
Denis Manson
Francesca Tuzzeo

Rights
Lana Beckwith
Rachel McCarron
Agnes Rigou
Hany Sheikh
Mohamed
Zoe Shine
Aisling Smyth

The HarperCollins Distribution Team

The HarperCollins Finance & Royalties Team

The HarperCollins Legal Team

The HarperCollins Technology Team

Trade Marketing
Ben Hurd

UK Sales
Yazmeen Akhtar
Laura Carpenter
Isabel Coburn
Jay Cochrane
Alice Gomer
Gemma Rayner
Erin White
Harriet Williams
Leah Woods

And every other essential link in the chain from delivery drivers to booksellers to librarians and beyond!

YOUR NUMBER ONE STOP

ONE MORE CHAPTER

FOR PAGETURNING BOOKS

One More Chapter is an
award-winning global
division of HarperCollins.

Sign up to our newsletter to get our
latest eBook deals and stay up to date
with our weekly Book Club!
<u>Subscribe here.</u>

Meet the team at
<u>www.onemorechapter.com</u>

Follow us!

 @OneMoreChapter_

 @OneMoreChapter

 @onemorechapterhc

Do you write unputdownable fiction?
We love to hear from new voices.
Find out how to submit your novel at
<u>www.onemorechapter.com/submissions</u>